LONG RIDE BACK

LONG RIDE BACK

A NOVEL BY

JOHN JACOB

THUNDER'S
MOUTH
PRESS

NEW YORK

Copyright © 1988 by John Jacob
Published in the United States by
THUNDER'S MOUTH PRESS,
93-99 Greene Street, New York, N.Y. 10012
Design by Loretta Li
Grateful acknowledgement is made to the
New York State Council on the Arts and
the National Endowment for the Arts
for financial assistance with
the publication of this work.
Portions of this book were
previously published in *Triquarterly*,
Other Voices, and *Whetstone*.
First Edition
Library of Congress Cataloging-in-Publication Data
Jacob, John, 1950–
Long ride back: a novel/by John Jacob.   p.   cm.
ISBN 0-938410-46-6: $19.95.
ISBN 0-938410-47-4 (pbk.): $9.95
1. Vietnamese Conflict, 1961–1975—Fiction.   I. Title.
PS3560.A248L6   1988   813'.54—dc19   87-25364   CIP
Distributed by
Consortium Book Sales & Distribution, Inc.
213 E. 4th Street
St. Paul, Minnesota 55101
612-221-9035
Manufactured in the United States of America

Thanks to the editors of *Triquarterly, Other Voices*, and *Whetstone* for permission to reprint sections of this book in slightly altered form; the Illinois Arts Council for support before, during, and after the completion of the manuscript; and my friend with the telling in-country name *Black Death* for invaluable insights.

FOR
Martha

FOR
Luke

FOR
Katy

memory is the shadow that stays

—LANCE HENSON
"Song in Autumn"

LONG RIDE BACK

It is September and I am fighting the heat. Everyone I talk to mentions the beautiful weather we're having.

Every night I sweat and sweat. I lie on my back, propped up on the mattress on the floor, legs out of the covers. Later it gets cool. In the morning I am hot again.

I decide that I am sick again. I get up late one night, past midnight, dripping sweat, and walk to the bathroom. The wind rustles the curtains. Moonlight shines onto my rocking chair against the wall.

My urine is cloudy again. I take two Flagyl tablets and two meclizine. The Flagyl will kill the bacteria and—if I take them long enough—me as well. The meclizine is for the nausea caused by the Flagyl. I can feel the bacteria running like roaches through my intestines.

3

It was September and hot. The rains were over for the week, but we were mired in mud all night. Leeches crawled over the tops of our boots and up the insides of our fatigues, stopping at the fat part of the thigh. All we could do was squash them and feel the blood and pus leak slowly down our legs.

It was hot and we couldn't sleep. Once a red flare lit up our perimeter from our side. The lieutenant got on the radio and someone killed the flare. We smelled it the rest of the night.

Whenever I am in a hospital I am awake when the nurses change shifts. I see them walk quietly past the darkened rooms, usually discussing food. Each time I learn who my ward or floor nurses are. The new ones offer backrubs. The older ones know not to walk into the center of the room— they stand near the rails of the beds with their watches and thermometers, their IV bags.

I had better IV technicians in the jungle.

I am fascinated by the night noises. I cannot discern the patterns of leaves blowing incessantly in the trees against the screened windows. There are walls containing me. I fill my mattress with sweat and fall away into sleep sometime in the morning.

It is October suddenly and the leaves have fallen onto streets and sidewalks. The weather is threatening, attacking, violent in its fury. Tonight it is dark at seven o'clock and the wind turns my umbrella inside out. No one walks the street in this storm. By midnight the rain has stopped but the cool air rushes in my window, and I hear the storm, not sense it, as I had in the jungle.

4

I sit straight across from the window, straightening the intestine out. Almost, dropping off into sleep, I am cooled. Almost.

Kathleen lives in the building and invites me to dinner. I accept, if she will let me take her to the theater—the movie theater. She accepts and late one afternoon we meet downtown.

We walk to the Fine Arts Theater to see Hitchcock's old *Rear Window*, revived from the dead, re-released. I remember seeing it with my parents and sisters, and I have seen it since on television.

The theater is chilly and we leave our coats on. The movie is just what I remembered. Occasionally I glance at Kathleen. She watches with a slightly furrowed brow, crossing and uncrossing her long legs. We are both cramped into small seats with no leg room. During suspenseful moments she clutches the armrest, or my knee, unconsciously, and quickly, then lets go. Her attention does not waver.

After the movie it is dark out and cool. Kathleen insists we take a taxi to the restaurant she has chosen. She stands back in the doorway while I prowl Michigan Avenue for an empty cab. Once inside, she instructs the driver to take us to Café Bohemia. It is, as my friends in college used to joke, *très élégant*.

We don't speak as the taxi whips down streets, scattering pigeons and pedestrians. Kathleen holds an index finger to her lightly glossed lips and crosses her long legs. I think that she is *très élégant*.

Café Bohemia does not serve "Bohemian" food. It has forever been located on seamy Clinton Street, just west of Union Station. If you walk by the corner it occupies around six o'clock any night, you're likely to see about a dozen people: maybe a cab driver waiting for a fare, the restaurant's doorman, maybe a half-dozen well-heeled restaurant patrons, and a few bums at work. My friends in college would have said it was *qu'est-ce que c'est?* incongruous, to us.

We join the dinner crowd waiting to be seated in a huge anteroom. Kathleen has me check our coats. She is prepared to impress the dinner crowd, and me, I suppose.

Kathleen is almost six feet tall and in very good shape. She has lately joined a health club, and she takes it seriously, swimming or running almost every day. She wears her very blond hair very short in front, longer and layered on the sides, and very long in back, a striking combination. Her tight black dress is stylishly long and unstylishly low cut. The men at the tables near ours are very interested when she leans forward across the table to make a point about the movie. I sit back and watch, interested. It is the scene that is interesting.

Kathleen's green eyes stare fully into mine.

"It was Grace Kelly's first comedy role and the only film in which she showed her command of sarcastic humor."

I weigh her earnest words carefully, wondering what Stuart Kaminsky, the film professor at Northwestern, might say.

I say, "Jimmy Stewart looked out of place with that cast on his leg. But his voice was still great."

Kathleen says, "Raymond Burr's inspired performance—so offbeat for that time—established an entirely new direction for the villain in American cinema."

I study her. She is leaning precariously far across our tiny table in her tight low-cut black dress. An abundance of pale, pure flesh stares me right in the face. Her blond hair is so perfect. Her green eyes carry subtle highlights. The light gold chain around her neck glitters.

She starts in again about *Rear Window* and its appropriate place in American cinema. I continue to sip from my wineglass, finally mentioning at a slight break in the monologue, "This appears to be pretty good stuff."

Kathleen looks at me as if I had slapped her. I think to myself, *Qu'est-ce que c'est?*

"Don't you think?"

"Yes. It is very fine wine. Do you want to go in for dinner now? I picked Café Bohemia because of its exotic dinners—really good food too. I recommend the venison, or buffalo steak. Venison is in season. They also offer a fine pheasant dish, and other fowl. Sometimes they have very rare items, such as antelope. Let's go in and take a look at the day's menu, shall we?"

She is still very earnest. The hurt look has been replaced by this new need to examine the menu, to see how exotic her dinner is to be, to join the elegance in the dining room.

I think maybe she's having a seriously earnest problem keeping all of her bodily parts within her dress, or so it appears, and maybe she needs to stand up to adjust herself.

As she rises she smoothes her dress and remarks, "Maybe they have some 'big cat' steaks in this week."

I am rising and continue to rise, to stand up straight, and when I am standing apart from the table and the people around me, I am back in the jungle, standing in the shade of a tree, hurriedly dipping a piece of fatigue cloth into a pot of lukewarm water and fastening it, dripping, around my head, tying it in back, like a pirate in a movie, getting the helmet back on over it as fast as I can, listening for the incoming, watching Pfc. Ray Sharp standing in the

7

sunlight with a long knife that is his nickname, with his helmet on the ground, with the knife in one hand and a scratching, clawing, scrawny village cat in the other. The sun is in his eyes and he is talking to himself.

Kathleen is waiting patiently. I am standing still next to our table. Her skin is so pale, so white. The chain glitters around her neck. I know her green eyes are upon me but I can't meet them.

The sun is unbearable, the heat, the humidity, the days and days of "paddy patrol," the weight of the packs, the AK-47's, the salt tablets driving us to filthy waterholes, forgetting helmets, weapons, caution, the second lieutenant losing a leg at the second waterhole two days ago from the *punji* stick, though the chopper took him out whole, his weak grin flashing in the deadly heat and sunlight, but we knew. We knew about the leg. We knew he wouldn't be coming back.

Kathleen is starting to look concerned, starting to edge her long body around the table, the pale skin ablaze under the subdued light, the chain glinting, inching, edging closer. Watching me. Those green eyes. That pale, so pale, skin.

So hot that day. Sharp, muttering to himself. The village cat with the wild green eyes. Scratching Sharp's arm, the welts dripping single droplets of blood across his pale chest. Sharp stands there in the sunlight, his favorite knife in his hand.

Kathleen parts her lips to speak.

Sharp mutters loudly now and his hand comes down viciously in a fast, cutting arc. I can feel the water dripping down my neck and onto my shoulders and chest. I can see the blood spurt from the cat's neck where Sharp slashed the jugular. The cat shrieks twice, convulses, throwing blood all over Sharp, into the dust of the village. Sharp keeps muttering, holding the swinging body.

Kathleen is reaching for my arm. She is so pale, so beautiful, so elegant.

Cat steaks.

Sharp cut it into strips and threw the carcass into the bushes.

I walk toward the door and out into the cold. A sharp wind bites down hard on my lip. I hear her call after me, faintly now. Kathleen is an echo. I walk toward the train station, shivering.

It is July. The summer has been very humid, even at night. The days I go in to work late I try to stay in bed, but all I do is sweat. The dreams are lengthy and complex. After I wake I sit up and continue them, force a resolution, settle an issue.

The nights I wake I hate people who intrude into my life.

It is July, ten o'clock on a Tuesday morning. I've slept in running shorts, ready to go out. I sit up until every vestige of dream is well behind me. Pill bottles line the lower shelf of a bookcase near the mattress. I contemplate them for several minutes before I choose a pill and swallow.

The radio is on outside, FM, the station with continuous rock and roll. I am up and stretching, hamstrings, thighs, shoulders, quads.

In college two friends and I played games. One was the creation of our own code, in French. We all had five or six years and could read fluently and speak fairly well. It was not just *très élégant*, not a natural phrase or two. We made up expressions, to suit an occasion, or to suit a sense of propriety—"what sounds right, Jack," Rizicko used to say. And Brooke used to titter in a high, intelligent laugh and tell us we were so *dégoutant*.

So we used to sit in class and construct little phrases that had nothing to do with anything, so long as they *sounded* right.

The philosophy professor would discuss the relationship of the self to "outer phenomena" expressed "hermeneutically" and one of us would mutter *"entrenous,"* or *"voulez-vous?"* Someone would answer a question and we'd scribble and pass the note: *Ca va?* or *Très bon* or *C'est vrai*. Smiles and laughter across the back rows of classrooms.

It stuck with me. I listen to rock and roll outside the window and think these things through, conclude that they are true—*c'est vrai*.

The hallway is immaculate. An unseen cleaning person takes care of it every day.

I snap my weighted gloves on and pick up bits of conversation from apartment doors closed and ajar.

There's one flight of stairs, darkened even for this time of day, and then the outer double doors.

Susan from the third floor is playing the radio, sunbathing on the sparse lawn in front of the building. She is built, my acquaintance Stern once said. She knows it. She is the color of light wood, and she exposes as much as she can. It gets boring seeing her in the same place almost every day, playing her radio, toying with her sunglasses, folding her towels, waiting for the police cruisers to park across the street while the cops have a leisurely lunch, checking her out.

She glances up behind the shades, her dull dark hair falling out of the barrette. A fine figure of a woman, I think, *c'est vrai*. She smiles her shark-white teeth. I nod. She props herself up on her elbows better to show herself off. I stretch the iliotibial bands on the sides of both knees, holding my feet, one at a time, up against my butt. The game. Stern said, "She has great tits." I didn't deny it.

But I am off down the street at a 6:30 per mile pace. *C'est vrai, c'est vérité,* I say, taking a lungful of air.

I feel like I cannot breathe. Heat sears my throat like a long barbecue at home on a July day. The corpsman runs over, holding his helmet on, offering a drink from the only canteen we have left. I don't know him, but he's a stupid bastard to share his water like that. I don't tell him. I am afraid if I open my mouth, the thirst will envelop me, drive me out of the rice field and into the clearing where Wood bought it.

The corpsman never made it in to check. Wood is probably dead and I know the corpsman is dead. I call out the code to see who's left so they won't know how many of us there are, how many are left. Anyone who answers "Yo!" followed by a "Sound off" is okay but sees someone either wounded or dead. I make it nine left, seven down, the corpsman dead and Wood lying facedown in gently twisting grasses, so peaceful, so silent, an outstretched hand still resting on the machine-gun bandoliers.

I think, Wood, you are an asshole to volunteer to bring up ammo after a year's tour. You learn. You should have.

I want an ice cube in my mouth. I want a tall glass of ice water, straight up. I am so thirsty, I heard nothing when the corpsman bought it.

It is October—the Moon of the Falling Leaves, a friend once wrote to me from New York. In October I stay out late and walk the streets of blowing leaves. Clouds ride the sky with strong velocity, obscuring the moon off and on.

I have been running in the morning since late March.

11

The summer has been hot and humid, even for Chicago. Only a few of us go out during the hottest parts of the day. It's a test, a fight against yourself.

I stay up later at night in October and run less often. The pain in my lungs and muscles eases other pains, so I continue to run, but less often.

It is October, late on a Saturday night. I sit at the window sweating, looking at the books stacked behind the bottles of pills. The lights are all off. The trees are silently bent outside. It is late, but I turn the television on.

The late night movie is *Hang 'Em High* with Clint Eastwood. I notice the great supporting cast: Ben Johnson, Bruce Dern, Ed Begley, Strother Martin, L. Q. Jones.

Eastwood is driving cattle across a river, alone, when eight riders appear on the bank. They splash across the river where Eastwood stands, wondering what they want.

Begley is their leader. He asks where Eastwood got the cattle. Eastwood says he bought them a few hours before and can show them the bill of sale. Begley asks for a description of the man who sold them. Eastwood replies, but his description doesn't fit. Three of the men rope Eastwood like a stray cow and take his gun.

Then Begley says, "Hang him."

They drag him across the river, throw a noosed rope over the limb of a tree, put it around his neck, hoist him onto a horse, whack the horse on the butt, and let him dangle.

They watch for a moment as his neck twists and his toes dance in the air. Then they ride back across the river.

Within a minute or two Ben Johnson, the federal marshal, spots the man hanging and gallops over to cut him down. Johnson gets Eastwood breathing again somehow, then takes him to the prison wagon. The other passengers stare at the permanent rope burns on his neck.

Of course, Eastwood takes it from there, tracks down the eight men, and kills them all. That's okay, though, because he's become a federal marshal himself.

It is now very late, but I am not particularly sleepy. Tired, yes, but not sleepy.

The television is off. Outside my window there is a massive reddish haze on the horizon, indistinct, but permeating the background of trees, single airplanes, a star.

Most of the yellow leaves will fall soon. There is no stopping it.

The sweat collects around my shoulder blades, in the curve of the small of my back. I take my shirt off, hold my head in my hands, close my eyes, try to reach into the realm of real and dreamless sleep that avoids me so perfectly.

You could see the sun and moon up in the sky at the same time some months. During the rains you'd see neither. The rest of the time they looked like two opaque balls, just sitting there, watching.

Marcolski had taken the point for a quick patrol into a nearby forest. The trees were massive, tall and thick, and fungus grew out of the rot of the bark.

There were five of us, not even a squad, no radioman even, no medic. I don't remember the others, just that all three were new, grunts sent up to replace the wounded and the crazy.

We had sent Simple Sherman back two days before the patrol went out. Simple and I had slogged the jungles and forests for three months, a long time for anyone then.

He had been talking to himself for about two weeks. Never anything too preposterous.

I had pitched a tarpaulin shelter against a bombed-out wall big enough for the two of us. Simple spread his kit out onto a blanket one night—grenades, knives and machetes, rounds of ammo, a couple automatic pistols he had taken off bodies.

He spread them out and began playing "choose weapons." He mumbled numbers and names to himself as his hands swept across the blanket, now touching a firing pin, now a silencer he had picked up in an alley brawl in the base city to the south.

I was on guard duty and tried to ignore him. Water kept condensing on the lip of my helmet, dripping into my eyes or mouth. Every thirty seconds or so I'd whack myself on the head to shake the moisture free.

Simple counted his weapons and I hit myself on the head. No wonder the C.O. and a medic came over before dawn began to break to see what the problem was.

Simple wouldn't talk to a C.O., not since the latest fragging up north. Our new man was smart, though, I give him credit for that. He carried an M-16, no sidearm, and camouflage paint on his face almost all the time. No bars on the helmet or shoulders, either. No radio, no radioman, unless he had to have it. Pair of mismatched fatigues. A bandolier of M-60 rounds no officer would ever carry.

They came quickly out of the fog and past the question on my face until they were next to him, listening to him talk, to run on and on at the mouth. Water dripped off my helmet into my mouth. It tasted like rank swamp water and rusted iron.

The C.O. didn't know what to make of Simple. No one ever bothered explaining to him why we all called him Simple Sherman. It made no difference.

The medic stood quietly against the bombed-out wall and watched the C.O. try to talk to him. The medic—from a broken-up airborne unit up north—wore his boots even at night and carried a pistol. And he wore his helmet, even though he was "off" and could have been sleeping. He seemed amused to watch the lieutenant try to get a simple answer out of Simple. Every few minutes the medic would light a new cigarette or glance over at me and wink.

The C.O. looked like he had just spent a month in the rotten jungle. He smelled like raw rice and dead fish, like old damp tobacco, like mold. His beard had grown in crooked and scraggly, and it helped him look mean and older than he was—that and his bandoliers and the gun he always carried in the crook of his arm. He had a cigarette butt stuck between his teeth. The printing stamped into his dog tags was turning green. He tied his boots on only halfway up but tucked his pants carefully into them. Water pooled beneath his green T-shirt and stuck. About the only things that weren't really disgusting about his appearance that night were his eyes—the quick, penetrating, quizzical eyes that took everything in while I tried to think how I'd get Simple out of this one.

Simple kept touching the things in his pile. I knocked myself on the head and water sprayed about. The smart-ass medic grinned. The C.O. stooped down and started talking.

"Hello, Sherman. Nice night tonight."

Nothing.

It was hot and humid, a night not unlike the days a month or two away. This C.O. probably hadn't felt them, seen them.

He tried again.

"So, Sherman. Nice collection of—stuff you got there," and he reached to pick up a Russian clip, when Sherman's hand snaked out and knocked it away. Then he returned to his sorting.

15

I decided to watch the C.O. and not interfere.

"Come on, Sherman. Just want to check out what you got. Maybe there's something you want to sell—"

"No. Nothing to sell." Simple kept his eyes low, hidden in the darkness of the wall, the darkness I began to feel in Simple's too-calm gestures. The tone of his voice. The angle of his jaw even.

I knocked water from my helmet.

"It's lights out, Sherman. You should be asleep."

"I should."

"Let's roll the duffel up and call it a night."

"No. No, I have something to do."

It was as if all the darkness of the nights in the jungle concentrated themselves into his speech, into the faint tremblings of his hands.

"It's late, Sherman." The lieutenant was ready to do something. The medic unbuttoned the flap over his .45.

"It is," Simple said.

Then his left hand slid around an old rusty villager's machete and cut upward in a slow arc, so slow we watched it like we were watching some kind of demonstration.

Then Simple was up and swinging. The lieutenant blocked the huge knife with his rifle barrel and ducked under the next swing. The medic had his gun out of the holster and on the way up, trying to aim, when I slapped him hard on the cheekbone with the butt of my machine gun and he went down.

The lieutenant hit Simple low and I hit him high and the machete flew free. It took us several minutes of furious fists and feet before he lay quietly on the ground, alone, his cache spread around him in disarray.

The C.O. and I sat watching him. I could hear the medic groaning and swearing somewhere close behind us.

Finally the C.O. turned and looked at me.

"Jones, I want you to escort Sherman to the infirmary. Take his stuff with him. I'll send over the papers while you're there. And I'll take your post for an hour."

I looked hard into his eyes and I guess he saw the cold question there.

"I won't send him back on a wounded slip. Just R and R, some time at base hospital, maybe even Hawaii."

I looked hard at the eyes and knew he was telling it straight. I got up and wrapped all of Simple's treasures in the blanket. The medic's face was half bruise, half pulp. I figure his gun must have flown over the wall. He sat swearing, staring at the lieutenant and me.

I helped Simple up and brushed his fatigues off, handed him his helmet for the long walk along the perimeter.

"And Jones—give me that machine gun. You can carry my rifle a ways."

I handed him the gun and slung his light rifle over a shoulder. I walked Simple a step or two, helping him across the mortar holes; then turned back to the lieutenant.

"We call him Simple Sherman, sir. That's what he goes by—all he goes by. For those transfer papers."

I hesitated and the C.O. nodded.

Then I said, "The longer you're here, the darker it gets at night, sir. Like tonight. Dark, wouldn't you say, sir?"

I looked directly and deeply into his eyes and never saw a twinge.

"I wouldn't know about all that, Jones. But you're right about tonight. Sure was dark, like the report said."

I thought I saw the hint of an understanding on his face that, coupled with a lot of luck, just might save this man's life.

"Yes, sir," was all I said.

I led Simple away. He walked slowly, like he was very tired or had just woken up. As we left the light of the position, I heard the lieutenant one last time.

"Jones, when you get him to the infirmary, tell the doctors I have a medic coming in for a few stitches. Seems he fell in all this rubble and cracked a cheekbone."

I smiled a little smile in the dark when I heard swearing back by the position. I never saw or heard that medic the rest of my tour.

Simple was singing "We're the army, can't be beat/We can sleep right on our feet" from boot camp, and I hailed the next guard position with the code words.

Simple went home two days later for good. Three months, Simple and me. I never saw him again.

Four days later and the patrol was sweating it out. I knew Marcolski was out there somewhere, and the three new guys were fanned out behind me, hot, sweaty, pissed off, scared. But I didn't have time for it.

I walked slowly through the lush jungle rot. The birds screamed in my ears. As long as I heard that scream I knew we were all right.

I pushed the helmet up and mopped my forehead with a bandanna tied across my left hand. It was a brace for the machine gun's kick.

This was the third patrol in two days. My pants stunk. My boots were falling apart. The constant moisture sucked them to pieces. Usually I wore a fatigue shirt with long sleeves to ward off bugs, but it was too hot. I wore a camouflage issue T-shirt. I hadn't shaved in days. The stubble gave way to finer hairs beneath my chin. My hair hung long and dirty in back and on the sides. I had cut it in front with my boot knife. I had to be able to see. Had to. The ID tags irritated me. Insects buzzed in a horde around my right hand, around the oiled and greased gun pointing obliquely at the ground.

When I stopped I heard the other three come up on me at the sides. They hadn't been watching, or didn't know better.

I yelled out, "Twenty yards. Back and out. You all stay twenty yards back and twenty yards out on the sides. And twenty yards from each other. And wait for the point man to report back before you come clanging up here again."

After their noise, my voice was nothing in the jungle. Jungle noises almost never stop. Only when something is about to die. Only then do the noises momentarily cease, until the death is enacted. Then more cacophony, more screaming. I was almost used to it.

I heard noises again as they clattered back and over to both sides of me. We had two wide men and should have been stacked three deep in the middle—Marcolski, me, one of the new guys.

I shifted the machine gun across my shoulder and cut past what we called a "razor," a plant with leaves sharp enough to make you bleed, to shred skin.

It was slow going. We were supposed to penetrate this side about three thousand meters to look for enemy infiltration. Great plan. If we found it, we had no radio and would probably all be killed before we could report back. And if we didn't, it was a waste of five men for half a day.

I stepped out of the brush into a tiny clearing before the nearest stand of trees and saw the body on the ground. Army fatigues, a helmet. He looked just like one of us, from a distance. That's what they wanted us to think. That's what Marcolski must have thought.

I saw the shadow first and cocked the machine gun, looked up and saw Marcolski hanging from a little tree.

19

Hanging by the neck. From a tiny little jungle tree. The head was bent to one side. I didn't look long at his face. The rope had cut so deeply into his skin on one side, you couldn't see the rope—just the blood running across the veins in his neck. They had cut him before they hung him. They had cut him all over, like a piece of meat.

The birds never stopped their clamor. I eased the ratchet forward on my gun and thought for a moment about the ID. Then I backed away. Just let those birds keep cackling, I thought as I backed away.

I was in the bush, backing away from two bodies, one shadow. He was the point man, but I had been a few hundred meters back and had never heard a thing.

I kept backing up, through the razors and bird shit, into plants that held you like something wet, something rubber. I backed away, sweat pouring into my eyes, the gun playing out in front of me, hearing those three near me, knocking down plants with gun butts and swearing until the man in the middle saw me and stopped. The other two stopped. I avoided their faces, turned, gave the thumb to start back the way we had come, and I led us out of the rotting jungle at the point, with those three kids not even knowing what we had left back in the midday heat of that jungle.

It is early on a Tuesday evening and Stern and I sit across from each other at a little table in Maison del Largo. It's a windy October evening. You can hear the sweep of the leaves and the tremendous gasps of wind whenever the door opens, whenever the masses of leaves blow up against a window.

Stern is drinking beers, dipping chips into a little pot of some green stuff. I have a Coke whose ice I keep swirling with a little red straw.

Stern is twisted in his seat like an animal too big for its cage. I sit so I can see the diners in the next room as well as anyone who comes in the front door.

We don't talk.

The bar is behind me but empty. We take up one of the six tiny booths that are technically part of the bar. It is not dark in the room but it is not bright either. Through ornate grillwork I watch the elegant people a half floor below dine. They eat things like steak and lobster, fancy salads, quiche. I swirl my ice and think they are all so *dégoutant*.

Stern had called me at work and had suggested we meet for a drink, which he knew I never did. But I surprised him. I thought, So what? I've got some time. We'd met on the street in the rush hour crush and found a quiet little place in this restaurant. Now I didn't have very much to talk about.

Stern is staring at the Lebanese bartender when he says, "How about those Rams?"

"Yeah," I say, an eye on him, an eye on the door opening and the lightning in the sky brightening the street outside.

"Can't believe how they're playing this year."

"Yeah, sure is incredible."

"Shows what a new coach will do."

"Sometimes."

"Whaddya mean sometimes? It always happens when they bring some new dude in. New offense, new defense, smart trades, good draft."

"Not in Chicago."

He considers it a moment. "True."

We sit quietly. Stern cracks chips in the dip dish. I rattle ice cubes around in my glass.

"So when are you gonna come out and play a few downs for us again?"

I remember my last game, the blood in the dust, the heat, the sweat, the itch to get in on a play, other things.

"I don't know. Give me a call when you get a game up. I'll think about it."

"Haven't seen you out for a couple years now, isn't it? God, you used to *be some*thing, playing that rover in the middle. Even scared some of the big guards from the joint."

He pauses. "You know?"

"I know."

Stern turns and watches the storm outside through heavily grilled windows. He has finished his third beer. I am still playing with my first Coke. I see people hurrying up and down Michigan Avenue. A young woman pauses at the window, peering in, her eyes and streaked hair reminding me of a rat. Rats. They were certainly plentiful, I start to remember.

Stern says, "Another Coke? Something stronger?"

"No. No, not tonight."

"We'd better head out. Won't be any fun in that downpour. Want to share a cab to the train station?"

"Nah. I'm taking the el. Same as always."

"Yeah. Same as always."

He pauses and looks around, his hands fluttering helplessly in the air for a moment like startled birds. "How's Kathleen?"

"Kathleen?"

"Yeah. That beautiful tall chick from your building. You were going out."

"Kathleen's fine. We're not 'going out.' But she's fine, just swell."

Stern looks distracted by the lightning, shifts in his seat again. I finish my Coke and pull on my jacket.

"You ever get the notion to just split this joint? Leave town? Leave it all to the crazies? Those people down there. People outside. You ever want to just *go*?"

I look at the forks entering mouths, catch the gleam of silverware and gold teeth, trip off another bad memory but suppress it. I look out the window at the sheets of warm, steamy rain.

"Yeah, Stern. I do."

"To just *go*?"

"To just *go*."

We're quiet a moment before we get up, toss a few bills on the table, and take the door at a half run.

Stern dashes into the street after a cab and yells back, "I'm gone."

"Yeah, man," I say. "You are. I'm gone too."

And we are swallowed up by the moving street.

It is August in Chicago, the month of the continuing heat wave this year, the month of my birth. Everywhere you hear complaints about the weather. The office workers in the Loop line the streets in short-sleeve shirts and slack ties, leering at the girls in their shorts, halter tops, tight blouses. These men have been starved for a month like this and can hardly control themselves.

A local documentary on television tells us that eighty-seven percent of all men and forty-seven percent of all women go to the beach "to see or be seen by others." All of the beaches are crowded every day, during the week, on weekends. Oak Street Beach is flesh-to-flesh people. There are fights. The police get testy. A Michigan Avenue dealer hires a model to stroll the beach clad in a fur coat and the locals pick her up and throw her in the lake. She is finally rescued by the police.

When I finish lifting weights after a run I am down to my shorts. Sweat pours off my arms, chest, back, runs little trails through the hair on my legs, collects in the hair that reaches toward my shoulders and drips off.

The sweat feels good. There is something honest and clear-cut about it. And there is something more than relief about a cool shower this month, something else honest and clear—like a sunset on a hot day. The illusion is that it is hottest at noon. The truth is that it is hottest when the sun goes down and the sidewalks radiate that slow heat back into the air.

When I drop my weights and feel the muscles throbbing I remember a friend who had told me, "More than anything else, I hate to sweat." She had other problems as well. I don't much wonder how she is taking this heat wave.

On the subway sweat runs down the temples of the face, pools on the creases in the neck, collects dirt. People jam the subway doors open at either end to collect the breeze of motion. Women mop the sweat running into their cleavage. My friend Stern has made a point of noticing this practice.

Stern's great fantasy is to approach a woman on the street—or in a restaurant, or on a subway platform—a woman with a classic face, or incredibly good looks, or a significant facial feature, or all three—and offer her a feature film contract. But he wants to really be able to do it, to have the connections. And he says he wants nothing more from it. He wants the anonymous approach, the explanation, the brush-off, followed by more talk, the embarrassment of the woman, her ultimate acceptance, the phone calls checking him out, the pleased and ingratiating gratitude when she discovers he's for real, his offer is good, the image of Stern turing around and forever walking away.

"You like to put women down," I say one day during lunch in Grant Park.

"Not at all."

"You like women to be indebted to you," I say, watching a young couple perform tai chi under the oaks of the park in the midst of this heat wave.

"Only by their choice."

He is turned away, one eye closed to the sun, the other checking the women out as they stroll languidly by.

"Basically, you want to get into their pants."

Stern half-turns toward me.

"Only the lucky ones, my friend, only the lucky ones."

The heat continues no matter what games we play.

"Go, man, go! Go! Get this thing up!"

The words echo from sleep to wakening, sound familiar, feel like they're coming from my own mouth. I'm awake with the harsh words ringing in my ears. This isn't the first time, just the first time in a long while.

I sit up against the cool wall and hear the wind rustling the curtains. My hair drips sweat. The pictures that accompany the words recede from memory as I force myself awake.

It's still dark out. I prop the pillows beneath my head so I can look at the curtains moving in the wind, feel the smooth sliding of a breeze across my face, hear the whisper of air against fabric, the light clatter of the windowframe. A sliver of moonlight cuts in and out of the window, obscured by the movements of the branches between the bright sky and the darkened room.

I try an old trick from my college karate class to induce relaxation, sleep: starting with my toes and moving upward, I flex and tighten every muscle that I can identify.

They tense for a few seconds each, then loosen as I move along the muscle chain to my neck, even to my head—the muscles in my jaw, my chin, my brow. Then I relax and lie completely limp, hoping for a dreamless sleep. But it doesn't come, not right away. I twist under the cover to face the wall. It is cool, so cool to touch, to be near. I remember briefly the hot walls and windows of other apartments in other cities. This heat has stalked me.

Now the night takes me in. I lie still in the cool darkness and resent the coming of dawn.

I was the side door gunner on a converted Huey that had been flown our way under cover of F-4's. It was rare to see those birds up where we were positioned that time. When the chopper set down, we watched the Phantoms cut a slice in the clear blue sky as they shot back south. The Huey carried two pilots but no gunners, and the pilots carried the orders that had me on the left door the next day.

The pilots each controlled a bank of seven heat-seeking missiles. Both doors were equipped with M-60 machine guns, but this chopper had some extra firepower. Someone down south had hooked additional rockets into the pilots' electrical systems. It meant they had twice the firepower designed and could stay up a lot longer. My side of the chopper came equipped with portable Laws rockets—not just one for me, but five or six for the passengers to play with. We were a landing machine and hadn't been designed like some of the armored death boats that had no room at all for passengers. But the Huey was designed to drop and pick up troops. Someone had something else in mind for this Huey, and for me.

The pilots kept to themselves most of the time. I almost never saw them except when we were called out on a mission.

At first everything was normal enough. We'd go out on a radio call and drop a few squads into an open area around the northern foothills. We used only one door gunner then—me—and rarely had any trouble. Sometimes our guys would surprise the enemy in the trees and had to fight their way out till we could maneuver in for the pickup, but by the time we landed, the shooting was sporadic—snipers, mostly—and I'd spray the trees a couple of times while the guys climbed aboard.

Then, maybe three weeks after the Huey appeared, a jeep made its way to our base camp. We were located next to a large foothill, giving us an expansive view of the hills and mountains in all directions, as well as a pretty clear idea what was going on in the villages situated in the valleys. We were well dug in. We had access to the top of the hill and had mined the other side. We knew what it meant when the saw grass moved the wrong way, or when the colors in the trees were wrong. We had dug into the side of the hill, literally.

Our equipment was hidden under camouflage netting, including the three choppers. It took a few minutes to move out because of that, but it was far safer. We thought for some time that they didn't know exactly where we were. We sent sapper teams twenty and forty kilometers in all directions to cause havoc. They'd locate a village and go in at night, or not bother to go in, just leaving a trail of well-concealed Claymore mines on all the footpaths coming or going. We'd drop troops in a widening arc, mostly to conceal our position.

We were told we were there to collect and analyze intelligence, that incursions against the enemy were necessary for our base security. Then the jeep came in on an old trail pitted with holes and marked by green overgrowth, and some of us began to wonder.

We were all vets. We were all in for at least a second tour. We knew generally how far north we sat in that beautiful, stinking jungle. We had all gone through training twice. We all had been on sapper missions. Back in the base city, some of us had been city sappers, walking time bombs. We all knew the dirtiest tricks. But we also were all highly trained intelligence troops. Some of us had studied at the top-secret base at Monterey, California. Others, like me, had been tagged for this duty since coming over. No one at that base knew fewer than four languages, and most of us specialized in regional dialects.

The jeep came carrying four Rangers, including the driver, and a short, dark, hard man in tan fatigues and a black beret.

They all went directly to officer's mess, which was strange—usually one man went to report and the others got the informal tour of our camp. I always watched with amusement when our designated "tour director" pointed things out. The tour began with the latrines, an intricate set of small hooches actually set into a drainpipe that had been airlifted in. Running water from a nearby stream kept it clear and washed our leftover American smells deep down into the ground.

I had pulled the M-60 out and was cleaning and greasing it when the jeep rattled in. I sat on an old discolored tree trunk carefully chopped away and then camouflaged when we first arrived. I liked that M-60. It was about the biggest individual weapon anyone carried in those days. It wasn't new or a thing of any real beauty, but it served.

I watched them disappear into the camouflaged tent. The M-60 was ready, as it always was, but I rubbed it down some more anyway.

New guys. I didn't like seeing new guys. It usually

meant another mission, a tough one. Somebody who wouldn't be going home. I could see the same sense of resentment on other faces around the perimeter. Resigned resentment. We were the only game in town, so some officer kept changing the rules, switching the plays around.

The officers ate together and the rest of us fixed our own meals. That day fires were allowed, the notice posted that morning. I dug a can of stew from the pack I always kept within reach and set up the folding Sterno stove. I cooked and ate dinner on that stump, the M-60 on my lap. Something was different. We all knew it. The guys were chainsmoking their cigarettes and not talking.

Joey Ringo was greasing his knife and its sheath. It was the longest, biggest, meanest weapon I'd ever seen. He could use it too. And he wasn't talking either.

About 2200 Ringo and me and three other "good men" were summoned to officer's mess. We were noncoms, corporals, nothing special—except we all had dragged bleeding and broken squads out of the forests and jungles more than once.

One of the Rangers and the hard man in the black beret sat behind the C.O. The other Rangers might have been asleep somewhere, might have been working out the next day's plans out in the copters.

The Ranger sat impassively watching mosquitoes attack the netting around the room.

The C.O. outlined it nervously and quickly. He wanted Ringo and me in one Huey, another two men in the other, and a ground patrol commanded by our visitor.

We were to infiltrate the northern jungle by air and ground as far as fuel and firepower would take us. There was only one objective: kill anyone we found.

Our C.O. wouldn't command. The Ranger, a captain,

would control the air. The stranger would move things on the ground. We'd go at 400 the next day. The C.O. asked for questions.

None of us was the shy type, but we all knew why we were supposed to be there: intelligence. This was a different kind of mission. And we had all gone on missions like it before, but not so well-planned, not so massive, not on orders from an HQ we never saw far to the south.

The Ranger's name was Cooper, we were told. He kept staring at those mosquitoes, like he had never seen one before, almost, waiting for questions. After a couple of minutes he said, "I don't imagine any of you boys been on a mission quite like this before," in a snotty Southern accent, eyes on the walls.

I looked at the new, hard man, whose name was also Jones, just that, no first name, no rank, just Jones. He looked back.

Ringo said, "'Scuse me, Captain, sir, but you don't really know *shit* 'bout what kind of missions *we* been on. Sir."

Our C.O. just sat back and watched.

Ringo fingered his knife. Cooper slowly turned bright red and finally said, "I'm told that you are *Ringo,* boy. That right? Well, you're just real lucky you're not going to be *alone* in that copter tomorrow with me. Your friend *Jones* there will be joining us. 'Cause if he weren't, *you wouldn't be comin' back*—in a recognizable piece."

Ringo was on his feet when the new man spoke, calmly, quietly, but quickly, like most Englishmen do. He was British all right. No mistake.

"Mr. Cooper, Mr. Ringo. We really do not have the luxury of time to discuss this any further—nor can we deal with it in any other way, I'm afraid. The mission is too important. Mr. Ringo, you have your assignment and I trust that you'll acquit yourself as befits a man with your service record. You will have Mr. Jones here on the other door. Mr. Cooper will coordinate rocket strikes from your position when I call in coordinates from the ground. Mr. Pacheco here will accompany me. The other helicopter will 'mop up,' I believe you put it. The ground troops have been notified and will be ready at four hundred hours. Helicopters ascend at five-thirty hours." He paused. "*When* you get back you may continue this discussion. Understood?"

Cooper nodded quickly and returned to his staring, this time at the ground. Ringo sat down but never said a word. The C.O. dismissed us and we shuffled out; Cooper and Jones stayed behind. We headed for the holes dug into the hill where we slept. Everyone was quiet. Finally Ringo tossed a rock into my hole and I stuck my head out.

"That Cooper asshole is *dead*, man. I just hope he stands a little *too* close to my door when we're touring the trees tomorrow."

I didn't pay much attention. That's how Ringo was.

"That guy Jones is British, Ringo. What's he doing here?"

"Ah, maybe he's an Aussie. We've seen 'em before."

"Yeah, but they talk differently. And wear uniforms. And have real names. And ranks. And no black berets."

"Yeah. I don't know. C.O. sure acted funny. Maybe we'll find out by tomorrow night, if they're done with our special services by then."

"We'll see. Hey. Joey. I take the left door. It's the only one my M-60 likes."

"You got it."

No one slept well that night. Even the perimeter guards were restless. Lights burned late in the officer's mess that night.

Sometimes the dreams from that night return, even now. After we got back, Ringo always called that day "El Destructo," and we talked about it, even though we shouldn't have.

It is September, early morning. I drift in and out of sleep. I see tracers burning a red tattoo through the morning fog. Both the moon and sun sit in the sky, motionless, streaked with scars from the tracers.

A tracer fired in daylight is like the memory of gunfire, but there's nothing like tracers in morning fog.

Is it a dream?

I sit straight up and peer through the blowing curtains. The sky is streaked with colored clouds and a light flickers in the corner of my left eye. I quickly grab a gelatin capsule from my bookshelf and swallow it without water.

Now I wait for it to go. The headache always comes anyway. The real fear is the dream of a day I cannot control.

I ride the elevated west late one night. The late trains are always two cars, and only two cars. The conductor always rides in the same car with the motorman.

We pass the Pulaski stop. I ride in the car with the conductor and motorman. Businesspeople pack our car. Light marijuana smoke fills the other car.

At Pulaski a man gets on but refuses to pay his fare. The train has already left the station and the conductor talks to him but the man will only say that he has no money and cannot pay.

The next stop is Cicero. The conductor tells the motorman what is happening and the train is stopped yards short of the Cicero platform. No one can get off, even if he pulls the emergency cord, because we are *live,* on top of the third rail. Every few seconds sparks jump up around us, hungry.

They are waiting for the police to arrive at the Cicero stop. They cannot pull the train up for fear the man will bolt out the door as soon as we reach the platform.

No one really wants to get off at Cicero. Everyone wants to get off at Austin, the next stop down the line, normally a two-minute run from Cicero.

It's late and the people in my car are getting irritated by the delay. They ask the conductor if we can't please just move, but he says no. They bang on the motorman's door but he keeps it closed. A man asks when the police will arrive. The conductor shrugs.

The man is young and looks old. His clothes are clean but torn. He wears old high-top basketball shoes, torn cotton pants, a sweatshirt, even during this heat. And a black sport coat over it. His hair is braided but incorrectly, making his head look off balance, always tilted to one side.

We sit and wait. The people in the other car are pressed against the window glass, pointing and laughing. A few sit still. In our car we stare at the man and at the conductor or look out the window into darkness lit by auto headlights. Eventually, one or two try to sleep.

The man stands by the door, not nervous or afraid, not high or drunk. He leans an elbow upon a metal support, lightly, almost delicately. He does not look at us. We look at him.

A man yells out to the conductor. He waves a crumpled dollar bill in the air.

"Hey, man. I'll pay his fare. Here's a dollar. Just take it and let's get going. We wasted too much time already."

The conductor says, "I can't do that, man. He's got to pay. You can't pay for him. Anyway, we already called the police."

The man says, "Christ, what bullshit" and stuffs the dollar into a pocket. Some of the other people haven't heard what the conductor said, or don't care. They throw money around, offering to pay the fare.

The man next to me sits, staring impassively at the littered floor. He doesn't move.

The people in my car tire of this and stare out the windows. The laughing people in the other car sit back down, subdued. The electricity on the line falters, plunging us into the half-light of emergency systems. The conductor's radio crackles in code, in speech. It is all beginning to remind me of some bad times, when we hear on the radio that the police are waiting on the platform.

The motorman inches the train ahead. The man standing in our car stares at the wall. The man next to me sits quite still. I have started to sweat, lightly, as one might think of a soft and short spring shower. People sigh and wait.

It's over in a few seconds. The policemen don't even bother to talk to the conductor. They step onto the train and force the man off, each pushing him out the door by his shoulders. The motorman starts the train as they cuff him.

Some people on the train smile at one another. Others wake and prepare to get off. The people in the other car are subdued.

The man who offered to pay the fare stands by the door and says to the man next to me, "You never moved. Never even looked around."

He looks up, finally, and says simply, "Trick I learned in Korea."

The sweat is gentle but it won't stop. Some things don't change.

34

Three of us are stripped to the waist, digging. I don't even remember what—latrines, sandbag enclosures, holes to sleep in.

I remember there were no mosquitoes. That was unusual.

McMichael was digging like it was the only thing on his mind, probably was too. His hole was two feet deep in minutes. His muscles glinted in the bright sunshine.

Mail call arrived and we stopped—but not McMichael. I got nothing but stopped to rest anyway. McMichael kept digging.

The other guy had a letter from his sister, from Cleveland I think, or Cincinnati. He sat and read and read again and flashed something silver at us, something that came in the envelope.

"My kid sister's into war protest. Sent this little button along for me." He half-smiled. The button had a tiny picture of several black-pajama-clad figures harvesting rice above the inscription, "They might be Viet Cong but they live there."

I read it out loud once, then picked up my shovel. McMichael paused and said, "Let me see that."

The kid handed the button to him. McMichael looked at it for a moment and then straightened the pin out of its back. Then he jabbed the pin right into his chest. A small trail of blood ran down under the eerie silver emblem on his tanned chest.

Then he kept on digging.

*Kathleen has invited me to have dinner with her at Boc-*caccio's. We meet at the restaurant early, not even six yet.

She's arrived before me and sits at the bar. She is an object of considerable attention. Still, both seats next to her are vacant. I stand in the gloom of the doorway for a minute to see how she handles herself.

Tonight she is wearing tight designer jeans and custom-made walking shoes, Herseys, they look like. She wears a tight white silk blouse with a tie at the neck and no bra. From my angle I can see the muscles of one breast pull as she lifts her arm to stir her drink. When she rests her elbow on the bar I can see the nipple standing out against the sheer fabric, inches from her thin arm.

She wears a single thin silver bracelet on her right wrist and a runner's watch on her left. It's not ostentatious—perhaps a Casio J-50. Her golden hair is bright even in the muted barlight, falling down her back and upon her shoulders but short enough in front that I can see a very blue vein pulsating in her temple as she chews on a swizzle stick.

Four men at the bar stare at her. Two men at one of the tables have moved their seats so they can glance over whenever they want. Some are more overt than others. Some steal glimpses of bouncing breast when she moves. Others sit and stare, nursing drinks, not taking their eyes from her.

She seems deep in thought but also aware of them. Her eyes stay on her drink, on the rows of bottles behind the bar. She doesn't turn when the door opens, even though I am late, even though the door has opened and closed several times since I arrived.

I hang my jacket near the door and ease into the seat on her left, the side I had been facing. Quickly, she places her hands palm down on the bar, tilts her head to one side, and smiles, coyly I suppose, her large mouth all teeth and gum, her lips poised.

"Hope you haven't been waiting long. There's a mob on Michigan Avenue."

"Not at all. I've been here only a few minutes and have been drinking this glass of exquisite wine. Would you like a glass before we dine?"

Dine, I think.

"I'll just wait until dinner, Kathleen. Finish yours, though. I'm in no hurry."

"Hurry? Oh, I hope you're not."

She shifts on her stool so that she faces me and presses both fine-boned knees against my right thigh. She leans forward, breasts bouncing with every movement, every wave of her hand. When she lifts her glass to her lips her right nipple grows taut against the silk, then relaxes into the shape beneath the blouse when she sets the glass down.

All of the men have turned away and have resumed their conversations, or they stare off into space—all except one, who continues to stare incredulously, first at Kathleen, then back at me. I don't want to have to deal with this man. I suggest we go downstairs to the dining room.

Kathleen bounces off her stool, leaving several carefully folded and creased dollar bills under her glass. She doesn't carry a purse but keeps a wad of bills in a front pocket. As we walk to the tiny flight of stairs, Kathleen leading and me following, I catch a glimpse of movement from the bar. It ignites something within me, and as I turn toward the bar and see the finger pointing at Kathleen and watch that mouth form a coarse smile and the ugly word that follows it, I am stepping toward him and somewhere else, lost in time. I step in a slowed motion into a dark time before I reach him.

Ringo and Jim McCoy and I hadn't had time off for four months. When we finally got liberty, we were sent south to the city for ten days.

37

Most guys got a week every two months, so we didn't quite know how to feel about it.

Ringo said, dodging the street vendors one morning, "It pisses me off. We sit in those holes up there for four goddamn months and they give us ten fuckin' days. Gratitude. Shit."

McCoy said, "Joey, Joey. You should be *pleased* to get this *generous* liberty of *ten* whole days *and* nights in one of the most exotic and beautiful cities in the world." McCoy stood six foot six and paid no attention to most of the world beneath him, including the little boys who tugged on his pants asking if he wanted his boots shined.

I said, "I'll take it. Why don't you go to HQ and complain, Ringo? I'll take the time when it comes." I zigzagged around old women on bicycles and checked the shoulder holster for my gun.

"Jones, you take too much shit. You need to dish more out so you won't take so much. You gotta be like me, Jones."

"Oh, God. The day I gotta be like you is the day I check out."

McCoy said, "What's it to be, gentlemen? What is your pleasure to be today?"

Ringo said, "We been here two days already and hardly moved from that 'apartment' of yours, Jones. Jesus Christ! I thought it was okay till I went upstairs last night and ran into that snake. Curled himself right around my legs. What kinds of friends you got based here anyway, Jones?"

"Joey—Joey. You were scared of a little twelve-foot python? Okay, maybe fourteen. Shame on you. If you'd have asked, I'd've told you about old Cornpone."

"Cornpone?" Two voices together.

"Yeah. The snake. He's been Bob's good buddy over

here for more than a year. His landlord stays out of the place even when the rent's overdue. All the MP's stay out no matter what kind of hell's going on. That's why we're staying there, man."

"Thanks a lot, Jones. You're just *too* interested in our welfare."

McCoy took us on a meandering tour down the main boulevards, past the free markets and the black markets in alleys and doorways, onto streets Ringo and I had never heard of, much less seen. The city was small and dirty and ugly but on foot never seemed to stop in any direction.

Most of the city smelled of rice and green vegetables. Some more affluent streets smelled of fish, and the cleanest street was paved in cobblestones and sported chickens in the shop windows.

The residue of cordite filled the air on the city's outskirts. Sandbags and spent shells littered the alleys and even some streets. We began to ignore the buzzing of helicopters coming and going, the drone of fighters and bombers and troop transports, the rattle of jeeps and convoys bumbling down the angled streets.

It was April, I think, the good weather preceding monsoon. Everything smelled dank—damp and dark, even on the brightly lit streets. McCoy and Ringo sensed it, too, I could tell, but it was our liberty, so none of us brought it up.

To the east of the city, ornate, three-story houses still stood. They were usually surrounded by gates or concrete walls—those the sappers hadn't hit. Some had green tile roofs, complicated gutter systems, scores of pearl-white wind chimes.

McCoy knew his way around the entire city, including this old French side that I would come to know and understand years later.

After a while we stopped talking completely and took it all in. I suppose we knew then that it wouldn't be this way forever. Couldn't. It wasn't that we felt we were a part of history. There was simply a sense of finality to the gradual destruction of a magnificent city, a sense of ending to some of us who had been sent there to end it.

Near the old French quarter McCoy guided us to a bar and restaurant. He called it the best food and drink from here to Honolulu, or Peking.

Ringo picked up the banter again. "McCoy, you never been to Honolulu."

"That's not true, Joey." He looked down on Ringo, out of place in those white starched civvies. "I did HALO training there."

I stared at McCoy, all six and a half feet of him. "*You* don't have HALO training. You never made a deep drop in your life, you asshole."

McCoy just smiled. "I did the training, Jones. But they said I was too tall and gangly. Get all caught up in the chute lines, you know. So they kicked me out after half a day and flew me straight here."

Ringo stopped and looked at him. McCoy opened his mouth and laughed and laughed.

It was a two-man patrol, not by the book. Sharp and me. No radio. AK-47's lifted from the village the company had just burned. The lieutenant called it recon, but to us it was just bullshit, or maybe suicide.

Fifteen hundred meters north and then fifteen hundred more west. We knew some guys would have gone fifty meters in and sat for an hour, then come out downstream. But not Sharp. And not me.

We waded through the river waistdeep, weapons held

high above our heads. We didn't talk: hand-signaled a left turn, a stop, a snake coming fast through the water.

We were ten minutes into the river when Sharp signaled fast to me, threw me his rifle, and reached into the tree over his head with his left hand and pulled a knife free from its sheath with his right. In a motion he cut up into the tree and I saw the spitting snake's head fall into the water. Then its six-foot body fell writhing onto Sharp, who pushed it off into the water, sank his arms to the elbows into the river to wash off the blood, and signaled for his gun. I tossed it to him and we kept wading.

We had been drinking for a while, but not a lot for over there. Most of us got sauced really quickly, but not that afternoon and evening, not us, not that time. We had dinner, spicy, hot rice with thin, pale vegetables and a chicken bone or two thrown in.

I was leaning back in my chair against the wall near the back door so I could see the front door. Ringo faced the bar. McCoy sat facing the other two walls, studying faces at the other small tables.

I don't remember much of our conversation there. Sometimes I awake from a dream in the middle of a phrase that one of us spoke then, back in the old city, reliving it word for word, feeling the hot breeze from the ceiling fan, sweating it out. But I don't remember much. I remember McCoy most of all.

McCoy told us that this was the best bar to find women in the entire city. Ringo and I were too tired from the jungle to show much interest, and even McCoy didn't seem too excited. But we waited to see these women. So far everyone in the place was male or clearly someone else's property.

41

I was leaning back in my chair against the wall when the girls came in through the back door. There were five of them, two almost blond, the others very dark. They were all dressed differently but everyone in the place knew their business. It was part of their demeanor, how they stood at the bar staring into drinks or looking vaguely about the room.

There were no blondes in the city. Now we knew what McCoy had been talking about. Still, we didn't move. Even McCoy, facing away from them, kept staring at the tables, a glass of whiskey balanced in one huge, scarred hand.

The din in the bar subsided but didn't stop completely. Everyone watched the five girls closely. I saw Ringo stare at one of the blondes. Her hair was stringy and showed strands of brown in the dim light. She was about fifteen, dressed in jeans and a soiled white shirt with no buttons. Her hands hung from the large open sleeves like dead things. I could see the curve of a breast and the nipple's outline against the cotton shirt. The other nipple, pink, protruded from the front of the shirt. Ringo kept staring.

They had a leader. Not a "madam." A girl who looked a little older and smarter in the crinkles at the corners of her mouth. She wore jeans and a halter top, and strings of pearls and necklaces around her neck. I had seen striped scars on her back when they had walked by. She was tall but small-boned, small-hipped, small-breasted. Eurasian.

An old, thin man approached one of the girls and said something to her. She looked at the Eurasian, who simply stood with her lip curled. Then she opened her hand. The man took bills from a pocket and placed them in her hand. She kept gesturing for more. He kept piling the bills in her hand, a look of hope, or surprise, on his face. Then suddenly she turned her palm upside down and let the money flutter to the floor. Then she laughed. The other girl turned her back on him and he recovered his money on his hands and knees at the Eurasian girl's bare feet. He walked quickly out the front door.

Just as quickly, two men got up and followed him out. Ringo had seen it and gave me a look. I nodded, still leaning back where I could see everything. McCoy stared into his glass, suspended between fingers like a little toy.

The quiet in the little bar added to its stifling quality. Suddenly I wanted to be outside in the fresh air, no matter how badly it smelled. I wanted a breeze to cool my face. I wanted to swing my arms widely through the streets, walking with my friends, without worrying about protocol, or sappers, and I wasn't sure which was worse. For a moment I could see myself sitting up against that barroom wall forever, rigid, faking a relaxed pose, waiting. Interminably waiting.

"Come over here, you little white-assed cunt. Bring your friends with you."

The voice came from the corner opposite me, rough, drunken, very American. It was difficult to see the corners of the room. Smoke hung in the air, occasionally moving in lazy swirls when caught up in the slow circling of the open-bladed fan in the ceiling. Bodies were packed tightly into tables, making distinctions among them difficult.

But I had seen the five Americans when we had first come in, and I knew it had to be one of them. I had noticed the clothes, the cigarettes, the gold wedding bands, the beard on one of the men—all as I had been trained. All in a glance. Pause, take it in, pause, file it away for future reference. That reference was now. I could see only a couple broad backs against sweaty white shirts.

One of the girls looked quickly over at the men and

then looked back at the Eurasian girl, who stared stonily at the bar.

The voice came again. "Come on, baby. We got good American dollars. We want two of you. *NOW.*"

It was drunk, that voice, but measured, and I knew by the shift in her eyes that the Eurasian girl understood. She glanced at two of the dark-haired girls. They walked slowly across the room, as they had been taught.

The Americans hoisted the girls onto their table, bought them drinks. Ringo and I watched and McCoy sat quietly facing the other way. The Americans kept drinking. Full bottles disappeared. The Americans laughed and kicked over tables, chairs. They took the girls' blouses off, one slowly, the other a loud rip in the deepening still of the bar. Ringo and I saw them stuff their hands between the girls' thighs, watched the girls' faces never change expression.

It was night. The people in the bar had thinned out. A short, skinny man who spoke French to us kept coming over with more bottles. We just looked at him and he backed off.

McCoy made his move just about the time one of the Americans had a girl spread-eagled on their table. The others held her ankles and wrists and he sat on top, humping, his pants hardly down to his knees. He grunted and groaned and she was still.

McCoy stood up and dropped his glass onto the floor. I could hardly hear it break because of the noise across the room. Ringo and I were ready and stood up. We pulled bills from pockets and dropped them onto the table.

McCoy turned and faced the bar. I kept my eye on the back door and Ringo moved over to watch the Americans, and the front door as well. McCoy walked up to the

Eurasian girl, who peered into her drink like there was something wrong with it. She had her back turned to the American's table. McCoy leaned over and whispered into her ear.

I watched the back. I wasn't sure where it led, or how deep it was. I braced myself against the wall and stuffed my hand into my shirt, against the cold heat of the gun butt.

One of the Americans across the room looked up and saw the three of us, especially McCoy, I could tell, all six-six of him, and kept his eyes up.

McCoy was peeling off bills and giving them to the Eurasian girl. She kept her hand out, not looking at him, and he kept filling it up. Ringo looked at me, motioned across the room, and I nodded. He had seen the American too.

The Eurasian girl tucked the bills somewhere inside the inner part of her belt and before I knew it was gone out the back door. It was almost as if she had never been there. Ringo started for the front door and McCoy followed, holding the hands of the two blond girls he had paid for. I followed them, watching the table of Americans and the girls they had bought, the girls who were being raped on top of the table while everyone watched and no one—not even the girls—said a word. I saw the one who had looked up nudge the man next to him, who pointed at McCoy and said something to the men he was with.

Ringo was at the door, opening it, when we heard one of them say, "Not so fast, you cunt-sucking nigger. You ain't goin' nowhere with them two *American* girls."

Everything in that bar except the ceiling fan stopped. Smoke swirled around the door, where the hot breeze from outside drew it back and forth. McCoy still faced the door.

45

Then the two blond girls began to twist away from him, but he held on to their arms until they turned even whiter than they had been.

I backed slowly away, angling toward the bar, closer to the Americans without facing them head on.

McCoy then said, in a voice that permeated the room, "If somebody in here just said anything, which they *may* have, I cordially invite him to stand up and repeat it. To my face this time."

In one movement everyone at that table stood up. The girls remained sprawled on the table, covering themselves with scraps of their clothes. And when they moved, I moved from the bar behind them, and McCoy pushed the two blondes to Ringo, who shoved them quickly outside. McCoy walked over to that table slowly, giving Ringo a chance to come back inside and angle to one side of the table.

The biggest man there also had the biggest mouth. He started to open it, when McCoy moved like a man half his size and put his fist squarely into that mouth. Ringo was behind two of his friends and had his gun out, waving it crazily, smiling, shaking his head. They got the message.

When McCoy had moved, the two men I was near grabbed for ankle holsters. I kicked the one nearest me in the throat and he went down choking. The other one tried to dive under the table but I laid him out with a solid kick to his kidneys.

McCoy's single blow had wrecked the man's face. It was bloody pulp: shattered teeth, strips of darkened skin hanging, the nostrils clotted over.

McCoy stood there quietly and then motioned with his head for us to move for the door. Ringo backed out, still smiling and swinging his gun around. I backed out after him into the freshness of the night, holding the door for McCoy until he signaled to me to let it close.

The two blond girls had huddled around Ringo, sand-wiching him between them. They looked frightened be-neath their makeup, their required boredom. Ringo had holstered his gun and stood grinning, an arm around each girl.

I waited by the door and then walked out into the dusty street, sucking in the fetid night air. Even it was refreshing after the bar.

McCoy had stayed inside.

I heard vague noises from inside, nothing more, for the next five minutes or so. I knew they all had guns—and so did McCoy—but there was no shooting. Maybe they re-spected the new odds. McCoy had his own method of settling this dispute, though he never once talked about it later.

Then we saw McCoy come around the side of the building. He saw my glance and just said, "Back exit." He looked the same as he had when we walked in a few hours ago: nothing out of place, very sharp, no cuts or bruises. But there was a look in his eye that I can't describe.

He grabbed the two girls by the hand and dragged them after him. We followed, Ringo and me, as he short-cut his way across town to the bungalow we had borrowed for liberty.

I don't remember much about that trip, or that eve-ning after we left the bar. I remember the heat and the smell of the air. I remember that we didn't talk all the way back. And when we arrived, McCoy went right up to the second-floor steps, still dragging the two girls breathlessly behind him.

He stayed up there with them and Cornpone, the snake, the rest of the week. He must have sent one of the girls down for food. Ringo and I didn't bother him, didn't question him.

The day we were to fly back north, the girls were simply gone and McCoy wore his stone poker face all the way to the air strip. Then, when we were tossing our duffel on and hauling ourselves aboard the Huey, his mouth split open in a grin, and then he was laughing, laughing as hard as I had ever seen anyone laugh.

So Ringo and I started laughing, laughing until we were crying, shaking the ship till the copilot turned around and told us to can it or we'd never get off the ground.

That made us laugh even more. Finally we stopped, but that gleam lit our eyes.

I said, looking right at McCoy, "You cunt sucker."

He looked back.

Then Ringo said to McCoy, "You nigger."

McCoy just looked back.

The gleam was there when he said "Fuckers. Fuckers!" to no one in particular. He was looking down through the side door as we swept up. We balanced our guns on our legs and settled in for the long ride back.

Sharp and I cut through the jungle at an angle, knowing if we went directly across we'd be stuck behind the company. Maybe that's what they wanted; we didn't know.

You get used to the plants that stick to your skin, to the vines that knock your helmet off and your gun out of your hands, to the constant dampness clinging to your boots and fatigues.

You remember the smell of the fungus beneath the fallen logs, climbing up even the healthy trees, mashed underfoot.

There's usually something dead in the jungle. All dead things carry a certain, but always different, smell. The snake in the river was quick. I smelled the sharp nasal quality of fresh blood, and then it was gone, sunk into the water, which carries its own smells.

That day Sharp motioned me over to watch a long constrictor squeeze a large trail rat to death, slowly, slowly cutting off the paroxysm of its muscles. A nest of baby snakes crawled near their mother. They lay in a twisting tangle while their mother slowly squeezed the life from the rat and then sucked it into its mouth, the jaws widening and growing until they could close on the rat whole.

We turned to go and our sudden movement must have startled the big one. She disgorged the rat, still whole, slightly digested, right into the nest of smaller snakes, who tried to swallow more than just a foot, or an ear, or the rat's face.

It smelled like a wounded grunt I'd dragged aboard the chopper while I fired tracers as cover into the hillside. Once inside, he smelled of a wound beginning to attract infection: not infected yet, new, but covered with fungus and mud and filthy torn fatigues for bandages. I'd kept firing long after we were safe just to keep the smell of powder in my nose, more powerful than the stink beginning to rise from the man's leg.

You can taste the humidity in the jungle. It can soften your beard so you can shave with a good knife and no water.

Sharp and I let the water fall into our mouths from our noses and lips. We sucked at it the hotter we got because we knew we shouldn't stop.

We glided through the brush, looking for any enemy sign. We went through almost side by side, neither riding the point nor breaking a path clear for the other.

I guessed we were only a few hundred meters from the trail the company was following, when we heard the voices

49

and both immediately folded at the knees. I looked at Sharp, hunkered down in the broken bamboo. He was turned slightly sideways, probably to hear their voices better. I took my helmet off and rested my gun across its inside so it wouldn't get too wet and jam on me. You can hear better without a helmet, obviously, but a sniper can kill you more easily too. The voices were calm. I didn't expect any snipers.

We had to make them and fast. If they were ours, we had to clear out and let them know a company was coming through. And if they weren't, that company would come slogging down that trail any minute now, figuring we had cleared it out for them.

I pegged them to be Montagnard, but we had no Montagnards working with us anywhere in the area. I picked up some phrases; Sharp seemed to be getting their general drift, too, which didn't sound very good for us.

He gave me the sign of the knife hand across the throat, an old Special Forces sign for enemy. I nodded but held a hand up for him to wait; I wanted to be sure. The Montagnard usually worked *with* us, and I wasn't excited about killing a half-dozen potential friends.

I had heard the dialect before but kept missing the meaning of words, phrases. Most of it came through, though: they were.rebel mountain people fighting anyone who came through their land. I tossed a stick at Sharp, who was quietly changing clips in his rifle from the short clip for patrols to the long banana clip, much harder to carry through the jungle. He kept working while turning an eye toward me.

I motioned us in closer, and he looked at me like I was crazy. I held up fingers on both hands, cocked an eyebrow, shrugged. That was our sign for "I don't know." He knew

I wanted to see how many there were before making a move.

And we both knew the company would be down that damn trail in minutes.

We crawled ahead, trying to avoid the bamboo that snapped like toothpicks and reverberated in our eardrums like bursts of gunfire. I slung my rifle upside down on my back so I could stuff leaves, dirt, moss, anything off the jungle floor, into the webbing of my helmet. I smeared the rest onto my face and arms. Sharp had rolled his fatigue shirtsleeves down and wrapped a camouflage issue bandanna over his nose and mouth. All I could see were his eyes in the underbrush and the gleam of a knife he nervously pulled back and forth from its leg scabbard.

We could hear them clearly from about thirty meters; I could see a couple of them pacing around in the high grass on the side of the rutted path that wound through the foothills. One carried an AK-47 with a banana clip; the other held an M-16 and gestured toward the west. As far as I knew, we didn't have anybody west. Maybe they did.

Now Sharp and I both could hear them clearly, and they meant bad news for us, and the guys coming at them down the trail to the south.

I counted five altogether. I picked up little bits of their conversation. They were a patrol sent out to walk the trail, looking for anyone on their land who didn't belong there: Chinese, Americans, other Asians, gunrunners, the local opium detail. It appeared they were unaware we were sending a whole company their way.

I couldn't divide them up to kill because two of them kept jumping around, babbling in that high-pitched dialect of theirs. I waited, face almost in the dirt on the jungle floor, knowing we were losing time.

51

A tiny piece of rotten wood bounced off my helmet and I looked over at Sharp. He held up three fingers and motioned with a sweeping gesture to his left. I nodded. He wanted the three on the left. The two crazies were mine.

Crazies were the hardest to kill because they were unpredictable. You never knew which way they'd jump, if they'd surrender, if they'd walk up to you with a hand grenade, live, in a pocket. They'd shoot their own people if it would give them an edge. Still, the ratio was right. Three normals for Sharp; two crazies for me. There was no other way to do it.

I gave the finger sign to go and we both belly-crawled forward, Sharp angling off to his left. I kept straight on, wondering which one to shoot first. The one with the AK-47 was shorter but stockier. I figured he couldn't run very fast. I couldn't see the other one too well, but he had the M-16, and I thought maybe he should buy it first just for that.

I could begin to see the other three clearly now. Two sat back on a rotted log; the third peered off west, his back to us. They all wore camouflage fatigues far too big for them.

Sharp was maybe ten meters away, still in the thick of the jungle foliage. I was almost at the edge of the trail and had begun to smell the men. They smelled of jungle, grease, cigarettes, dead fish. I saw that one of them had a box of grenades slung over his shoulder.

We stopped and looked at each other, then gave the thumbs-up sign. It meant move in exactly five seconds.

I tensed the muscles in my legs and felt the blood pounding in my temples; my abdominal muscles tensed and relaxed with each breath, with each second. Tensed and relaxed. Tensed and relaxed. Then sprung to life as I wrenched myself in one movement off the jungle floor, saw

Sharp do likewise right on time from the corner of my eye, and charged the remaining few meters.

We started firing at the same time. Even before I saw the man with the M-16 go down, cut in half, I saw Sharp's bullets riddle the log the two men sat on. Then my man started jumping—jumping up and down like he was crazy, digging in that box for a grenade, and none of my shots hit. They spit dirt at his feet and cut off into the air over his head like a crazy lead shower that rained and rained with no effect.

I saw Sharp charging out onto the road, cutting down his third man, looking around the log for the other two, and I knew there'd be a grenade at his feet if I didn't move.

I broke through the last of the underbrush and held my rifle by its clip and butt, running for the man standing there screaming, fumbling with a Russian grenade. I caught him in the stomach with the first thrust of the gun and he dropped the grenade. I tried to yell and nothing came out, but Sharp had seen and dove headfirst back into the brush. I ran a few meters, ticking the grenade down, and then jumped for a clear spot near the trail's embankment. The grenade exploded, driving me down into the dirt like someone had grabbed me out of the air and slammed me hard to the ground.

I peered up over the rain of dirt and stone and saw what was left of the Montagnard patrol. The bushes stirred to my left and Sharp emerged, eyeballing me the quiet sign. He was staring at the log he had dusted, moving steadily, silently, hands down by his boots.

Then I saw it too. Movement. Just a little, tiny movement, but enough, on the other side of the log from Sharp. Where's your gun, I thought. Sharp was advancing without a gun. And mine—it had been thrown clear when I made my leap. It lay half buried in dirt and silt a few meters away.

Sharp was almost upon the log, and he had drawn one of his knives from a boot sheath. As he stepped over the log I saw a blur of color and the Montagnard was on his feet, a Chinese survival knife in his hand. Sharp stopped and appraised him. It looked like he may have taken a round in the left shoulder, but it didn't seem to bother him. He switched hands with his blade while Sharp stood still, straddling the log, holding his knife blade edge up like the experienced cut man he was.

I remember other scenes, a gallery of sight, sound, and the smell of blood. Always that smell of blood.

Knife fights are usually very fast. They size each other up and make a move. Usually that first move decides it, one way or another. Fifteen seconds, maybe a few more. Compression. There is no luxury to think about what you're doing.

Sharp waited and the Montagnard feinted ahead, drawing Sharp forward. I crawled to my knees and tried to find my gun. The Montagnard had Sharp in close and kicked the knife from his hand, smiled slightly, then lunged at Sharp, who waited, poised, watching for the mistake that was the smile, the loss of concentration. He let the man come. I saw my gun stuck in the brush a few meters away. Sharp let him come, and when he made his slow lunge, still smiling, Sharp didn't move a muscle but to pull a second blade from his shoulder sheath, a bright double-edged blade with a black grip. The smile fell away but he couldn't stop and Sharp motioned wildly with his empty left hand to distract the man and then he cut him across the neck, left side, front, right side, in one semi-circular motion.

It's always surprising that men contain so much blood.

The Montagnard fell at his feet and Sharp moved out

among the other bodies, checking them for a pulse, his second blade ready to finish it. I had my gun and found Sharp's back in the jungle, almost as if he had left it there on purpose. I didn't ask.

We checked and rolled the bodies into a pile silently, watching the west for movement, listening to the birds and insects that had resumed their insistent thrum. When they stopped again—just as they had when we moved on the Montagnards—Sharp and I stepped back off the road into the jungle brush. We were covered with blood and moss and clay and fit right in. Sharp's bandanna had fallen down, making him look almost human, if you can call the way we looked then human.

We saw him about one hundred meters to the south, walking the trail like a fool, not crawling through jungle grass. I couldn't tell who he was at first, but then I recognized the leather sling on the M-16 and knew it had to be Andrews, an eighteen-year-old corporal from Tennessee. Shit. Corporal at eighteen.

Sharp and I exchanged a look and smile. We'd let this sucker point man walk right up to us. The trouble was, a nervous man suddenly scared can do foolish things. So we dug down into the dirt and moved an old log in front of us to intercept any stray bullets.

Andrews just kept coming, not seeing how the trail was pitted and scarred from bullets and grenade fragments, not smelling the blood or the spent rounds, not listening for the birds. He walked slightly bent back, foolish for a point man because of the larger target under the helmet. Andrews had proven to be a real killer, though; that's probably why he walked the point. The lieutenant, dumb-ass that he was sometimes, probably hadn't bothered to send out flankers. He probably thought Sharp and I could handle it.

So Andrews came abreast, still not seeing, not hearing,

not feeling what had happened at his very feet. Sharp started coughing as loud as he could, and I started babbling nonsense in Montagnard.

Andrews dropped into a crevice off the side of the road. I have to give him credit for that. He put the trail's ridge of dirt between us, and he didn't just shoot at the noise.

Then it was quiet. Too quiet. The birds and insects were still, except for the mosquitoes going for the blood all over Sharp and me. I looked at Sharp, who just cocked an eyebrow up.

I had this quick little flash of young Corporal Andrews, eighteen, pulling the pins off several grenades and sending them our way, so I yelled out.

"Andrews, you dumb-ass. You forget the patrol sent out?"

No answer.

Sharp yelled, "Come on, Andrews, how do you think we know your name?"

Still no answer. That did it for Sharp.

"Andrews, you are one dumb mother-fucking Georgia asshole. Sharp and Jones here, you hear me, stupid? Jones and Sharp, recon. Pull your half-assed head up out of the dirt and get your whole ass over here or I'll show *you* just why they call me the cut man."

I was trying not to grin because the mosquitoes were thick around my mouth. We heard a noise, a soft and slow movement from the trail, and saw Andrews's gun pop up, then his head.

"Over here. We're a couple meters in."

He pulled himself up, finally, and walked our way. We crawled out from behind the log and walked to meet him.

He stopped when he saw us, muttered something under his breath.

Sharp said, "Hey, man. Where's the company?"

"Maybe a mile back. Shit, what happened to you?"

"A *mile*? You're on point a *mile* ahead of the company?" I couldn't believe this.

"Well, maybe less. I always get ahead."

Sharp and I exchanged weary looks.

"So what the hell happened to you guys?" Andrews just kept staring at both of us, from head to foot, up and down. It just wasn't worth going into.

Sharp and I sat down on the ridge and slapped mosquitoes while Andrews walked officiously up and down the trail, upset because we wouldn't talk.

Sharp and I heard them before Andrews had an inkling. They made more noise than a whole regiment of the enemy. Andrews walked back down the trail and signaled them up. Sharp and I sat still on the ridge, slapping mosquitoes. The lieutenant motioned Andrews down the road and sent out a couple of flankers, then stopped near us for our report. I could tell he knew more than Andrews, watched his eyes as they roamed over Sharp and me, the pitted trail, the remnants of clothing and spots of blood where we'd dragged the bodies off into the jungle. The eyes finally narrowed to slits, and Sharp saw it too.

"Okay, let's have it. What went down here?" The lieutenant was motioning the men on, past the dead patrol that would have ripped the company's balls to pieces before we could have killed them.

We knew we'd answer for it later, but it seemed like the only thing to do at the time. Sure, sometimes the lieutenant made us forget he was a plastic man, created at some ROTC center back in the States. But that day he was a dumb, ignorant fuck.

Sharp said, "Fifteen hundred meters north," hitched up his gun and gear, and started after the company.

I said, "And fifteen hundred meters west," slung my

rifle barrel facing down across my back, and followed a few meters behind Sharp.

Then we both yelled back, without turning around, "Sir!"

He looks up, surprised to see me so close, in his face really, his smile diffused and slanting off, the word probably past his remembrance, echoing for me everywhere in the bar, the word from that bar so many years before, the word itself a bad taste in my mouth.

I see Kathleen's surprised look from the corner of my eye, but now all the men in the room are watching me, not her, not dreaming up their ugly little words, not this instant, and I see them react when I push the heel of my palm into the man's face. They jump, tic, swallow, scatter.

He's off his stool and regaining his balance as the blood flows from his nose onto his bleached white shirt. His look is of anger, pain, annoyance, a drink too many, he probably thinks. But he backs away and leaves, muttering. The others stare. The bartender casually wipes the blood from the bar. I return their stares until each drops his gaze, returns to a drink or hushed conversation.

Kathleen is next to me, one breast tight against my right arm. She starts to ask a question but I take her hand and lead her to the dining room stairs, promising her, "Later, later." She walks pinned to my arm, her breast firm, undulating against me with each step. I glance finally at her face, to remember her in this place, and see the fine blue vein throb below her silky blond hair. She looks me in the eye with concern, then places her other hand on my shoulder. I touch that hand slowly, gently, probing the length of the fingers, the short nails, the fine skin and bone.

I wake from sleep, silent, quiet, alone. It is dark, the branches of trees scrape at the windows, and I know I have been dreaming.

The wind is a squall outside, blowing in, but I don't move. I breathe slowly through my mouth to calm my racing heart, reach down into the ball I became in sleep to pull my socks up.

I don't know the dream but I know of it. My eyes close once more and I try to remember or forget and succeed at neither. It is a dream I talk to myself about in a code, one of many such dreams that prey upon stormy nights, hot afternoons, odd times when I let my guard slip.

To be simple, I tell myself it was the cut man dream. I give it a name and release it into the night, and release myself into the fear that sleep brings.

Stern and I are in Lincoln Park. I run and Stern watches the girls on bicycles and roller skates.

I sit under a tree, resting, cooling off, drinking a beer. Stern sits a foot or two away but in the sun, the sunglasses reflecting the deep, cool calm of Lake Michigan.

It's a nice day and the girls are everywhere: Girls in bathing suits, body suits, halter tops, tight muscle shirts, shapeless sweatshirts, short shorts.

I alternate beer and water while Stern pulls at a tall one under his longing gaze.

"Heartsick?" I ask.

"You better believe it."

"I thought you doctors could have your pick. Nurses, patients, grateful relatives, candy-stripers."

He peers over the glasses to see if I'm kidding. I don't smile but I know he sees it in my eyes.

"Right. It doesn't work that way. Especially not with the nurses."

I remember the jungle hospital and the nun bathing my sweating face and bare arms and chest without a break until they dropped a package of medicine by parachute. I never knew her name, couldn't even talk until after they airlifted me out.

"It's just this nice weekend, Jones. You know, we probably won't have anything this nice till next spring."

He pulled long and hard at his beer. I chugged the rest of my water and waited for the rest.

"Got the strangest case in a long time this week. A guy was referred to us by the north suburban medical center I told you about. He had a car crash about eighteen months ago—real bad. Killed someone in the other car, but it was their fault. Anyway, my new patient had a broken rib, a few lacerations, and severe contusions to his head. So they patched him up, did some minor repair work, and released him after about a week. Pretty soon his wife calls the medical center and asks to talk to a psychiatrist, which she does.

"She tells him that she doesn't even *know* the guy who walked away from the accident. He was totally different in behavior. Treated her with diffidence, and he had always been a devoted and doting husband. Treated their three kids badly. Seemed wrapped up in his work but couldn't seem to understand it.

"So she talks it out, and the shrink calls the kids in, who verify her story and add to it, and finally he calls the man in, but he refuses to have anything to do with a shrink.

"By this time the wife is almost crazy. She feels like she's living with a total stranger. Nothing is the way it used to be. She thinks she's really going to lose it if something isn't done."

Stern pauses for a pull and follows a set of legs along

the cinder path. I'm getting cool, and change shirts, then sit back to listen. Stern talks well, engagingly, no matter what he says.

"Finally the guy agrees to see a neurologist, not a shrink who doubles, but a straight neurologist, someone he knows—or knew. So he gets the battery of tests, X rays, skeletal exam, CAT scan. They show some brain impairment—minor—but also a completely abnormal series of electrical impulses in the brain. Nothing that will severely affect him, understand, not now—but evidence that he had changed completely, that he had almost no memory of his life, job, wife, kids, education—no memory that he chose to *use* anyway. He was like a slate that the accident had wiped clean. New life, new interests, new goals—and all of this without really knowing what had happened or was happening to him. That's why he was irritable, had so many problems at home.

"He separated from his wife after a little less than a year. Just couldn't give her a life, a man he didn't even know. It was a relief for the kids, I guess, it had been so bad.

"So now I got him, and probably the rest of the family too. There's no way they're gonna put it together again, but I have to try."

I turn and look out at the lake. Far off in the distance the tiny white sails move, jumping as the boats break into the waves that lap at the rocks a few feet away. Today the smell of summer has returned—the green leaves equal in number those that have turned, and the moss on the rocks looks healthy, new, ready to grow. The sun strikes sharply off the water, the whitened rocks, the polished driftwood along the shore. Each wave is a stab of light so bright I look away.

Everything is a drone, a single indecipherable sound. I try to focus on objects, distinguish them, but they run together in a swatch of white and color, color and black. Not a blur, but a white and black spotting, a series of multiple little dots, like what you see when you fall asleep and awake under the glare of the sun.

Stern's lips move, his hand gesticulates, but his eyes are twin pools of blackness. I start to sweat heavily, soaking the clean shirt through. I know the eyes are white, cloudy, filmy white, but still white behind those glasses.

My throat dries and stiffens. I fight panic, digging fingers into the dirt, twisting an ankle out in front of me to forget, but it isn't working, not this time. I am as helpless as I was once and this time surrender completely to it.

The room was white. Sometimes I'd think the room was really black, dark, and that we were told to *think* it was white, but that wasn't so. Somehow I knew it. I knew it was white, white as the snow I hadn't seen except in pictures for so long, white as ice, the kind that crusted on my windows at home, white as the silence that they forced upon us.

Sometimes they left us there, alone; I don't know why. Sometimes I think it was to force us to think about the white. So what happens when you *have* to think about a color, or, that's right, the absence of color? What kind of games are we playing here? How far back into memory and personality and—and I knew this is what they wanted, after all, this is what they craved—vulnerability—*vulnerability*—did we go? Too far. Too far for some of them, carried out still or babbling.

I had my own way. I thought of the story by Conrad Aiken, the classic, indecipherable little short story "Silent

Snow, Secret Snow." I tried to remember passages but could recall only the tone, the dry, wry way Aiken talked of the boy and his world of white snow, of silent snow, of whispering snow, of the final story that would be told.

It was a world of fantasy white, snow and crunching leaves and voices that interrupted the boy's very secret, very pleasant world.

Of course, the doctors and the others in the room understood the dreaming and focused upon it for their own purposes. I suppose they detected a gleam behind my half-closed eyes or saw a finger pulse with alarm when I was supposed to be asleep. They used it like they used us all those days, however long it was.

They called it the clinic. Even later, after we were out, at the debriefing at the hospital, everyone referred to it as "the clinic." It was no clinic. It was the torture room, just that, plain and simple. The white torture room, and well-designed it was.

I emerged from that place. Maybe it would be like waking up in the hospital a completely different person. Their side wanted it and our side wanted it too. Some people will abuse you, the song says. The new song. There were no songs over there, not in the jungle, or in the white room. There was a radio at base hospital. It played ? and the Mysterians and Sam the Sham and the Pharaohs and we all wanted to go home to this place we no longer knew.

" . . . One of the strangest head cases I've ever seen. Totally bizarre. Don't know if, what I'm going to do with this guy. And his family—wrecked, you know. . . ." Stern continues his monologue as if he were lecturing a pathology class.

It's red and unfocused where I've sat staring too long at the water. I sit up and lick my dried lips. It was a dream, no, worse than a dream. It was right here, among so many people. And Stern just kept right on talking.

I shake myself and break the bond the sweat has formed between those days and these.

"Head case, you say?" He wasn't expecting any interruptions and is flustered, slows down, stops.

"What? What's that? Oh, my latest case, that got you interested, Jones?"

"I wondered why you kept—keep—referring to this man as a 'head case,' that's all.

"Well, that's simple, old man, it's because that's exactly what he *is* and probably always will be."

"Will be *what*, man?" Stern doesn't like this. It's too much like a confrontation, a test of his expertise.

"He'll always be living his life out of his head, man, and a changed and rearranged head at that. It's no big deal."

"Yeah." I watch the people stroll through the park alone, in pairs. Flashes of white off the concrete, the bright legs of untanned girls.

Then I say, "You ever treat somebody *not* a head case, Stern?"

He turns and looks, cut by the tone in my voice, then hurries to grab his stuff and follow after me across the grass.

I'm moving, heading for a drinking fountain and then a fast train ride home.

I hear him behind me, running to catch up, panting. I hear parts of it—"figures of speech, all my cases are, this most recent, where are you—" and though I know it's rude and though I know I've done it before and though I know he's a friend of mine, I leave him easily behind.

It's so easy. And there's a song about that now too. I don't have to count the bugs on the mosquito netting to the tune of "96 Tears" anymore. Isn't everything so easy these days.

I'm at Tut's on Belmont on a Friday night. The place is packed and it isn't even late yet. Smoke around the stage area makes it seem even smaller than it really is, which is small.

This is the house of the Blues on the north side. The south side is legendary for those who've played there, and most have made the trek up north as well: Buddy Guy, Junior Wells, Junior Manse, Bo Diddley, Muddy Waters, Little Sonny, T-Bone Walker. There's too many to remember.

Jim McCoy had called me and asked to meet me here. I hadn't known what to say—never did when things like this came up.

"Come on, Jones, been so long we have to get together. Discuss old times. Huh?"

"Sure, Jim, sometime. I don't know if I can make it Friday."

"Man, you *gots* to make it Friday. My kid brother Jimbo's playin' with one of the bands—nothin' regular, but he was *invited*, ya see, not just another jam session for the boy. I told him I'd scare up some of the boys to see him play."

I thought about hanging up and walking, a nice long one into Oak Park to clear out my head. It felt like fuzz collecting around my ears. I swallowed some stale water in a glass by the phone stand.

"Who else you invite, Jim?" It came out kind of hoarse, kind of throaty, kind of dark and suspicious, but I couldn't help it.

65

He paused before he answered.

"Just some of the old guys, Jones—not everybody from the war like last time. Just some people I know. I don't think you know any of 'em 'cept Swanson, Jack Swanson. He's okay."

Yeah, I thought, that dude is okay.

"Promise me this won't be like Pheasant Run that time, McCoy. I don't need that kind of scene, you understand."

"Hey, my man, no way. Nothing is gonna happen. Like I say, Swanson you know, and he's cool, and the three of us can just have a few beers with my friends and hear my brother play. No big deal. Anyway—be good to see you after that time. You know?"

"Yeah, Jim. I know. Okay, Friday night when I can get there. Save a table or I'll save one for us. How many?"

"I 'spect six'll do 'er. This is cool, Trav, good."

"Jim."

He stopped and waited. I could hear his deep breaths coming through the line and could imagine him, all six foot six of him, waiting for another dumb-ass question, but not really minding, either, knowing somehow that it mattered.

So I just said, easy as striking a match, "What's your brother play, anyway?"

McCoy sighed in relief and laughed.

"He plays the black man's instrument, brother. He blows the harp."

I nodded, smiled to myself.

"So how will I know this dude if I show up late?"

McCoy laughed and laughed like he used to. He couldn't stop laughing.

"What. Come on, McCoy. Can't be that funny."

He was laughing and I could hear him crying. "No,

can't be, for *you*, Jones. He's playin' with the Nighthawks on Friday, man. You know them?"

Nighthawks sounded familiar but I had to say no.

"Well, never mind. It's just that they're all *white*, my man. You dig?"

I did.

So I'm at a little table not too close to the bands so we can talk, trying to hold the table till McCoy shows up. This is becoming increasingly difficult as the place picks up, packs the bodies in.

A group of punks bop over and slam themselves into the four vacant seats. One of them is tall, blond, in basketball shoes and baggy pants; another is short and acne-scarred with metal chain and earrings hanging all over him. He must be Son of the Road Warrior. The two girls stare at me. One is short and dark, in plastic sunglasses and cute black vinyl booties. She's carrying cameras and light meters and tape recorders around her neck. The other has natural red hair and glossed lips, heavily made-up eyes, a skeleton body.

I go, "Sorry, but these seats are taken."

Blondie says, "Yeah. Who's taken 'em?"

No laughter. These people know how to act serious.

"I'm saving these seats for some friends who should be here any minute."

The guy with the pitted face is looking over my old brown leather jacket.

The short girl lights an herbal cigarette and says, "Blow, man. You don't save seats at Tut's this time of night. Where we gonna sit? Look around. You see anyone else savin' seats for anybody?"

Her awful-smelling smoke hangs in the air around her pudgy face. A worm, I think; a pasty, fat little worm. Turn that log back over.

67

I go, "Look, my friends are not exactly—gentle, understanding types, unlike myself. I really think you'd better find seats somewhere else."

The other girl says, "That's cool. 'Scept there just *aren't* any other seats. Are there?" She stares at me, purses her glossed lips, runs a hand across one bare shoulder.

The herbal smoke is nauseating. I see the bright white skin, look over at the stupid plastic shades, see the smoke being sucked into that mouth, watch the blond play with his ponytail.

I want out. I want to breathe and not have to go through this. I don't want to do anything to these people. I don't want McCoy to do anything either.

The voice droned on and on as if the speaker never breathed, never coughed, never took a sip of water, never paused to consider.

"What do we do with the maggot? Why, we are repulsed, of course. But why? And what do we do? Do we step on him? Do we stand back and hope he goes away, burrows somewhere into a hole in the ground and never raises his ugly white head again? Do we?"

The voice was metallic, echoing off the cinder block walls, off the steel doors. I thought of the snow outside the walls, outside the doors, the snow that would fall and accumulate in spite of the sun and the dripping heat.

The table and chairs were white. When I was allowed, I'd place my fingers on the table and slowly, carefully, stealthily, chip away a tiny piece of lacquer from the table's edge. I had almost a meter of cheap metal uncovered before they caught me and sent me to the little room for meditation.

"You are no better than maggots to us. You are the

same pasty white, carry the same dirt, the same odors. You scratch and claw and grope, all for nothing. You would be blind as maggots if we allowed you outdoors. Blinded for life, just for leaving your new home here. You do like it here, don't you? You must like it here, because this is your world now—all of it. The clinic takes care of you. No one else cares. Not now. Not anymore. The clinic feeds you and provides your clothing and a safe, secure place to sleep.

"But ask yourself why? *Why?* We could have let you die. We still can let you die.

"Attendant number three. Choose a patient and sit him in the chair."

I sat numbly thinking how cold the snow was making the big white room as one of the guards walked back and forth before the table. I could see the polished black boots. How quickly the snow would blanket them, suck them in like living things, cut that guard off below the knees, where he'd bleed to death in the quiet, whispering snow. All of that blood would run deep but be buried, covered over forever by the cold, by the white.

Some of the other men sat staring at the walls or the floor. The white intercom box sat high in a corner, its white wire mesh like an albino spider web. Guards came among us and pulled our hair or pushed our faces up or tilted our heads between their small, gloved hands until we all were forced to stare at the man shoved into the white chair, his neck and hands and feet secured by white steel bands.

The intercom buzzed but I tried not to listen. It hissed instructions, croaked at us, droned on and on until the guard the box called "attendant number three" appeared with a white flour sack that moved. The guard reached in with his gloved hand and removed a large black rat, the only dark thing in the room, with yellow eyes and saliva dripping from its mouth and a white cord tied around its neck and one leg.

The box droned and droned and the smell of the rat permeated the room. The guard tied one end of the cord to the base of the chair. The rat had six feet of cord. He ran and tugged and sniffed, then jumped up onto the man in the chair and seemed to look him right in the eye before he bit.

The box exploded with noise. Screams filled the room. One man's head was bashed again into the table. Another man who had vomited blood onto the table was removed. The table was quickly cleaned. I watched the rat on the man that I had known and saw a blur of snow on a mountain, the fierce winter wind whirling from the box on the wall. And then it was over and everything was as it had been, and the droning metallic voice hovered in the humid, cold air.

"There is no reason for you to have to hurt yourselves in this way. We seek to help you, to remove you from your chosen status as maggots. You have a choice. You have free will, the will to create and define your own freedom, if only you will choose to take it. . . . "

McCoy and Swanson and two other guys are standing to one side, looking at me and the punks at the table. McCoy is smiling; the other two are smiling; Swanson has absolutely no expression on his face. That's how he was at the football scrimmage last year. No expression till he was hit late and out of bounds.

The punks don't notice until Blondie turns to me, waving a ringed finger. He stares at McCoy, half a foot taller and a hundred pounds heavier, the single hoop earring swaying as McCoy's grin widens. Blondie blanches and stands up. McCoy is dressed in black leather from head to foot. He places a hand gently on Blondie's shoulder and says, "Now, I don't want to cause any trouble with you or put you out in any way. Am I doing that?"

The other three are gathering packs of cigarettes, matches, cocaine spoons off the table and trying to be cool.

The blond one says, "No. No, sir. We just stopped for a smoke and will be going."

McCoy's face freezes in mid-grin. "You know, boy, they used to try to call me 'sir' in the army. I didn't like that. Not one little bit."

Blondie can't get up because of the massive hand on his shoulder.

"I'm sorry—my mistake."

McCoy slowly eases off and the blond one gets up and edges away with the other three. McCoy and his buddies erupt in laughter, then sit down. Swanson holds his great stone face intact and stands for a full minute, watching them go.

The weather turned vicious before we knew what was happening. You live in rain and mud until that is all you know, that and the slime clinging to trees, the fungi growing on anything that didn't move.

You don't know a monsoon until you live with one, or several. We had guys turn down liberty all year to advance their names on the list so they could get out for a week or two when it hit.

Sheets and sheets of foul-smelling rain pelted down through the trees, through the thatched hootches, through jackets and fatigues and underwear and boots. We pulled wool blankets over our heads at night on guard duty. Some guys would strap themselves in, pulling web belts tight around their legs, waist, chest, shoulders when they went on duty. They looked like sodden gray mummies with helmets and beards.

One night my duty started at 200 hours, a short shift because of the miserable conditions. I pulled my boots on in the hootch I had built into the side of a rock pile—at least there was no soil to collapse on me in the middle of the night—and forgot about the inch of water sloshing with every step. I had a machine-gun nest for my watch, so I left my gun behind, just carried a sidearm and a few grenades.

When I came up on the post the guard was sitting up straight, peering into the forest, wrapped up in those blankets. I gave the sign and crawled down into the hole, already a foot deep in water, but he didn't move, just kept staring out there.

Finally I tapped him on the helmet and it fell with a splash into our hole. He had a neat little slash on the side of his neck where the jugular runs. I guessed it had happened hours earlier; the rain had washed the blood away. He must have been tied into those blankets when the sapper closed on him, and he couldn't do a thing. His hands were free but they had not moved from the cold stock of the machine gun.

Of course, the sapper was long gone. It was a message for us, that we were too far north, that we didn't belong, that some knew how to live with the monsoon. It wasn't us.

Command issued orders against strapping into the blankets and put out double guard teams for a few nights. We never saw a thing.

When the rains slowed or cleared for an hour or two, the winds would rattle our bones. It wasn't the cold so much as the humid penetration of the dampness into our joints, right to the marrow in our bones. You don't know arthritis until you've lived through the monsoon.

I am reminded of it when I shake and burn at night, twist and turn in what should be sleep. And I remember the grunt propped up in blankets with his powerful machine gun, the blood drained from his body like something altogether natural.

I nod to the two guys McCoy introduces, shake hands with McCoy and Swanson. Swanson looks at me. I hope it all hasn't caught up with him.

"So, big bro' McCoy, where's this little brother of yours?" I think, keep it light and on track, and we can split in a couple hours with no pain, no trouble.

"Hey, Jones, don't you know rock 'n' roll? He's backstage rappin' with the band, where he belongs. Tunin' up. Dealin' with the groupies. He'll be out, you know, later, when the dudes decide they're ready to play."

I look at Swanson. "How's the construction business, Jack?"

Swanson has light brown hair and delicate features— light skin, a small scar under one ear, eyes almost white, they are so blue. He folds one hand upon the other continually, folding, refolding, but not nervously, just a repetition.

He looks vacantly in my direction and says clearly, "I've been out of that business for about six months." He looks around the room, folding his fingers onto the back of his other hand.

"So—are you working, Jack? Taking a break, maybe?"

You have to go slow and light with Swanson. Keep him steady. Talk but don't push. Ask but don't pry. McCoy is peering intently at Swanson when he answers.

73

"I'm working again. It's a pretty nice job. I'm a teacher's aide at a school in the suburbs."

McCoy drops the leather jive pose and quietly says, "I didn't know that, Swanson. Why didn't you tell me? That's cool, man, great."

Swanson doesn't smile but says, "You never asked, Jim. Anyway, Jones has done some teaching, so I figure he knows what I'm talking about."

McCoy and I trade looks. We've never seen Swanson so quiet, so docile, even. I think maybe he's on tranks—tranquilizers—but that probably would be good for him.

I'm about to respond when the Nighthawks come out onstage to a round of applause, whistles, boot stomping. They pick up their instruments and begin to tune up. McCoy's brother isn't out there.

I lean over to talk to Swanson before the set starts.

"So you've gone into teaching, eh, Jack? Sounds like you'd enjoy it."

"Well, not *into* teaching yet, but helping out. From what I see, I'll like it."

Swanson sits deathly still, doesn't move a muscle as he speaks.

"Where are you teaching?"

"It's a little suburb out south, Country Club Hills."

"Heard of it. Somewhere. So what kind of classes do you have—or homeroom—or whatever?"

"The school is grades one to five, and I'm the aide in one of the fifth grades. I mark papers, prepare assignments, help the kids in art and gym—just about anything they need."

"How do they feel—the kids—about having a *man*—and a guy your age—being one of the teachers?"

Swanson sips a drink as the band tunes its way through

a little pick-up of "Shake Your Tail Feather." He looks at me with the first real expression I've seen tonight, a sort of amused appraisal.

"You know the issues, don't you, Jones? I guess I should have known you would. Well"—he looks around the room for a second—"they were surprised at first. Not at my age. I don't think they really know how old I am, how much older than the other aides. But because I'm a man, yeah. At first. The only other male teacher around is the half-time P.E. teacher. You just gotta work around it. You know what I mean."

I know. The band warms up on an instrumental number that I don't recognize. We have to yell over the noise of the band, even though we're back from the stage. McCoy and his friends are into it, but Swanson and I keep talking when we can.

"You know, Jack, I really don't know much about the kind of teaching you're doin'. I taught for a while at the high school level. Since then it's been all college for me. So I *don't* know what you're doing."

He pulls on the drink and looks vacantly around the crowded room. He sighs.

"Yeah, but it's all pretty much the same thing. The kids might be a different age. They might not even be *kids* in college. But you still have to think a certain way, act a certain way, figure out how to get them to work for you. Even in high school and college. It's not automatic."

I haven't thought about high school in a long time, but he gets me back there, and I think about those days a little before the emcee steps up.

"Okay, everybody, you know who the guest attraction is tonight, a rhythm-and-blues powerhouse playin' just this gig in Chicago, the mean and hungry *Nighthawks*!"

A cheer rises from the crowd, people clap, slap hands, pound their feet on the floor, rattle the tables and chairs.

A guy from the band who's been sitting alone on an amp steps up to the mike and says quietly, "Hi and thank you, I'm Mark Wenner and we just want to play some blues for you."

That's all and the bass player starts a line. Wenner selects a harmonica from his back pocket and sucks in the first few notes of "Shake and Finger Pop." It's an old classic and I know without even looking that he's blowing a Hohner Marine Band, key of A. Same harp I used to play back in the 60's, so long ago.

Wenner is a good harp player, sucking and bending notes, not blowing much. Even some of the good harp players don't understand what you can get out of the low register if you bend or waffle a note, shifting and sliding across the holes.

It was 1969 and the Chicago Democratic National Convention was a memory. I was asked to sit in with some local musicians at the University of Illinois Chicago Circle Campus, to warm up the crowd for the big names. The main attraction that year in Chicago was The Young Lords, the Hispanic gang then getting into politics.

So we had James Hildebrand on drums, Rich Zywicki on bass, JoJo Kern on rhythm guitar and vocals, Elmore Grace on lead, and me on harp. We all came from different bands or session work and only a couple of us had ever jammed together. We had no rehearsal time. Local SDS leaders had called three of us. The Lords had asked for JoJo and Grace at the last second. One hundred dollars each for an hour and free lunch, finally confirmed just the day before.

I was living in a studio apartment on Sunnyside at the time, in between "real" jobs. The SDS offered to give me a ride to the school union. I told them sure, why not.

So Anna Friedberg picked me up in a 1960 two-door Chevy, full of rust and grime. She stopped outside the building and honked. I pulled a T-shirt on and picked up my bag of harps on the way out.

Anna Friedberg will live forever in my memory from just that day. She sat all sprawled out, every little inch of her, maybe five-two, behind the wheel, looking bored. She wore heavy brown boots and rough blue jeans without a belt, a blue workshirt with holes in it at the elbows and shoulders, and a tightly rolled bandanna around her neck. Her body was really sort of nondescript—nothing outstanding but nothing missing, either. It was her face that day that I remember best.

She had calm but angry green eyes that peered furtively from behind a pair of silver wire-rimmed glasses. Her brown hair hung around her face, strands and light curls falling almost to her shoulders. She probably washed it last week. Her nose was small with tiny but distinct nostrils. Her mouth was large, capable of the widest smile, but set in a line at the time. One tiny ear peered out from the strands of hair. Her brow was furrowed in three tight lines that crisscrossed the cool blue blood vessels of her forehead, and her light, almost blond eyebrows turned in toward her nose.

She sat sprawled behind the wheel, the motor running. One foot was pulled up toward her crotch, where the boot lay on the splintered plastic upholstery like something dead and discarded. The other booted foot was planted squarely in the center of the passenger side. I squeezed one leg in under hers and fit the other up against the door and slammed it shut. I put a hand out the window into the breeze and shoved my kit between the window and the dash. She held the rims of her glasses for a moment between her left forefinger and thumb and then pulled the glasses back away from her eyes, farther onto her nose. It made her eyes seem even more distant, but piercing, burning from inside.

She said, "Hey, man," put the car in gear, and we were gone. She had moved her right leg to drive but the other leg stayed curled on the seat. She drove with one hand, her right—just a few fingers, really. Her left arm dangled out the window. Once in a while she'd pull strands of hair out of her eyes or mouth.

Her voice was quiet but gravelly, sort of how you'd expect Janis Joplin to speak back in those days. Not put on, though.

I didn't answer her because she didn't seem to care. She just drove—switching lanes, passing on narrow streets, darting up alleys and through truck loading zones.

Anyway, she knew my name and why I was going down to campus. Probably no big deal to her. Finally, though, I felt a little awkward rolling along the city streets with someone at the wheel whose name I didn't even know.

"So what's your name?" I tried to put it as casually as I could.

She looked over at me as if I had interrupted something important and she wasn't very pleased with it.

"Why do ya want to know?" She tossed over her shoulder as she screeched around the turns on Lake Shore Drive.

I really wasn't in the mood for sullen banter.

"Forget it."

I tapped my fingers on the hood, felt the wind pull at them, then pulled them into a fist.

I noticed a little smile creep into her annoyed expression.

"Drive, he said. That it, Jones?"

Our eyes met and locked for a moment, amused.

"You read poetry, huh. Creeley. I suppose the Beats too. I thought all that artistic stuff was 'counterrevolutionary' to you guys. You know what Bobby Seale says. Eldridge Cleaver. Right?"

She just drove for a minute, then opened up.

"Hey, man. I'm not gettin' into it. I'm just your friendly local free ride downtown. But I don't have some party line to follow. Seale and Cleaver don't tell me what to do, or Dellinger and Davis. I don't know where you're at, man, some weird musician or what. Different strokes for different folks, some middle-class trip. But *I* know what I'm up to. Women have a new place, and maybe that's *your* place, brother. I don't know you, what your bag is, nothin'. I just know me, and I don't talk your 'revolutionary' line."

She was gesturing with one hand and driving with the other, her hair blowing up in her face, the leather of her boots flashing in the noon sun. Wild. Wild woman.

"Hey, lady, or woman, whatever you want. I've heard this shit before. I don't even want to know *you*. I just wanted to know your name. Like polite small talk, ya know? But can it. I can do without it. So drive. I'll just take the ride. No speeches, questions. Okay by you?"

I guess I got pretty mad, who knows why. I usually didn't talk like that to strangers, not in those days.

So she drove. I rode. The sun was hot and glared through the windshield, glanced off the steel of downtown Chicago, stuck my T-shirt to my back with a bath of sweat. The wind whirled through the air, kicking newspapers around, blowing dustballs up the curbs onto sidewalks against the gray-suited, well-heeled businessmen who gritted their teeth and closed their eyes against it, like pale, turgid turtles.

Scraps of paper and cigarette ash blew around at my feet. The vents near the floor picked the dust up and the flow of air from the windows forced it back down.

We fought it out with other cars in the Loop. She drove either with a foot and finger or with her whole body. By the time we were on Congress headed west for the campus she was leaning forward, beating on the horn that wouldn't work, rocking the steering wheel, screaming out the window.

"Move it, you fucker! Get your ass out of my way. Shi-*it*!"

She never looked my way except to make a lane change. An irregular smear of dirt ran down her cheek onto her neck. Drops of sweat fell from her temples. Some intense young woman.

I was getting a little annoyed myself, though. By car, my place should have been about half an hour's drive at the extreme. We'd been on the road almost an hour and it was almost one, almost time for me to go on.

"Fuckhead," I muttered at a guy who jammed into our lane only to decide to change again, slowing us to fifteen miles an hour. We missed a light and I banged my fist on top of the car. I heard a light cough and thought I saw her smile, then drive on.

We were finally about to make the turn onto Halsted, when a bus ran through the yellow and left us stranded in our lane.

We both yelled "Asshole!" after the bus at the same time, looked at each other, and smiled. Then she said, "Okay, man. My name's Friedberg. Anna—Friedberg. And I know who you are."

"Okay, Anna. So you got a name. I'm sorry about the hassle, but you're SDS, right, and not too friendly, at least not at first, right, and you know that poem by Creeley, it seems, right, so—"

"Yeah, yeah, point made. Yeah, I'm all that. But it's not like being a Ritz cracker or something. And we don't all look alike, have natural rhythm, dance to it, you know what I mean?"

She made a crazy dragging turn to the left the split second the light turned green.

"Yeah. I'm no expert on SDS, much else either. Just trying to be friendly."

"So Jones—you're Travis Jones, not some bum who likes to hang out and hassle radical young women, right?"

We both laughed as she pulled into a university lot.

"Call me Trav, or T.J. They used to call me T.J. in school, high school. Some people still do. Or just Jones. Hell. Anyway."

"Anyway—we got to move, man, we'll be late for sure—anyway, just why are you doing this gig?"

"Say it was for money and free lunch. What'd you say to that?"

She grabbed a canvas bag—used Swiss gas mask, I could see—and I grabbed my harps, slammed the beat-up door, and ran across the street toward the Union.

"Good question. I guess that's cool, if you need the bread. It ain't bad pay."

She paused and looked up at me. Out of that car, she was small, in spite of her boots—a little over five feet tall, and skinny under those nondescript clothes. Her hair hung free everywhere and the dirt streaks remained.

"But I get the feeling it's not just the money. Eh? Somethin' else?"

I wanted to think about that one, about her asking it, so I grabbed her arm and said, "Five to one. Let's make a run for it."

We sprinted across the grass next to Hull House and up the second-story steps, two at a time, charged through a door propped open, and through the concourse toward the Illinois Room on the third floor.

We were in our third day in the trenches. Sharp and I had dug in together, lifting the silt and mud and sand out with a caved-in helmet and regulation "survival" shovel. No way that thing could help you survive over there.

The rain was pretty bad but the winds were worse. They'd die down for an hour, maybe two, then rise again, peaking sometimes at eighty miles an hour or more. You couldn't dig in that kind of wind, so you'd stop and find a sturdy tree to prop yourself up against.

That's how the Hmong tribesman did all their farming, lashed to rocks and trees so they wouldn't fall off their land. But that's something else.

That morning Sharp and I had dug out of a little hole thatched over our heads with bamboo. It was just a two-foot hole for sleeping till we could get the real one made. The rain and wind both had picked up that night. We had heard the weird moan of the monsoon spilling out around us, huddling us deeper into our hole.

We were up at 400 to check the perimeter guards and raise the relief out of their holes. Not too far from our dig, way inside our perimeter, we found a Pfc. dead, his head just hanging to one side, lashed to a tree. He still had his helmet on, chinstrapped tight. His fatigues were soaked with water. But he was the most ordinary-looking dead man I had ever seen.

I could see that Sharp was stumped. No blood, no shrapnel holes, no artery cuts. Then we saw the binding across his chest that held him up against the tree. Sharp cut him down, and when he fell a great pocket of air whooshed out of his body. Sharp stepped back, but I was on him, pounding his chest for something, trying to raise something other than his last great lungful of air. Nothing.

We figured his hootch had blown away in the storm and he had been caught in the winds. He must have found himself a sturdy old tree to tie himself to, so he could get *some* sleep, even if standing up. His big mistake was that he had lashed himself on with leather cord and tied it tight and in double knots. After he had fallen asleep the leather—maybe a piece of a villager's abandoned fish net—began to dry out when the rains stopped and the cooling winds continued. And he had probably awoken in time to feel his heart and lungs being squeezed like sponges, probably called out to the watch, the words lost in the gale, his frantic attempts to untie the knots useless, his reach for the boot knife not long enough.

Sharp and I figured it the moment I stopped trying to raise another lungful, without saying anything.

They say that a baby who has been beaten to death looks like a rag doll. This man, all bulky in his gear and fatigues, tall, with a beard coming in, with an automatic rifle on his back, this man, ready for whatever he was there for, looked like that.

Sharp went to find the C.O. Probably get pissed off at being woken up. We needed a burial patrol. Someone had to write it up, send it down the line. Explain it, in military language, something they would understand.

I stayed and clipped his dog tags off and draped them

over his gun. I don't know what I saw in that face. Maybe that's what scared me. It wasn't fear, or anger, or peace. Just a blank look. Not even a stare. He was like a department store mannequin, but one I probably had talked to. I really couldn't remember him, but we might have talked. Now, just a face with nothing on it. Eyebrows, a nose, lips—nothing. Just nothing there.

Later I dreamed about him: sometimes just the face. Sometimes I'd wake clawing at my chest, suffocating, the bands of leather tightening around my chest in sleep. Once, they put restraints on me in a field hospital so I wouldn't yank the stitches in my back and shoulder out. I woke in those restraints and went wild. It took three French nuns and two soldiers to get me back into bed. The doctors had to throw seventy stitches in me just to close the new wounds. That night they started leaving a nurse next to my cot in place of the restraints.

Sharp came strolling back as I covered the Pfc.'s face with branches to keep the flies away.

"Captain wants us to finish diggin' our hootch and to get in there as soon as possible. New watch is notified."

I started to walk away.

"Jones."

"What?"

"Captain wants to see us about this."

"I thought he wanted a hootch, soon as possible. Monsoon's coming up again."

"He said do it when he's done with us."

Sharp stood on one foot, balanced, looking closely at me.

I spit.

"Shall we do it, then, Corporal Sharp?"

He pointed to the camouflage tents with his belt knife.

"After you, Corporal Jones."

I hate it when I dream and am caught within the dream, a hand or a leg there, the mind here. You feel helpless. It isn't the dream. It's a different place. In the dream you have the freedom of the mind's will to take you into the past, to rearrange the present, to predict the future. When the dream goes bad, all freedom is sacrificed and you're in some twilight zone that won't release you.

I am dreaming, drifting higher and higher from deep sleep to that moment when I am suspended between dream and waking. We're in the north country and the patrol has been decimated. It's Sharp and me and the new C.O., just sent over from the States, Captain Quigly. We all call him the Q, usually behind his back. He's the closest to a spit-and-polish man I've ever seen over here.

The rest of the patrol is hidden in the fields down below. The Q wants to reconnoiter up on this mountain, just a brown spot on our map. Then the mortars come in and damned if they don't blow the fields to pieces. Round after round, volley after volley, and the smoke is so thick, we can't see where they're coming from, or if any of our guys are still alive.

But it's a dream and the shelling lasts forever. Sharp sits on his helmet behind a tree and carves four-letter words. I just stand and watch. The Q, pasty-faced, paces and paces, his mouth open, but no sound comes out.

He left the radio down there. Maybe that's okay—they can call for support with their exact coordinates. But we could have called it in. I'm pissed off that the Q is so stupid. But I can't tell the dream to stop. I can't control it. It keeps playing this scene over, the three of us helpless on the mountainside.

They asked me what I dreamed about. The voice came over the intercom in the ceiling and while my eyes got used to the glare of the room, someone came in and left a cup of brown tea. The voice was gentle but insistent. I studied the cup, its smooth contours, no cracks or breaks. The voice intruded. I thought of a woman's breast, a breast that is never flawless but so beautiful, so perfectly shaped to be itself. I thought of the breast of a girl from school—always firm with muscle, always brown, the nipple always hard to my touch. I could hear snatches of the questions, only fragments, and I sat there smiling until the box cut off with a final crackling and I was left alone in that white room with that cool, perfect cup.

So Sharp and I went to see the captain. We'd been through this before. I just hoped he didn't try to field-decorate either of us for anything. It got tiring explaining to them why we said no, why we didn't want it.

The captains had a big camouflaged tent on the hill perimeter, protected on two sides by hill and sandbags and on the others by buried machine-gun nests. The tent also contained the radio and the terrain maps of the surrounding countries—piles and piles of huge colored maps, others rolled up in cardboard.

The captain was young, a little older than Sharp and me maybe, but still young. He sat by the radio on a hammock slung between metal poles. He wore fatigues and seemed to be growing a beard. He was my third C.O. in three months: reassignment and snakebite took their toll.

We stood at a sort of attention. He seemed to be studying a map, but I saw his eyes flicker and glance about and knew he had just been sitting waiting for us.

He stood up and said in a monotone, "Sharp. Jones."

We said simultaneously, "Sir."

No enthusiasm. But he knew that's how we were, so he

looked at us only briefly, then stood with a hand running up and down the smooth aluminum pole as he spoke.

"That was Pfc. George Ambrose Eckerly you found out there. First tour. Fifth month here. Fourth week up here with us."

He stopped and looked at us.

"Either of you know him?"

We both shook our heads. I saw something on his face then, a glimpse of relief perhaps? I couldn't be sure, and he went on.

"Well, without going into the details, which, as good soldiers you need not know, and which, as gentlemen, such as you are"—Sharp spit phlegm onto a bug crawling near his feet, then resumed his stance of relaxed attention—"such as you *are,* you probably do not care about, I intend to recommend Pfc. Eckerly for the Bronze Star for Valor."

We looked at each other, Sharp and me.

"I will, of course, need your reports and signatures on the supporting documents. I will send my recommendation back by courier at twelve hundred hours today, so you are both relieved of duty until then to work on your reports. That's all."

But he stayed there, and so did we, the two of us slouching at attention, the C.O. running his hand up and down that shiny pole.

Finally Sharp spoke up.

"Pardon me, Captain. I don't care what kind of recommendation you make for this kid, he's dead, but I don't think our reports can be of much use to you. That man just made a big mistake in the storm last night, that's all there is to it. I cut him down from a tree he had lashed onto. And Jones tried to bring him back, but he was long gone. He lashed himself to a tree, see, and when the rain stopped—"

The captain stopped him with a glare.

"Now, listen to me, Sharp. You, too, Jones. I've had it up to *here*"—hand at his neck—"with your backtalk and your asshole attitude. Was up to me I'd send you both back. Or out alone on long patrol, maybe."

He smiled.

I said, "That's been tried before. Sir."

The smile dropped into a scowl.

"No more horseshit. This is how it's going to be. I want that star for Eckerly and I'm gonna get it. You write it up that he caught a load in the chest in crossfire during a black attack."

I said, "Come on. A black attack in the middle of a monsoon? Who'd believe that?"

"His father will. And so will the brass. They don't know a monsoon from a spring shower. But that ain't your problem or your concern. You give me the report I want. That's the only thing you have to worry about."

Sharp was fingering the Moray knife sheath he wore around his neck. He was looking at the ground. I was staring the captain hard in the face.

"Who is Eckerly?"

Sharp's voice had a peculiar light tone, resigned, about it. He didn't look up.

For a minute I thought he'd answer, but he closed his mouth and narrowed his eyes.

"That's all, men. I want your signed reports as soon as possible. Then you return to trench duty. Or we can find you something more pleasant to do. Now, that's *all*."

He turned back to his map. We watched him and slowly shuffled out.

Sharp stopped a few meters from the tent and said, "I could peg him from here when he comes out the door."

I surveyed the distance and decided that he could, too.

"Or incoming could get him."

"Shit, you never know. But not in this weather."

"Maybe a black attack."

"Yeah. Oh, yes. And at high noon too. Oops, sorry, sir, nonregulation attack, sir, pardon me, sir."

We walked in the general direction of the quartermaster's tent. He had the forms and clipboards.

I kicked over a pile of mud. "What do you make of it"

He fingered that sheath. "Some kiss-ass."

We stood outside the tent for a while. I watched the recruits brought up the week before try to clean the mud out of the muzzles of their guns.

Sharp finally ducked in, muttering, "He won't live long out here. Not this far north."

I followed him in and saw the man in the black beret from the corner of my eye.

I dream a dark dream. One of the men is tied down in the mud and they are throwing handsful of mud over his feet, his knees, his stomach, finally his face. There are three of them but it seems like there are more. A man walks up, all black, in a coolie hat, and as he passes by he guts two of them with knives from his sides and kicks the third in the face.

There is heavy machine-gun firing. It is so loud in my ears I almost wake, but then retreat. It's so loud because I hold the M-60 a few feet away, spraying the thin thatch huts in the village. I can't see my face. It is smeared with the blackest mud.

The man in the coolie hat scoops up the man on the ground, cutting him free, and throws him over a shoulder, running for the trees. I follow running backward, spraying the village, the brush, anything. Little dots of red and yellow appear before my eyes and I stop to look at them.

They are soundless and spit thatch and mud up onto my clothes. Then I back away again.

When the man in the coolie hat turns, I follow, hoisting the gun up to run, and I see the vacancy in the carried man's eyes, and I think that I must know him, but then realize that I do not. I tap the other man on the shoulder and give him a sign. He throws the man down and slaps him hard, while I rip his neck chain off and dig through his pockets. He slaps him again and again and then I hear the gunboat overhead in the clearing, and I drag the man in the coolie hat away, leaving the M-60, spiked, behind.

The black and green gunboat hovers and the door gunners are tracing patterns through the trees.

Daylight breaks through and I can't focus on it, but we make it, that much I know, smelly and filthy in that ship banking like hell out of there.

It is a face that I thought I knew, but didn't know. Couldn't know. The sun comes up suddenly, as if it had been hiding for a long time.

"See, none of that was what was supposed to happen." I speak in a hushed tone that is absorbed and enfolded in the dark corners of the room, in the rich mahogany of the walls.

Four men sit in the room, three in plush leather chairs, the fourth on the floor, leaning his head against his hand. He speaks softly and tiredly.

"That's right where you're wrong, my friend. It was all supposed to happen. Why do you think they kept sending more and more of us over there? On some whim? You were trained and retrained and it never even changed, did it? How many guys did you train, Jones? I don't mean in dress at the camp down south or up in Monterey. I mean *there*, in the mountains and the villages and the paddies—how many did you help? And every time you did it you helped the thing keep going."

I walk to a window. The room is on the second floor of a spacious suburban home. It is gray outside, late October afternoon weather. The leaves are stripped from the trees and lay defenseless on the ground and in the street. An occasional car goes slowly past. Everything is slow, and dark, and oppressive. Even the tired young men in the room. I have heard so many like them talk about the war, their adjustments, the noises that startle them, the crowds they cannot face.

I remember the great movie *Halloween,* probably because of the weather, the coming of Halloween. Jamie Lee Curtis plays a high school girl who will be victimized by the boogeyman before the night is over. But what I remember best—and most—is the gray day, the dreariness of the sky as she walks home from school, the look on her face when she lies alone on her bed, thinking, thinking about what only the innocent can know, before unknown, sudden terror strikes.

I get over it, I think, and decide to leave. One of the men is saying, "Sure, it was just like a tiger cage, maybe not that fuckin' filthy, but there was shit lining the bottom. They wanted to break me. And they did, in a week." His face is red but vacant, in contrast to his expensive suit and French-cut shirt. He's one who has learned to adjust.

My leather jacket is hot as I take the stairs down, but I zip it up outside. The wind is starting. Clouds blow quickly overhead. It's fresh in my face.

I scuff through leaves and am reminded of my first fall back, and of that woman who got me through, or at least pushed me to a new place—Anna again, Anna Friedberg. I wonder where Anna is now and what she possibly could be doing.

91

The wind is cool and biting and I welcome its strength against my facade.

The Illinois Room probably holds a thousand people if they pack them in. They were packed in that day we rushed up the escalator stairs, flashed our temporary ID, and found ourselves going in opposite directions: me for the stage, Anna for the rear of the room.

I shouted through the crowd, "Where are you going?"

She flashed the ID over some heads and said, "Concert security." I stopped but couldn't see her. I could hear the band tuning up, smelled sweat, cigarettes, marijuana. I was about to turn for the stage when I heard her voice, saw the top of her head: "Hey, I'll see you after, Jones. Give you a ride home." Then she was gone and I needed to be on that stage.

I knew all the guys. They handed me a "Chicago mike," a big vocal microphone with omnidirection and two or three inches of flat pick-up cells—the absolute best for harp reproduction. James Cotton never used anything else.

They kept tuning and I fiddled with the bass and treble of my amp. Someone had stashed a couple of bottles of whiskey behind it. I blew a note or two and noticed they had wired my mike to another amp across the stage— stereo-effect. Good sound men. I blew some scales.

The bass player called us in and said we'd do "Hell Hound on My Trail" to lead off. The crowd was restless; I kept hearing cracks about white boys playing the blues. We cut the solos and did the short version.

We were situated on a small stage in the center of the room. We were maybe two feet off ground level, and huge potted plants sat next to our amps. A portable lectern had been moved from center stage but sat on our left. Picture windows were at our backs. It would have been nice had the crowd come to see and hear *us*.

We did that first number and huddled by the drums. JoJo Kern was already drinking wine out of a brown paper bag. I split a bottle of Gatorade with the drummer, Hildebrand, and Kern and I agreed we'd better play rock and roll if we wanted to make it through to our free lunch—and our paychecks.

Then Kern suggested "96 Tears" and Zywicki said Yeah and I wasn't at all ready for it, not that sudden, out of the blue. I told them I'd sit it out, there was no harp piece in the song. Hildebrand looked surprised but they were cool about it. Grace said he'd do the organ changes on guitar and I walked away behind the amps as they cut into it.

I opened the curtain and looked out across Halsted Street, toward the south and east parts of the city. Trucks poured along the streets exhaling brown and black smoke in the heat. I could see the parking lots and tried to pick out the Chevy but couldn't

They reprised the song. The audience had gotten into it, and they kept repeating the chorus with its beautifully repetitive chords. It was hot and smoke rolled my way, pressing me up against the window, my own sweat plastering my shirt to my ribs and shoulder blades.

I couldn't see the lake but I knew it was blue, blue where the water meets the sky and rolls on and on endlessly. The sounds and the sweat and the smells burned into me like a hot knife, the one Sharp had used to rip open my pectoral muscle before the poison could infuse the nerve with its power. Sharp had ripped it with the hand of a crazy man, but I'd seen the eye of the surgeon as his hands worked the muscle and the liquid came pouring out, a green viscous fluid intermixed with my blood. Green, green, what they used to kill us over there, and never the same thing twice.

Sharp and I were split up after we turned in our reports. We sat a few feet from each other while we filled them out but never said a word. Mine was all numbers: hours, patrols, patrol number, base number, bases, the kid's serial number, weather reports. All that before the narrative. I never saw Sharp's. Mine read: "Victim of environment; odds heavily against the survival skills of normal soldier— no matter how good." God only knows how the C.O. dealt with that and translated it on the master report for the Bronze. I had the feeling Sharp's was a little more acerbic and dead to the point. Maybe: This fucker practically committed suicide. All I know is the next morning we got different orders and saddled up with new small patrols.

I was sent to a Sergeant Lewis, a good enough soldier I'd seen in the jungle from a distance with other patrols. Lewis just looked up from his plastic pouch of orders when I reported and told me to go sit in his tent and relax. He had three other new Joes to round up. Two were late and the third hadn't "volunteered" yet.

I dropped my pack in the mud under the tent canvas and sat on it. I always arranged the kit so a flat tin plate lay near the top with a rubber tarp on top of it: a little bit of cushion when the waiting came around. And the waiting always came around.

Something different was happening. The lieutenants were spending more time studying their orders. More patrols were heading out in all directions. I could hear the radiomen all the way across the compound. Static was coming through. The snipers were all being dispatched with foot patrols, even the two or three who were always positioned in the trees around our base. But nothing had leaked through the grapevine.

I saw Sharp walking south with a seven-man patrol. They were just outside of camp and they had a point man already, and Ray rode the eastern flank. Two snipers slogged along through the mud with him.

Lewis ducked under the tent awning, looking tired already. He slapped mosquito juice onto his neck and looked me over.

"You know there's a move on, Jones. You're a smart dude. Maybe you know even more than I do. Who knows. But you know I can't tell you much. All I can tell you is you and I are going out with two new guys and a recruit from SOG who's been here less than three weeks, first tour. In spite of SOG, I'm not impressed. And then I've got you. Potential sergeant by now if you'd only taken the promotion. Twice. Curious. Want to tell me why not, Jones?"

I looked away and Sharp's patrol had been sucked up by the brush. A mist hung over the trees and steadily, slowly, it dripped down, like a cheap shower you can't fix. Lewis was okay, but I had no reason to talk to him.

"Well, I figured it'd be that way. You're a smart one, no matter what you use your brains for. Just promise me you'll *use* 'em, when you travel with me, okay?"

I grinned and knocked the moisture from my helmet.

"Sure thing, Sarge. No matter the condition, it keeps on tickin'."

His mouth lay in a flat line but the gray eyes softened. He motioned me up to look at a tiny blue map pinned to a cork bulletin board.

I have a cork bulletin board a lot like that now in my apartment. It's on the bedroom wall next to an expansive window that looks out toward a huge old maple tree. A

95

chair sits several feet away, but within clear view of the upper branches of the tree.

Tacked to the top of the cork are two tiny gold and two tiny silver medals from a track meet at Northwestern University a couple years ago. A good memory. Below them are a couple of commercial photos—color—of me plodding along in a couple of races in Chicago. Thumbtacked around are several ribbons from little local track meets and road races. And in the middle there are photocopied training tips from a running magazine. There's plenty of free and empty cork space.

I have a little desk up against the window, with a small lamp, a phone, some stackable files. I usually throw dirty elastic bandages and sweat bands on the desk to dry out. Sometimes I swing my typewriter around and use my desk to hold papers. Most often I sit back in my chair, or sit in the typewriter chair at the desk, just looking out, watching the thousands of leaves in that tree, shimmering in the sun, dripping in the rain, shaking in the winds that come up late at night.

I have dozed off in my chair. My legs dangle over the side of the overstuffed chair, a "let's-get-rid-of-this-thing" gift from my mother when I moved into my own apartment in college.

The day and night are hazy, indistinct. I resist the automatic impulse to check my watch, with its built-in light. Let the night be, late or early.

It's late October and still the leaves hold on. The wind in the leaves sounds like surf, or the gentle push and pull of water on rock. I had heard the same sound at the Indiana Dunes not long ago.

For a moment I think of Kathleen in the apartment below. My eyes open but I force them shut. Sometimes I'll take the memory rather than chance the new occasion. Tonight I will let her lie, no doubt curled naked or in just a T-shirt in her huge bed, one leg pulled halfway to her chin, her hair disarranged on the pillow, a blanket pulled up to her chin or thrown off in moments of hot dreaming.

A kind of blue haze settles down upon the cornea. Not the red of the sun, or the black of certain darkness, or the white I avoid when awake, but a cool and restful blue, the meditation on blue, blue the metaphor and the sign.

For me it is no sign, and if it is metaphor, it is metaphor for itself. It is alone but suggestive, even of other color, and I wonder by now just how awake I can be.

The quieting of the leaves is the color of sleep. Tomorrow is soon enough, isn't it, to think of tomorrow, and memory, and the moods that sweep me away more and more each day. *Blue* is the story for tomorrow, and I know as sleep approaches that I will be ready.

*Mornings I lie in bed on top of the sheets, usually sweat-*ing, replaying the night, the dreams, the half sleep. Images drift and tumble about and are dispelled.

Today something brings to mind a movie I've now seen on TV two or three times, always late-night. I can never remember its title, but it has a small, good cast, including William Holden, Peter Fonda, and John Phillip Law.

Fonda, Law, and another man are all Vietnam veterans who live in the same town. Once each year they leave their kids and their wives behind and head into the wilderness to hunt.

The movie begins with Holden dropping his granddaughter off with Fonda's wife. There's a quick flashback to the girl's mother's funeral. Her father also died at the same time. We assume a car crash. Holden's going out of town and needs a baby-sitter. By coincidence, it's the same week the boys are heading out.

The three drive toward a deserted chain of rivers, acting very macho and manly along the way.

As they near the little dock, they spot an attractive woman with a man in her car. They force them off the road. Law rips them out of the car with a .44 Magnum at their heads while Fonda flashes an ID for a second, tells them they're under arrest, and pats them down. Then they drive off, their captives in back and the third man left behind. He drives the woman's car into a river and watches it sink.

At the dock the man tries to escape and gets beaten. The man and woman know these guys aren't cops. They load their gear and the two people into inflatable rubber rafts with motors and start deep into the chain to where their cabin waits, alone and isolated.

The man considers escape but has no chance. Fonda takes the woman inside, manacles her leg to a post, and tells her to clean the kitchen. They lock the man in a bedroom while they unload.

That night the three get drunk and play poker. The man and woman argue about escape, getting hold of a raft. Finally the woman goes out to drink and play with the guys. She goes to bed with Fonda. The next day, they tell the man and woman, is the day of the big hunt.

These images are all clear and distinct, down to the colors of the boats, the sky, the rocks shoring up the dock.

The way it always was, the colors were indistinct. With memory, everything was tainted with mud, its colors, its heaviness, its solidity, its stench. Mud was the color of dysentery—the fat, frothing shit that sent friends home. You were lucky if you leaked blood to clean your bowels out. I remember the brightness of the blood and the medic who said, "Long as it stays bright, man, you know you're okay."

The next day they're all hung over except the man locked in the bedroom. Fonda goes out to take a swim and the woman tries to go with him, but he shoves her back inside the house. Her strategy failed. And her man has watched it all through a chink in the wooden wall of his room.

Later they sit them both down and explain the hunt. They'll get full packs (food, water, a knife), a raft with motor, and twenty minutes. Then the three will follow, but armed only with hunting bows and broad razor-tipped arrows. Same hunt as every year. That's what the 'Nam taught them about "big game."

Much laughter and hilarity among the three. Much sweating and cursing between the two. The man grabs his pack and splits. She follows and tries to go with him, but he throws her out of the boat. She climbs ashore and hides in an old abandoned barn near the house just when the twenty minutes are up.

It seeps in, then creeps around the edge of consciousness; then it's there.

Ringo was walking through a village that our F-4's had just strafed and dusted. Everyone on the ground was dead. But there was a little barnlike hootch suspended from several trees about forty meters ahead.

Ringo was on point. I had the left and some new guy, a private, I think, the right. Ringo had ten meters on us. The rest of the patrol was back in the grass in case there was a live nest somewhere in there.

I whistled to stop Ringo and gave him the palm down,

for caution. He kept going, each pace slower and shorter than the one before. Finally he was almost under it.

Smoke from burning thatch drifted in the humid air. I could smell the rancid sweat from the new guy, that and the grease all over the action of his gun.

Ringo turned and gave the high sign. Then he inched underneath the straw and stuck his gun barrel up through the floor, softly, slowly, carefully, almost daintily. I saw his half smile and the arm going up, the fingers trying to form the sign, when a branch broke—pop!—brittle as dead wood back in the States on a crisp fall day, and the next thing I knew the kid was crumpling into the ground, holding his helmet on tight, and spraying the thatch with long bursts. Ringo dropped straight down, digging his face down into the hard clay while straw and dried mud and sticks rained all over him.

The kid had an MZ-84 he had picked up on a body count patrol. He kept raining 'em in there, and finally I ran over and dragged Ringo out by the arm. He was screaming through lips dark with dirt and blood from when he hit the ground.

"Stop that fuckin' son of a bitch. What the fuck's he doin'? Didn't he see my sign? Stop him, Jones. You gotta!"

Ringo's eyes were scared, wild, wide, dark pupils swimming in white.

He said it again as the bursts clipped the silence of heat, of fear. "Make him stop, Jones, or I'll kill him!"

I dove onto his arm as the burst hit the trees over the kid's head. Then we hit the ground and rolled over and over, trying to claw his rifle loose from the other's hand.

But that stopped him. Smoke poured from the muzzle of the machine gun cradled in the kid's arm. He watched

100

us, bewildered, leaves still raining down upon him from the trees.

Ringo broke free and jammed his bare hand down onto the baked clay six, seven times. Then he sat back on his heels.

"You fuck. You poor dumb fuck who just don't know what the hell you're doin'. C.O. sends *you* on the wing." His voice slowed, calmed, leveled off.

"Okay, soldier. Go check it out. That bolt you must have heard was just a twig. A fuckin' twig. Go check it out."

He picked up his helmet and gun and walked back toward the patrol, now emerging from the brush.

"That's where the villagers stashed their *kids*. All of them. Go see what an MZ-84 does to a *kid*."

The new kid just stood there, the smoke circling around him. I sat down on my helmet and looked up into the sky. The clouds were yellow, the sun red at midday, the air a sickly green.

Throughout jail, marches, sit-ins, demonstrations, walks in the park, bed, special moments just the two of us shared, I never once really told Anna what it was like. Of all the people who should have been told, she never knew. But she did know. She wasn't some anarchist, black-flag-waving bimbo from River Forest, Illinois, or Shaker Heights, Ohio. She wasn't stupid, or gullible, or pretending to be what she wasn't. She just didn't like letting people in on her own personal pain. Not many people, anyway.

Not too long before the Kent State strike we sat in the window of her apartment, legs dangling out the window, music on low, a bird on a wire not ten feet away. We sat like that for a long time before she talked.

"You know, Jones, this fits. Nice."

I nodded.

"Two years ago if you told me I'd have a life like this, I would have laughed—fast and hard. I was on my way overseas. Almost, anyway."

I looked over, searching for something in her demeanor that said she was lying, not seeing it. I was so tired of looking.

"You think that's strange, don't you? Well. Maybe it is. But you know how things change."

"Yeah. I know."

Sunlight dipped and swayed among the leaves on the trees across the way.

"Did you know I was a nurse. I *am* a nurse. Got my degree, training at Hines VA Center."

Little surprised me, but that did. I wouldn't have ever pegged Anna for a nurse—the uniform didn't seem to fit, if nothing else. But in those days, and even days since, lots of things fit that didn't seem like they should.

"I wanted to go over there. I thought I'd seen it all at Hines. I thought I had something to contribute. Corny shit, huh? Well. It's true."

We sat while she smoked a cigarette. I sensed a question behind this but didn't know what it was.

I said, "We didn't see many civvies over there. Rare stuff."

"I know. They discouraged it. But they let some of us come ahead. I was supposed to be one."

The record changed and the breeze grew warm.

"What happened?"

"I don't know. I just know I couldn't go. I could sew up a man's stomach—saw plenty of gutshot at Cook County for that—but I couldn't go. Maybe I was plain scared. Chicken shit."

"Most of the soldiers were chicken shit. At first and later. All the time. You should have known that."

"I think I did, but it didn't matter. In the end, it was me, my expectations. Something fell apart. You know?"

I waited.

"I actually decided when the jet was ready to leave. Not before. All my stuff was in cargo. I just stood there and stared at the plane's exhaust and finally the C.O. climbed on, gave me one last look, and closed the door."

Comings and goings were the hardest, and I hadn't known that she had been through one. It broadened what I knew. How I felt.

"And after that no more nursing, SDS, demonstrations, new lifestyle."

"You did a three sixty."

"A what?"

"A basketball player goes up to dunk the ball and twists three hundred and sixty degrees in the air and then jams it in. Three sixty."

"Well then. I guess I did."

We both waited. Me for the reasons for that 360. Her to learn what she had run from. But we didn't talk.

Bob Dylan sang "Go 'way from my window/Leave at your own chosen speed," and the bird walked gracefully along the wire, and she didn't talk. And I didn't either.

The three run out onto the dock to reconnoiter. They see the froth from the motor bubbling across a far bend in the river. Fonda says he'll take the land route across a high ridge. Law and the other guy follow the man in a raft.

The girl comes out and scrambles into the house. She breaks into the gun cabinet, finds a shotgun and shells, and goes back into hiding in the barn.

The man knows he can't outrun the bastards, so he

beaches the raft and leaves it. He strikes out across the ridge. Somehow he climbs above Fonda and drops onto him with the knife. In the scuffle Fonda loses the bow and is cut. But Law and his buddy show up and scare their prey into the bush. They wait him out until he breaks across a sandbar and shoot him down. That's when they hear the speaker on the stereo back at the house broadcasting a tape, calling them in, calling out their names.

Law and Fonda can't figure it. It must be the girl. They jump into the rafts, leaving the third guy to walk back. As soon as they're halfway, there's the sound of a high-powered rifle, and he sprawls dead on the sand. They hear it; something's gone wrong. They split up. Fonda takes the long route back. Law will look for the girl.

Law beaches the raft and is about to explore the house, still blaring his name in the voice of a man he does not recognize. Then he sees the barn and snakes around the back. He catches the girl looking. Her first shot is wide and the second is in the air as the arrow penetrates her right breast. The barb comes out her back. Law grins, takes a step, and the report of a rifle echoes in the silent landscape. He drops to his knees, amazement in his eyes, blood at his mouth, and stays there.

Fonda's heard it all. He approaches the house quietly, using all his skills. He dives through a window but the house is empty. Someone has put a recorded loop on the tape deck so it will play over and over. The volume is up to full.

Fonda can't understand the message. He leaves the bow and takes a high-powered rifle. He goes to find the one who made the tape, and Law.

He sees the girl's body a few yards from the barn and walks cautiously in that direction. Then he hears the voice, calm, soft, calling him in, speaking his name, saying, "This time your little annual game is over."

Fonda walks around the shadowed barn, turns, and sees Law hanging by his shoulders from a grain stick.

We see a man's black boots and green camouflage pants and hear a bolt's click. Fonda whirls but he's too slow. The rifle drops him hard in the upper chest and he sits down, eyes bulging, looking up at Holden. As he dies, Fonda says, "Who *are* you?"

Holden looks at the drooping body for a moment and says, "I'm the father of the woman you killed last year."

We get credits as he motors off in his own rubber raft. That's when you remember the little girl, the granddaughter.

I stand at the far southwest corner of Columbus Park and watch the football drills. The cool has come upon us with the waning of fall, and I pull my jacket zippers tight against it.

They're just kids, but they're already into it all. Headcracker drills—two men butting helmets until one gives ground. Two-on-ones, where they hit low and high or on both sides together to get the man to lose ground. They even have a blocking sled.

The wind and cold cause my knee to ache, the scars on my side and back to burn.

I hear the swearing, the crunch of helmets and pads, the coaches' screams to "Hit, hit it again, hit him harder!"

I can't help but think of other voices at other times talking it up to me. And later, far away, whispered or scared voices like these all around me. And voices in other tongues I didn't know but came to know.

It's all there together as the sun goes down and the

wind comes up higher and stronger. I turn away from football and watch the sky, its quick clouds, and the trees in the park. It is so peaceful here, now.

After that second version of "96 Tears" I went back onstage. The rest of the band looked at me and I looked at the audience. Then I picked up my harp in "A" and bent the first couple of notes to "Shake Your Tail Feather" and we were off. We went right into "Little Red Rooster" and they dug that too. The roar was tremendous after that one. A security man motioned to us to keep going, pointing to his watch. We didn't know. But it looked like some delay with the program, and we had the audience, so let's not lose them. That was the attitude.

People packed in around the stage, jammed up against the amps, cut off any path we might have had out of there. Some girls were dancing on the vents that ran along the windows around and behind us.

I thought we needed a long one, something to give us each a solo, maybe multiple solos, to stretch it out, keep the thrill going. I looked at Kern and yelled "I'm a Man," he grabbed his mike, and I blew the first four fast notes. Zywicki and Hildebrand were both right there and we were rolling.

After the first run-through Kern and I traded the vocals, and I blew and blew that harp till the reeds cut out and bent, and I had to switch to a Bluesmaster, key of C. We synced up for the last eleven notes and the long, held final that Hildebrand drove through the floor with his bass drum.

More cheers, applause, stomping. We were all up, smiling, soaked in sweat. I took a gulp of Gatorade and wiped sweat out of my eyes and from my forehead and neck.

I could see Anna up near the stage, together with a

number of other security people all wearing red buttons. Some wore leather or blue-jean jackets. These were tough-looking dudes, I thought, and that included the women. There were maybe twenty of them in that line, and seven or eight were women. Anna led her half, standing firm against a pushing, shoving crowd. We had almost gotten them too up.

Anna and the guy across from her gave us the "cut" sign, so theatrical there and then, and I saw him looking from his watch to the back door, where another group of security people stood nervously, waiting. Very elaborate, all this.

I yelled to JoJo that we should split, pronto. He yelled his thanks to the crowd, the guitarists unplugged, an equipment man crawled onstage and cut the amps, and we were down and running along with our "escort."

I could see the joints being passed around in the audience, bottles in brown paper bags. This rally wasn't purely political—at least not for everyone.

I hitched a finger through a loop on Anna's jeans and she turned with a look that meant trouble till she saw who it was. I screamed above the din, "Just tryin' to stay close." I saw her smile again before we collectively shoved our way to a back entrance, out, and down the steps to the second floor.

The head of security—thin guy with shades—handed each of us an envelope—SDS letterhead, of all things—thanked us, and gave us a room number where we could eat if we wanted. He also passed out red passes in case we wanted to get a good look at the main speakers for the day or sit in.

Then they were gone, all but Anna and a very young girl named Liz. At least she looked young. We were starved after that set, so we wandered across the Center looking for our room with its free lunch. JoJo walked ahead, keeping a hand on Liz's arm or waist no matter how many times she picked it up and took it off. She was a very patient girl. She even kept smiling through all his moves.

Anna and I walked behind. I saw her smile at the two of them but wasn't sure why.

The other guys lagged behind, discussing plans for other gigs, even talking about us getting together to play. For the moment I let it lie.

Anna said, "You guys were good."

"Thanks. Crowd pumped us up. We had some fun."

Silence. We threaded our way through knots of students, teachers, street people.

"So you two pulled us as your detail, huh? Wouldn't you rather be back in there listenin' to the rally?"

"Our 'detail'?"

Sometimes I just couldn't switch, make the smooth transition, especially back then. Sometimes it seems like being over there has been the smoothest piece of my life so far. I tried to make the switch but didn't always make it.

"Sorry. A word I used a lot once. I mean you're responsible to usher us around. We can find this room by ourselves, get some eats, maybe come back upstairs. Or split. No hassle." I don't know why I was doing this.

Anna was looking at me, hard for a moment, like something invisible suddenly was showing.

"Hey, Jones. It's no big *duty*, ya know. I'll split when I'm ready. I'm gonna go back up when the feature attraction is on. Till then I can use some food myself."

Sweat pooled under her eyes. She must have been steaming in those clothes. Even out in the halls it was hot and humid. I stopped at a water fountain and shook out a malarial antibiotic. She watched. "Aspirin," I said, and swallowed it down.

*The jungle hospital was little more than a series of camou-*flage chopper tarps sewn rudely together and strung up by blackened aluminum poles. The only undamaged, at all modern thing in the place was new, unripped mosquito netting for the five or six really sick guys. I don't know where they got it.

One of the bad ones was Chinese. Someone had posted a guard on him even though he was unconscious and delirious, muttering in his sleep every night till I thought I'd know him better than he would ever know himself again. Except I was in and out myself and can't swear by what I think I know.

Who can?

Those first nights they pushed it into me by vein, run in with the glucose and injections of Adrenalin. They tried to pump me up to a stable level but I wouldn't respond. I had a wound in my shoulder, another from my left side around to my back, and malaria.

I never found out where I was or where the French nuns came from. I don't even know how long I was there. But I remember bolting up in the middle of the night only to be pushed back down by a gentle hand. Other times I'd wake and search the darkness for something, anything familiar, and catch one of them sitting not five feet from me on a folding camp stool, alert, hands clasped together, eyes gentle but concerned, probing my eyes for signs.

Was it just pain they searched for? Or was there something else to such diligent vigil?

They rarely spoke. Once, when I was lucid, a doctor checked the dressings and adjusted the drips on the IV. I saw him shut down the sodium bicarbonate. One of the nuns listened intently to him, speaking rapidly and quietly in good French—not the pidgin stuff we heard in the cities or even in some of the villages. But French from France.

109

I picked up a little, talk about fever, rubdowns, poor supply of alcohol, something about evacuation.

Then I passed out.

I remember the eyes of one of those nuns. They were blue with green sparkles. Her hands were ridged with veins, but she was still a young woman. The hands were gentle, but it was the eyes I remember. There was a light within them that kept me going till the day I heard the choppers coming in. Two tall men ran into the tent and picked me up. Other patients were being slung over shoulders, IV bottles hooked onto their belts.

These men wore no uniforms, but they were neither American nor French. Just as I was hoisted through the chopper door I saw the officer in the black beret speaking hurriedly to the head nun, who only looked quietly and patiently at him and nodded. He handed her a package and she nodded again. I could see it was a satchel charge and tried to cry out, but I was too weak.

As we lifted off, I saw the nuns standing in a little group, being sprayed by dirt and dead grass, looking up at us.

I saw that woman's eyes lock onto mine for the last time.

Sometimes the eyes possess a haunted look, a deep and purposeful gaze that shrinks and cowers in fear as it is held. It's like the unhappy smile that sours the longer it is maintained.

I can see the look come and go in Jack Swanson's eyes even while we're just sitting there listening to the blues. After "Shake and Finger Pop" the band goes right into "Born in Chicago" and gets a tremendous hand from the crowd. They're tight, and good. Wenner has a good voice for the blues and knows his harp. He knows when to ease up and when to lay down a long solo line. All the Hawks get their licks in, though, even the drummer. Tight, good music, even as my mind drifts off, to Swanson, to 1969, to the jungle, to everything that's come between.

I remember one of the outposts where we had time to put up corner guard towers. It was sometime around Christmas back home, and music drifted up from the sandbagged gun pits. The alert was off, so everyone was quiet, sitting on their helmets listening to tapes.

Somebody had a tape put together by his little sister. She was in high school by then, but she was still a "little" sister. And it was strange, those songs spliced together: Barry Sadler's "Ballad of a Green Beret," Bob Dylan's "Like a Rolling Stone," something by The Doors, some Judy Collins. He played that tape and we all sat quietly, listening. The guys in the guard towers paid no attention to the perimeter. One looked out at the sky. Another put his gun down and held his head, helmet and all, in his hands.

Before the tape ended the guy's sister came on and talked to him. She said she was sorry he'd be gone for Christmas, that she hoped we could make it white somehow for him, that she missed him.

It was such a young voice, so girlish. You could just about see her talking into the microphone, sitting in a cozy Midwestern living room somewhere, surrounded by books, records, all the things we collect. She was probably a blonde, a budding young woman just staring out at life with a smile.

She ended by saying, "That's about all I have to say this time, Bill. Remember I love you, and Mom and Dad do too. You know that. I wanted to save this last song for you and all your friends. Turn it up *real loud* and get home

111

soon." And fading in from the background was Country Joe and the Fish, with the Fish Cheer ("Gimme an F. Gimme a U. Gimme a C. Gimme a K. What's it spell? FUCK? What's it spell? FUCK! What's it spell? FUCK!"), followed by the "I-Feel-Like-I'm-Fixin'-to-Die Rag."

At first we were all pretty quiet. I didn't know most of these guys, and I was the ranking man in the pits at the time, so I just sat and watched. And they watched me. And as it went on I couldn't help myself. I smiled. I laughed. At that the compound was up for grabs. They'd stand up and link arms and sing along. They'd call for Bill to rewind the tape over and over. They'd scream out the Fish Cheer till they were hoarse.

No one moved from the C.O. tent. They gave that Christmas to us, and we took advantage of it.

The music comes back in, slowly, from one ear to the other. Swanson is looking away. Ringo rattles his rings on the table. His friends are about ready to do some signifyin'.

It's loud in there. I wonder why Swanson is so cool, so calm. It's not the Swanson that I knew from the jungle, from the city his first year back.

A line of sweat has broken out across his forehead, and he folds and unfolds his hands. But his jaw is relaxed. He's listening, or reliving times I don't know.

The band is playing "When a Man Loves a Woman" and it quiets down some. I look around tables. Some people look at the band. Others look down into the darkness of their drinks. They even lower the lights a little on this one. Swanson is looking up, but not at the band. I can't follow his line of sight.

I'm tired. Tired of always being on guard, tired of my "social obligations," tired of not getting any sleep, tired of working and moving and acting normal through the sicknesses and memories that visit me.

I didn't want to come out tonight, but Ringo made it sound important. He doesn't call very often, considering we live in the same town. The get-togethers are fewer, shorter, stranger as time passes.

He called me at home. I was reading intently, developing a headache, and almost didn't hear the phone. I kept reading as he talked and finally I agreed, as much to get him off as anything.

It was a short article in an education magazine for teachers: the sort of thing used to provoke class discussion in generalist college courses, or among advanced high school students. Its text, under the title "Did Nightmares Kill Them?":

> In the last four years, 17 men and one woman, all in good health, have died mysteriously in their sleep in various U.S. cities. The one characteristic they share is that all 18 were refugees from a mountain town in Laos. Doctors who have investigated these deaths say that there is no sign of previous illness nor any evidence of a murder or suicide attempt. Cause of death has been recorded as "irregular heartbeat." Doctors are therefore faced with the question: Why would a perfectly healthy heart suddenly stop beating properly? One possibility is that the 18 Laotians may have been frightened to death by their own nightmares. Is it possible that memories of their wartorn homeland and the tensions of adjusting to life in the U.S. had made them fearful? And could these very fears have provided terrifying dreams that led to their deaths?

I took the article with me to my rocker before the window. Everything was still. Usually a wind came through. Usually there was a distraction out on the lawn—girls sunbathing, kids break-dancing, someone fighting or making a buy. That day, nothing. The stillness was as great as the deep mirrored finish of a deep, quiet pond.

I drummed my fingers on the magazine and noticed a white sidebar to the article. Someone—probably one of the kids I tutored—had ripped out the beginning of the article. The sidebar read:

> Dr. La Berge plans new tests on the *healing* effects of dreams. First, volunteers would have small cuts made on their arms. Then, through lucid dreaming, they would command their body to heal one arm faster then the other.

I put the magazine on the table next to the rocker. *"Lucid dreaming."* It was disturbing, something from my past that I couldn't quite dredge up.

Someone walked by the building with a radio playing "Dancing in the Sheets." The music stopped for a moment, several moments, then continued through the stillness and down the street. It was quiet again. I was left with thoughts: so simple, isn't it? Thoughts. Nothing more.

Wenner is into a lowdown version of "Bright Lights," very funky. The lights are low. I can't even see Pete Ragusa, the drummer. I see a cymbal shine occasionally. Zukowski is like a mime, perfectly still except for his fingers. Thackery walks about the stage, making the easy transition to "Memo from Turner."

I lean over and whisper into Swanson's ear. "We should talk. Tonight? Get together later this week?"

Jack considers, still off somewhere but coming back for a moment.

"Let's wait to see after the set." He's dripping in sweat, though it isn't very hot now that the lights are down and the crowd is settled in. I nod.

I give Ringo's chair a kick and raise my palms in question. Where's the famous little brother, anyway? I don't ask but he knows. He grins widely and shrugs. Then he just says in a half voice, "Wait up, brother. Show's just *about* to begin."

I smile a weary little smile and lean back in my chair.

As soon as I get home I grab the pill bottles from the bookcase, select two pills, and swallow them down with a glass of milk. The suit coat gets a hanger. Everything else is thrown into the bedroom hamper. I change to nylon running shorts and sit in my rocker near the window, letting the warm early evening breeze slip over me, fighting the sleep that is inevitable, that I invite in the slow movement of the rocker, in the resting of my head against its back, in the closing of my eyes.

I hear voices. Outside? On the street? I am sweltering hot. The voices make no sense. They pause and pick up in volume, intensity. I hear them plainly but see only shadow, red shadow, black shadow.

"We have no other medicine."

"His temperature is already one hundred and five degrees."

"You've done all you can. Now it's up to him."

"No! One can never do all one can! I shall stay with him through this, until I save him, with God's help, and with yours—with your medicine—or he dies! You do not believe in God, Lavey; you'd better believe in *me* or get that medicine."

"Sister. I have told you. It is up to him."

A silence, a faint buzzing, an intolerable heat.

"Then leave us. We will win *this* war."

115

The blacks and reds begin to focus, to become distinct, awash with cooling sensations across my stomach, my chest, my arms. I feel myself rising, coming out of this state, then dropping back down into it.

Swanson and I talked between sets, during the softer blues. I'd stop and watch Wenner blow. McCoy was watching Swanson and me, I knew that, but I didn't care. His gaze was tough, hard to avoid, and I was just about to say something to him when Wenner stepped up to a floor mike and said, "Now, a special guest of the Nighthawks and Tut's. Hear it now for Jimbo McCoy!"

There's scattered applause, including mine, but Big Brother McCoy was pounding on our table and foot-stomping till the drinks spilled and his friends joined in, both smoking and grinnin', ready for the act.

I leaned way over and shouted into Swanson's ear, "How the hell can your *brother* be named 'Jimbo,' man?"

No one was on stage yet. The shallow blue spotlight darted around.

McCoy grinned his grin. "I got to talk to you some other time 'bout that, Jones. Right now I got to dig my little brother, wherever the hell that little punk *is*."

McCoy stood up, his massive frame blocking a piece of the spotlight.

Then we saw him up on the stage, a harmonica cupped over a Chicago microphone. He drew the first few notes in so deliberately I knew they were going into Willie Dixon's great song "Spoonful."

In the blue stood Jimbo McCoy, at least as tall as his big brother, dressed head to foot in blue denim. Jimbo looked every bit like Jim except he had a massive beard that made his head look even bigger than it really was. The way he swayed back and forth, eyes closed, as the bass line picked up, drums came in, lead echoed the harp, and Wenner played riffs off him, it was like he was in a trance. Or trying to put us in one.

The rest of the set it continued. He let Wenner take the vocals. He just wanted to play his ax, and he did, on every song. He was good—good as Wenner. They traded lead and riffs and counterpoint like gentlemen, but we all knew they were going at each other. It was the real blues, harmonica heaven.

Swanson quieted down and listened. We all did. Even McCoy stopped his grinning and let himself be drawn in by the music. It was sharp and kind, gentle and persuasive, raw and violent. The Nighthawks filled up Tut's that night with sound, with a pure music I still remember.

But that night I thought too much about 1969, about the days in college, about the time before the jungle. It gets painful sometimes. It was hard that night.

In the middle of the second solo from "Delta Blues" I left. Swanson looked surprised, but he was somewhere else too. I shook hands with McCoy, told them both I'd give them a call. McCoy just nodded, just like he had after Pheasant Run, just like he had when he heard so long ago that I was going home. McCoy never spoke when he really knew.

I nodded to his friends and lingered at the door. Sweat dripped from Jimbo McCoy's beard. He was bent far over, sliding his hands across the top of the mike, bending half-notes, going to the low register and the high.

He could cut Wenner on the harp. And he could cut me.

Outside, the cool wind struck me full in the face, fanning my jacket out behind me until I pulled it in tight against my sides, wrapped it around me against the wind, and walked, pulling the air into my mouth against clenched teeth, wanting to be out of there but not sure why, or where I would rather be.

It's not dark yet. A faint light lingers outside the window. I don't know how long I've been awake. I hear a phone ring somewhere in the building. Someone slams an apartment door. Birds flock into the upper reaches of the tree outside the window. The smell of charcoal drifts in. I glance at my watch. Not yet 8:30. Should I sleep now, more? Should I surrender myself to the night? As I think it, I know it sounds absurd.

I spend so much time remembering, now more than ever before. It's almost incremental. The further away I get, the older I get, the more I dwell on the faraway, the long gone. I would like to think about Duncan, innocent and comfortable Linda Duncan, but I can't focus on her.

Kathleen must be downstairs in her apartment about now. I haven't seen her in several days, but she has routines. Right now she is placing her perfect body beneath the shower head. She will just stand there for ten minutes, letting the water bead off of her silky skin, wet her hair in the back, flow smoothly down her legs.

Then she'll step out and let the air dry her skin. She may stand before the window, lights out behind her, and look out. She may lie down on her back on the couch and read a magazine. *Fiction Quarterly*, maybe, or *Film Quarterly*. She'll get up to fix a soft drink or to go to the bathroom, padding the carpeted hallway naked and elegant. Always elegant, even with her damp and scraggly hair, the scar on the lower half of her right breast, the sore nipple chafed from running into a strong wind that morning in a cotton T-shirt, without a bra.

Her wounds, her damage—they are cosmetic on her. Wounds. Something always comes up, brings it up. This time I fight it off.

The rocker is cool. The sweat has been dry for some time now. My legs feel cool, the light breeze against the soft hair of my shins.

I walk into the bedroom and pull an old race T-shirt from a drawer, stretch it on, tuck it into my shorts.

There are papers, files, legal briefs strewn across my desk. I pull out a file and look through it, sitting cross-legged on the floor. Keep occupied. Wait for Duncan. Wait for anything.

*Of course she didn't believe me. If there's one thing I re-*member about her best from that first day, it was that.

We walked down the hall.

"Hell, that wasn't aspirin."

"Who says?"

"Come on, man. Didn't look anything like any aspirin I've ever seen."

"You, of course, have seen it all."

"Come on, man."

"Tell you about it sometime."

"You will."

"I *will.*"

"I know you will."

I didn't understand. She spoke softly, petulantly.

We ambled away the lunch hour, munching on sandwiches as we explored the campus. It didn't bother me to leave the guys behind. It didn't bother her to leave SDS behind.

We wandered south to Taylor Street, then back. Anna's boots clattered on the cement.

"You're a subtle dude, Jones."

"Now, what's *that* supposed to mean? Should I feel good or be scared?"

"Scared?"

"Scared."

"What of?" She stopped, hands on hips. Through it all, the clothes, the glasses, the talk, the pose, even the truth, I saw her as she was when she was eighteen. Hips, shoulders, waist, breasts. The hurting eyes. The woman she was.

"Nothing. Nothing."

The air around her face seemed clear as a wave cutting in off Lake Michigan. Like snow before it touches the ground. I could read her eyes, mouth, dimples in her cheeks. A picture to be preserved.

"We better get back to check out the main attraction," she said.

She hung on to the moment like she hung on to my shoulder when we squeezed our way through the crowd outside the Union. Then she snapped back into place, into the pose.

"Shit. You're right. They said they didn't have enough security as it was. Let's go."

For the second time that day we ran across the asphalt and grass and up to the third floor. We were stopped once but Anna impatiently flashed a little red card and we were sent by.

The crowd was alive in that big room. Smoke was dense. Anna pulled me over to one side.

"They want me to watch for The Man. Wanna help?"

There was nothing funny about this gig for her, that was certain. Her mouth was set still in a line, but I saw light and something—happiness?—in her eyes.

120

"Anything you want me to do—man. Just put me where you want me."

She smiled. It was really some smile. Shit! It was the best smile I'd ever seen. Too bad I didn't know it then.

"You just stay over here. Most of these people know you were in the band. No one will look twice at you, including The Man. I have to move closer to the stage in case something goes down."

She clomped heavily away, then turned with a sort of cockeyed grin.

"When it's all over, you want a ride home?"

I'm sure my grin was just as awkward, just as true.

"I sure do."

She walked away and disappeared behind the amps.

Lucid dreaming? Is that what they call it? I didn't call it anything when they wanted me to explain who I was and how I got to the clinic. They said the white was peace, and the black and brown and green awaited just outside the door.

Once, locked into my little box, I must have seemed dead to the world. The guard opened the door and let the smells in, the heat, flashes of red and yellow upon my closed eyes, the notion that I could live without the snow.

The snow was silence, but so was the heat that brought my sweat pores back to life.

On the hardest days in the clinic I remembered the French girl. It helped. The day they used scopolamine and atropine together I sent myself back to a day in high school, the local park, flying kites with pretty short-haired Susie Kemp. All I could remember were her smiles, her long arms, the long legs dashing across the burned grass, trying to get the kite up.

I sat under a little tree with sunglasses on, practicing for later life. Kemp let the kite drift, tied the string to a branch, and sat down with me to look wordlessly into the dark blue sky.

It was the French girl's silence. It was the stillness of the girl in the parking garage whose boyfriend ripped her blouse from her shoulders. It was the searching after words by the European girl who pressed herself against me, needing a tutor. It was the dark vacuity in my face when they cut all the surface skin from the American in the box next to mine. He screamed forever but I never heard him, then.

Fever came on but I broke it every night. They couldn't understand it. They wanted it to grow inside me, but I dreamed it into oblivion. It would catch on later, but not then. They should have bled me. I would have closed the wounds with dreams.

Linda Duncan curls up against me, concentrating on the TV. The TV is set back into a bookcase in the living room, surrounded by heavy hardbacks.

The room is dark. Light flows from the TV screen, drifts in the open windows from the streetlights, falls dully into our room from the light in the bathroom.

We're sitting propped against pillows in a corner of the room. Duncan has a glass of white wine within easy reach. My glass of water settles steadily into my hand.

It's become cool, but I'm still in my shorts. Duncan changed to running shorts, sandals, and a halter top tied behind her back. Every once in a while she'll talk as we silently watch the flickering images, sometimes looking up at me with those eyes framed in the wildest curls. The eyes are questioning or bemused, or both. She concentrates on the movie.

It's Sergio Leone's *Once Upon a Time in the West*. Henry Fonda, Jason Robards, Charles Bronson, Claudia Cardinale. My favorites, though, are Woody Strode and Jack Elam as gunslingers who never talk. One of them lets water plop onto his hat monotonously from a leaky faucet. The other catches a fly in the barrel of his gun.

Fonda is a heavy, one of the few he's played. You don't mind seeing him die. Robards has to die, too, but he's probably the best character in the film. Bronson is himself.

But what's exciting is the music. Ennio Morricone wrote each of the character themes, including Bronson's "Man With a Harmonica."

I am rubbing Duncan's shoulders where the blue veins pulse under the tanned and freckled skin. Her curls fall onto her neck, around the tied bow of the halter. She puts a hand on my chest, presses both knees against my thighs. All of her skin is so cool, so tan, so smooth, so supple.

There's a commercial. She sets her head on my shoulder.

"Nobody came in for tutoring, eh?"

"Nope. Their loss."

"Yeah, today it would have been. Linda Duncan, honors student, topless tutor. I bet we'd get more business with that kind of PR—topless tutoring."

Her fingers stroke a design across one of my nipples. She moves one of her legs across mine.

"You should have stuck around, Jones."

"Oh, did you have a good time without me?"

She looks up, brushes the curls away from her eyes with her hand.

"I can show you."

"I think you will."

Her skin is getting hot—not sweaty, but warm, flushed.

123

Her hand moves in a wider arc. She rests her other hand on my hip.

But the movie resumes and she slows her hand. The other hand moves away from my hip to scratch her leg.

The Harmonica Man plays only when someone is going to die. He isn't playing yet.

I ask her, "What book did you bring over tonight?"

"It's good subway reading. Heidegger's *The Essence of Reason.*"

She's watching the movie. I'm watching her, every gesture, and listening to the musical cues. She's very relaxed, cooler now.

"Something for a class, or for Philosophy Club?"

"Neither. Just something I pulled off the shelf a couple days ago."

"Northwestern Press, I suppose?"

"Yeah, I think so. Phenomenology series."

She scratches again. I move my hands down her shoulders to her arms. Her palm pushes down hard on my nipple. Her other hand is on my hip. I move my hands faster but lighter.

Duncan breathes deeply. I feel her breath on my chest. The music from the TV is changing. Her curls are in my line of sight. I watch her fingers slip under my shorts at the hip. The Harmonica Man blows. I untie the bow from the halter and it falls down to her waist.

She buries her face against my chest, sucking on the nipple, and I hold her head hard on that spot. Her fingers fan out under my shorts. I push under her shorts and hold her hard against me by the ass.

I let her head go and she pulls hungrily at my other nipple. With my free hand I encircle a breast, squeezing the nipple, running my fingers across and around it.

I move my hand around under her shorts to the front

124

and she stops, looks at me with wide eyes, then pulls my shorts down with both hands.

As her head drops to my crotch I can see her tan breasts pulsing against my torso. I squeeze hard with my fingers, everywhere, she with her lips, and the Harmonica Man plays.

Each year, at this time, race organizers put on Run the Boulevard, a twelve kilometer race through downtown Chicago. It's a kind of odd distance—7.4 miles—and takes the runners down Michigan Avenue, through Printer's Row, across Grant Park, and up a surprisingly steep little hill to the Standard Oil Building.

Most of the city's good runners turn out. I've told Kathleen a tale or two about the race and she wants to run it this year. She keeps asking, but I haven't said what I will do.

Two years ago I got to watch the people before the race and after. I stuck around quite late, fascinated by the scene.

I've seen bits and pieces of racing and running psychology other times: race organizers sending runners the wrong direction, unmarked courses, awards presenters drunk at nine o'clock on a Sunday morning. But two years ago was like a clinic. Duncan should have been there to study it.

She sleeps like a baby in deep dreamless sleep, limp and relaxed, the rising of her left breast the only sign that she breathes.

The day was a bit warm for the season, late October-early November. Because it was near Halloween, a few of the two thousand runners wore costumes, or parts of costumes: killer bees, bunnies, a fully-suited chicken.

The elite runners, the runners who tried to act elite,

and the runners who wanted others to think they were elite were running brisk strideouts up and down Randolph Street. As usual, women who had no intention of running a step lounged around the start in new shorts and nylons, or Puma sweatsuits. Their hair was perfect. Some even smoked cigarettes.

There was the usual shaking of hands, checking out the T-shirts and the muscles on the other runners, furtive glances at running shoes. Nike and Saucony were very popular. Only one runner besides me was wearing Kangaroos. One girl wore a pair of Reebok aerobic shoes.

The city opened a recreational center for a change so runners could stretch out, get a cup of coffee from a machine, and go to the bathroom somewhere besides the middle of the park.

The stretching routine alone is bizarre. The men come in to do situps on a carpeted floor. The women engage in intricate gymnastics that prove their flexibility.

But the bathrooms are the best, at least pre-race. The stories you hear as you wait in line are outrageous. Someone is always talking about the marathon he ran the week before, always to a guy who's never run one. Someone else offhandedly remarks that he was out running the course during the week, then tells us all if it's okay or not, accurate or short. And someone else is talking about his weekly mileage to a guy who runs down his list of injuries, capped by his partying until four A.M. the night before.

And they wonder why some runners never race, and why some leave racing after a few years in the pursuit of speed and distance.

We lined up on a bridge and I got to hear more great conversation. Excuses, laments, predictions, bad jokes.

Everyone always moves up to the starting line when the countdown to the start begins. It's stupid, because we all pack in too tightly and consequently all get poor starts. Two years ago it happened just that way.

After a few minutes of jogging along, watching the heads in front of me bob up and down, I made one of a series of moves, up onto the sidewalk and past the throng. I quickly settled into my pace, which leaves room to breathe and little more.

The race itself was uneventful. I'd been there before. I jockeyed for position against a few runners I knew. And going through a narrow underpass, I had to throw an elbow or two in retaliation. Anything goes in the gloom down there, and Chicago runners have gotten tougher over the years. They're like track runners, some of them—oops, sorry about that elbow, gosh, sorry I cut you off on that turn.

After the circuit of the city and the thrill of running in the middle of Michigan Avenue while onlookers gaped at so many people allowed outside in their underwear, we finished up a hill, which put my quads to hurting, but all you can do is charge it, lean down into it, bear down. I crossed the line in 48:44 and clicked off my watch. It was a good time for me. It's hard to compare because the distance is so unusual.

Runners streamed in, some pushing it and sprinting to the clock, others just happy to have made it. An ambulance sped away from the medical tent. I drank cups of water and wandered down toward the tent with free samples from race sponsors: Diet Pepsi, boxes of fruit, yogurt, even cereal and coffee.

It was a mob scene in there. I'd seen it before, and I'd been there, grabbing bananas and cans of Coke to take home. Not that day. Hands grabbed the cups from workers' hands, ripped open boxes, pushed and shoved more than in the race.

I sat down on a little hill with a couple more cups of water, loosened my shoelaces, pulled off my wristbands to dry in the sun. I leaned back against a little tree and enjoyed the still, the people all around me talking up the race, the aid stations, the mile markers, the split times, anything you could possibly imagine to complain about.

I sat there in the sun and took it all in. I knew I would race again, but I wasn't sure why.

An hour later some of the runners were still around. I was in no hurry to go anywhere myself.

I listened as a young woman explained to some new friends that she had turned to running when her marriage had gone sour. She'd told the judge she couldn't accept custody of her two children because of her commitment to running.

I sat under that little tree and closed my eyes, listening to the little birds cry above the noises of the people around me.

I wake trembling, jittery, disoriented. The sheet has fallen to the far corner of the mattress and I'm alone there. I stare at the ceiling for a moment and breathe in.

Duncan sits in the rocker across the room, reading. I can hardly see her face through the crazy ringlets of hair jutting in every direction. She sits very still on the rocker, concentrating, her nude body not moving, the book held out, bringing her breasts up and out.

I reach over to the bookcase and shake pills from two bottles into my mouth, swallow them down with my glass of water.

Duncan's seen me move and glances over, tenses her muscles as if she were caught, surprised, somehow, then reads for another moment and closes the book on a bookmark. She sets the book on the floor—her muscles are all so firm and fine—and she sets her arms on the rocker's arms and looks at me.

I used to think Duncan is a tease, but now I know it's all personality.

I'm naked and uncovered and she knows she's got me turned on.

"Hi, Jones."

"Hi, Duncan."

So much for repartée. She makes a point of looking at my crotch.

"All ready to start the day?"

"You want some breakfast, Duncan?" I start to climb off the mattress and quickly, like a lithe, springing animal, she's up and out of the rocker and kneeling next to me, pushing me back onto the pillows.

Her eyes are enormous so close up, framed by the delicate hairs that curl all over her head.

She places her hands on my hips and leans over me, her breasts like pendulums bouncing back and forth when she moves. She looks me full and hard and sweet in the eyes.

"Thank you, Jones. I think I will help myself."

As her head drops I grab onto a breast and flatten it in my palm. I wrap the fingers of my other hand around her curls and relax, letting the sunlight and shadow melt into a single color around me, Duncan's deep tan lightening with it, the objects in the room dissolving into the color, into heat, pure heat, into blood flooding the brain.

Ringo caught one in the throat on the Hmong trail to the Mekong. He had the point, as usual, and I was on the flank a little behind him when I heard the dull series of cracks and saw him spin around three or four times in place, a crazy marionette out of control, all green and brown with a

129

pop gun in his hands and a tin can on his head. Then he fell.

I called back on the radio, "Pitcher hit by pitch. Pitcher hit by pitch, repeat, read. Batter in the box, behind the plate. Just one. One or two."

The transmission cut in asking for confirmation, coordinates, and a repeat, but I cut it off, dropped my pack, and ran straight across the grass, not bothering to weave or dodge, just running as fast as I could for where Ringo went down, firing my rifle full auto, spreading the shots across the area in front of Ringo. I had to shoot at an angle from my hip and I knew it wasn't accurate. I just hoped I could move fast enough to avoid the sniper and the return fire from the company down the trail.

I heard what sounded like a cough and saw that the other flanker, Franklin, had laid down some smoke between me and the heavy brush and trees up ahead. I turned once and saw him spraying the trees with his AK-47 and talking on his radio at the same time.

The elephant grass was high, so high I had to sling my rifle and try to hurdle through it. I hadn't heard or seen Ringo since he went down so quietly.

Then I saw a flash of silver—dog tags or a gun barrel—just as the rockets from our rear came hurtling into the underbrush ahead. The ground shook with each explosion, and the brush caught on fire.

I lay with my hands over my helmet, trying to orient myself. I heard small arms fire from both directions and knew I had to get to Ringo fast.

I found him less than six feet from where I had belly-flopped. His gun lay a foot away along with his pack. Somehow he had dropped both and rolled away, knowing an enemy patrol would go for the gun and supplies first.

Ringo was covered with clumps of grass pulled out of

the ground. He had clicked his radio off, but it lay near his head. His eyes were closed and his legs were drawn up against his chest.

As I pulled him over I smelled cordite, smoke, blood, and sweat, but not the fecal smell that always accompanies the bodies of men shot down violently, quickly, and without warning. Dead men.

One hand gripped his pistol, the other his boot knife. I pulled them free—should he wake up, I didn't want him mistaking me for the enemy—and looked at the neck.

Ringo's hands, face, neck, and torso were soaked in blood that continued to bubble from the wound in his neck. It looked bad.

I quickly checked his pupils and pulse. He was out but his heart was strong. My pack was back across the middle of the firefight, so I was stuck with my own ingenuity and whatever Ringo might have had in his kit. I kept a little bit of everything in mine, even on the flank, but plenty of point men left the regulation supply behind and carried only morphine ampules, extra ammunition, and maybe some extra water.

I ripped his pack open. He wasn't much of an exception to the point-man rule. I threw the cartridges into the grass, grabbed the canteen, ampules, and a couple of extra headbands.

I opened the rubber cap on an ampule and inserted the needle into a vein in his arm, then tapped the glass end of the ampule with the butt end of his boot knife. The broken vacuum sucked the contents of the ampule—several grams of pure morphine—into his vein.

Just then I heard the tremendous *whump!* of a mortar shell. The first one hit too deep, over the trees. Another *whump!* and we were sprayed with dirt by a shell that hit only a few meters away.

I scrambled on top of Ringo's legs and clicked the radio on. "You're rocking the pitcher, lobbing onto the mound. Pitcher down. Relief pitcher on the mound. Readjust. Readjust!"

Another shell exploded, a few meters to one side. "Outfield! You're rocking the mound! Readjust! Outfield! Get those fuckin' mortar shells into the trees! And get a Medi-Vac in here now!"

I clicked it off and soaked the headbands in water, then cleaned the blood away from his face first, so he could breathe, and to check for dum-dum shell fragments. His face was clear. Then I worked on his neck. The bubbling had eased into a mild but continuous trickle. He had already lost a lot of blood.

After I cleaned it away I saw the source of the blood. It looked like he had been hit by a single bullet, inside of the carotid artery but outside of the throat. It had passed through clean as far as I could tell.

I rinsed a headband free of blood and pressed down hard with it on the wound. I tried counting to three hundred for five minutes of heavy, steady pressure but was distracted by small arms fire. It was advancing from the south, from our side, but I thought I saw something move in the smoke to the north.

With my other hand I stripped his shirt away, again checking for wounds. All the blood had come from his neck.

Then everything happened at once. I heard a chopper, looked up, Ringo sat bolt upright, the smoke blew off from the chopper's rotors, a figure stood up just meters from us dressed in black, I lunged for Ringo's gun, and Franklin broke through cover firing as he ran, cutting the man in black down.

Franklin kept spraying the elephant grass while I held Ringo's head up so he could breathe. I applied more pressure to his neck. Ringo looked up at me with a kind of wonder, then reached down and held tightly on to his sidearm.

Franklin directed the chopper in. More flankers had come up and were returning fire. The trickle continued from Ringo's neck, but much more slowly.

Someone from the company vaulted through the grass, dragging my gun, radio, and pack. Someone else moved up to check the body in black where Franklin had dropped him.

The chopper landed a couple of hundred yards to the rear, and two medics and a gunner jumped out and sprinted to our position. The gunner wasn't wearing a helmet, just a blue headband with fresh cigarettes stuck into it. He talked to Franklin while the mortar and rocket fire doubled, obliterating the entrance to the forest ahead, and blowing up this piece of the Hmong's trail of escape.

One of the medics took over the pressure while checking Ringo's pulse. The other one snapped together a folding stretcher. Ringo held tight to his gun, even when the medic told him to relax.

We lifted him onto the canvas stretcher with his gear. I heard one of the medics shout to the other over the din of the rotors, "He's got his tags all right."

I said, " 'Course he does. What does it matter, anyway?"

The medic looked at me like he hadn't noticed me before, then just said, " 'Case he buys it going out of here. Sniper. Stray bullet. Infection."

I just looked at him and said, "You jerk."

He shrugged, signaled to his team, and they picked the

stretcher up. I clapped Ringo on the shoulder but the morphine had him and his eyes looked over to one side, unfocused.

The medics sprinted for the chopper while Franklin called in more firepower and their gunner ran behind them, spraying the grass in a deadly arc.

I crouched on my knees and watched the ship lift off, carrying Ringo to some ramshackle "hospital" stuck in the hills, maybe like the one I had just gotten out of.

And Franklin and the company and I would follow the trail of the Hmong, all the way to the Mekong if we had to.

Some of the trees were trip-wired, tied to old Claymore mines they'd stolen from us or that had failed to blow. They'd tie a filament line to the mine and bury it, then stretch the filament taut in front of a tree, right about where a resting man might lean.

They literally tried to catch us napping.

One particularly hot summer day in my first tour, four of us were sent to recon a little village near the only fordable point in the river. It was too quiet down there, and our planes had spotted men working in the fields. There shouldn't have been any men anywhere near there. They all should have been drafted, killed, or living in the mountains.

As usual, I was the only corporal around, so I led the three privates down the hill toward the village. I don't even remember the men so well—lots of names and faces from that time. But they were young, I know that.

We walked in two staggered lines down the grade that ran to the river. I couldn't see anyone through the sparse brush and occasional stand of trees. We walked slowly, me on the right flank with a recruit behind me, the other two privates fifty meters to the left. A quick burst of automatic

134

rifle fire or a grenade would get one or two of us at the most.

I thought about stopping at the treeline directly above the village, but there's a limit to the number of times you can talk about strategy, about being alert, about being careful. So we walked on and in.

The village was a set of hootches and old issue canvas stretched across saplings. There were three or four large, communal cookfires. The whole setup was above river level by two or three feet. I noted the hard clay of the overhang near the river and instinct told me to check it out. But when we cleared the trees, all hell broke loose.

We were bunched up, only twenty meters apart and vulnerable, when a young woman ran out of a tent stark naked, shrieking excitedly in what I knew was a Hmong dialect. And I know my guys had no idea what language or dialect she was speaking. They were all watching her run across the clearing from the tent to a hootch on the other side of camp.

The flank man was on his knees cocking his rifle. The other two were rushing up while I screamed to them to stay back, to move back to the trees. Other women, fully-clothed, ran out of their huts, then screamed when they saw us and tried to run back in.

Chickens and pigs ran amok about the clearing. Another second or two and that flank man would open up, I knew, so I ran over and knocked the gun from his trembling hands with the butt of my gun. He looked up, surprised, but hardly angry, and I crouched down next to him and yelled to my rear, "*Sit on it!*"

The other two hit the ground, guns up. Old villagers and animals ran about the dusty pathways between huts until all was silent.

I crouched on my heels and listened. I could hear the

sweat dripping from my chin and elbows onto my gun. The birds and insects came back, loud, in a minute. I could hear the river rush over rocks, where there must have been a manmade portage, beyond and just below the village.

Sweat collected on my eyebrows but I left it alone. I said to the private on my left, "I'm going to talk to somebody in that village. Take your gun back and if you see me in trouble, spray the area, then clear out." I was up and gone before he could ask questions.

You can tune all your senses in when you really want. That's what I did that day. I hadn't seen any men, so I wasn't very worried. But our reports were usually accurate.

I walked slowly to the hootch the naked girl had entered, ducked, and dove through the doorway to one side, finger steady on the trigger.

There was a low fire—embers—in the middle. The air was foul with the smell of dead and curing fish. Then I saw through the smoke and mist the racks of split green wood covered with fish.

Two women huddled together across the fire from me. One was old, shapeless, dressed in light cotton. The other was the girl, still naked, her small breasts thrust forward as she sat back, her arms behind her. As I sat looking, the old woman tried to cover the girl's groin with a strip of cloth but the girl pushed her away.

I ignored the girl, turned to the old woman, and spoke to her in Hmong.

"Soldiers?"

She said there were none—none but us.

"Men?"

She paused, but it was enough. I saw it in her eyes. She said there were none, none but us.

I unstrapped my helmet, sat it on the ground, and wiped sweat and smoke from my eyes with my headband. I held my gun loosely cradled in my arm. I asked her how many women were in the camp.

She paused, but only to count to herself. I watched her eyes. She said there were eight or nine, waiting for relatives from the south until they could safely cross the river into another country.

That seemed odd. I was sure the portage was there, already built.

The young woman sat still, staring at my face. I asked the old woman how many like her were in the village.

The old woman didn't answer, but she didn't look away, either.

I had already added it up and was trying to figure how to bring the recruits in right, so they wouldn't all get killed and me in the bargain.

I just thought one step ahead of what I made up as I went along.

I smiled at them—made sure they saw me look long and hard at the girl's body, smoky and dirty but also young and firm—then slowly stood and ducked out of the hootch.

The tent she had run from was about thirty meters to my left. I casually put my helmet back on but didn't strap it. I put a cigarette in my mouth. My gun lay in the crook of an elbow, pointing about at the treeline.

My three young recruits were lying flattened well outside of the village, but I could see the humps of their helmets. I walked slowly toward the periphery of the village, clumsily veering to my left as I walked, like I was drunk, or taken with the heat. I knew I had to say something and soon.

"Come on in." I waved them up. "Visitors must be upriver." All three stood and advanced, none carefully, none listening to the silence around us, the absence of insects in the trees, none noticing I was carrying my gun like I never did, in the crook of my right arm, not my left. They just came in walking easy as if they were on Main Street on a hot summer's day, and that's all I should have expected from them.

I slowly eased a match from my shirt pocket but couldn't get it lit. Two of the men kept coming straight in. The other veered off, but only to pick up a little trail to the side of the makeshift village, near the treeline. Easier walking, I guessed.

All three kept coming, guns pointed in the air, not even watching the village or the trees, just plodding on in.

I eased another match from my shirt pocket and palmed a grenade off my bandolier in one quick movement. I turned away from the tent and dropped the spring, counting, my hands cupped and coming to my mouth with the match to light the cigarette.

I had time to scream "Down!" before I flipped the grenade into the tent and dove to the side of a huge old cooking pot, holding my helmet on when the grenade blew.

The other three had kept on coming, and suddenly found themselves walking into a rain of wood and canvas and metal fragments, and blood and skin and bone.

I was quickly onto my knees, ignoring them, looking at the hootches, swiveling my gun around as if it were mounted on a turret, checking the other tents, watching the trees, the brush, the trail down to the river.

I heard a ratchet fall into place and screamed back at the two now flat on the ground, "Don't shoot!" For a moment I could see them spraying the village into oblivion. I didn't turn—couldn't afford to—but kept watching, waiting to hear the women cry out. If they did, we were in trouble. But a minute passed. Nothing.

I looked around. The two behind me were buried nose down in the dirt, but they'd waited to fire. The one on the flank was pressed up against a tree. I could see the muzzle of his gun and the white of his face. I called in Hmong for everyone to come out, told my men to watch the huts and not move.

The women slowly crawled out of hootches and tents, even the one who had been naked, now wearing an old shirt that hung to her knees.

"Everyone in the middle. By the big cookfire."

They were too close to me. I wanted some room if I needed it, if one of them wasn't Hmong, or was kin to the man I'd killed in the tent.

They moved into a little group a few meters away. In English I told the flank man to hold a bead on them, then repeated it in dialect. They hadn't seen the man on the flank, just the three of us who had come straight in. I told the other two to walk all the way in, slowly, and to spread out. I went to look at the hole where the tent had been.

There had been just one man, that much I could tell. He was blown up pretty badly. Thank God the river brought a breeze that washed away some of the smell. I didn't stay long, but long enough to see the bent and riddled stock of a Chinese machine gun.

And then I remember, vaguely now, questioning the women, looking closely at each of them, especially the girl in the shirt, to see if they really *were* Hmong, asking about the man from the tent, explaining to the two recruits that the woman probably had been raped by the single sentry, that if he had been one of them, they would have at least cried out, maybe even tried to kill me.

Those two wanted to know how I knew there was just one, how I knew he was watching from the tent, what I found out inside the hootch, how this and why that, and I wearied from it all, and that's why I still blame myself for what happened.

I turned to the flank man too late. He'd been holding steady for so long, he had to rest, I guess, and I saw him take the helmet off, lay the gun down, and then place the helmet on the ground, and I knew what he was going to do next but couldn't do a damn thing about it.

As if in slow motion, I yelled at him not to sit down, and he had an idiotic grin on his face as his body slowly sank down on the helmet and then back against the tree for rest. The women saw it and ran for cover and I pushed my men hard, in the chest, and they crumpled onto the ground, and all I could do was watch that smiling face move down and back against the tree. I dropped down and pulled my helmet over my ears, but our eyes seemed to lock for one endless moment before the inaudible click and the flash and the roar where he had sat against the tree. Then he was gone, him, his helmet, the gun, the tree.

The women had known. They had known and didn't tell me, I thought as I jumped up and began dragging them out of the brush, from behind trees, throwing them like dolls into the dirt in the middle of the clearing.

The other two men looked up at me, not knowing, not comprehending. Three recruits, one dead, two stupid. Hell, I knew we were all that way once. But I didn't see it quite that way at the time.

"Claymore mine trip-wired to the tree. Classic trick. Probably ringed this village with 'em." My voice was suddenly so tired, so tired, but I knew I had to tell them.

One of the men stood and said stupidly, goddamn stupidly, "Claymore? One of ours?"

I just looked at him and said, "Go see what's left of your buddy."

I turned back and scrutinized the faces. Dull. Motionless. Waiting. Waiting to see what I'd do next. All except one, that is. The girl. There was a glint in her eye—almost nothing in those black eyes, but still something, enough, enough to tell me she knew things that I didn't want to know.

I dragged her by the arm around the cookfire, then yanked her to her feet and ripped the shirt down the front, tore it off her shoulders, jerked it away from her dirty, trembling body.

The other recruit seemed to wake up. "Jones, what the hell are you doing? You said these people were refugees, you said—"

I snarled, throwing the shirt into his face, "I said, I said. They probably *are* refugees. *She* probably is too. But they knew. They didn't tell me, and I speak the language. And *she*—she probably more than knew."

I could hear the man over in the trees retching, and I spun around and cracked the naked girl in the head with my gun butt. She crumpled to the ground, blood soaking into the dirt. Then that recruit came at me and caught the muzzle of his gun in a blow to my neck. We looked at each other eye to eye.

"If you killed her, Jones, no matter what the fuck else happened here today, I'll get you for it."

For a moment I almost dropped the gun, almost thanked God for a decent man out here in this sodden jungle, almost thought maybe he was worth it. He had sand, they used to say in Iowa. Then I remembered where I was and how stupid he was. It's nice to be a moral man, but not if you're dead.

I spoke softly, deliberately, but I knew he couldn't miss my meaning.

"Now, friend, I want you to go get your buddy and, when he's through being sick, hightail it back to HQ. You boys watch yourselves, now. Bring back a couple snipers, medics, and intelligence. They'll want to talk to our ladies

141

here. And no, my friend, she's not dead. You better hurry, though. If she comes to before you get back, I'll be forced to ask her a few questions myself."

I guess it all finally sunk in. He backed away, grabbed his gun, and went to find our third man.

I yelled after him, "Stay away from the trees."

They left on the run. I stood quietly in the middle of a ring of women's bodies, watching the path to the river, wondering how long before I could close my eyes again.

Linda Duncan sits up on the back of the park bench. I ease my shoulders against the wood, careful of cracks, splinters.

The sun glides in and out of cloud cover, shining off the lake one moment, disappearing the next.

I can feel the cool wind even through my leather jacket. I stretch out and shove my hands into my front pockets.

Up above and a little behind me, Duncan moves her face into the wind, letting the breeze rustle the curls around her face, showing patches of white next to tan, where the sun never penetrated in summer.

We've been sitting in the park for an hour. We walked through the sand near the water until the lake breeze grew too cold for us. We sat under a tree and watched the waves curl in and die until the ground grew cold and stiff.

I look across to where blue meets blue and ask, "You know anything about sailing, Duncan?"

From behind I can hear her light little laugh, then her "No."

I could fall asleep, even in this awkward position. There's no one else in the park. It's quiet, and I like the chill, the toughness of the Chicago weather.

"Why do you ask?" She slips down next to me on the bench, stretching out until her legs are almost even with mine. Almost. I look at her face, hidden in curls.

142

"Just wondered what you really know. What you're interested in. Secrets, Duncan, all those secrets you've got tucked away in there." I grab a fistful of curls and tug gently on them, drawing her face close to mine. She smiles, a beautiful, bold smile. She holds nothing back—nothing I've discovered so far. She links her arm in mine, an oddly old-fashioned and romantic gesture, not really her, but not false either. She looks openly, fully, into my eyes.

"You want to know what I like, Jones?"

I look off into the distance, but something in the smile, the tone, brings me back. I look at her and sigh.

"What *do* you like, Duncan?"

"Philosophy and sex. Not necessarily in that order." She laughs loudly, the sound ringing out across the deserted park. She nudges me in the ribs. Her face is so radiant, so open, so calm, so trusting, so certain. She isn't a beautiful woman, but she sure is great-looking.

"Okay, Duncan. I'll bite. Why—"

She interrupts, laughing, poking me in the ribs. "Later, boy, later." The sun sparkles off the ringlets in her hair.

"Right. Later. But why philosophy and sex?"

She jumps up off the bench and strikes a pose right out of a Levi's 501 Blues commercial, chin in hand, elbow on blue-jeaned knee, the long, skinny leg something to see.

Then she takes a few steps out of a gymnast's routine, so ebullient I start to wonder. Her chest jostles freely beneath her loose nylon sweatshirt.

"Philosophy and sex are the only two things I know that no one understands." She smiles, pouts, strikes another pose.

I laugh, this one time a great booming laugh that floats up into the air. I jump up and strike a pose, leg up onto the concrete post behind the park bench.

"No one, Duncan? Not even *you*?" We're both smiling, grinning, as we walk carefully around each other.

"That's for you to find out, Jones." She laughs, spins around. I jump up on the bench and raise a hand into the chilled air.

"So tutor me, teach."

She jumps up next to me, wraps an arm around me, and raises her other arm to mine. We wrap fingers together, laughing, squeezing each other tightly in the dying sunlight, against the chill, the wind, the low lapping of the waves on the rocks. Against it all for as long as we can.

Again Patrick bugs me. He seems to know how.

"I don't hear much about your work these days, Travis. What's up?"

"Not much, Tom. Why do you care?"

"Hey, I'm concerned. You can't let a promising career filter away. Talk has it you're hardly in the office anymore. I'm surprised I caught you in today."

"Consider yourself lucky."

"Travis. Come on. I'm worried about you."

I remember Miller. He would have said, "Bloody well unlikely." I don't say anything.

"You there, Travis?"

"I'm here."

"Don't want to talk, huh?"

"Perceptive of you."

"Just take a piece of advice, Travis. Leave the jailbait alone."

I sit stunned. It is so stupid.

"You know what I mean. College kids? You've got better sense. Fact is, I'm having a party next weekend—"

I hang up. Past the bookshelves in my office I can see

144

the storm clouds building in the sky outside. I've opened
the window a crack and papers rustle on the desk.

Black clouds rise and fall in the eddies of air outside.
This is exactly how it was when I stepped off the commercial jet. Home.

I shake two Vistaril into my palm and swallow to forget.

McMichael was huge. I knew some big men over there, but
he was a giant, maybe six-six and two-forty. And he wasn't
a simple guy, or a stupid guy either. The time I was with
him he did his job, all the jobs given to him, didn't
complain, and didn't question.

That was also the time of no questions. We wondered
about our orders in terms of the area—the little theater we
were in, the borders that defined our lives, the likelihood
that we'd come out of it alive. But mostly, like McMichael,
we just let it be.

It was tough being a corporal. There was no way to
refuse those first two promotions. Sergeant was the tricky
one to avoid.

Most of my friends were your basic grunts, almost all
privates or corporals who intended to stay there. We had to
be tough but understanding, unquestioning but supportive
of the men.

And we had to be ready to switch units, companies,
patrols, all at a moment's notice—at least up where they
positioned guys like Ringo, Franklin, McCoy, Swanson,
Miller, McMichael, Sharp, and me.

Some of us I could figure. Others made no sense on
paper or in the field. McMichael was one.

His vital statistics were all correct, but he was like a
pack horse—all power and good instinct. He was no killer,
no SOG recruit, no Monterey man. He had come out of
Alaska, and before that he was from a farm in Iowa.

145

McMichael was the only soldier I ever knew who came into our elite units from down south without some kind of haircut—only private to do it, anyway. Miller, for God's sake, had been dropped in with a full beard. But he was a corporal.

The first time I saw McMichael was the day he reported. I had sniper duty far out in the forest and spotted a dust trail to the west. It was small and coming straight in, though, which meant it was most likely one of ours. I knew the coordinates of the old camp trail, checked them by the moving stream of dust with the spotting scope I'd mounted in a crook of a tree, then signaled to my counterpart across the forest.

We used mirrors, no radios, and changed the codes every day. We never knew till nightfall who the other man had been. Could be your buddy, or the guy you hated the most in the whole outfit. The point is, it shouldn't have mattered, and it didn't.

My job was to confirm a friendly face by surface and precede it in. They all came by jeep or air, though Franklin had walked in unannounced after swimming for two days—by night—up the Mekong. Big foul-up, lots of swearing, tightened security. But they had asked for a frogman and gotten one.

It wasn't hard to cut through the woods to confirm the nature of our little dust cloud, then orienteer in. I could move faster on the wooded trails than any jeep on the pitted clay roadway to our south.

I was waiting for them where the road forked a few kilometers from camp. Unfriendly faces always paused there, uncertain which way to the camp. But sticking to their directions and the significance of this point in the roadway were made explicit to all our drivers, a hand-picked lot.

146

If the vehicle slowed, if anything at all seemed amiss, we would kill them here.

I had rubbed clay into my face and mud under my eyes to cut out the sun's glare. I had a rock ledge above to protect me from grenades and shells, and I hugged another rock in front of me.

The engine revved and came spinning around the turn. I knew the driver by sight and he was turning the right way, so I relaxed and had a look at the man jostling around in the seat next to him, his very special delivery. This guy was almost as big as the jeep. He wore fatigues like the rest of us, but his hair was almost shoulder-length, held back from his face by a long corded black sash. The barrel of his M-16 lay across one knee and squinted off into the forest. It was like having a swivel machine gun in the front seat.

As the jeep went by I took the forest route I knew so well. I was in camp and had checked in at least five minutes before the jeep chugged the final few meters over rock and decaying log. The C.O. knew about his recruit, so he didn't say anything other than his stock little speech to each of us when we reported in. Except talking to McMichael meant looking up, not down or straight across.

McMichael stood in our cooking area, twice as big as anyone else in the unit, taking up enough space, it seemed, for half a patrol. His hair blew back in the breeze, and the mosquitoes were plenty frustrated by the day's beard on his face and down his neck. There was life in the eyes. I knew McMichael would be okay.

The words are like a mantra that you push so deep into your consciousness they will remain there forever. The cut man. Just words, but the associations of those years, all the terrible things that happened, go with them.

It is November and I sleep a listless sleep, longing for

the heat and humidity of summer because they made the night a clear moment, one darkened series of hours that I had lived through and understood.

November brings the cool winds to massage me into deep, dreaming sleep, the sleep of memories, ghosts, and demons.

The cut man used to sit in his little hole, sharpening his knives until morning. He'd oil the sharpening stone with sweat if he had to.

The cut man was the kind of thing—*thing*—we used to think about on the dark moonless nights of summer, years ago. We were all kids once. And those fears were the kind that turned knees to Jell O and started fingers tingling. But that was all because we didn't know anything yet.

I sit wrapped in blankets sometime past midnight. I've given up on sleep. A replay of my thirteenth summer— long since banished from thought—is selected to play. How that works I don't know and can't control. I'm in the memory's grip and thrall as much as I ever was at Monterey, or in our northern camp, or on special patrol upriver from the tributaries of the Mekong.

And if you try hard—really hard—you'll have the same memories of the same years. And the nightmares that are inseparable from them.

Even as the rain flowed out of the sky like blood gushing from a new bullet wound, I could feel my own sweat rolling down my legs from my crotch. It fell from my back and caught where my shirt was tucked into my pants. I had tied a long cloth headband into the mesh on my helmet and let it fall over my neck and shoulders. I thought it would keep me drier in the storm, but it only soaked through and dripped irritably onto my back.

Through the rain I saw the faces, all looking intently at me, waiting. The rain was so heavy I could see its vertical lines in front of their faces.

There were Miller, Franklin, McMichael, and Lewis. But Lewis had been hit and lay a couple meters away, the rain draining blood from the deep thigh wound. He was conscious but couldn't, or wouldn't, talk.

We were huddled in a stand of trees. Miller had draped extra strings of green and brown moss around us, hanging from the trees and trailing off onto the ground.

It was Lewis's patrol but now I was ranking man. I didn't even know what the objective was. Lewis had saddled us up, the most experienced men in camp, and led us through the forests at angles, checking compass bearings and reference points every kilometer or so.

We'd been out about an hour when the rains hit, and as soon as Lewis turned to say something, he'd caught a couple slow dum-dum rounds in his legs. Another burst shattered the radio that he had dropped. Miller lobbed a grenade into a deadfall and blew one of the snipers out into the trees. I gave them our sign and took off through the forest, zigzagging around trees and brush barricades, knowing it wasn't mined, hoping they could get a bead before the man with the sniper rifle got lucky. I could hear his slow bullet *thuds* behind me, at my shoulder, and then all of them but Lewis opened up.

When the firing stopped his body fell thirty meters to the forest floor and I double-timed back.

So that was it. Lewis incoherent. No radio. No mission information. Hazy ideas of where we were. No idea how many more snipers, or regular army out there.

For a moment I lost my concentration and gave in to the smell of powder and sweat and blood and fungus and fear.

Then McMichael picked Lewis up and slung him across his shoulders.

Miller whispered, "For God's sake, man, he'll bleed to death like that. We've got to patch him up."

I came alive and tried to smell a wind, a sign of direction. "Bandage the legs fast, Miller. McMichael's right. We've got no time to be nice about it."

Miller started to cut Lewis's pants away.

"Fix him up the way he is, Miller. You've got one minute. All that firing will attract company damn fast. We'll backtrack and then hug the forest perimeter south. At least we'll meet someone that way."

And Franklin said, hefting McMichael's MZ-84 on his shoulders, "Yeah, and they'll probably kill us."

Miller had been quick: antibiotics for the legs, morphine, a bit of amphetamine to keep him awake, and bandages over the torn and bloody fatigues. Already the blood was seeping through, but the rain washed it away as fast as it could pour out.

It was one of those moments that you don't forget, that come to you in dreams. You know you made it back, and you know how, but either you don't remember that or don't care.

The decision was mine and it was a guess. It was those faces that make it memorable. And that damned sweat rolling down my legs, mixing with the tepid rainwater, sloshing into my boots as I gave the sign to move out.

Years later, Anna Friedberg. I remember that first day so well. And so many other days.

We went to my place and listened to Slim Harpo records. And, in time, her place to hear Big Brother & the Holding Company. My place for Paul Butterfield. Hers for

Quicksilver Messenger Service. And both poor little apartments for Dylan and the Dead.

There was the day we drove to Iowa to test her new gas masks. She drove us to the corn fields outside Cedar Falls and had me lob cannisters in at her. Natch, she didn't understand that you need to change filters, so she got a lungful.

I met Rennie Davis at a rally. John Sinclair. Cha Cha Jimenez—that first day, in fact. All stories in themselves.

And Anna and I trashed the ROTC building on the University of Illinois Chicago campus.

It was hot that May day in 1970, after the "official invasion" of Cambodia, after the surprise and anger and fear of Kent State. I still remember all those young, surprised faces in the crowd, so outraged that someone—or maybe just the war itself—had brought the war home, finally. Dead people in a parking lot, draining real blood.

There was terror in their eyes, just like I had seen it so many times before, twelve thousand miles away.

Friedberg was in the middle of the rally, giving her rap. I had worn my blue jeans and bandannas and walked the outer circle of the crowd, looking for cops. That was my job. No one was better at it than me.

The microphone buzzed and crackled and then, for some reason, the crowd was running across campus—past the Circle Center, other buildings, Halsted Street—to the ROTC building.

She was in the lead and I ran along the flank. It seemed very familiar. When we arrived, someone told the ROTC cadets to clear out. The megaphone man gave them five minutes.

All these actions were carefully planned, almost orchestrated, the result of hours of meetings and arguments

151

about strategies and tactics that I couldn't stand. I learned early to split.

I found out too late about the "plan" for ROTC headquarters. I just looked at my watch, looked around for plainclothes, tried to locate Anna, pulled a bandanna up across my nose and mouth, and led the charge into the building.

Cadets had tried to barricade the front glass doors with old wooden desks, but we just pushed them away. It was dark inside. I sent a couple girls downstairs to the basement to check it out and to lock the fire doors shut with chain.

The rest of us charged the steep stairs. The main corridor swung right and I sent everyone that way while I moved into the classrooms on the left.

As I walked through the door, a cadet leveled a rifle at me and said in a loud but very shaky voice, "Don't move! You're not taking this building!"

So there we were, the cadet barely mature enough to shave and in his regulation browns, and me, older and more tired-looking, in faded Levis and a day's growth of beard that he couldn't see. Him and his rifle and me and my eyes glaring out from beneath the blue bandanna.

So I said, real fast, "Okay, boy. Let's drop the blood on the floor right now if it's got to be that way. That gun will take chunks out of me and drop 'em all the way into the hallway."

I saw him blanch and look down and I yelled in his face, "Put the gun down and get the fuck *out*, kid," and he placed the gun carefully on some chairs and ran like hell right past me.

I was sweating up a storm. It was hot in there. I heard the splinter of wood and knew someone had found the fire axes. Then I heard a siren. I yelled down the hallway, "It's

The Man!'' grabbed a wooden chair/desk combination, and led the charge down the stairs.

At the bottom I hurled the chair through the plate glass and it shattered. Glass was still dropping as I ran through it, ahead of the trashers and the police.

"They wonder why you're over here, McCoy. Maybe you better go dig a hole on the other side."

McCoy looked at me like he might laugh or cry but hadn't decided which one. He kept digging.

I could hear some of the names, the comments. Mostly I saw the looks and smelled the sweat of fear somewhere in our little patch of dirt, surrounded on all sides by tall sawgrass.

We were three very loose patrols, really just fifteen men out on a perimeter setting up an ambush. Sharp was on the far side, pretending he couldn't hear, helping Ringo drop the heavy machine gun into its camouflaged hole.

McCoy and I were digging our own defensive trenches for the night side by side. We were cross-cover fire for the machine gun. The men talking to themselves—six vets— were digging in to support our mortar, handled by a guy named Davis, who watched the grass with field glasses and heard nothing in our own encampment.

We dug the ditches long enough for our bodies to lie flat, deep enough to cover with grass, wide enough for a man and a gun, nothing more. We were used to it, so we dug slowly, knowing we had till dusk before we had to cover up.

The muttering stuck out. It belonged somewhere else. I threw my shovel and knife down and straightened. McCoy knew my intentions and grabbed me before I could take a step. He turned me away from the group and we stood watching Davis watch the high grass sway in the wind.

153

"Don't you know by now, Jones? How many years, man? Watcha gonna do on the outside if you let 'em get to you here?"

"They're ours, McCoy. That's what bothers me. *Ours.* They can pull this shit any*where* else and with any*one* else. But I don't appreciate it *here.* That's all."

McCoy looked off into the distance. This was something we had never gotten into, never had to. Davis swiveled his head slowly in an arc, the big glasses fastened to his face. He'd pause whenever the grass seemed to move just a bit too much.

McCoy looked back at me. "Understand, Jones. *I* am the only one who should be pissed off here. Not you. And not them. But this is it, man: those guys are *bloods*, dig? They're all vets just like you, but they're bloods. They know what this war is for, Jack. It's theirs, it's mine in a way you can't ever understand.

"I'm a blood, man, and that's something you have to get into. No matter what else happens, I will always be a blood just like them."

Davis was focused on a stand of grass that stood unnaturally high and green.

I turned and watched the six of them pitching dirt into the pile behind them. Two of them were watching their rear, two were watching Davis, who had frozen in place, and two were watching McCoy and me.

In a monotone Davis said, "Someone's out there. Stand of taller grass." I told him that McCoy and I would go. McCoy slipped two grenade bandoliers on and I walked over to the holes the bloods were digging, reached down, and spread thick black dirt over my face and hands.

Then McCoy and I crawled out. The last thing I heard was one of them saying, "He's no blood. No way." And someone else answering, "Don't matter to me. Let's go finish—"

We took care of the problem with our knives and walked back in.

The mortar and machine gun were set. Someone had finished our holes, McCoy's and mine. The six men were quiet, digging into their positions, covering up.

McCoy grinned his grin. We sunk in and pulled the grass down over our guns and waited.

. . . As soon as I hit the street I pulled the bandanna down and walked to the outer edge of the crowd that had gathered. I spotted the Chicago policemen in plain clothes and the feds taking pictures and circled around to one side, making sure there were people in front of and behind me.

Then I saw Anna and some of the people from her collective. Before I could get to her she had charged up the stairs of the building, followed by about three hundred friends, supporters, hangers-on.

Someone chained the door from inside, flashed the V for victory, and disappeared.

The police had been around the whole time, plain-clothes mixing in the crowd, men in blues sectioning off the streets, quietly placing white barricades between the building, the rest of campus, and the stores across the street. Now they moved in, but slowly, obviously not looking to arrest or bust heads. They formed a line between the crowd and the ROTC building itself.

I drifted back along the curb and found a tree to sit under. It would be a waiting game here, too, at least for a while.

Not too long after the police moved in, a megaphone

called down to the street from a little window on the building's top floor. The voice proclaimed the building "liberated" and called for someone to send up sandwiches.

The police response was to bring in their own megaphone, to tell the crowd to disperse, to threaten those inside with arrest for criminal trespass to property if they did not leave. The police promised no arrests if all protestors left the building within twenty minutes.

There were a few minutes of silence. During those minutes someone brought a box of food and soft drinks to the base of the building. They managed to haul it up by rope during the momentary truce.

Then I saw Anna in the window, the megaphone pressed to her face. She told the police and the crowd that the building had to be occupied in response to the illegal invasion of Cambodia and the killings at Kent State and Jackson State. She said that those wishing to leave would exit by the fire doors and, by agreement, were not to be arrested. The remainder, she yelled down, would maintain their passive resistence to illegal police interference on their own campus. They would leave only under arrest.

I stood up under my tree, where no one could get a good look at me, and cursed her stupidity.

Then the fire doors opened and more than two hundred students and other protestors poured out into the parking lot before the doors were slammed and chained shut behind them.

That left fewer than a hundred inside. The police repeated their demands. Anna repeated her statement. Then both sides were silent.

I knew it wouldn't stalemate. That would have been too simple. Neither side could let it go like that, could just let it slide.

And that, in the end, was why Anna and I didn't make it.

So I waited in the lengthening shadows, munching on Hershey bars. Like old times. Someone had a guitar inside and was singing. Some of the students outside had sat down in the asphalt parking lot. They ate sandwiches, watched the police line, called up to friends inside.

I saw the unmarked vans roll in and couldn't do a thing about it. We had reached an agreement, members of the local collective and a few of us: some of us had to stay untouched, unarrested, unphotographed, to continue our work. And some would deliberately go to jail. And others could decide depending on circumstances. They called these different groups cadres.

I was one of the few to stay completely clear, untouched. My job was to create situations, like taking the ROTC building, then disappear. Anna's job was the opposite: she spread the word about our actions in lockups and youth camps and national guard compounds.

The students sitting in the parking lot didn't know how to look, or listen. So much passed them right by. The jungle had taught me so much, and I used what I dared to remember in the war we fought in Chicago, and later in Boston and Iowa City and Ann Arbor and elsewhere.

I heard the sound of many men in those vans and was back in the trees, when the loudspeaker ordered us to disperse as the police in riot gear poured out of the vans, the sirens started up, the police on the barricades grabbed the protestors closest to them, and the panic set in.

I could smell it forty yards away, that stench of fear that is so astringent.

People were running everywhere, but the police were only coming a few yards past their barricades. I saw one of them talking to a fed with binoculars and a camera around his neck.

The police rounded up a few students and tossed them into a hot squadrol and let them sit. A pair of cops were at each of the doors of the ROTC building. Their drill was sort of funny: one of them would crouch down, gun drawn and aimed up the stairs of the building; the other would break the glass completely away from the chains on the inside of the door and try to cut them off with huge boltcutters. None of it worked, and the two cops would back away, one holding a gun, the other a monstrously large pair of wire cutters.

When the pairs of cops retreated, a cheer went up, first inside the building, then outside. A few of the cops grabbed people who strayed too close to police lines, or to the building, and dragged them away.

I knew I should go back to Strike Central, the Art & Architecture Building, to find out what was happening across the city. This campus was coordinating strike activities throughout the city, at Northwestern, even at junior colleges deeply entrenched in the suburbs.

We had taken the Student Union, the Chicago Circle Center, before we split for the most obvious target on campus, the ROTC building. And it had been a good action. We had an eight-story building, access to food and water, enough people to control all exits. Our math people had started to get into the computers in the Center—no academic information, but enough payroll and service account data to knock the whole school down for months.

But just as we began to get it, just as my group had sealed off the toughest access area, the cafeteria food delivery entrances, collective leaders emerged from a meeting and said the administration had proposed a trade—can you believe it?—and they had agreed.

In exchange for the entire Center we'd get the A&A

building, a monstrosity isolated in the middle of campus, surrounded by grass and art objects and flood lights. And they had accepted! We'd also get shipments of food as long as the strike action continued, and water and electricity would be kept on, but at minimum levels.

I stood back in the shadows and laughed. What a farce. What a tactical mistake. We had given up bargaining power—the police couldn't have taken it back from a couple of thousand pissed-off kids without serious violence—for security. The A&A building was a labyrinth of small rooms containing nothing of value to us. But we had our base, alright, and our locked doors and free food and flushing toilets.

And I should have been down there now, figuring strategy for tomorrow. I should have let Anna and her group get busted, go bail, and then, as Dylan would have said, "They'll put you on the day shift."

But I didn't leave. I hung around because this was the action tonight.

Kathleen has set the dinner for Avanzare's, one of her favorite restaurants not far from the old Water Tower. Her voice is concise on the telephone, though I wonder why she's calling when we live in the same building.

"I thought we could meet here for a change and go downtown for the occasion. You won't be working on Saturday, will you?"

"No, but—"

"Fine. Reservations are already made, in your name. I hope you don't mind."

"No, that's fine, but—"

"Yes, Travis, what is it?"

The October night is clear. The windows are open only

a crack, but the wind still rushes in and chills the sweat pooling on my back.

"Are you downstairs?"

She pauses for a moment. It is very unlike her.

"Yes."

"Why didn't you come up to ask me? Why'd you have to use the telephone? Sprained ankle or something?"

"I just thought it would be better this way. I didn't want to disturb you."

I think about Linda Duncan. For that matter, I think about Jack Swanson, and Ruth, my secretary, who had been over for drinks the week before.

"Something you want to talk about? Ask me? Go ahead. Ask now, 'cause I want to have a relaxing dinner."

My voice is hard and rushed, but it equals the chill I had heard. Her voice immediately warms.

"Oh, no. There's nothing. It's just been a while since we've been together. You still haven't told me if we can run that race together. And there's other things that I thought—"

"Ah, Kathleen. Dear Kathleen." She is a sweet one. "We'll talk about our plans at dinner. Will that be alright?"

"That will be fine, Travis. I'll look forward to it. Why don't you come down here at about five? Dinner's at seven, so we can have a drink—or whatever you're having these days—before we leave."

"Fine. Five on Saturday. Maybe I'll see you earlier."

"I'd like that. I'll be in and out. But drop in whenever you want. You know where the key is."

I think and think. Nothing.

"Uh, right. I'll see you."

" 'Bye."

I can see her thoughtfully hanging up the phone, standing at the window with a finger on her lips, or sitting in a chair with her feet tucked under her, pushing her beautiful blond hair off her neck, thinking about Saturday.

It's almost Halloween. I remember the Halloweens of my childhood, special times for me.

I dwell on memory. There are blocks set somewhere deep in the recesses of my thought, or my moments of no thought, that beg to be removed. It's as though each memory is a key to a door that must be opened, or a piece of a complex puzzle that begs to be completed.

And in the last year the keys and the pieces have multiplied until I cannot distinguish dream from daydream, thought from fantasy, simple recollection from memories terrible and hidden, finally brought to light.

There's nothing I can do about it. I met with Swanson. I have had meetings with those of us who walked out of the jungle. But the little things pile up that I do not understand: the black beret, the nun, the "clinic," Lavey, "El Destructo," the French girl, the cut man.

It would be so simple to solve it all, to become the cut man again, to do a Jack Swanson in the middle of Chicago. So clear-cut. So clean. So frightening. And I think of Pheasant Run that night and shelve it, knowing I cannot run from my memories forever.

But tonight the Flagyl and the double dose of codeine do no good, and I sweat and chill, sweat and chill.

I remember Halloween as damp, cold, rainy sometimes, misty. Piles of dead leaves in gutters. Late, after the trick-or-treating and, later, the parties, sitting outside alone in the dark, feeling that the night was mine to own, to walk in, to feel and smell.

The world changes but Halloween stays the same. And

I know even that is not true, not right. The world changes but only my memories stay the same. Bring them on, then. No use fighting them anymore. Let them come.

I lay down to face the night without the white, the yellow, the blue pills that have lined my brain for so many years.

Franklin was probably the best soldier I knew over there. He could take orders and bitch about them later if he had to. He pulled his weight. He handled more weapons expertly than anyone I ever met. He knew the people, the terrain, the weather. Best of all, he took care of his own. You could talk to him and get across. He always protected his squads, no matter who was in them.

He was quiet, not obvious like lots of the corporals over there. He handled his rank well too. He wasn't like Sharp or me about that. He was a corporal because he was promoted, and that was that. He never said so, but I think he would have taken sergeant if they'd kicked him up.

Franklin, Miller, and I were sitting around one night at HQ in the northern zone. Up there we had nothing to do at night. Some people played cards. Lots of cards. Some told outrageous stories—lies, just lies. But the key was to establish a veneer of truth to draw your listeners in. Then pour on the bullshit. Nice little recipe. Lots of them were about firefights. Some of them were about sexual exploits, over there or back home.

It was tough talking about home. You could go only so far, say only certain things before some guy would get pissed off, or scared to be up there, or sad. The sadness was the worst. Anger and fear we could control. The guys who started in on a good bawdy tale and ended talking about wives they hadn't heard from in months were truly sad cases.

We were all that way one time or another, but if you dwelled on it you sat in some crowded base hospital while the doctors asked you questions, questions for which there was only one answer: I want to go home. And you felt like a shit because you were lying in a bed perfectly healthy, physically, while double amputees on your ward were being fitted with arms and legs before they were sent home.

Anyway, there was nothing to do, and the three of us were sitting around on little mounds of dirt doing it.

The one thing we could do was talk. Bawdy stories, stupid jokes, great business ventures for back in the States. But the best form of recreation, the only art form I know of to be highly refined and developed in the jungles of Southeast Asia, was the monologue. Few grunts could do it right; the chopper pilots were known throughout the countries we occupied as the monologue experts. But no matter who you were, when you were on, you were on. If you built up some momentum, you could really go.

Like I said, Franklin was a pretty quiet guy. He spoke up when he had to, and not much more than that. We were sitting on these piles of dirt excavated from our little sleeping holes dug into the side of that big hill, playing with our bayonets. That's about all you used a bayonet for over there. If you couldn't kill it with automatic weapons fire, then it was too damn close for a bayonet.

Of course, there is an exception to every rule, and our exception was Ray Sharp. If you think he was good with a knife, you should have seen him with a bayonet. But he was on recon farther south when Franklin pulled out the stops.

He started talking, not asking questions, just kind of rambling on, and after a few minutes it sounded like a full-scale monologue coming on. You keep a respectful quiet during the occasion, interrupting only when absolutely necessary. But you let Franklin go regardless. There was an

163

earnestness about him, something to respect. So we let him talk.

"She was the best-looking nurse I've ever seen. It's almost worth picking up a piece of shrapnel to see her again.

"She told me she had never seen a wire wound before. You know, that happened during the sapper attack back in the city, when they cut the transformers and tried to take out anything in uniform. I know *you* were there, Jones."

I nodded, looked away, waiting for more.

"I was caught coming back through an alley when the lights went. Bang! On one second, off the next. I was wearing my greens and knew something was up even before that first explosion, way off on the perimeter of the city.

"I jammed myself back into a little niche in the alley wall and pretended I was dead. I didn't move, didn't know if there was someone waiting for me in that sudden darkness. I groped my hand around on the concrete wall and grabbed as much mud and grime as I could coax out of the cracks. It wasn't much. What I got I smeared onto my face, neck, the backs of my hands.

"I figured I was six blocks from the apartment I was using. That was a problem too. I wasn't on base, which was both good and bad. I knew my place was secure, but maybe they knew about me. The place was always used by guys on leave, always greens and fatigues going in and out. I tried to figure it as best I could while the explosions picked up across the city, coming in closer and closer to my puny little position.

"Well, boys, I had to make a move. The longer I stood there, the more vulnerable I would be once I had to move. I figured out the fastest, most direct route back. I also figured I had a better chance on the streets than in the alleys. There'd be more light, I could tell who was who, and any of our guys out would see my greens and let me by— maybe even help me get to base.

"See, base was maybe three miles distant. If it had been closer, I would have headed there straightaway. I know your move, Jones, that night—fuckin' bold, too, to get onto base. But I decided I'd better pick up some heat at my place before trying to link up. All I had was a pair of survival knives clipped to my boots.

"So I unclipped one and hooked it onto my belt, unclipped the other and carried it as I inched along the mortar wall, through all the filth they had thrown out their windows into the gutter, out onto the abutment. 'Course I was stupid enough to forget that it led onto a bridge, one of those funky little sandbag-and-spit jobs we'd put in to cross a rivulet of garbage and other liquid shit—mostly our own—and, as we all know, gentlemen, bridges are number one targets in a raid.

"I sprinted like hell across that twenty feet of trembling dirt. Didn't even look under for sappers, didn't feel around for wires connected to plastique. A few flares were up, and the burning on the south end of the city lit everything up pretty well.

"As soon as I cleared the bridge, the whole little platoon of bridges around me started going. Blowing. You guys know that little stream they called a river . . . well, all the interconnecting bridges had been mined, probably that day, in daylight. I never saw a sapper or NVA anywhere near there. I figure they used our own C-4 on us, stole it out of the compound. Maybe even bought it on the black market.

"Well, running that bridge had cleared my mind a little bit, and running the gauntlet all the way home seemed like a reasonable thing to do. So I took off like Charlie was on my tail and gunned it down the middle of the street.

"I heard some of our gunboats going up, heard small arms fire on the east and west. It seemed like only the north was open, which was strange. Should have started there and worked its way in.

"But you, Jones, I hear you figured some of that and took a detail in that direction."

He was into his rap but he looked at me closely. I glanced at Miller, who was balancing Sterno cans on his bayonet, and dug deeper into the dirt with mine.

"Yeah, I had a thought. But I want to hear about the wire, and this extremely fuckable nurse friend of yours."

"I'll say." He was off again. It seemed funny how excited they got, the men, no matter the rank, to tell these stories. They spoke faster and faster. Their eyes literally glistened as they spoke, as if they never knew where the stories would lead, as if the deed were the only thing, as if the sad and sorry endings were an unexpected surprise, something come up out of the past without their knowledge or permission, something they hadn't bargained for in the telling.

I'm no storyteller. Not over there, not here. And maybe that's why I'm in the shape I'm in today. For me a memory is more than a real thing.

Franklin, the quiet one, had opened his eyes wide with excitement. He punctuated sentences with short, hard thrusts of the bayonet. I saw its blood groove fill with the sweat from his hand.

"Well, fuck the north, I said, cannonballin' down the street past a few drunks and opium smokers passed dead out. I kept runnin', knew they could be sappers faking it.

Motorbikes, bicycles, fruit carts had all been abandoned. All sitting in neat rows on one street and blown to junk, still smokin', on the next.

"I was only a block from my place when I turned the corner and ran straight into an old man and a young woman. They threw up their arms and whispered, '*Chu Hoi, Chu Hoi*,' you know, over and over.

"I can just imagine the sight—a tall American drenched in sweat and covered with moss, mud, and filth, carrying a heavy knife blade side-up like he was looking for business, running smack dab into these two, probably just trying to get underground, or out of the city.

"The man was tall and wore an old shabby suit. Looked like a shop owner. But the girl wore her working clothes, skirt slit to the waist and blouse with slits over each breast.

"But did I care? No way. I just wanted to be gone. They were surprised when I spoke to them so fluently in their own language, but they listened. I told them to get off the street, to avoid the bridges, to head north or to our base. They nodded and ran up an alley to the north. Last I ever saw of them. It only occurred to me later that I probably could have found a lot more out by asking them questions than by giving them advice, but that was later.

"I could see the apartment from the corner. I hung on to the lamp pole as it flickered. There was something wrong. I could see something . . . it looked like two or three forms moving slowly, slightly, in the shadows . . . near that rundown hootch we called an apartment. One of them lay flat beneath the stunted tree in front. The other two flanked the doorway. I could see gun barrels but no faces, no uniforms, no insignia.

"I didn't know if they'd seen me burst around the

167

corner or not. I hoped they thought I was just another villager running to safety. But they were waiting, all right, and I wasn't about to let them get me so easy.

"You should have been there, Miller. RPG rockets flew so thick you would have sworn they were big flies. What you could have done with a 'borrowed' RPG. God! Well, off the point."

Franklin swallowed and took a breath. I saw a faint smile on Miller's face as he flipped the bayonet in the air, catching it by its handle every time. Like most of us, he had "blued" his bayonet a deep black so it couldn't be seen.

"I was determined to get inside, give those assholes some of their own business, then split for base. I had an M-16, sidearm, pair of bandoliers, and a nine-mm Browning automatic in that place, and I wasn't moving till I had 'em in my hands.

"I crossed the street to the alley that ran behind my place. I knew they might be waiting there as well, but I figured there'd be fewer. I was hoping for just one, and that's what I got—though it turned out not to be exactly what I was counting on."

I remembered most of all the unbearable heat from chemical and gas fires, and the smells: rubber, metal, hootch grass, livestock, and human flesh. I pitied the corpsmen I saw who scurried from body to body, looking for someone to pump up with an IV and instant transfer orders. But that was me remembering, not Franklin.

"I sprinted through the alley to the back entrance. All I had was that knife, and the other one at my waist. I made a run for the back door, thinking I wouldn't be any better off by slowing up, and knowing I could knock the flimsy door flat with my weight.

"All I felt was a stinging sensation on both shoulders.

Then I was on the ground and my arms hurt like hell up high somewhere, I could feel something hot and wet mixing with the sweat on my back, and I took time to wonder what happened. I was ten meters or so from the door and hadn't heard a thing. Before I could move, something black jumped onto my chest, forcing all the air from my lungs.

"He had a knee on my sternum and another on my left arm and was twisting a garrote around my neck, slowly, as if I were a doll that couldn't move. I saw his face, his tight mouth, his dark eyes, and felt the wire slip around my neck.

"One arm was free but was turning numb, but when I brought it slowly up behind his back, I could see the knife still in my grip. My fingers were glued to it.

"He wrapped the ends of the garrote across each other and was raising my head for the final twist when I pushed the knife as hard as I could into his back. I must have hit his spine, though, because it didn't go in very far, just raked across bone with a sickening clatter as I let the blade fall.

"Immediately he dropped the wire and arched back, pulling his knee off my arm, and he pulled the knife from its shallow stick in his back. He looked at the knife like he had never seen one before and was turning toward me with the blade in his hand when I snapped the other one off my belt and shoved it into his gut with all my draining strength. This time it stuck, deep, and I gave it a last twist and then rolled to the side.

"He dropped the knife, looked into my face as he fell toward me, and didn't move. His eyes stared, flat, into mine as I got my breath back, felt around on my shoulders for the damage.

"It was blood that was running so freely down my back

and chest and into the street. My hands were going numb from loss of blood, but I could still trace the deep cuts in both shoulders. I knew how close to my neck he had come. Maybe his height had done him in. Maybe it was the awkwardness of my running stride that made him miss. I'll never know.

"All this was fast and very quiet, but I didn't move quick enough, couldn't move quick enough, taking the knives and garrote and rolling his body down the alley. As I was struggling with the back door I suddenly felt something small, and cold, like an ice cube, on the back of my neck. But I knew what it was. I just kind of slumped over, tired, drained, waiting for the click of the bolt and the searing heat of the bullets.

"They never came. Next thing I heard was a voice saying, in good old American, 'Keep 'em raised. Stand up straight. Where'd he get the greens, Hooks? Turn around, scumbag,' followed by the same in that dead sapper's language, so I turned and saw two guys from SOG and a third man dressed in black, wearing a camouflage-colored beret. The others had helmets, and all three were pointing machine guns at my head.

"Remember those orders that we got that time—when, two years back?—about never trying for a body shot when you could take him down by the head? Great old time, those days down south. Jeez.

"Right away I gave it to 'em by the book: name, unit, assignment, code for that day, all in an order they couldn't question. I didn't want to get taken down by some scared grunts, SOG or not.

"The Americans lowered their guns, but the guy in black still had a bead on my forehead. One of them started to laugh but stifled it to a chuckle. The other stuck a cigarette in his mouth and was about to light it when the man in black grabbed his hand. He spoke in French, so fast even I couldn't pick it up, holding that gun on me now from his side.

"The American with the cigarette tucked it into his helmet webbing and spoke quietly and quickly to the Frenchman, once or twice pointing at me and mentioning my name. The other SOG man vanished into the darkness.

"I was so weak I fell back onto the doorway. The Frenchman stopped talking then and strapped his gun onto his back. The other SOG came back into the dim light cast by fires and explosions moving slowly in our direction. The Frenchman put an arm around me, hefting most of my weight, and took a quick glance at my tags. I heard him mutter my name and thumb the two soldiers our way, then kicked the back door in. He carried me to the only sturdy chair in the place and dropped me carefully into it.

"The Frenchman went to the front and took a position near the tiny side window. One of the SOG's took a similar position at the back, blocking the shattered door with an old trunk and the breakfast table. The third man helped me out of my shirt, examined the deep wire cuts that still bled, and poured sulfa powder onto the cuts, then bound them tightly with gauze and tape. When he brought the syringe from his hip pack, I asked, 'What you plannin' to shoot, my friend?' He told me the first would be morphine, a few grams, the second a couple million units of penicillin. I told him I'd take the second. The first could wait. He was surprised but went along.

"As they watched and worked they filled me in. They had been sent to bring me in—units like theirs had spread throughout the city as soon as they had word that sappers were in the city in force and more than the usual number of booby traps had been set.

"In fact, those shapes I'd seen in the front outside my

apartment had been *them*. Their orders were simple: bring me in, back to base, with all my stuff. I told them I was ready.

"From my kit I tossed around a camouflage paint stick, painfully pulled on a long-sleeved black turtleneck, and collected my 'stuff': a bandolier of grenades, for the Frenchman; a pack full of C-4 and some lightweight plastics, just a bit less stable, for one of my new SOG friends; the old fifty-caliber machine gun that came with the apartment, for the other SOG; and I grabbed my illegal thirty-eight to wear on my hip, my even more illegal forty-four that my dad had shipped over, in a shoulder holster, and my issue M-sixteen.

"It was almost light as dawn outside and small arms fire was closing in. We conferred, broke out the front in five meter staggers, and ran like hell for the darkness of the building down the street."

He broke off when the guard shift changed. We changed shifts a lot, used odd hours, two-man perimeter patrols, strange stuff like that to confuse the enemy the few times they found us. And usually it worked.

The guys who'd been burning their eyelids out staring into darkness fell into their private little holes and were asleep immediately. Their replacements began the lonely three-hour vigil. At this camp you couldn't even smoke on patrol within the base. There was a lot of twig-chewing and not much else to do or think about except to watch. That's how HQ wanted it.

"Well, we knew where we were and where we wanted to go. The Frenchman knew the quickest route to base."

"Say, who was this Frog, anyway?" Miller asked, smiling.

"Never got his name, man. Even after that night and the next day, when we were together almost constantly. All

I could find out—and this was later, a hell of a lot later—was that he was ranking, from some special unit that had never pulled out—not even after Dien Bien Phu. S'posed to be only a few of 'em around, kinda like the first 'advisors' we sent over, right?''

I thought of the ranker in the black beret and no insignia, the one they referred to only as Jones. Never sir, or major, or captain, or whatever. A Britisher. And I thought of the man Lavey out at the jungle hospital, the nuns carrying the satchel charge as we flew off—and I missed part of Franklin's amazing, continuous account.

''. . . But we knew we still had blocks to cover on open ground and not much ammunition. I was bleeding through, could feel it, but there was nothing to do for it then. We crouched alongside a little well to plan the next sprint, when six of 'em came runnin' straight at us, draggin' a Russian machine gun and carrying two RPG's. We were ready to cut 'em down, when we realized they weren't comin' for us, they just wanted to use the well for cover. So I hunkered down with our guys and listened to the talk not four or five meters away, the strategy for the machine gun and the rockets. They were hunting for soldiers like me—guys living off base or caught outside somewhere, trying to get back in.

''They were supposed to establish a stable position with the big gun and one RPG while two of them roamed the area with the other one. I flashed it all with hand signals to my new friends. We were plastered flat into the mud at the well's base, just hoping one of them didn't smell us, or inch around the well for a better look 'round.

''We had to take them out quickly and quietly. The two SOG's unsheathed their knives and I pulled the garrote from a pocket. It was as good as a knife to me. I'm no cut man like your friend, Jones.''

173

"No one is," I tried to drawl lightly back.

"And Frenchie produced a nine-mm Parabellum with a silencer, both from a holster rigged inside his shirt. Dirty tricks, man.

"We each sweated a monsoon each time Frenchie turned the silencer tighter into place. The miniature rachet sounded like a pistol shot to me.

"He gave the timing signal and we each knew how it was supposed to go down, who was whose. 'Course, it don't always work that way, and it didn't this time, either.

"My responsibility was the man closest to me, on the far right. My SOG friend would take the one next closest. The other four were for Frenchie and the other SOG, one by knife, three by silenced bullet.

"We went. I saw two startled blackened faces leaning down over the machine gun. One reached for the trigger and the other tried to stand up. I heard the muffled thump of silenced bullets hitting flesh and gut to my left as I let instinct take over and looped the garrote around both their necks together, then twisted one wire over the other with all my strength. My new friend had immediately gone for the third from the right and was pushing his lifeless body to the ground when I heard the *snap!* of a neck, and then I was falling backward, the weight too much for me, the struggle by the second man too fierce.

"I saw my buddy turn his back on me and spike the machine gun with an iron rod. The other American was hefting an RPG and rocket bag over his shoulder. My second man was almost free, and I was sure they'd forgotten about him. I was sure all four of us were about to be killed, the three of them shot in the back, me slowly strangled to death.

"Then the Frenchman was by my side from nowhere

with his big gun stuck in the second man's abdomen. He fired once, twice, odd little sounds really, and that little pumping noise of his big gun tore the man almost in half.

"But he didn't even pause, just pulled the smoking barrel away and sprinted for the next dark shadow in the street. I picked up the second RPG and the pack of rockets and followed. The two Americans brought up the rear.

"From that point to base was one shit of a fight, boys. Nothing like it, before or since, not even up here. Took me a while to figure out the RPG, but once I had it down it was smooth. You can literally watch these suckers fly out of your hands and impact. It's a strange feeling.

"We got to the base and shored up the lines. You know all about that part, Jones."

I chewed vacantly on a splinter of wood and nodded.

"What was it, two days? before we cleared the area. Then we swept the city."

"Thirty hours, Franklin. Not two days." I didn't like glorifying what we'd done. Franklin usually didn't either, but it was the adrenaline, or maybe boredom, talking.

"From when you busted back into camp, maybe so. It was *a while* is all I know. 'Course, I didn't go with you on the sweep of the city. That's when I met the greatest-looking nurse I'd ever seen. Maybe the greatest-looking *woman*, even. Nice too. Some things are hard to compare. She had short blond hair cut kind of raggedy, like a shag she held back with a bandanna. That was a shock. She was like one of us that way. No cute little cap or hairnet or scarf or pins or barrettes. A folded bandanna keeping the sweat off her face and the hair out of her eyes and away from her hands as she worked.

"She was short, too, about five feet, I guess. You'd never notice her in a crowd unless you saw her face—pale

175

blue eyes, almost transparent. They got darker when she concentrated, like she did on me. A small nose, little ears stuffed behind the black strip of cloth around her head, and a wide, wry mouth that always had a little upturn on one side or the other. She had big eyelashes—natural—and fine eyebrows. And a constant dimple in one cheek."

He paused. "She was something."

Miller's voice came out of the dark. "That's it? Go on, my boy. Tell us more. She had to have more than that."

"I guess so." He sounded different, brought down to earth somehow, more reserved, more like himself.

"Well?"

"Well, she had one of the greatest sets of teeth between here and the States."

Miller snorted, "That ain't hard to get done." Franklin ignored him.

"Pearly whites. Perfect. When she smiled, the dimple opened and her lips flared, and it was pink and white, and you stared at her like there was nothin' else around."

Miller. "Which, in this case, probably was true. What about her body? Good jugs? *Playboy* material, or what?"

There was another pause, and when Franklin spoke, his voice was lower still, and more measured.

"I didn't look at her that way, Miller. I know it sounds like BS, being over here so long. But I just didn't. Not her. Some others, yeah, plenty of others. But not her. But thinking about it now, I'm certain she'd qualify in any contest you can imagine."

We were all quiet for a moment. Then Franklin murmured. "Jones? You still awake?"

I thought about where it was going to go and then said, "Sure."

"What do you think? Was she something or what?"

"I think you skipped the part about your wire wounds

and what she said about 'em. That's how you got onto this whole thing to begin with, you know.''

He perked up. "Yeah, yeah, right. Well, she was standing in a hospital tent for walking cases, low priority—that's how I noticed her, really—she could actually stand up in one of our tents. Anyway, she was working on some guy's hand or something and didn't even look at me, just glanced at the transmittal form that said something about deep cuts on both shoulders. So she snipped the thread she was using to sew up his hand and told me to take my shirt off and wait.

"She did a great job on that guy—shrapnel in both hands. 'Course, he and every other guy in the tent were just sitting there staring at this woman. And it wasn't like there were no other nurses in there, either.

"She taped the gauze down, signed his green slip, and told him to go find his company. And then she gave him a great big smile. The guy kind of stumbled out the door.

"She laughed, we all laughed, and she turned to me, reading my injury report. She nodded and then looked up. Her eyes caught mine, square on, gentlemen, and you could hear bells all the way to Shawnee Mission, Kansas. God! What beautiful eyes. What a classic face.

"In a second she was running a probe over the line of caked blood and pus on the front of my left shoulder. She looked at the cuts very intently, front and back, on both arms. She was frowning. And that's when she said it.''

I was very tired and had guard duty sometime early the next day. I muttered, "That was the big moment, eh?" and wrapped myself snugly in my poncho.

Franklin continued as if he hadn't heard me. I imagined the cartoon stars in his eyes. He was entitled. Any of us was entitled.

"Yeah. She said she had never seen cuts like that

before. Not in her life, not in her career, not since she had come over. She kept circling them, this time with antiseptic and gauze, looking for one place to stitch.

"'I can't stitch around your whole shoulder,' she said. I told her not to worry about it so much, it would stop bleeding. I told her it didn't need stitches. That was a mistake. *She* was a nurse, I was told, whereas *I* was just a crazy soldier who'd almost had his arms cut off but still stayed out fighting and wouldn't report to the hospital.

"You know when those cheap trashy books talk about a woman's eyes *blazing*? Well, they were right. That pale blue turned dark and shot off sparks in the tent. Some of the guys being treated or waiting laughed and she jumped on 'em quick, told 'em to can it or get out of her tent. I'll tell you, the place was dead quiet in an instant.

"So she swabbed 'em down, put some butterflies where the bleeding was slow but consistent, put pressure on the strip points where the wire had dug deep. In each shoulder she threw a couple heavy stitches where the wire had met the bone.

"'How did you get this?' she asked. 'Garrote,' I said, pronouncing it like the Frenchman had taught me. We'd fought well together, going in and on base. But that's for another night."

I heard Miller mutter "okay" with the heavy syrup of sarcasm, but Franklin went right on. He was on a roll, a real tear. I had never heard him like this, never did again. I thought maybe he'd dipped into the amphetamines we all were issued, but that didn't seem to be it. He wasn't jumpy like you get on Dexamyl and the other shit we carried. He was for real, just his low voice carrying out into the night air.

"Get this. She asked me what a garrote was. Man! She

didn't much enjoy the answer, either. Well, finally she'd wrapped and taped half my arms and chest. She wrote out orders for my C.O., spent some time at it. Then she sealed it. The guys were giving me the eye. All she said was, 'You're not going home, but that's not because you shouldn't. Give this to your captain and tell him you cannot use a gun for two weeks or you'll pull everything out again and probably get infected. That reminds me. Drop your pants.'

"Now, boys, that had to be one of the hardest things I've had to do in this poor excuse for a war. But I did it, she injected the penicillin in a second without a blush, and continued with her 'orders' as I tucked everything back in place."

Miller and I had to chuckle at that. I was almost out, but it struck me.

"'No guns,' she repeated, and sighed. 'I'm sure he'll still send you out there on patrol, but these are *medical orders*.' She slapped the orders down on an equipment table. 'And tell him I want you back here every two days to check these wounds! Next!'

"Hooting and applause broke out in the tent, and she gave me a gentle push toward the door—and a shy little smile that flashed those teeth, showed that dimple. Man. I walked the wrong way till the perimeter guard sent me packin' toward my unit.

"And sure as hell I was sent out on patrol. Should have seen the C.O.'s face when he read the orders. Talk about fuckin' red. But he followed 'em all right. He made me carry the RPG to flush out sappers in the French Quarter."

I was suddenly awake, alert, at the sound of those words. I had buried my days deep, but the mention of the

179

Quarter, then, and me with all my defenses down, brought it back up, quickly, like taking a bullet and watching yourself bleed, knowing there was nothing you could do.

I knew thinking about it again too much would ruin me. I focused on my time with Sharp. This time I prayed for the cut man dream and in time it was answered.

Franklin droned quietly on.

"RPG kicks your shoulder all to hell and she saw that when I came back in. Healing left shoulder, bleeding right. She was not pleased. Even called the C.O. on the phone, then and there, and dressed him down. Got away with it too, 'cause she'd been a captain six months longer than he had.

"I was under her personal care, boys, almost a month . . . God, what a month! I remember times . . ."

I started out thinking and sometime, I can't say when, ended up dreaming about the cut man. And, strange to say, that dream probably saved me that night.

I watched the ROTC building and I watched the cops huddle to discuss their move. There was no doubt they'd make it. It was an issue of how, and when.

About two the next morning the cops began to congregate behind a couple squadrols parked at an angle in front of a bar. The street was quiet, and I knew it was about to go down.

I moved in a little from the position I had under the trees. I'd been sitting stock-still while the curious on-lookers had gone home, the barhoppers had quit for the night, the commuter students had grown weary of the wait and left, the hardcore had gone to A&A for the next day's strategy.

I knew some of the students and others sitting in the parking lot, waiting. Most of the SDS were inside, at the

A&A building, or were designated, like me, to do everything to stay clear and out of jail. Most of the Weathermen were in exile. The SDS was split about that. Anna and I had a problem about it.

A fire department car pulled up and four firefighters with giant boltcutters piled out. They were smart. They had positioned themselves out of sight of the two places where those inside the building could have seen them—the front doors and a side window where Anna's bullhorn sat, quiet.

I decided it was time. I ran up to the lot and told them it was going down, and *now*. I saw Anna's face appear in the window, heard the crack of a tear-gas gun, and started pulling people up off their asses, telling them to clear out. I grabbed the steaming tear-gas cartridge, threw it back as far as I could, looked up and caught Anna's stare, pulled the bandanna over my nose as the gas cannisters fell around me like stones, pulled a girl who'd been sleeping on the asphalt to her feet and slapped her ass, pointing her in the direction of campus.

I hadn't seen the undercovers on the flanks. They were in the parking lot before I could move. I heard the bullhorn up in the ROTC building click to life but couldn't understand what she was saying. I dodged the cops and their clubs, and I had to leave some of our people in the lot. They were just too slow.

There was one cop between me and a clear path back onto campus. He was big and beefy and carried two nightsticks, one in either hand. I knew they were weighted with lead drops on their ends.

I turned back once, in time to see the first wave of cops charge the stairs in front of the building. Another was flowing my way, and more cops had circled around the building to cut us off.

I turned again and ran hard at the man, heard Anna's voice on the bullhorn screaming "Go, man, go!" And I ran for all I was worth right at that cop, which I knew would surprise him. Hell, I'd done the same thing in the jungle— throws off equilibrium. So I charged him and just as I closed on him I saw the fear and the smirk and the contempt all thrown together in the features of his fleshy face, and he raised a club to protect his chest and another to crash down on my head, and I faked with my arm, bringing his eyes up, then swept his left leg out from under him. As he fell I clipped him with an open hand on the top of the head to make sure he'd stay down. I heard the *whoosh* of air expelled from his lungs and the heavy, angry shouts of the other cops, and I was gone into the maze that defines the campus.

I passed some of the people I'd sent back and yelled at them to get the shit out, head to the A&A building, where they'd be safe. Once in there, all faces look alike, and the administration had promised no police interference.

Some of the younger cops were doing okay. They were still in the hunt. And they were ignoring everyone else and going for me. I saw two of them running an angle toward A&A and knew that would be cut off. I hurdled rows of bushes they'd have to go through or around and let adrenaline take over. I cut south, toward the open amphitheater where we'd kicked the rallies off, a fast little plan taking shape in my mind. I put in my fastest sprint through the concrete of the amphitheater, knowing somewhere north those two cops would be cutting my way, turned onto the grass in front of the library, and reached for the lowest limb of the short but leafy tree planted there. I swung myself up, held my heavy breathing still in the bandanna over my mouth, reached over and stilled the shaking leaves.

A few moments later three of them pounded into the

open, stopping a few yards from me. They didn't talk but were breathing in gasps. They waited, and within a minute the other two ran up and stood, heaving.

I moved a branch down an inch or two till I could see the group of five men, four plainclothes and a uniform.

One of them wheezed out, "Where could that little shit have gone?" No one answered as they stood doubled over, catching their breath.

"Maybe we should try that A&A building," the uniformed cop said.

"Hey, that's off limits. You know what the lieutenant said." It was one of the younger cops, a guy with long hair who must have been on loan from vice, or gangs, maybe. Then I thought, maybe he's been planted as one of us. I couldn't see clearly but chose not to chance moving anymore.

The oldest guy there—he'd held up pretty well in the chase, actually—said, "Fuck that, kid. He took one of us down. We get him any way we can."

The young cop had some grit. He stood his ground. "Not the A&A. We do that and the campus will blow. This is Strike Central, Sarge, and if *it* goes, the city goes." He paused and looked at the other men. They listened, not agreeing, not shouting him down. "Let's do this. Someone goes back to report. We split up and send two through campus looking. Hell, he could be as tired as we are and bedding down in the grass somewhere for all we know."

The "Sarge" wasn't real happy with the kid giving suggestions, that I could see. Some things never change.

"Yeah, hotshot, and what about the other two?"

"Put them somewhere outside the A&A if you want. In plain sight. So everyone will know we've been straight."

"And if the asshole shows up?" Sarge's voice was heavy with sarcasm, but the "kid" was up to the challenge.

"Why, Sarge," he smiled, patting him on the arm, "I think you'll figure out something to do."

The five of them moved off, some laughing, someone swearing. And I had the distinct feeling that they were going to take the kid's advice.

I waited awhile in that tree. It had grown cooler. I could feel the smoothness of the bark on my hands and the dew from the leaves against my neck. The moon glowed weakly to the north. When the wind blew, lightly shaking the branches, I remembered the war. It seemed like old times.

For thirty minutes or an hour, or whatever it was, I was strangely content. I didn't think about the police, the bust at the ROTC building, the strike, my responsibilities. I laid out in that tree and didn't think. It was like being a kid again, run away and hidden for all time and space, and not caring about the consequences.

Tracers ran in a line like a long piece of rope on fire. They lit up the night for seconds at a time, but only in the muzzle flash from the jungle and the bursts of flame of each bullet as it struck the ground.

Mortars made their little mechanical sounds when the shells ignited. We were using shrapnel loads. I could hear the pieces splattering through grass, leaf, wood, flesh.

The fire and the sounds were hypnotic; that was their danger. Somewhere behind the lines there were men trying to kill us. I tried to focus on that, and Sharp kept yelling at me to keep my head down when I'd stare up at the rocket fire in the air.

I was thinking about a girl, a girl caught in it as much as or more than me. I didn't know her but I planned to. It was a very silly thought, and very foolish.

I was trying to push her to the back of my mind, when Sharp rose up and sprayed the grass right next to me. I saw the short body fall, heard Sharp yell, "Grenade," and then Sharp's shoulder was in my rib cage, driving me down into the soft dirt.

The explosion rained dirt over us. Lucky the dead man had fallen on his own grenade. His parts were well distributed, but I was starting to not notice, to not particularly care.

A flare went up and our machine guns cut in, a cacophony of sound drowning out everything but me yelling, "Thanks, Corp.," to Sharp.

He drilled a burst into the elephant grass and yelled back, "Anytime, *Sarge.*"

First I gave him the finger, then I pointed proudly to my sleeve. And then I opened up with the extra M-60, tripod intact, spraying an arc over and over until the tracers vanished and the mortars fell silent and the medics sprinted out and the only sound was the hisses of the dying.

It was my job to come in. I'd done as much as I could on the outside, caused as much directed trouble. I wanted to find out about the ROTC arrests, and I needed something new to take up my time.

I never joined the Veterans Against the War. It was too much of an Organization. Capital "O." I had my own ideas about how to protest and resist and just talk about the war, the jungle, the relentlessness of it all. And I had my own ghosts to contend with. Still do. But then, back then, I had fewer than I have now. You learn later what things really mean and what they are worth in the "real world," the life over here, thousands of miles from the jungle where we made the rules and lived by them.

I dropped noiselessly onto the grass and lay for a moment, breathing and smelling, breathing and listening,

185

and sensing, like I used to do. Then I made my move to the A&A building. I ran low to the ground, from a tree to a concrete post, from the stairs to the second level catwalk that ran across the campus to one of the black kiosks that held campus bulletins. I blended into the dark and took the most direct route. You can't travel straight across campus; there are buildings and chained-off plots of grass in the way. But even going the long way it would have been only a five-minute, leisurely stroll.

And I knew there'd be two cops sitting for me somewhere in the dark. They'd agreed to leave the doors clear, but that meant they could be anywhere.

I moved around Lincoln Hall and flattened myself against the building. Light came from the irregular smoked glass of A&A. It was diffused, muted, no help to me.

In spite of the darkness I picked them out right away. One knelt behind the bushes a few yards south of the east door. The other one had pinned himself between a security wall and a trash receptacle. He could cover two doors if he were quick. That left only two doors open: the second floor, which we had secured to be an exit from the building only, and the main entrance on Harrison Street. They were smart to leave that one uncovered. I'd have to walk at least three blocks under streetlights and in the glare of traffic to get in that way, and only a fool would try it.

So that was the dilemma. I knew I could outleg either cop to the door; the problem was getting the security people inside to let me in before I was grabbed. All of the doors were heavily guarded.

I pondered the issue there in the dark and finally decided to go for the one against the wall. I could charge for one door, then cut and hit the other. At least it was a chance.

I had pulled the bandanna up across my face and had

inched to the closest edge of the building. I was counting breaths and shaking tension from my hands, old tricks, when I heard shouting and running, laughter and singing, and all the demonstrators from the ROTC building came straggling across the lawn from the east.

They must have scared the shit out of the cop over there, facing the other way, because he just cut and ran, over to his partner, who came out of the shadows to stare at the motley crew.

I didn't know what had happened, but it was my chance. They were knocking on doors and passing security people when I pulled the bandanna back down and sprinted in among them. The cops never noticed.

Some of them were laughing so hard they were crying. I saw one of the old-line SDS security guys from way back, Paul Taylor, and fell in next to him as we squeezed through the door.

"Hey, Paul, what the fuck. I thought you were going to stay and get busted."

The tears rolled down his pale cheeks and he grabbed my shoulder and thumped me on the back.

"We did, man, we did. Oh, I can't talk. It's too funny. It's too great. You gotta hear Anna tell it."

"Anna. She's here too? I didn't see her. You mean they didn't bust *any*body?"

He sat down and shook with hysteria. I was almost laughing just from looking at him.

"I can't talk, man. Anna's gonna tell everybody what happened. Oh, man!"

I left him to his fits of the giggles and pushed through the crowd. Everyone was milling around on the first floor, in the concourse, the only big area not designed like a maze. People were hugging each other and the ones who had been out were tearing into sandwiches, cookies, whatever they could find out of the machines and from the food committee.

I finally saw Anna talking to security and operations people and was almost to her when she raised the bullhorn to speak.

"Okay, people, quiet down. This is one story you have to hear, start to finish. And this is what happened. Who knows what the pigs will say or tomorrow's papers print?

"As you know, some of us were involved in a ROTC action this afternoon and evening, on this campus."

Cheers and whistles. Anna stood on a riser and I leaned against the wall to her right. She couldn't see me.

"We sent in a team to trash the building"—more cheers—"and another group to occupy it. The Man gave us the choice to vacate and we sent a bunch out. Hope you're all here right now!"

Applause. Everybody but security and some people sleeping in one of the art rooms was listening, and there must have been seven or eight hundred packed in there for the night.

"A cadre stayed and locked the doors. We decided we'd submit to arrest in memory of the brothers and sisters at Kent State and Jackson State!"

Cheers, whistles, hands clapping, hands slapping. Anna punctuated her sentences by stomping the heels of her boots down. She glowed with excitement. She looked tough. She looked good, maybe the best I'd ever seen her.

"So we stayed and had a rousin' *good* time. I saw some of you out there in the lot, and we appreciate your support. Special thanks to the dude with the basket of food and drink we lifted up to our window!"

Again, cheers. Applause. Whistles. Boot stomping. Hands slapping.

"But we were serious about this action, and we stayed

put. The pigs waited till the streets were clear so no one would see them bustin' any heads, then they charged the building and snapped our locks.

"We were aware of the bust goin' down from some faithful people still waitin' in the parking lot. Those of you here, power!"

Fists filled the air and now it was quiet, eerie in the huge concrete building full of shadows, where Anna's voice rang out, crackled through the megaphone, and echoed hollowly around the walls.

"The pigs took us out. We were sitting—nonviolent, man—with our arms linked together. They used their billy clubs on the women we had by the door and dragged all four of them out first. We haven't seen them since. After the killings in Ohio and Mississippi we are concerned and have people checking on them right now."

A low murmur. Somewhere, far up on a catwalk and across the building, someone played "For What It's Worth" on a guitar. I heard a young girl singing.

". . . All of us. We were dragged downstairs, slapped if we opened our mouths, and literally thrown into three squadrols they'd backed up to the front entrance.

"They took us to headquarters at Eleventh and State. As we stepped out of the vans they made us put our hands on our heads. They marched—what?—all fifty of us?— whatever number into the station and it was pure chaos, man. I mean, they'd busted a few of our people in the lot for assault and were bookin' them, they had people in there from every campus across this fuckin' city, because we have *shut it down!*"

Cheers, screams, whistles. Same low guitar, same woman singing, counterpoint, in the same building but so far away from all of us.

"So some great gross fuckin' sergeant in fancy dress

189

blues, shined shoes, big gun, the works, dig it? comes over with his clipboard and his papers. Squadrol cops just say we belong to him, turn around, and leave.

"The big man doesn't know what to do, right, so he marches us over to an elevator bank and tells us to get in. It takes four elevators to carry us. He calls upstairs and says they better be ready to process sixty or seventy punks and hippies."

Snickers, catcalls.

"Then he reaches in, punches twelve on each of the elevators, and lets all four of 'em go up. Well, my brothers and sisters"—she's in top form, flushed with the thrill of it all for her, for all of them, or maybe not quite all; I see a few unsmiling faces out there, a few weary bodies slumped against desks facing the other way—"well, it takes about half a floor for us to drop the hands, a floor to check out the wounded, and a couple more floors to talk over how we did what we wanted.

"All four elevators stop on twelve at the same time. The doors open. And there are no cops there. I peek out and see them all shuffling papers behind their desks, probably figurin' some of their buddies will escort us over. They *all* figure that. Then it hits me. The greatest plan, and the simplest in the world. The biggest embarrassment for the Chicago police department since the '68 convention. I look across at the brothers and sisters in the bank across, they look at the people next to my elevator, I give the sign for one and have to cover my mouth so I won't bust out laughin'.

"Next thing you know, all of us are heading straight back down to the first floor, trying not to be hysterical all the way down.

"Clunk! First floor, doors open. Now, see, I just wanted to harass the heat, keep them workin' overtime. But when we got down there, there was nobody waitin' for us! The doors opened and there we were, fifty peace freaks, uncuffed, unprinted, uncharged, standin' in four elevators and staring at one another in disbelief.

"There was only one thing to do. I said, 'Let's split' and we were gone, walking quietly through the front doors of the CPD's headquarters into the night. Soon as we made sure we were all clear, we ran for it—ran all the way here, broken into small groups. Never saw a cop except outside on campus."

It was exhilarating, really it was, even for me. So bold, so crazy.

"So we did it all tonight, brothers and sisters—took the ROTC, got busted, walked away. We're back for more tomorrow. *More strike!* Thanks for your help!"

Cheers, whistles, laughter. When you're actually *there* and involved, it isn't boring, doesn't get stale. You think back, and sometimes wonder how you made it through so many carbon-copy rallies. The room was buzzing, picking up in noise and intensity.

"One more thing, people. Committees need to go to work now to prepare for tomorrow. If you've been working here while we were gone, you should be set, except I want to meet with the press people. I want the story to go out the way it happened.

"Leaders of Arrest & Bail will meet in 204 in half an hour. And anyone working the outside, the hit–and–run people, should meet at three in"—she leaned down and one of her "aides" whispered in her ear—"classroom 350. Strategize. Okay! *This night belongs to the people!*"

She clicked off the megaphone and bathed in the lights, a couple of cameras clicking, the fists thrown her way high in the air, just all that activity for which she was responsible.

191

She was walking toward the art tables where the PR campaign for the whole city had been mapped out, when she saw me. She whispered in the ear of the same guy while eyeing me, handed him her megaphone, and came over to lean next to me. I chewed on a toothpick, staring her down.

"Damn rousing speech, Anna. You got what it takes."

She didn't say anything at first.

Then, "I saw you take that cop out. Think they know you?"

I tapped the bandanna around my neck.

"Nope."

"Good. You played your role, man. You did good."

"Thanks, boss."

She stepped away.

"What do you want me to say? You've made your choice and I've made mine. You're valuable to the movement. So are all those who refuse to be photographed or busted."

"Compromised."

"I don't see it that way."

"No, you don't. And I don't see sittin' in that fuckin' building for half a day, getting beat up and busted, and then running away in the night. Why didn't you bring your hundred people out to help *us*, to divert the heat from other actions? They're closin' down Sheridan Road up at Northwestern, you know that? The more heat we keep concentrated in Chicago, the better their chances of gettin' it done. They're boarded in at DePaul but they're surrounded by heat. We have an extra hundred to send into the Loop, Grant Park, wherever, we can draw them away that way too.

"Same damn thing at IIT, Mundelein, Loyola. You know, it's not like everybody believes in this thing like we do. We gotta make a *move*. We can't play games with the media, Anna. The Days of Rage didn't work."

"It's the same old thing with you, isn't it? I don't know why I talk to you anymore." Her lips and face were drained of color. I saw a trickle of blood leading from her collarbone down into her gray T-shirt. There was a dark pool showing high up on her chest.

"This was important, Jones. You might not think so now—might never think so. But I know it was important. It *is* important. I can't explain it to you again."

"Anna, I think before your meeting you better talk to the medics. I'll walk you up the stairs."

She laughed and pulled away.

"Man." She looked at me as if for the first time, a funny, appraising look. "I can take care of myself." It was final, the tone of that voice, final.

So I said, "Yeah, you can. Always could, always did. I think we split here, Anna. You gotta go your way, I gotta go mine."

She looked at me closely. Then the color returned to her cheeks.

"You mean about everything."

"I mean about everything."

She sighed a heavy sigh and looked me over. "There's no changing you, is there, Jones? There's never been any changing you. I don't know if it's the war or if it goes back further even than that."

I looked her firm in the eyes. Something in me hurt, and my head was buzzing, but I always knew it would end this way.

"What's for you, then? Will you stay with us, work with us?"

I didn't have to think about it. "I'll stay. Evasion and

Escape Committee. But count me out of the executive committee meetings."

"Okay." She looked sad, and small, and not half as strong as she really was. "It was good while it lasted."

I laughed. I was bitter about a lot of things then, so I said it: "Isn't it pretty to think so?"

She stood looking at me thoughtfully for a moment, then raised a fist halfway and whispered, "Good-bye, Jones."

I didn't move, just said as calmly as I could, "Friedberg."

She walked quickly away and out of my life.

The strike ended within a week. We gave the building back in exchange for total amnesty and a promise that all classes at the university would spend the rest of the term discussing war issues: the economics of war, the history of war, the psychology of war, the French occupation of Indochina, police intervention, police actions—whatever the classes had been about, now they spent some time focused on the war.

It was similar on other campuses in Chicago. Most went about their business. Northwestern had seceded from the Union and never ceded back—not to this day.

I traveled some, helping the antiwar movement with my expertise in hit-and-run, information systems, debugging telephones, and weapons. I wasn't into weapons use but weapons identification, so I could tell the demonstrators what to expect.

In Iowa City—home of the University of Iowa—early that June a bomb exploded in the student union and I left quickly on the bus. In Boston I fought the mounted police outside of the Sheraton, where Spiro Agnew was eating dinner. They rounded two hundred of us up against a chain-link fence and waded in, clubs swinging. Four of the two hundred got away. I was one of them.

In Madison the library blew from a light charge of C-4. We fought the police with garbage can lids. My people stood their ground while we were gassed. Some of us had masks, and those of us who didn't, soaked their scarves in water and draped them over their heads, slowly backing away, not getting caught.

The Free Clinic in Berkeley stitched me up after the Man clobbered the leaders of the Free University. They burned the acres of vegetables planted earlier in the spring. When I left on a plane, all that remained was a plot of ashes and dust, surrounded by rolls and rolls of barbed wire.

I returned to Chicago toward the end of June. It was strange living with—and off—other people, but it wasn't so strange compared to my life overseas. It had the same sense of rootlessness, of never belonging but needing to. So I returned to the city I called home.

One of the older guys from the cadre told me about the ceremony scheduled for the last Sunday in June on campus. I knew she'd be there and decided to go.

They had called for a final graduation ceremony of the Free University of Illinois at Chicago Circle. They had gotten permission to use the amphitheater, which was no big deal because it was a Sunday. Those days there were no classes at all on weekends.

I walked over on the second floor walkway toward the library. She was in the middle of the open air theater, at the bottom, standing behind a microphone stand and table. Two of her friends were there with her.

It was late afternoon and quite cool for late June. I sat on the cold concrete steps near the top and pulled my

Mexican poncho over my legs, wrapped it under me, and watched from behind my little tent.

There were maybe a hundred people in the place, scattered in groups of two or three. It was not a very impressive turnout. A few of them smoked joints. Most of them were cold and not enthused. Probably like me, they were tired of speeches, rallies, pep talks. But they were there anyway.

Anna had cut her hair very short. She wore overalls and tennis shoes. She looked cold, and tiny, and out of place.

She was arranging papers on the table when I sat down. One of her friends had just finished speaking. There was a bit of applause when he stopped. Anna stepped up to the microphone and scanned the faces of the people around her. She didn't look at me, just kept scanning.

She spoke about the significance of the spring term at the university. She told us it was an important beginning in preventing the normal discourse of higher education or, in other words, teaching the subjects of war. ("We won't teach war no more.") She talked about the strike committees, the results of Kent State, and the actions that followed. It became a kind of drone in the chilled air.

Anna was more strident than when I'd left. I sat still and listened as best I could.

She was concluding her remarks, thanking people, speaking of the actions planned for summer, when she recognized me. She didn't stop, never missed a word in her rhetoric, but she stopped speaking to the crowd and ended talking to me alone.

"I'd like to thank the cadres, most of whose members could not be here today because they are working against imperialism across the country. They afforded us the opportunity to attack the war machine, the system, in ways that would have been impossible without their dedication to their work. We have been able to develop a multipronged attack on that war machine.

"We honor all of the women and men involved in these actions and activities. Those of you present should feel secure that your place in history"—she paused and gave me a ghost of a smile—"even if anonymous, is secure.

"We have diplomas here for all of you. You are all graduates of the Free University. We have many names on our lists but will limit them to those present. If you have participated but your name is not called, please stop at our table and we will provide you with a diploma.

"As you move down to pick up your diplomas, we will be sending around several jugs of wine and loaves of Italian bread, donated by Giovanni's on Taylor Street."

She passed a grocery bag around at the bottom steps of the amphitheater and slowly bottles of wine and huge round loaves of fresh bread traveled up the steps to us. Meanwhile one of the men she was with read off names. Some of the people scattered throughout the area went down for the flimsy pieces of paper handed them.

I watched the tops of the stairs for police photographers but saw none. One of the men standing directly below me might have been a cop. He wore a yellow windbreaker and sunglasses and he chain-smoked. But he never moved, so I figured he was harmless.

Anna was busy signing some papers down on the table. Her head was buried in her work; she never looked up at me. She kept on writing, I shivered when the wind blew in, and the names were sporadically called off.

I took the wine and bread from a girl in jeans and a T-shirt. She smiled shyly, shivering, holding her arms after she gave me the food, and I asked her if she wanted to share my poncho. She blushed and said thanks but no, then sat back down a step or two away. I chuckled and drank.

The calling of names stopped for a minute, then Anna stood up. She looked around the circular area and then straight up at me. She was holding two pieces of the flimsy white paper.

"Finally, before the graduation ceremonies close, I have two diplomas for a distinguished guest and advocate for peace. To receive the Master of Arts in Tactics and Strategy and the Doctor of Arts in Peace Mongering—Tom Smith."

She pointed at me. I knew she'd seen the Windbreaker man or someone else who could compromise me. Loyal to the end, I thought as I got up slowly. Some of the people were lost in their own little worlds, the end of the strike for many. Others looked over as I walked quickly down the amphitheater steps and up the two steps onto the concrete dais.

Anna's eyes sparkled a little as she handed me my diplomas and we shook hands the "power to the people" way. We held it a little longer than is customary.

She said, "T. Jones. My man."

"Friedberg," I drawled, smiling.

"We've been hearing about some guy travelin' the college route, demonstratin' and leadin' actions just about everywhere, man. Knew it had to be someone I know."

She laughed quietly and low.

"Listen, Friedberg, we should—"

She cut me off. "You'd better move along now, *Smith*. Places to go, you know. Choices to make. See what I mean?" Her head bobbed up toward where the Windbreaker man had been. He was gone.

"Right you are, boss."

198

Then we both just waited, looking at each other like two high school kids out on a date.

She said softly, "Be cool, man. Be true." She touched my shoulder where the scar was. I held her hand there.

I said, "You too, man. You too," and was off the opposite way I had come in, climbing to the second level east, making fast time.

A folksinger had come down. She was wearing buckskins—coat, shirt, vest, boots. She sang "I Am a Man of Constant Sorrow" as I jogged along the parapet wall, desperately trying to not look back.

I wouldn't see Anna again, but the changed refrain of that song would haunt my many free hours: "I'm goin' back to Illinois/Place where I was chiefly raised."

I'd gone back, and I knew it was to stay.

Jack Swanson had been back sixteen days before he went wacko. He'd gotten a commercial flight into San Francisco like I had, transferred to Chicago in an hour, and there he was, standing waiting for a bus at O'Hare Airport, hours, only hours out of his last jungle patrol. They hadn't bothered to debrief him because he had been good at his trade. Model soldier. Mostly he killed people.

His parents had died when he was a kid. He had a sister somewhere, but she'd been raised by a foster family and never had answered his letters once he went overseas.

He'd lived alone on the north side of Chicago, on Byron Street, a little one-bedroom apartment. But that was long gone now, just like everything else he ever knew.

Intelligence had known we were from the same area, and they'd given him a number where he could reach me. Trouble was, I'd been cut loose only three months earlier. When Swanson got off that plane, I was in the hospital, undergoing malaria treatments.

Later he told me he called from the airport, from the Palmer House downtown, where the bus had let him off, and from the room he rented in Evanston. He had gotten on the el and taken it as far north as it would go.

I really don't know how he made it sixteen days. But on that morning of the sixteenth day he dressed in his jungle fatigues, strapped on a pack, tied his hair back with a headband, and painted his face, hands, and arms green and brown. He laced up the boots and went out looking for the enemy.

And maybe that's all he would have done, that's all that would have happened. The problem was he found it— he found the enemy.

Somehow he wasn't reported to the police all that time he dodged across deserted residential streets, ran across lawns of the rich and near-rich, popped off a search-and-destroy in the middle of suburban Chicago. Maybe it was too early in the day for anyone to notice or care.

He had the unfortunate luck to be sneaking along some street, moving from bush to bush, when he heard a woman's voice, and she wasn't exactly happy. When he heard the man's voice in response, it clicked and he was back there, crouching in the saw grass with the enemy within striking distance.

The voices came from a house just ahead. Swanson told me about it once, when I went to see him in the psycho ward, and never spoke of it again, to anyone, doctors included. And most of it was a quiet, lucid, exceptionally clear and detailed description of every movement, every sight, every sound.

A high wooden fence surrounded the yard from which the voices came. It was eight feet high and well-made, chinked tightly. The knotholes had been covered with plastic wood. The edges of the fence abutted the house. A garage sat against the wall across from the house.

Swanson flattened himself against the garage after checking the fence for holes. Nothing on the street moved. Swanson could hear the voices clearly now.

A woman was muttering, almost moaning, sort of like whining. And after each female sound a male sound, harsh and low, followed.

She said something like, "Not *now*, Charlie. No. No! I didn't invite you over for that."

"Why then, baby? Come on, baby."

"No."

Sounds of squirming, flesh on flesh. We'd all heard it often enough over there to know what it was.

"You're just teasing me, baby. Not nice."

"I'm *not*! I just wanted to talk. I didn't say what we might want to do tonight. But not now."

"Lori, baby, you're so beautiful I just can't help myself. Here, let me help you. . . ."

"No! I don't want to do that! Charlie—Charlie—"

What snapped it was the crying, the beginning of the low weeping. And maybe the name too. That day, it would have been a bad name for anyone: Charlie.

Swanson had the duty. He was on response patrol. Maybe I would have been out there, doing something crazy like that myself if the hospitals hadn't snapped me up. Sixteen days back, a pocketful of money, and nowhere to go, no clear idea what to do.

Jack did what he was trained to do. He scaled the rear of the garage and peered down over the edge. And he was *fast*—a few seconds.

From the tip of the garage Swanson's blackened, red-eyed, cloth-bound head appeared. He scanned the yard after he saw the two people on the wooden swing. No other people. Two exits—one into the house, the other into the garage. Beach towels set out for sunbathing. Barbecue. Lawn chairs. That's it. Back to Charlie. Charlie and Lori.

The two of them were all tangled together on the swing. It was huge, sturdy, anchored into the fence. The seat creaked as the girl tried to push him away. He was just a boy, but we had seen too many killers who were just boys. She was just a girl, but over there that meant you were a woman.

They had blond hair but Swanson didn't notice, didn't care. He saw the boy with his pants unzipped, shirt off. The girl's blouse was unbuttoned and pulled off one shoulder, pinning one arm to her chest. Her breasts were tanned, small, jostled in the struggle. The boy held her by the head with one hand while he tried to move her shorts down with the other.

Swanson didn't pick up the sentences from the struggle, just the sounds. They were sounds he had heard too many times before, in jungle grass, thatch huts, bars, alleyways. Always the same, when a soldier, either side, could get his hands on a woman.

This girl Lori wouldn't scream, and Swanson had seen that too. Somewhere from before the jungle he understood why, but it didn't matter. This was patrol, and there was someone to deal with.

Swanson wasted no time. He swung his body forward over the roof's peak, slipped a knife from a leg sheath, and skidded down the other side. A gun would have been nice, but he'd done the deed with knives before. This was no different.

They didn't see or hear him until his body softly hit the ground and rolled once. Then he was on his feet and the girl saw him first. She shrieked, a scream that must have hung in the air like weight. Charlie turned, dropping his hand from her head, leaving her shorts unzipped, pulled halfway down one hip. His eyes bulged at the sight of that wild man standing there, some *thing* risen from a nightmare, and they both moved at the same time.

Swanson took the few yards in a second, and the kid jumped off the swing, zipping his pants, turning for the door. In a second Swanson had him in a lock, his beefy arm wrapped tightly around the kid's neck, the point of the eight-inch blade pressed against his back until pinpricks of blood popped out. He held him quietly and looked at the girl.

She had pulled the shorts up and fastened them. She'd pulled her blouse back on, but her breasts hung free, forgotten in the sudden horror of the attack. She covered her mouth with one hand and backed slowly away along the seat.

Swanson told me he questioned them both in all the dialects he knew. When they didn't answer, he wasn't surprised. He'd seen it before. So he tried French. The girl, he said, looked like she understood. Not the boy. Swanson could smell the warm urine released by the boy as they stood there, could see the pools of sweat draining off the hollows of his back.

She wouldn't answer, so he tried English. The boy got hysterical.

"Man, what, what, who are you, what will you do I wasn't doin' anythin', this is my girlfriend she invited me here why, where did you . . . " Swanson moved the knife to his throat and told him to shut up. The boy broke down and wept. But Jack had seen that before, too, half the time an act to make him drop his guard, give the enemy the advantage. Swanson easily held the sagging body up with one arm.

203

He talked to the girl.

"Okay, Lori, he isn't going to hurt you anymore. I knew I'd find him if I kept looking. That's my job, Lori, part of my job. You don't have to be afraid."

He looked at her face and at her breasts. She pulled the blouse together and said, "Mister, I don't know what you're talking about. I don't know how you know me, my name. That boy isn't bad. He's a friend of mine. I invited him to come here. My parents are out of town. Please let him go. Please leave us alone. We haven't done anything to you." On and on, he said later, teeth chattering like it was winter.

But still he didn't let the kid go. He didn't believe her. Sometimes the enemy told them to use a story or they'd be killed. He didn't want her to believe the kid, the little punk. He thought about it and dropped him hard onto the flagstones leading between the garage and the house. The kid didn't move.

The girl didn't move. Swanson just stood and looked at her, tan and blond and half naked, and he saw other women sitting just like she was. He stood holding the knife for the longest time. Then he saw the freckles on her skin—her arms, her chest, her neck. The knife slowly slid down toward its sheath while he watched her, while she tentatively stood, while she took one fear-and pain-filled step toward the house, while Swanson pulled the boy to his feet and brushed him off, wondering a little at the camouflage stick on his own arms.

The girl saw her chance and dashed into the house. The boy stood still, waiting, while Swanson brushed off his pants, examined his back, turned him around and looked him in the eye.

Swanson was sitting on the swing when the police came. They chopped a hole in the fence and sent in their version of SWAT. They threw Swanson down on the ground and spread-eagled him with the muzzles of their rifles. They searched him and interrogated him and finally dragged him out of the yard, cuffed and manacled. The last thing he saw before being thrown into the police car was the girl's face in a window. Her large blue eyes were wide with fright, and tears streamed down her cheeks.

I found out about it the day I was checking out of the hospital. A government agent, some fed from an agency whose name I was supposed to have forgotten, came to see me. He told me about Swanson. He asked about my health. And he mentioned as we walked down the wheelchair ramp that a Sergeant Hooks from Special Operations Group had killed himself on a farm near Omaha.

I could feel him watching me, but I just kept walking, thinking of the white snow, the pearls my grandmother used to wear, the color of my first girl's breasts.

He handed me a slip of paper. One side had a phone number and address for Swanson. The other had Hooks's army information and his parents' address in Nebraska.

Without a word he got into a drab government car and drove away. I walked to the lakefront, folding the card into squares. I put it in my pocket and walked across Lake Shore Drive to the grounds of the water treatment facility. No car could follow onto the lush grass. I sat under a willow tree by the water, my little pack of stuff from the hospital still on my back.

The fever started again and I took a pill. I looked out across the still water toward the city and felt the tears burning my eyes. Only this time I didn't know why. There were just too many reasons.

Cocktails in the afternoon? My friend from school would have found it *très dégoutant.*

I walk downstairs, dressed in a blue, three-piece suit, a blue shirt and tie, dark shoes and socks. Quite the outfit for the el ride downtown.

"Walk on the Wild Side" by Lou Reed comes filtering through the door of the apartment next to hers. I stand quietly for a moment, listening, thinking of a night alone on Rush Street, wondering how it all will go tonight. I push the buzzer.

Kathleen opens the door and invites me in. She is impeccable. If I didn't know her so well, I would be impressed.

Her hair falls in heavy shag waves on her temples, on the sides, and hangs shimmering down her back. It's been fluffed up in front. She wears a single hoop earring from her right earlobe, with a small turquoise pendant hanging down from the hoop.

"Come in, come in. How have you been?" She smiles, pearls, a radiance lighting up her eyes, and steps back from the door.

"Not bad, you?" She motions me to the couch.

"Good. Want a drink, or anything?" I'm taking my coat off and she's heading for the kitchen. Running magazines cover the low coffee table, along with *WomenSports, Games* magazine, and two literary magazines, *Alaska Bar Rag* and *Mojo Navigator*. Eclectic woman, Kathleen.

"Pepsi." I sit, page through *Running Times*. She returns with two wine glasses, one with Pepsi and ice, the other a white wine and ice. She sits on the couch next to me, one arm back against the wall.

Kathleen is wearing a very short white skirt and no stockings. The skirt rides halfway up her thighs. Her loafers are the same color as the tan of her legs.

She's also wearing a fashionably large black blouse with sleeves cut off above the elbow and a deep and wide neck. I've seen women on Michigan Avenue in them, always with another blouse or even T-shirt on underneath.

Not Kathleen. When she leans over to pick up her glass, the top of the blouse slides down and her breasts flare against each other in the opening. They're too big to actually fall out, but they come close. Her nipples are pink, erect, surrounded by the pink of the nipple area and a very small white strip of untanned skin.

I wonder about this woman. I wonder what she has in mind after dinner.

I wonder what I have in mind after dinner.

She pulls her legs up under her, not bothering to hold the tight white skirt from hiking up even farther.

"I haven't seen you out running the last few days, Travis. I'd hoped we could have gotten together, put in a few miles."

I stir the ice around in my glass with a finger. *Dégoutant.* "Well, I took a few days off—lot of work, late hours, some pains in my knee with this cool weather. You know how it gets."

"Yes. Oh, I did call you at the office but you weren't in. Court, I guess."

She stretches her arm out and the blouse falls open at the shoulder. She has excellent muscle tone. She may be, overall, the most beautiful woman I've ever met. There's a lot I don't understand about this—but I've been there before.

"Listen, Kathleen. I don't spend a lot of time at the office. Or in court. Or—it just varies. I've been seeing some old buddies lately. I tutor kids. I conduct client interviews in scuzzy apartments all over this city. I don't always have time to run, or be in my office, or leave messages, or be available. I'm sorry. I just don't."

I'm hot, pissed off, but also sweating through the tight-seamed shirt. Kathleen shifts quickly on the couch, letting her knees slip out against my leg. She leans over and holds my hand. The breasts are perfect, so perfect, like the rest of her. Her nipples are only inches away and are calm and flat pink highlights surrounded by white, then brown, then black.

"Travis, I'm sorry. I just wanted to talk. I won't call you at work if you prefer."

The way she puts it always gets me. Tonight, everything is going to be smooth, soft as her silky hair, a nice time. I really want to have a nice time.

I pat her knee in a brotherly way. I've had practice. Then I pick up my drink.

"No problem at all. How'd you like the Olympics?"

Safety. She talks for half an hour about rhythmic gymnastics, the first women's marathon, cycling, any sport you can think of.

I ask, after she's filled our glasses again at the first break in the speech, "How'd you like the announcers? How'd you like your namesake, Kathleen Sullivan?"

She runs her hand through her hair impatiently. She looks out across the room to the spacious window brushed by the branches of a large maple tree. Her tan runs right up to the black underwear beneath her skirt. She looks thoughtful, then angry. She turns back to face me and I notice the little turquoise pendant on her earring is a snake with rattles and a tongue but no eyes. I've never seen it before, or one like it. It's engrossing, and ugly.

"Kathleen Sullivan is the most overrated sports reporter I've ever seen or heard. She could have done well paired up with Cosell in the boxing pavilion." The green eyes flash and sparkle and Kathleen stands up, pulling her skirt down, unable to stop the blouse from slipping off one shoulder or the other. I take the hint.

208

"Shall we?" I say, carrying our glasses to the little kitchen and setting them on the bar.

"Why not? It's about time if we want to make our reservations." She's shorter than she often looks because of her shoes, but she's all flesh, leg, shoulder, neck, cleavage.

"It could get cool tonight—you wearing anything over that?" I'm pointing from the kitchen door and my finger accidentally pokes her softly on the breast.

She smiles up at me and says, "Nice of you to notice."

"My pleasure. Hard not to."

She says, "Good," then rolls up her sleeves and adds, "I see your point. And I hope to see more of it later," then walks briskly to the closet, takes out a gray leather jacket, and dangles it over her shoulder.

She clicks out the light overhead, and opens the door. "Shall we?" I pick up my coat and follow her out.

We walk in silence to the el. Innuendo, hands touching, the small sexual moves, the slim, tight thighs against me, the pulse of her breath against the fabric of her blouse. I could dwell on it for a long time, and it's been a hard hour to concentrate on conversation. There's just so much of her there, so close at hand.

Kathleen is having trouble getting into her tight leather. She tries to get it on over her floppy blouse and almost pulls the thing down to her waist. She doesn't even look up as she tucks her breasts back inside and pulls the jacket down to try again. I step behind her and hold the collar and sleeves up so she can just slip backward into it, and that works.

She zips it up when the train comes but insists on sitting in the outer seat. She is so tall that she has to cross her long legs in the aisle. We talk about running and ignore the stares and laughter.

We change trains at Washington and I hold her hand as we walk through the dank tunnel. She is surprised and searches my face for a clue but I just keep walking, staring straight ahead, swinging our hands into the air.

We take the subway two stops and get off at Chicago and State. It's windy when we emerge from the tunnel and I button my jacket so it won't flare out behind me. Kathleen latches onto my arm and I don't say or do anything. We walk down Michigan Avenue talking about wine, sleeping bags, stereo receivers. It's like the traveling Playboy Advisor.

Avanzare's has the reservation, in my name, and I order a half carafe of white wine. Kathleen has draped her jacket over the back of our very secluded booth that she had requested in advance. She's taken her loafers off and tucked her feet beneath her. It's impossible to look at any part of her without seeing the radiance of her skin, all natural, no makeup except maybe around her eyes.

Someone sits down at a table across the room, someone I've seen in court. I can't place her. She's very well done, perfect for this place, for this whole area. She wears a black dress slit in the middle and sheer white stockings, white star earrings and tightly curled, long dark hair. She doesn't look our way.

Kathleen sets her long fingers over my hand. "I want to know about your tutoring," she says, leaning close, letting the blouse fall open in the middle.

I drum my fingers on the table. "Okay. What do you want to know?" I look around, wondering about our menus.

She runs her other hand through her hair, leaving it looking windblown and free.

"How much time do you put in? Who do you tutor?

Who do you work with?" She rattles them off as only Kathleen can do, so quickly, so earnestly.

I give her a basic rundown of the students, the facility, where the tutors are from, my hours. It's really the standard stuff I give to people who call to ask for appointments but aren't sure what they are getting into.

"So not many hours a week, huh?"

"Nope."

"Would you like to work there more?"

"Nope."

"Meet any interesting people?"

"Oh, the people are something. Some of them you would not believe. It's probably the one really unpredictable thing about the work—all those stories, all those problems and strange ways of seeing the world. It tires you out because it's a heavy emotional load, but it keeps you coming back."

She shifts her legs out and crosses one over the other, leaning a knee against my knee under the table. She leans over a little bit closer. I glance at her eyes. Her lips are poised with another question but the waiter has come with the menus. Kathleen looks it over, and I look her over.

I have to mutter under my breath as her nipples harden and then relax, but she doesn't look up, only says, "Hmmm?"

"Nothing, nothing. Lots of good stuff to eat, that's all."

"Well, Travis, what sorts of *stuff* are you going to order?" She's set the menu down and is gazing into my eyes. The busboy is filling our water glasses and taking a long time to get it done. He's gazing somewhere else with a look of astonishment and happiness. I almost hate to suggest he's filled four water glasses for us, which should

211

be enough, but he's just a kid. There's a limit to how much he should see all at once. I wave him off.

"Don't know, babe, really don't know." I contemplate the menu as Kathleen offers her recommendations.

"Right. Why don't you order for both of us?" She thinks that is a *splendid* idea. We talk some more about racing strategies and tactics. Her questions are precise, clipped, direct, practical: quintessential Kathleen.

It's only when she's explaining the origins of herbs in our French onion soup that I wonder what I'm doing here. I could be out walking the streets, or watching the clouds traveling before the full moon from my window, or watching the uncut version of the great Japanese film *Yojimbo* at the Biograph. Instead, I'm sitting in a secluded booth at a fancy restaurant with the all-American woman telling me about herbs from the south of France.

I think about my friend Duncan. She's probably pondering the complexities of Merleau-Ponty's brain, lying in bed in her sweat suit, a slight grin lighting up her face.

Kathleen changes the subject. "I've been thinking about something and I want your input, Travis. I want you to access this problem and give me a solution."

I really wonder sometimes how her brain can possibly exist within that body.

"I'm all ears." Slang and other idioms drive her crazy.

"It's Heisenberg who has been on my mind."

"Heisenberg?"

"Yes."

"You've been sitting around thinking about Heisenberg."

"No. I haven't been sitting at all. It's a problem that comes up when I am out running."

"We may have running in common, but not Heisenberg."

She leans her elbows onto the table on either side of her curried chicken, hunches over, and her blouse drops open in front. Again.

"Just listen. I'm sure you can help me."

"I'm sure I'll try."

"Heisenberg postulates in his uncertainty principle that reality is subjective . . ."

"Sounds right to me."

"Will you just *listen*?"

I can see she's getting excited, so I nod and gaze soulfully into her blouse. She doesn't seem to notice.

"He discusses reality in scientific terms, but if you strip all the rest away—"

Which is what you've already done to yourself, I think—

"You learn that he is concerned with either the *velocity* or the *position* of the particle, but never both."

"Of the particle."

"Yes."

"Alright, Kathleen, so what exactly is your question?"

"What do you think of the mutual exclusivity inherent in such a postulation? Is it necessary? Can reality be viewed in terms of some combined compromise of the explicit halves of Heisenberg's theorem?"

I look into her eyes and see the sincerity, the probing, the inescapable fact that she is concerned with this issue and really wants to discuss it over dinner.

"Alright, Kathleen. You want to know what *I* think about this, right?"

She nods and swings her legs over against mine. Most of her left breast, all of her left shoulder, and half of her chest and back glow in the candlelight. The snake pendant swings blindly from her ear.

I say, "I've got a friend, guy who lives in Chicago now

213

in fact—we go back a ways, a number of years—anyway, this guy, name of Billy Priest, used to play wide receiver for the New Orleans Saints. Not a big guy, maybe six foot, one-sixty soakin' wet. Didn't usually start, either. But he had fingers like a frog's tongue. They'd put him in on third and long, and back then you could use stickum on your hands to help you catch the ball.

"Saints were a poor team, lost a lot. But no matter. Priest would get a pot of stickum and a stick and slop that stuff all over his socks and the tape on his ankles. Like Freddy Biletnikoff. No big secret. Then when he'd go in the huddle he'd just reach down and smear the stuff all over his hands, on his wristbands, even his elbows. He told me he once caught a ball on his *arm*. The ball just fell on there and the stickum wouldn't let go. Big play for the Saints too.

"I know you're wondering what this could possibly have to do with your problem, aren't you?"

She tries to look involved, but I see a kind of fear in her eyes, a ghost of the look I saw when we first saw each other after Café Bohemia. It's a scared, hunted, outclassed look.

"No, Travis. I trust you. Please continue with your story." She drains her wineglass and I fill it with what's left of mine.

"Well, Billy was something. As I say, we go back. We went to law school together, but we go back even further than that.

"Down to your question. I think my friend can serve to answer your question. Billy Priest is a wide receiver. He runs routes downfield and catches the ball. Sometimes he sees the quarterback in trouble—saw, you know, all this pro football was years ago, even though he can still play"—something clicks in the back of my mind, a phone call, something to do after tonight—"and he comes back for the ball. Sometimes he was lucky and let the stickum help out. But most of the time it's a timed pattern with that quarterback. Priest knows how many yards to run and then look back over a shoulder or cut inside or outside. The quarterback knows how many yards he's going to run and how long it should take him to get there. The ball's in the air when Priest looks for it. It's already thrown. It's all pattern, practice, a little instinct and luck, but precision timing.

"So as far as I'm concerned, Billy Priest may as well be this *particle* you're talking about. But if he wants to catch that ball—and he was one of the best in the game— he has to think about how fast he can run and how soon the ball will arrive—velocity—*and* where he'll be when he tries to make the catch—position.

"Velocity and position, if you want to use those terms, made Billy Priest a great receiver. Both of them. Not either/or."

I sip my glass of water, wave the busboy away. "That's what I think about your uncertainty principle."

Kathleen looks as if she's trying to understand something very difficult. She even reaches behind her and pulls the blouse down in back, moving it up in front. Her brow is creased in concentration.

"Is there a problem, Kathleen? Something I said you don't understand?"

She snaps out of it, shrugs the blouse off her shoulder again.

"Just one thing. I was talking about a theory, a principle to be applied to the idea of reality, the intellectual construct we've labeled with that name."

"So?"

"You're talking about football."

215

I explode into laughter, and faces from other tables peer anxiously our way. I grin at her with a wicked notion in my eye.

"Come on, Kathleen. You've read philosophy. What could be defined as more immutably real than football?" I laugh softly, look across the room at the woman I know, who gazes back.

Kathleen doesn't answer. We finish our meals and Kathleen orders coffee. She's obviously trying to work it all out in her mind, but I'm onto something else.

She changes the subject abruptly and we talk about movies—*films* to her. She wants to discuss *A Woman in Flames* and *Sanjuro*. I have some fun talking about the pyrotechnic inaccuracies in *Red Dawn* and the anthropological exegesis of *Sheena, Queen of the Jungle*. I know it's frustrating for her, but I can't help it.

Outside it's turned colder. Kathleen zips up the leather jacket, zips the sleeve zippers, buttons the collar. She's a mine field of goose bumps from ankle to thigh, and I wrap my suit coat around her on the way to the subway. Savoy Brown's "Skin and Bones" comes filtering out of the train tunnel.

It's all silence and small talk on the ride home. In spite of the cold, the night sweats have begun and I swallow capsules while we wait for the second train.

At our stop it's warmer because we're not near the lake, and Kathleen plays with the zippers on her jacket. She's unusually quiet. I carry my suit coat over my shoulder as we walk up the stairs to our building and pause outside Kathleen's door.

We crossed the Mekong River exactly at midnight. We had a captain with us for a change, and a couple noncoms. No lieutenants. They were scarce this time in the war.

Captain Cotton had been with another patrol when Ringo got shot up, but he looked pretty grim anyway when he heard Franklin's report. I was scouting fording locations on the river. All told, we might have had forty men, but once we crossed the river we'd have no support from the air and probably nothing on the ground either. And, as usual lately, the orders were sealed and known only to the captain.

He was a Southern boy, from Arkansas, and he chewed tobacco when he could get it. He was a nervous dude, too, but he could handle his load. The sergeants had taken Franklin and me aside, together with two Pfc's, to give us the dirt on Cotton. You had to do that in the jungle if you wanted to make it.

George P. Cotton, the P. unexplained during the time that I served under him. He appeared a year or two older than me, which was good, but that still was pretty damn young. He was the only officer I ever knew who put long thick patches of camouflage black under each eye, like a football player, to cut down the glare. 'Course, sometimes it made him look downright comical. You'd come into his tent with the recon maps and wonder who we were playing this week. It brought back memories for some of us, and that wasn't all bad either.

Franklin asked me before we hit the river about the raid that was legend among troops sent north of the border territory, far from where we were supposed to be. And I told him.

"The ugliest thing I remember about that raid—Ringo called it 'El Destructo' and the name stuck—was the asshole who ran the show, guy by the name of Cooper. Not like our George P. Cotton, that's for sure. Cooper was like a burr you get stuck under your saddle, but you can find a burr and throw it away. Not Cooper.

217

"By his order our troops assembled what may have been the greatest amount of firepower in one place ever seen in this little jungle 'police action' of ours. There were weapons I had never seen before and haven't seen since. We had backup you can't imagine. Makes this operation look anemic.

"British guy named Jones—yeah—ran the show with him. Never quite figured it out."

Franklin and I walked through the deserted village we used for base that night, collecting dog tags from all the grunts as they rubbed grease and paint into anything that would show when we crossed. More sealed orders just broken by Captain Cotton.

"I've heard a lot of stories, Jones. Never quite believed 'em. Outrageous bullshit. I mean, you can lie and then you can *lie*."

"Probably not lies, man. I can't tell you all that happened, and I don't want to know it all. I just know it was a massive strike, that we lost more men from our own copter rocket fire than we did from the enemy. I saw whole villages of just women and kids burnt to the ground, klicks and klicks away from intended targets. I think. I like to think that. If those villages were our intended targets . . ."

"But you had no *objective*? No hill to grab, village to defoliate, NVA totals to turn in?"

"Nope. It was the first I saw of the sealed orders, same things we saw in the captain's office a few minutes ago. From some HQ neither of us will ever know. In that weird bureaucratic code/language that makes no real sense."

"Those were the days you were with Ringo and Sharp, weren't they?" There was a trace of envy, of embarrassment in his voice, but it was true. We were three of the coldest hard-ass corporals in the whole goddamn war theater.

"Yeah," I said simply. "Sharp and Ringo and me. We put on a show, something Cotton won't allow. Fact is, man, you and I freelance now as much as anyone in the northern zones. They just can't let us go."

I wanted Franklin to feel good but it was still no lie.

He asked, "And tonight?"

I said, "Tonight we have coordination and a small but important role to play out. El Destructo was all show, all weapons and communications and bullshit that made some of us what we are now.

"We waded into Red Cross hospitals with flamethrowers because some of the sick and dying were hill people. We'd send mortar strikes in till you literally couldn't take a step without stepping into a mortar hole. I mean, there was just *nothing left.* Nagasaki over again to prove a point, new country, new ideas. *What* ideas? What *point?* Damned if I knew."

We threw the tags into a rucksack and stashed it in the recon hut. The guards posted above were smoking weak grade boo in a pipe. I said in a loud voice, "So the captain thought he'd stroll on over here at twenty-three hundred to see how we're doin'." Swearing came from above and two red-hot pipes came sailing over the edge of the hut, where I ground them into the clay with my boot.

We walked away and heard them yelling after us, like in stage voice, "Jones, Franklin, you total shitheads." What a laugh.

"We worked our part okay, three corporals together and on our own as a unit. We took out part of the supply trail with a line of C-4 that we rigged in the pitch black. I wired it while Sharp stood guard at one end with his knives and Ringo took the other with a silenced Browning."

"Illegal gun."

The whites of our teeth were all that was showing.

"Three of us took on squad after squad before the killing was over." Suddenly I felt those days in my joints and bones, a shock much deeper than a remembrance.

"Anything I didn't know about war by then I learned, fast."

We paused near Cotton's tent.

" 'Course, sealed orders are always new. Guess I'm not done learnin'."

Franklin patted me on the shoulder and we ducked through the khaki flap to report.

She's got keys out and I fumble for mine. She places her hand on my shoulder and unzips her coat.

"Please stay." There's something in her voice I recognize but cannot, absolutely cannot, place.

I don't really think long. "For a while." It's enough for her.

I beg off further drinks but she fixes us orange juice anyway. I thumb through her *TV Guide* movie listings till she sits down next to me.

"Nothing," I say disgustedly, "there's nothing decent on anymore."

She sips her juice, loafers kicked off in the kitchen. "No *Citizen Kane?*"

"Nah, no *Terror Train* with Jamie Lee Curtis or that great *When a Stranger Calls* with Durning, Dewhurst, and Carol Kane. Real solid class."

I strip my tie off and toss it on the chair with my suit coat and vest. Kathleen sets her glass down—the finest Waterford crystal—and moves against me, her arm running across the buttons on my shirt.

We don't talk. We both know the evening was leading to this, to something in the soft muted light coming from the lamp across the room, or in darkness.

She unbottons the top button and my hand goes automatically for one of her breasts. It fills my hand through the soft nylon of her blouse. She works on another button and I move inside her blouse, in the cavernous space of the little tent she chose to wear. If anyone could have filled it, though, it was Kathleen. I find her nipple and squeeze it tightly. She slips my third button free and we kiss, lightly at first, then wildly, tongues thrusting against teeth and sucking at each other's lips as she opens my shirt and I hold a bare breast in each hand, as if I were judging them for their succulence. I finger the right breast scar, then let it go. She doesn't seem to notice.

She slips my shirt off my shoulders and throws it onto the floor. As I run my thumbs around the aureole of her nipples, she raises her arms over her head and I yank the blouse from her body, letting the breasts fall down into my waiting hands.

She rubs both hands against my crotch. I remember her knee in the restuarant and then her question. All her questions.

I leave her breasts alone, but she unsnaps my belt buckle and draws the belt through the pants loops, adding it to a pile on the floor, unzipping my pants, pulling my underwear down, and grabbing my engorged penis with both hands. One hand rubs up and down the shaft. The other plays with the tip, spreading semen around and urging more to dribble out.

I want her as much as I've ever wanted a woman I could have. But there's some kind of gap here. It just hasn't made itself known yet. It's like waiting for Ray Sharp to talk, like the first day I met Anna Friedberg, like the French girl the last day I saw her.

I move my hand up, slowly, against the velvety skin of her legs, to the underwear beneath her skirt. With one hand I unbutton the skirt; with the other I slowly trace the pattern of the underwear across its top line. I let the skirt slip loose, pull her head down against mine, and rub hard against the hair I can feel around my fingers, between her legs.

That kiss might last an hour, for all I know. My one hand moves freely from her neck to her shoulders to her nipples and back up to her face, where I trace gentle patterns along her brow, her cheekbones, her fine chin.

Sometimes sensuality and lust are the same thing. This was one of those times. And still, behind it all, I knew exactly what I was doing. It was as if I were watching myself from across the room, as if I were orchestrating the whole scene, unrelated, uninvolved.

I slide my hand beneath her brief black panties and rub the mound of damp flesh and hair with my whole hand, then pull the panties down and move into her with two fingers. Immediately her hands tighten on me and I push her against the back of the couch. She lets go gradually as I move again and again, deeply, into her, and she holds me by the shoulder and the back of my head.

It's furious. She is sweating and the droplets roll between her breasts. One of her hands trembles uncontrollably as I go into her as fast as my wrist can sustain. I feel her orgasm shudder throughout her entire body, the goosebumps rising on her legs, her fingers dug into my hair, her head shaking back and forth. As the moan starts from her mouth I cover her lips with mine and hold her between the legs, softly, quietly, kissing her gently.

She shudders again and sighs and her legs relax. One of her hands reaches between my legs, and she guides my hand to her breast, where she rubs my fingers back and forth in the pool of sweat dripping there, across and around the nipple, over and across her scar. She plays that way, content, but when her hand begins its motion along my penis I pull away and bend down across her chest, licking each nipple in turn with my tongue, and driving back between her legs. I use three fingers this time. She starts to pull back, says "Oh, no" in a quivering voice, but I place a finger to her lips and she chews on it with her teeth.

I suck hungrily on her nipples and drive her legs and hips hard into the couch with my other hand. She spasms once, twice, chews my fingers almost raw, and I take as much breast in my mouth as I can. And I go into her again, and again, until she sits stunned on the couch, her eyes closed.

I slip out, finally, listening to her raspy breathing, letting her skirt and panties fall finally to the floor. I toss my pants and underwear onto the chair and remove shoes and socks.

Without looking she finds my penis and draws her hands against it. I play with the layers of her hair that fall down her back and shoulders. I've forgotten the questions, the restaurant, the suspicions, the rest, and I'm more than ready when she spoils it, when she says, in complete sincerity, "Travis, I want you to enter me. I want you to *penetrate* me with all of your force, with all of your masculine power, with everything that you know. Please, Travis, do it now!"

It's like a bad play, a soap opera, a paperback romance, but it's real. This beautiful, desirable, perfectly fuckable woman is sitting naked next to me after hours of everything *but* fucking and she has to say that. At this point it's very hard not to just ignore her. Very hard.

I sigh very deeply and not for effect, sit back, close my

eyes, fold my hands awkwardly in front of me. She senses it, looks up, tries to massage me between the legs, to lick a nipple, and I hold her hands and head away.

"I'm sorry, Kathleen. I just can't do it."

"*Why?!* What did I do? Or what is it?" She is in a panic. I almost laugh, but it is sad, not funny. Such a perfect girl. So beautiful. So smart. Really. But with such poor instinct, such a poor judge of character.

"It's nothing you *did*. You were really quite fine. It's just the way you said what you said. I can't explain it now, but it kind of wrecks the mood, the moment."

She is surprised, truly surprised, and perplexed, angry. Veins throb on her forehead and shoulder and left breast.

"I don't know what you mean."

"I know. And I can't explain it. At least not now. Believe me. I just can't."

I reach over and touch her hair ever so lightly, follow its sheen down to her shoulders. She is a lovely girl. Someday, I think. Maybe.

"Let me do something for you, then," she says, and leans over me, but I snap her head back up and shake my head.

"WHY??!!" She almost screams, beats her hands on the couch, then collapses crying against my chest. I wrap a hand around her slender back, run my fingers through her hair.

I say very quietly, "Kathleen, there are many things for you to learn about me. Many things. History. Give it time, Kathleen. Give it some time."

She hasn't moved, doesn't stop crying. I rub her tanned shoulders lightly. She calms, wraps her legs up next to mine on the couch.

"Let's put you to bed."

She looks up at me, the tears glistening on her cheeks, the light makeup down. And through it all she is still a beauty. We get up together, holding hands, leave our clothes where they'e fallen, and walk into the bedroom.

She closes the bathroom door behind her and I collapse into a chair by the window, across from the bed.

She appears a minute later, wearing a pair of Hawaiian print running shorts slit up both sides, New Zealand style. She wears nothing on top, and her large breasts bounce invitingly as she walks past the bed, over to my chair.

In the sudden light the long scar running the length of the underside of her right breast stands exposed, a cruel pink and white against the tan of the rest of her body.

She's washed her face and it seems to gleam in the moonlight. She's pushed her damp hair back so that it frames her perfect features.

I look her in the eye and do not waver. "Someday," I whisper.

She nods, strokes my hand a minute more, then pulls the bedspread off and climbs under the single blue sheet. She looks up. "You are staying, aren't you?"

I nod. "I'm staying."

"Come to bed?"

"Later. I want to sit for a while."

She's about to say something but she closes her lips. The curves and peaks and depressions she makes beneath the sheet are inviting. Finally she settles, turns away, and says, "I think I can wait. I will be waiting."

I say good night and watch the clouds and the tree branches. Her side of the building has long, overgrown ivy, I see. When I quietly stand up I see that she is already asleep.

I pad out into the living room and get the Flagyl and

the Vistaril from their bottles. I take them in the bath-room, clean up a little, notice the artwork from feudal Japan framed on her walls.

I climb onto the bed and let the sweat come, wiping it off periodically with a towel. This is the first stage. When the chills come I climb in under the sheet, pull the bed-spread up onto my half of the bed. I shiver, fighting it, praying for sleep, dreamless sleep.

Kathleen is facing me. She looks like a child somehow ... even her sophisticated bone structure, her full breasts, the dip at her waist, the hump of her hip, all seem so innocent and at peace in sleep.

I rest a hand on her hip and smile. Tomorrow morning might be different.

Exactly two days after we crossed the Mekong we crossed back.

Of the forty men who went across, twelve came back. Sergeant Rohn led the way. He was the only noncom left. Franklin had taken a piece of shrapnel below the eye. I'd patched it as well as I could, but I watched it bleed and pus when we took five every few hours.

I had a bullet flick across the fatty tissue on my back. Those folds are about a quarter-inch thick. Rohn told me that any other angle would have killed or paralyzed me. He taped it. Franklin made jokes about skipping stones across a flat pool of water.

Franklin and I carried Captain Cotton back across on a stretcher. He'd taken a bullet near the liver. Our medic was killed by a mine as soon as we'd gotten past the support area, so we all had to sew and tape each other up. I'd stitched the captain myself, alone. I could smell the bile right after he took the bullet and knew he'd leak his insides out unless he were stitched. I didn't want the few who were left to panic if they thought that Cotton would die on us.

Rohn and a private named Booker were the only healthy men left by the time we reached the river. Eight of us had taken bullets or shrapnel, one had triggered a poison-knife booby trap (but I'd cut him and drained it immediately, and it looked like he'd make it), and one had simply slipped and fallen down one of the hills the people were cultivating for vegetables. It was pitch-black that night and we suddenly had two healthy men, not three. The third had an ugly green-stick fracture.

Franklin and I tried to hold Cotton up over the water, but the current ripped at our legs as we walked, the mud sucked at our waterlogged, heavy boots, and rocks and dead wood tripped us up. Franklin could hardly see, so I went ahead, but every time I tried to lift the stretcher higher over the water my back would cramp and I'd have to slowly lower his weight. Franklin could do no better. But we made it across and stumbled in the dark into the deserted village.

We couldn't risk fires to dry out. All our gear except guns and first aid equipment had been lost across the river. We couldn't even risk a signal flare.

Rohn and Booker checked the wounded, shoved together for warmth into tiny bamboo huts. Franklin was asleep, the headband to protect the eye pulled across the top of his head and down his neck for warmth. I changed the dressings on the captain's wound, glad that Franklin and I had a hut to ourselves with the captain, glad that Franklin was asleep. The stench was overwhelming. After I'd changed the dressings I told Booker, on watch for our hut, I was going to the brush.

I took the old bandages and dug a hole with my knife in the sandy dirt and buried them deep. Then I went back

227

to camp and tried to sleep, hunched over an old wooden stool, on my stomach.

The captain was delirious and talked about home, the Arkansas Razorbacks, and then a jumble of words and things, one right after the other with no continuity— "Major, major, colonels, Colonel Lavey, *quatorze*, Paris, Paris in June . . . SOG . . . one firefight after . . . majors, captains, yes, the corporals are going too . . ."—until he was silent. I checked his pulse once. It was weak but there was nothing to be done.

I couldn't sleep. Once I thought I heard an APC, one of our big personnel carriers. It was the mosquitoes fighting over the bloody pus dripping from Franklin's headband.

It was a nightmare, like something terrible you think you see, see over and over and over until you really are seeing it, it's so bad, and so real. We had forty-eight hours of that.

They lured us right into a mine field and then dropped mortar shells every few meters to finish us off. I'll never know how they knew we were coming or why Cotton's orders had us take that exact route. It was suicide.

When they were bored with the shelling, maybe tired of hearing our men screaming from fatal wounds with no one to help them, then they sent a crack team of their own in to mop up.

The dead were luckier than the badly wounded. We couldn't get them out. I took my bullet while making the rounds of that filthy, blood-greasy field, collecting the wounded. Sending me was smart, because I'd been there, but it was the last order Cotton ever gave. Oh, we got him out alive. But he never spoke a coherent word after those two days.

Franklin and I huddled with Rohn and talked it up. We'd take as many men as we could, and we'd kill as many of the enemy as we could. Rohn asked for a volunteer to kill our own wounded. No one volunteered, not even Franklin, not even me. Rohn wouldn't do it, so we left them, some with primed grenades hidden under their bodies.

A sergeant who'd been gutshot had us mount the tripods on a pair of M-60's. He drew a hell of a lot of fire before they got to him. When we broke for the jungle growth by the river, I sent Franklin on ahead. Booker and I hung back. I had carried an M-203 grenade launcher all that way and wasn't going out without using it.

Booker and I were covered with slime and blood and dirt and gut, so we set up right on the path they'd take to follow us. As our men broke I saw a face and told Booker, "Feed me, man," and we took down the point and the flankers with a single grenade. After that it was nickel and dime. I had Booker feed me until the barrel smoked on my shoulder and he padded it with his shirt to cut down on burns. I looped them in like mortar shells, even sent them straight on target like a bazooka, till we were out of grenades and Booker helped me run to catch up.

I felt the sun before I saw it. Booker had dozed off outside our hut, and I felt something out there. Nothing stirred in the other huts. I slowly leaned the barrel of our last machine gun out the window and trained it on the tree line, braced myself against a support pole and felt the adhesions of my back wounds split open and the blood cascade down onto my pants, onto the floor.

Franklin's eye looked bad. The insects had been at it. I could smell the captain. But I had to watch. I tried to toss stones onto Booker's helmet to wake him, but he was out.

I saw a figure step out from behind a tree. I rubbed my

eyes and spit on my hands to get them working. I pulled the bolt all the way back as he moved away from the closest bush and cautiously crept in, close to the ground.

He wore fatigues and a black bandanna over most of his face. No helmet. AK-47 in both hands. I held off, wanting to be sure. Then I saw the SOG radio on his belt as he pulled up behind the big cooking fire, that and the string of moray knives hanging from his belt. I stared at that head that now wouldn't move, that waited.

I said, "I think I died and gone to hell. Tell me it ain't you, Sharp." He'd seen me and the barrel in the window clear across the enclosure, no doubt about that now, and he stared fiercely into the hut. He held his gun down so I raised up just a bit in the window. Then he saw.

He pulled the bandanna down and it was none other than Raymond Sharp, Corporal, United States Army.

"Jones, you dumb shit. What the fuck. Tell your people I'm comin' in."

He flattened in case one of the sleepy grunts was trigger-happy. I tapped Booker on the head with the barrel of the machine gun and he scrambled for his own gun, dove into the door of our hut almost right onto Franklin.

"What's up? What is it?" Franklin's good eye was already checking out the unnatural piece of landscape out by the cookfire.

"Booker, be careful about this. Corporal Ray Sharp, one of the best men we got in this pitiful army, is staring down a gun barrel at you right this instant. Wake Rohn up and tell the other guys to hold off. We just might have made it."

Booker sprinted to the other hut. We could hear them moving around until I yelled out, "We got help. That's a friendly face out there, personal friend of mine in fact, and he wants to come in. I suggest we accommodate him."

230

I saw Rohn slip out the window to cover—smart soldier—but knew Sharp had seen him too.

"Come on in, Sharp. We're just havin' a little rest here."

Sharp came in but ducked around the huts first to check for snipers by the river. Before I could even get up he was standing in the doorway, grinning from ear to ear. God knows what he must have really thought, what we must have looked like. I smiled back.

"Jones, you need a course in stealth. I saw that barrel come up before I even knew there was anyone in here, except your friend on guard duty." He handed me a cigarette. I tried to get up again but couldn't.

I grimaced as the pole dug into my back and replied, "Just doin' it your way, Sharp. Just doin' it your way." Then I pitched forward and passed out.

When I came out of it, Rohn was talking on Sharp's radio. Flankers had come up and were carrying men out on stretchers. Sharp was whispering to Franklin and pointing at the captain and me.

I tried to keep it light. "Boys, you've met." They saw I was awake. Someone had moved me and the captain outside and onto stretchers. Sharp hurried over as I went on. "Sharp, this is Franklin. Franklin, Sharp." Something pressed against my back, but it felt light and soft.

Sharp and I clasped hands.

"Yeah, I know this one-eyed dude." He looked me over, a little more seriously this time. "You got yourself into a hell of a mess this time, didn't you? Just shows what happens when I leave you alone for a minute."

"*Me?* Hell of a *mess! Me?* Least I'm not still the point man for some lousy patrol in whatever country we're in right now. Don't you believe in upward mobility?"

Sharp's answer was cut off by the sound of choppers

coming in over the trees. A weak cheer went up from a few of the men.

"Time to saddle up," Sharp said as he and Franklin took opposite ends of my stretcher and hefted me up.

"Hey, man, you're jivin' me. Just call those babies in here and save yourself. This clearing's plenty big enough to land in."

"The word is, my man, that we're too close to the Mekong. They won't risk comin' in this far." The sound of the rotors and blades remained constant, on the other side of the trees.

I couldn't believe it. They'd sent forty men across that river, two days into hell, and now wouldn't risk setting down to take out the few who'd come back.

Sharp carried the head end of the stretcher and I saw that look in his eye. He'd crisscrossed our grenade launcher and machine gun across his back.

"That sucks, man."

We walked awhile in silence. I asked Franklin about the eye and he said it would come around. I looked back and Sharp nodded. It was good to know.

And I asked about Captain Cotton. Sharp said, "You did what you could. I figure they'll try to kill some of that infection. The intestine isn't workin' right, either. They'll almost have to fly him out to a good hospital and fast. I *do* like your work, though." In a lower voice he added, "It's one thing to know how to cut. It's another to know how to sew it back up."

The choppers were loud and men were milling around the four gunboats they'd brought in. Someone had even bothered to throw out a perimeter defense while they loaded us aboard.

The corporals and sergeants rode together. Sharp looked over at Rohn as we kicked up dust and hovered.

"You did a hell of a job, man." Rohn looked at Sharp and smiled, just a little—the first smile I'd seen from him since we went across the river—then rested his head in his hands.

Most of us slept. I felt tired too. Sharp pointed to my back. "Two entries and exits but no fragments. Lucky it's clean. We gave you morphine when you were out and patched what you keep tearing open."

"Thanks for the morphine. How many ampoules did you use, anyway?" I fought to keep my eyes open.

Sharp worked on the string of his neck sheath with oil. "Enough. Knew you'd appreciate it."

"Well, Sharp, old pal, before I join everyone else in oblivion, tell me how you're here. You bring some patrol back north or what?"

Sharp stopped working on his sheath, laid it down, and hefted the knife, tossing it from side to side. There was no smile there.

"We went south on orders, sealed orders. All seven of us with a noncom. Good soldier." He paused and looked at the black blade as if it were a mirror. "I'm the only one who made it back. At the end, it was bad." His voice sounded hollow and distant under the constant chatter of the rotors, through my morphine haze. "I guess it's been bad all around."

I was starting to fade, but I heard him say, "They stuck me with airborne to round up missing patrols. I wondered if you'd be in one of 'em. I had a feeling I'd find you." He didn't have to say "alive."

My eyes closed and the steady machine noises were lulling me to an oblivion without dreams. Sharp leaned over and asked, "Jones? You still awake?" I nodded my head slightly, just hearing him. "I called ahead. We got a new C.O.—another one. A major this time. I talked him into assigning us together soon's they cut you loose from the hospital." I smiled and felt a hand on my shoulder before I was out.

Sharp and I weren't separated again. We served out our tours and "special reenlistments" we hadn't bargained on together and didn't split up till we were sent stateside, me to San Francisco, Sharp to New York.

Even then, we never did say good-bye.

The doctor scrubs up for his next patient and I button my shirt-sleeves.

"Travis, I can't tell you much more than that. Wish I could. You've just got so damn many complications, some from your service, some since. And we don't know enough about them."

"So it's medicines—drugs—from here on out?" My voice is even, just asking for the truth. We know each other well, my doctor and me.

"I won't say that. Certainly for now, yes. Research may say something. The recurrent malaria may stay with you all your life. The intestinal problems are harder to diagnose. The pancreas needs help, and your liver and kidneys and bladder are having a tough enough time doing what they're supposed to do."

He hands over four white slips of paper. "We'll keep you on the pain pills and the MAO inhibitor. But when you get a free weekend, try the other two—Ativan and Bentyl—together. Minimum of two days if it's to work. I'd give it a week."

I slip down from the table and offer my hand.

"Call me if you get a cure—for anything." We smile, but it's awkward.

"Don't worry."

I walk down the corridor and he shoves my folder into the door's clip. Then he calls after me, "And you call me if the fever goes beyond a hundred, or if you can't break those chills."

A brisk wind rattles my bones at the door and I call back, "Will do." The sun is out but it's still cold, prematurely cold. It's still October. And the dreams have gotten worse.

I sit on a step outside his building and swallow a Dilaudid without water. Women in greatcoats and fine white stockings parade up and down Erie Street. They are so absurd. I've seen a man after he was skinned alive, and now these women in their perfect clothes and hair.

I decide to skip work again and walk slowly toward the lake, catching the glint of the sun off the water in my tearing eye. It must be the wind.

Billy Priest and I walked Rush Street one hot night years ago, not far from the homes and condos of the rich and famous. Those were the days Billy was sick. I went along for the kick and to keep an eye on my man.

Billy had played football for the New Orleans Saints. And he'd fought in Vietnam. But we'd met in Chicago, at a semi-pro football game. He played wide receiver for the Cardinals and back then I was the free safety for the Eagles. We met when I hit him after he caught a dump pass. When he didn't get up I yelled over to the sideline, "Get this guy off the field. Let's play ball," and he slowly got up and looked through the cage of his facemask at me. Then he smiled and said, "Tough little bastard, aren't ya?" and walked slowly back to the huddle.

It didn't matter to me any, but he never went out of the game, and I had to give him credit for that. I hit him five more times in that game, hard, hard as I knew how, which was *hard*. He'd get up and look at me and walk slowly back to the huddle.

Our strong safety, Sanchez, came over to me and said, "That's Billy Priest you're knockin' on his butt, ya know."

"Who?" The name didn't mean a thing.

"Priest. Billy Priest. New Orleans Saints wide receiver, maybe 1960 to '65. All-pro his last year, before he was drafted. Funny. He always looked little on TV. And ya know, he really *is* little."

"I don't know him." I'd been overseas most of that time and never paid much attention to pro football back then anyway.

"Yeah, I think he can tell." Sanchez moved over to the line and I backed up, covering the middle. I was the "monster" back on defense, the rover, the wildman—most teams have a name like that for their free safety, the guy who covers receivers on some downs and on others can do whatever he wants—blitz, doubleteam, jam guys at the line. He lines up anywhere he wants, and usually is a killer tackler, and if not, intimidates, makes the quarterback nervous when throwing and the receiver looking over his shoulder when catching.

And I played that way. I'd crack guys right on the line of scrimmage. I'd block guys not involved in the play. If the ref was looking the other way, I'd give the guard or center a forearm shiver and look the other way when the stretcher came out. It was the only way I could play.

Years later, when I played and coached defensive backs for the Birds, a bunch of lawyers, deputies, a judge, parole agents, guards, even a couple ex-cons, I told them they had to do only one thing for me: come to play. They saw what I meant.

The University of Michigan always had a monster back. So did Alabama. The pros these days have something similar, but usually it's a linebacker. The Raiders had Ted Hendricks. The Giants have Lawrence Taylor and used to team him with Brad Van Pelt. And the Bears used to have the only monster safety combination I've ever heard of, Doug Plank and Gary Fencik. Sometimes Fencik still plays that way.

Anyway, this little receiver, Priest, played pretty well, considering he was on the carpet at Hansen Stadium most of the afternoon.

We won the game 21 to 17 and later I heard Priest talking to our coach in the locker room. He said it was his first game of semi-pro ball and he wanted to have a second. He wondered if the Eagles needed a receiver.

The coach must have been ready to kiss him, but first he looked at him, blank-faced, and asked why. Why the Eagles.

"Well, I'll be honest with you, coach. I never spent so much time on my backside since my rookie year with the Saints, or maybe Vietnam. You got a rover with 'T. Jones' on his jersey and I think I want to play *with* that dude, not against him."

I was untaping my ankles on the other side of the bleachers but moved to a bench behind the bank of lockers. I didn't smile much in those days, but I allowed myself a little one then.

After that we got to know each other. We practiced together. I took it easy on him and he learned to cut me at the knees pretty well. And we talked before and after practice and games, and went to a bar or two. Nothing regular. I was in law school (on the government) and needed breaks. Sometimes big breaks. So Billy and me

237

would go out, or sometimes take some guys from the team with us. For a long time—years—I didn't associate with guys from the offense. In fact, Billy Priest was the first one.

Anyway, after a few years Billy got tired of playing and quit. Just quit. One Friday he was practicing and that Sunday he was gone. Nobody, me included, could talk him into coming back. And he became a very hard man to find. We didn't see each other much anymore—maybe once in a while if I tried real hard to track him down, or if we met accidentally at a Bulls game. Then it was like old times.

In 1981 Billy decided to make a comeback. Just like that, same way, no explanations. He knew I played for the Birds and showed up one day in pads at a scrimmage in Columbus Park.

I was giving the defensive signals in the middle of a play when I saw him, still too short to sit on a bench with football players. It was August and hot and humid. We ran the scrimmage in pads and half jerseys, but the sweat poured off us into pools in the dirt, and we tackled in the mud.

His big grin caught my eye just when I'd called a strong safety blitz, which meant I had to cover a back and the tight end. The quarterback—Tommy Patrick, by no coincidence—dropped back, the tight end stayed in and blocked the strong safety, and Patrick dumped off to the fullback. I was looking half at him and half at old man Priest sitting there grinning, and I said, "Oh, *shit.*"

The fullback was a prison guard and easily the biggest man on the entire team. He ran right at me, tried to stiff-arm but I blocked it with a heavily taped and padded forearm, and I hit him. WHAM! It was the hardest, most vicious collision I can remember from civilian life. We were both still standing, wobbling a little, I think, and then the fullback started running again. I chased him and this time tripped him up by the shoelaces. He still had the first down.

I signaled to the bench for one of our new young PD's, public defenders, to come in and I took myself out.

I sat down next to Priest. He kept watching the scrimmage while I wheezed and felt for cracked bones. It was late, and only a little pool of sunshine lay on the field. The trees were still, as if oppressed by the weather. Locusts sounded from the bushes and grasshoppers from the tall grass of the lagoon.

Priest just sat there watching, talking to himself or me, it really didn't matter much, about the play.

"Not bad. Nice kick, shit! Oh, watch out, li'l return man. OH. He got crunched. I told that li'l return man to watch out.

"Looks like a real green secondary. Too bad they don't have an old cagy veteran in there to help 'em out. Not some flashy dude like 'The Hammer' Williamson, but somebody wily and smart, even if he is old and slow. Somebody like Brookshier or Jake Scott.

"That old safety made quite an impression on the fullback, yes he did! And what a hit! Unmovable object and all that good shit. Shoestring tackle. I love it."

I let him talk. Hell, I needed a rest, didn't want to talk law with the guys on the bench, hadn't seen Billy in a year. He looked like he was in good shape. He wore an old Saints jersey over his pads, and shorts. The legs looked good, solid and muscular. But it was Billy's hands that spoke for him. His fingers were long and the span of the palm to fingertip was amazing. He used to talk with those hands, about as well as he caught the football.

"'Course, what this team needs more than anything is a reliable receiver. Somebody who knows the routes, the tricks, the sucker plays. Somebody who's been there.

Somebody with good speed and good hands. Most of all, a wily, experienced dude who won't get stuck looking stupid out there. Somebody sort of like that safety I was talking about. And somebody who don't necessarily have to block real well."

He looked over at me and grinned and I grinned back. Before the afternoon was over he'd run the forty, run routes, practiced against the safety who went in for me. Priest burned him and was on the team. And he got paid for next week's game in advance. Some moves.

Looking back, I think the money may have been why he returned to the game. By those days semi-pro players made some money, usually only enough to pay for gas to games and practices. We made more, because we had the court behind us, and behind the court all the illegal betting that goes on in chambers, law offices, police stations, parole offices, and the joint itself. It was all so ironic. I never thought about it when I played. I was still the monster back and played—and thought—like one. Like Mike Mallory at Michigan in '83 and '84. Other times I'd think about my money coming from judges I faced in court and from cons I defended, always free.

Billy played only three years. He had gotten a job in PR for an insurance company after the war, and he'd saved a little money from his glory days in football, but he was hunting for money, especially that second year, the year we hit Rush Street.

The Nighthawks do a great rendition of "Bright Lights." The song starts, "Bright lights, big city/Goin' to my baby's head," and there was something about that scene that had gone to Billy Boy's head. He was into the lights, the jive artists on the sidewalks, the marquees, the girls, the fast cars, all that glitter.

We strutted—he strutted and I walked next to him—from bar to bar. He'd buy bourbons and I'd order Cokes. Billy'd laugh every time he asked what "his man" would have. I didn't even bother reminding him about the malaria. He was on his own roll, powder-blue suit and all. He flashed when he walked, flashed when he spun on his barstool.

We walked the strip. Billy was drunk on the gaiety and glitter, intoxicated by the scene. He talked to the strippers, ran a line down on the call girls. Style, he had style. But if you stuck close, like I did, you could see the edge to him, reactions just a second too fast, the mouth just a moment too loose. He'd prattle on.

"T. Jones, you're my man, we gots to do this more often, now, isn't *that* something, a looker, she should be up on that stage herself, but that's too lowdown and dirty for her, you know, man? She deserves the best. You see one you want, we can split this joint, go to a nice little place I know down the street. Yeah, talk to that pair of sweet things, Jones, *talk* to her."

One of the house girls was asking for drinks and sticking her tits into my face, giving me a good idea what special drinks they had in the back room tonight for $75. I pinched her cheek and said maybe some other time. She moved on down the bar.

"Now, Jones, don't you *be* like that, we're here for a little fun, don't get down so, boy, hey—oh, hey, I got to see a man, be back, keep my seat." He strutted over by the pay phones and a young girl took his seat. She looked me up and down and I shrugged my shoulders. Priest was talking into the guy's ear, and they looked right together, like two pimps signifyin'.

I got up and left a few bucks on the bar. The girl

snatched them up and put them in her shoe. Then she finished Billy's drink. I just said, "I'll be back for my money, honey," and walked away.

I leaned on the cigarette machine near the topless/ bottomless cage. This was young-stuff night and she was young, but she had it all in one place, and it wasn't her first night on the job. She puckered up and I pitched her a quarter.

I could hear them trying to talk over the blare of the music a few feet away.

"But I need the blues, man, I need the blues real bad," Billy was saying.

He was talking to a man about his age, his height, dressed like he was Billy's brother. He had a short, clipped moustache and rocked back and forth on his two-inch heels. It seemed like he never wanted to get too close to Billy, like Billy had a disease.

"Can't help you, Billy. I told you last week the *me-di-a* turned the heat up. Can't get it from suppliers. But we're working on it, baby. You got your T's, man. That's all I can do."

Billy tried to buttonhole him but the man stepped back.

"I got a hundred. Give me what you got, substitutes, anything," Billy begged.

The man smiled, making him look suddenly very old and used. "I got *nothin'*, Billy. *Nothin'*. I told you. I can't take your C-note tonight, Billy. But I'm sure I'll be hearing from you, won't I?" He reached a hand out, instinctively, to pat him on the cheek, but remembered and held it an inch from his face.

"Billy. I'm doin' all I can." He straightened his suit. I'd never seen Priest look so bad.

"Look. Guys I know freelance it, cocktail it, ya know?"

Billy shook his head. "Man. They mix it with some other downer, cold pills, caps of this or that. It goes, Billy. Try it."

He walked away, then turned and said, "You got nothing to lose." He disappeared past the girl in the cage holding her tits out to the crowd while the men whistled and the women pointed and sneered and the band played on, something dull and forgettable.

Priest stood a minute looking at the back entrance, then hurried into the john. I found him in the last stall shoving Talwins and Contacs down his throat. The latch on the stall hadn't even been locked. Billy turned and I knocked the drugs onto the floor and into the toilet, then dragged him kicking, trying not to scream, to swallow instead, over to the sink.

I held him over it with a knee stuck against his kidney and hit him on the back. Nothing. I could hear him trying to swallow. His hands reached back for me, grabbing at whatever they could find. I hit him again, this time on the back of the head. Nothing. I reached a hand over and pinched both nostrils shut. He stood stock still, then heaved out a huge breath. Capsules and pieces of capsules fell into the sink and I washed them away before he could reach for them.

"You motherfucker! You goddamn motherfucker!" I held him another moment, then let him go and stepped back. His fist hit the automatic dryer; I caught his kick and held his leg and twisted it. He grabbed the sink for balance.

Someone came into the john and I said, "Excuse us for a moment, won't you? We'll be out shortly." The guy took one look and split.

I held the leg till he stopped twisting, stopped swearing. I held it till he collapsed against the sink.

243

I stood against the wall. "Priest, that would've killed you."

"What the fuck do you know." It was a low, resentful voice I'd never heard before.

"I know plenty. It's T's and Blues. And you ain't got the pyribenzamine, the Blues. So you try Contac instead. I never thought I'd say this to you, man, but you are one stupid asshole."

I saw him glance up in the mirror, then look away. "It's my business, Jones."

"You invited me down here, to your stompin' grounds, Priest."

"My mistake. It won't happen again."

"Damn straight it won't. All those drinks and Talwin and Contac and you won't be bringin' *any*one any*where* for any*thing*. I know what I'm talkin' about, man."

"Fuck you."

"Okay, Priest, okay. What's worth savin', man? I know from the war."

The war is the one subject we both backed away from, so we respected it, knew any mention of it would be straight.

He said, "Yeah. Okay. So you know. It don't matter, man. I'm walkin' out of here, got my business, and you don't follow me." He raised up and brushed water off his suit, pushed his hair back with his fingers.

I was tired. "You got that right. I don't follow you. Your business." I spat into the stall littered with bright, tiny Contac particles.

He turned and walked out, never looked back. I looked at my face in the wall mirror. There was red in the eyes, the same red I'd seen in my urine for a month. People came in and looked me over, standing against the wall like a statue, like a silent hustler.

I walked toward the bar. Priest was gone and I didn't bother looking for him. I saw the woman who'd taken my money and when I walked past her, I yanked both shoes off and ran for the door, shoving one shoe into each suit coat pocket. She yelled and tried to follow me but the band was too loud and the floor too crowded.

I told the cheap pimp they called a doorman to find me a cab and flashed him a five. I was out of there in thirty seconds. In the cab on the way home I slipped free the money from the special clips hidden inside the shoes. I guessed maybe $200. I took the money and left the cabbie the shoes as a souvenir.

Within the month he called for help. I got him into a detox program at the VA hospital on the west side. And he got clean, off everything except the scripts the doctors wrote for him. One was Dilaudid, almost as potent as Talwin, but I didn't say anything.

He played football another year. He was slower but still smart. He took even longer getting up after a play than he used to, and Patrick started putting him at wingback, where there was less blocking in our system, and alternated him on downs. He still led the team in catches and helped us win the division.

Then he got hurt and didn't play in the league game, the one no one will ever forget, the one that falls like thunder into my dreams when they are innocent and finally free of blood and gore and violence.

He didn't quit because of injury. He just knew it was time to leave the game. At the time, I didn't think Patrick cared. I was wrong.

I run into Kathleen on the stairs of our building—literally. I hold her waist to keep her from falling. She's in an old sweat suit and her bangs are plastered to her head.

245

It's awkward. We haven't seen each other since the morning after Avanzare's. It's been only a week.

She steps up a stair and holds my elbow tightly, looks me right in the eyes. "Thanks."

"Anytime." I like her spunk. I like her wit and her style. I like her when the guard is down. Generally speaking, I like her a lot. But I'm through pushing things, especially with women.

I step down a stair or two and she calls after me, "Jones?"

"Yeah."

"I just got cable hooked up. Maybe you want to take in a movie at my place?" She pauses. I don't answer. "I make the popcorn, you bring the Cokes."

I peer up in the gloomy hall at her. The sweat pants are soaked around the waist and there's a big sweat stain between her breasts.

"I guess you might want to watch *Citizen Kane*, or maybe *Metropolis*." She shakes her head. "Okay. Maybe *La Cage aux Folles* or *Emmanuelle*." She smiles, the perfect teeth showing. "Then *Billy Budd* or some early Peckinpah." She shakes her head again, holding on to the railing while she pulls her sweats off over her Pumas. She's wearing her Hawaiian shorts. I notice the slightest paling of the tan on her legs.

"Actually, Travis, I thought you might want to come this weekend. Halloween is Wednesday, you know, but they've saved all the real classics for Friday and Saturday." She rolls the sleeves up, shakes the sweatshirt to cool herself off.

I'm onto her now. God, so weary. "Oh. I get it. A little *Psycho* and maybe the original *The Thing*. Hawks, you know."

She smiles a different sort of smile, one I don't know.

"I know," she says, leaning toward me. "Actually, I thought we could watch a real classic double feature: *Slumber Party Massacre* and *The Town That Feared Sundown.*"

She catches me and I know it. She almost giggles. I know I'm just standing there, mouth half open, looking *real* dumb. She's got class. I thought it late that night, again that morning after Avanzare's.

I just look around stupidly and say, "Yeah. Great idea. Tell me when."

She gives me the high sign and starts up the stairs.

"Kathleen?"

"Yes?"

"Are you busy tonight? I thought—I think it'd be nice of us to just sit around, no planned agenda, you know?" It sounds stupid, but I hadn't exactly prepared a speech.

She looks at me as if to figure my angle. There isn't any, and I hope she feels it.

"What time?"

"I'll be home by six-thirty. Anytime is fine."

"Okay." Neither of us moves.

"Kathleen?" Do I sound like I'm begging for something? Have I ever?

"Yes?"

"Stay as long as you like." Then I think, what the hell. Open it up. Get this friendship rolling. "All night, if you want." Pause. "I've even got some wine for the occasion."

She laughs, and that sure breaks some of the crust forming between us in that dark, moody hallway.

"Separate beds?" And laughs again.

"I've got a couch. But we didn't need it last time, so I don't see why we'd need it now." I grin up at her, probably a cat's grin.

"Keep your options open, TJ," she laughs, and dashes

up the last stairs and into her apartment. She's never called me TJ before, ever.

I take the stairs down quickly. It's decent to have a friend. Decent. Maybe you do need friends. Maybe.

I'm feeling good when the chill hits me at the door, but the sun's out and it looks great.

A woman is sunbathing in front of the apartment. Vain girl. There are goose bumps all along her back. She slips her shades down from her eyes as I pass and she says, "Hi, Travis."

"Hi, Susan." I walk a step and then stop and look down at her. As usual, she's up on her elbows, letting her breasts hang down into the tiny cups of her suit.

"You know, a friend of mine says you've got great tits."

Her smile freezes. She doesn't know how to take it, to thank me or tell me to fuck off. That's how I had it figured. I turn and start down the sidewalk, then turn again and say, "But not that great."

If the walls are white, so is skin, so is blood, so is dirt, so is shit. Endless. Endless.

They talked at us on the box till we slumped onto the white table. Guards would throw water on our faces to wake us up, then make one of us mop the table and floor.

I knew when the guards made mistakes and spoke among themselves in another language. I could understand them. Then it occurred to me that they must have known why I was sent to the northern zones, must have known about my special training at Monterey, must have known things I'd forgotten.

So I let them jabber without listening and I watched the warm snow fall onto my hands, my legs, my bare feet.

The cubicles were too small to stretch out in. Each had a bucket and an earthenware pot of water. The walls were white. The ceiling was white. One day they caught me pulling green grass into my cubicle from the ventilator holes at the base of the western wall.

They put me in the box, a smaller cubicle isolated somewhere in the middle of the clinic. It was a glaring white, some whitewash or paint different from the rest of the place. There were no vents—just creases in the walls through which air moved. Every day I put my ear to a crease and listened. The movement vibrated the eardrum and simulated sound, sound from which I had been cut off, even the sound of the voice box.

It wasn't the first—or only—time I'd been in the box. And there'd be more until the day the war caught up with the clinic and the helicopters carried away with them what little there was left of us.

The box had the earthenware pot, filled with water, but no bucket. When you were in the box, you had to be creative.

One time I didn't want to hear only the soft rasp of air inside my ear. I tore a sleeve off my uniform, tore it lengthwise, and spent the next few days rolling and snapping, rolling and snapping, until a guard must have heard me. My "adjustment," they called it, for that act, was returning me to the room with the long table, the other prisoners, the box that crackled and spoke.

A man died from beating his head against the wall. The guards removed us for an hour. When we returned, the man was gone and the blood spattered on the wall and floor had been replaced by a new coat of white.

The dreams started to come in white, sometimes white only, sometimes gray, sometimes harsh blacks and whites.

When I woke I'd smash my fist against the wall to see red, to know color again.

Toward the end, before they got us out, I had the cut man dream. Against my will. I tried to block it out, but it kept coming back.

The cut man sharpens his knives for a long time. He is very good at what he does. In fact, there is no one better. In the white world, the cut man has trouble doing his job. The conflict is what the box wants to hear, to sense, to feel. But it's too late. The walls come tumbling down and later, in the hospital, and much later, in the States, I can only wonder how much they knew, how much they did that will never go away.

In the cold, one sweats unlike in the heat. The dream is sticky, white with fear. I see a plane land and all of the corporals I ever served with standing together in a line, smiling, waiting to go stateside. The ramp is lowered and I sit in the plane's hatch behind an M-60, grinning from ear to ear. My teeth chatter with the heavy bullets biting into bodies until they are all down, all but one, Sgt. Rohn. I aim again but stop, realize he need not die, he is a sergeant, not a corporal.

He walks toward me, stonefaced, each step on the sticky asphalt heavier than the last, until he is on the steps of the ramp, smiling, thanking me for such an excellent job. But the face is not Rohn's, it's a face I don't know, and the dress uniform is different. This man is older and wears generals' bars on his shoulders. He extends his hand to shake and I try to cut him down with the machine gun, but it jams, and he smiles, and I go for the moray in my shoulder sheath, but hands hold me back, white hands with long white fingernails. I turn and see the grinning

250

face of Marcolski on one side and the smiling one-eyed face of Franklin on the other.

I wonder how long I scream, who can hear me. When the chills stop and the sweat is dry, I take a warm shower, think about calling Duncan. I sit naked next to the phone. The digital clock reads 4:40.

Six months after the Mekong, Franklin died in a crossfire between two units of our Marines. Rohn took a round in the jugular while walking point way up on the Minh Trail.

I prop myself up in bed, the window open more, anything to make it natural.

On the first day, I rode with Colonel Cooper and Ringo. The colonel kept calling for counts of confirmed kills. I started out guessing. As the day wore on and he kept asking, I'd tell Ringo I was thinking of a number between one and one hundred. He'd keep guessing till we had a bigger number than last time.

The colonel liked the constant chatter of our guns and our numbers. He forgot all about his threats and clapped us on the back when we deplaned.

On the second day I flew with the British officer with no rank, Jones, and the ranger with no identifiable rank named Pacheco. The system was different. We had swivel mounts on both doors, and my job was to run across from one to another as Jones shot the chopper through narrow gaps in a high mountain range.

There were no military targets. None. They admitted this "exercise" was of no real military value, but it would "help the war effort."

On our first run Pacheco sat at the rear, where a hole had been cut and fit with Plexiglas. Pacheco sat on top of some kind of radio device, a transformer maybe, and flipped switches as we lowered into the valley.

When we made our first strafing run, he pushed the black buttons wired into the switches, and the backfire of the rockets being released almost pitched me overboard.

I pulled the ear protectors back on but didn't even feel the reverberation of the explosions. I kept my gun smoking but yelled over the rotors at Pacheco, behind me.

"What'd you do? Aim those fuckers at the moon?"

He yelled back, though why he bothered I don't know, "Those weren't rockets you are familiar with, Corporal Jones. We've wired in a special system. Heat-seeking missiles."

Just as he said it the chopper was almost knocked into the mountain by a blast nearby. Three or four other explosions followed, spread out below.

Pacheco yelled to me, as if proud of a new, complicated little toy, "It takes a while for the sensors in the missiles to lock in to anything generating enough heat to trip the signal. Then their radar guides them down."

I stopped gunning and stared at him. "You mean we're using those on bands or villages or whatever of *people* down there, based on their *heat*? Nothing else? *Heat?* Kids? Women? Buffalo herds? Family sitting down to dinner? Here come the *smart* American bombs. You fat ass." Pacheco looked at me as if I were crazy.

Jones didn't look back, just yelled, "Corporal Jones, resume your gunnery position. We're passing back." He turned to check the flanks and his face was completely expressionless.

The next day I requested ground duty. Jones asked me why at the dawn briefing. "I'm more used to jungle warfare. Sir." He paced the mud floor for a moment and then said, "Right. You and Sharp then will lead search-

and-destroy missions. Same objectives all 'round. Do you understand?"

I nodded. At least I could pick my targets. Sharp and I saddled up. All he said was, "Weird group of fuckers. We stay alive out here long enough, *Corporal* Jones, we're going to see just everything."

"Haven't you seen enough?"

Sharp took point and I took the only navigable flank. Like so many other times, we plunged ahead of a scared little patrol into the jungle.

There are more men this time. There are about six when we start, but more keep dropping in. As usual, I walk around the richly paneled room, stopping now and then to stare out the window. The last days of October are chill, heavy with the promise of frost, a hard winter. The leaves stay on the trees but are brittle and discolored.

One of the men tries to make introductions, but it doesn't work because we come and go, and someone is always talking. There's a plush, fully stocked bar at the end of the room, and every time one or two of them get really ripped. Those who do, then sit, stone-faced, silent, or take the discussion over. That's when I leave.

I'm at the window listening to the wind and to their words, when two new guys come in. Our group leader gives their names, but I pay no attention. It's afternoon but gray, almost black. The leaves are hanging on in spite of the wind, which touches my bones in all the bad spots: shoulders, collarbone, knees, ribs above the left lung.

The conversation picks up in intensity. One of the new men is talking, not loudly, but well.

"We have to face the fact that we were systematically lied to. All down the years. From 1960—maybe before that—till 1975 and that 'last gunboat' bullshit. I've talked

253

to guys who fought with the French. And I've heard from other guys who did some kind of duty as late as 1979. Not CIA, regular army."

I can't see this man too well. He has a thick beard and short, greased hair. He punctuates his sentences with a hook where his right hand had been.

"I'm living on partial disability—or I *was* till asshole Reagan cut it back—and I saved my money all these years. I worked on magazines devoted to the war till I got tired of the hype, and seeing those high school kids line up to get the latest issue so they could read about the guns and the glory, even when we *told* them there wasn't any.

"I've researched the war, spent part of my life on it, maybe part that I would have had without this." He thumps the back of the hook down on a mahogany coffee table.

"Look, most of you guys shipped out long after I came back. My tour was '62 to '65. I would have gone another year but for this.

"I believed in it then. I don't know how, or why. They sent me north, to places most of you never even heard of."

I stare at him, move away from the window, closer.

"I saw things no one should be expected to see and come back sane, normal. You guys know all this. But I was there *years* before you guys. What I did—or failed to do— should have allowed you to stay at home, or at least be different. Just like some of you've been saying, it really bothers me that it was all a waste, for nothing. Nice little territorial dispute. Political war. Fight for the oil in the South China Sea. No one will ever know for sure.

"Listen, they promised me corporal and promoted me when I was only eighteen because I was a crack shot, could count the dead soldiers and civilians and sort 'em out, and because I'd walk the point every time. Even up north, in that no-man's-land, I'd walk the point.

"Good men with me, though. Wouldn't have traded them for the Marine Corps. Lots never made it out."

Some of the men murmur to themselves, get up to make new drinks. I look at the man again but stay behind the high chair on the far side of the room.

"Man, let me ask something." I speak as softly as I can.

"Shoot." He faces me and squints in the dimness.

"You said something earlier about the French, in the early years of the war. You mean around Dien Bien Phu, some of the last holding actions of the French troops?"

"I'm glad you asked. No, I'm not talking about that at all. I've talked to men who worked with French Foreign Legion and regular army as early as 1958 and as late as 1965. I heard of a French officer coordinating evasion and escape when I was there. Never met him. And soon after the stories came in, they dried up. People seemed afraid to talk about him. But yeah, I know about it firsthand."

"You said you were assigned north. How far, and why?"

"How far can you go in Southeast Asia, north? Don't ask me why. I can just say that I was there and did my job. Mostly I was a low-paid killer. Anything else, friend?"

"We were all low-paid killers, man. You're new here, but don't think you're special."

"Don't worry. I don't." He speaks more quietly.

"You said there were these French guys. Uniforms? Were they fighting? Or just advisors?"

"They weren't Lurps, if that's what you mean. But they sure weren't advisors, man. They wore our uniforms, I hear, and were in on missions in the north, undermining

255

actions, stuff with the tribesmen and natives up there. But listen, friend, don't pick on the French. I *know* the British were there too—not Aussies or New Zealanders. Intelligence officers from England."

I take a step forward, peer at this man closer, looking into the eyes, dull with a bright spot in the center. I can't make him out through the beard.

"How do you know?" The silence in the room allows me to hear the thrashing of the tree branches in the wind.

"I've talked to guys who saw them, worked for them, even rode missions together with 'em. And I met one of 'em myself, must have been '63, not too long after I shipped out. We never found out his rank. Someone said colonel. Someone said general, but that's bullshit. He dressed like the rest of us, could fly any chopper we had, used our weapons. Only thing was he wore this funky little black beret."

I know they're looking at me strangely as I move closer and continue to stare at this man. "You wouldn't know his name, would you?"

"Well, I figure they didn't use their real names. Why bother? No rank, probably no name. But he needed something for us to call him. Nothing distinctive. He just called himself *Jones*."

I'm maybe six or seven feet away, leaning toward him across the back of a convertible leather chair. (Nothing but the best for the troubled veterans.)

"That's my name too."

"Oh, well, I don't mean it's so ordinary it's an insult. I just mean he probably wanted to use a common name, that's all."

"What's your name?"

He looks at me hard, trying to place the face, the

features. "You missed introductions, huh? My name's Andrews."

It's hard to believe. After Sharp and I killed the Montagnard guards, the company had continued north for several days, but then we'd both been flown back for some sapper work across another border. But there is no doubt. It must be him.

"Corporal Andrews. Snot-nosed eighteen-year-old kid who walked the point like strolling down Michigan Avenue at noon in the summertime."

He's out of his chair. "I know you."

"Sure do. Company north of the known zones. A week's march without support. Never did know that Sharp and me had saved your ass when we flanked ahead on your point. Yeah, I know you too. T. Jones is the name."

He looks stupidly at my face, then lets his gaze glance down at my hands, my feet, maybe checking to see if I made it out whole.

I've been around plenty of amputees. You get used to changes. I walk closer and extend my left hand, which he shakes, hard and strong. Behind the beard and the greased, shining hair, I can see the baby-faced kid named George Andrews.

"Goddamn, Jones. I never thought you'd have made it out in one piece."

"Well, there were times when I almost came back in a bag, but I convinced 'em to let me stay."

It kind of cuts the ice, lets everyone laugh and get another drink. These chance meetings happen every now and then when we get together, even other times, but it's usually awkward. We don't know how to greet each other anymore. In some ways we're close, closer than brothers, but in other ways we remain absolute strangers, especially after a lot of years. It's tense. A good strong drink takes the edge off for most of them. If I touch a drop, my medicines will kill me.

Andrews faces the group and says he'll talk about it more later. He wants to talk to me.

But I say, "Listen, man, I really can't stay. I got things going on, too many things." These meetings always make me nervous. It's like I'll have to admit something that I don't want to admit, find out something I didn't know and don't really want to know.

And meeting Andrews makes me even more nervous. It always happens when I run into one of the guys from the war when it's totally unexpected. Give me a couple of days warning and it's no problem, not on the surface anyway. And it's not like it happens all the time. There aren't enough of us left.

"Okay." He smiles a little, looks at me like he's putting it all through his personal computer. "I know what you mean. We can do it some other time. You pick the day." He's scribbling his phone number and address onto a scrap of paper, but I put my hand out and stop him. He's remarkably fast with his left hand.

"We'll do it. We will. I have to ask you something before I leave."

"Yeah, okay, go ahead."

He sits on a barstool and grasps a shot glass, then lets it go, with his hook. He does it over and over, without looking at it, like flexing a muscle unconsciously, watching me instead.

"Tell me what you know about Jones."

"That's right. The British dude."

"So you *knew*. You knew he was British too. You've known all these years."

"I knew he wasn't an Aussie. That's all. I heard the accent. That would be pretty hard to miss.

"And you talked to him, spent time with him. Listen, your reputation preceded you to that little jungle foray. We knew about the 'professional corporals' deployed out there. You weren't just grunts like us. You were door gunners, sappers, ordnance experts."

"Man." I sigh. It's like the lie that grows and grows the more it goes around. "There was no difference between me and Sharp and Ringo and lots of other guys you never even heard of, and you, and all the guys in your company. We took the same trails, crossed the same borders. You were a corporal too. All I know is I didn't want another promotion. I studied languages at Monterey so I traveled a lot. All I know is that I got a lot of assignments. It wasn't like I wanted them." I pause, look out the window at leaves that cling tenaciously to branches. "Believe me, I didn't want most of them."

"Well, we'll talk about it sometime. I know about you and some of your buddies. You can learn a lot when you got nothin' else to do."

He gives me the level look, the dark-in-the-eyes look of a man who's spent too much time in the jungle. And too much time afterward thinking about it.

"You may know some things, and you may think you know some things. Whatever. I want to know about that British officer."

"So do I. What makes you think I know anything else about him?"

This is getting tiring, dangerous. And I'm losing my patience with Corporal Andrews. "Man. I don't know what your problem is."

"I got no problem. I want to know why you're asking

me questions about some British C.O. that you fought with when you know fuckin' well I never said a word to him." His grip tightens on the shot glass.

"Humor you, asshole. Fine. I rode door gunner with him from a mountain base. Me and McCoy. It was heavy fire. That's all I know."

"The shit it is. How do you think *I* was taken out over there? Got this 'prosthetic device' instead of a hand?"

I don't answer. I get up and shrug into my coat. Like so many vets that I meet, Andrews has lost it. I guess, one way or another, we've all lost it.

Suddenly the shot glass shatters in his metal grip, showers the bar with heavy pieces of glass. Everyone stops talking, looks our way. The perspiration stands out on Andrews's face. He calls out after me as I move for the stairway.

"You want to know who you were gunning for, who you were protecting? A colonel in the SBS—Special Boat Service. Most elite British commandos there are. *Why*, Jones? Why were the British *and* the French *and* God knows who else over there to begin with?"

I start down the stairs, not wanting these questions, not wanting to know any more about the man we called just "Jones." But I had to ask to see what he knew.

"I'm gonna call you, Jones," Andrews yells from the bar as I step out into the cool of autumn. "I'm not gonna let you go this time—" And his voice is swallowed up by the clang of the heavy metal door and the absolute emptiness I feel inside.

Late that night I sit in the rocker, sweating. I throw the wet towel across the room, knock over bottles of pills on the table. I'm fucked. I will sweat away the rest of my fucking life. I feel like slicing open my guts and letting the bacteria run free.

It's not hot, but the wind has shifted and brought a last warm front for Halloween. I'm stripped down into shorts and socks, waiting for the chills. When they hit, they take over. I'm too exhausted to wait till they come to put on the socks. I'm pissed off, ready to take them all on. Fuck the medicine. It never works anyway. I'm ready to fight all by myself.

Someone rings the front doorbell. It reverberates like the box on the wall in the white room. I'm slipping too far into the past but can't do a thing about it.

The medicines bring with them torpor, the tendency to drop one's head to the side and not lift it up again for five full minutes or more. Other effects are less predictable.

The ringing continues. Now it has a pattern—several seconds of ringing, pause, several seconds of ringing. When the chopper dropped down next to the clinic, I heard it and thought the box on the wall had finally slipped a tube. The small arms fire sounded like the sounds I'd heard when the attendants would hold one of us and dislocate an arm, a shoulder, a knee, then pop it back in, and keep doing it and doing it and doing it. . . . I recognized the rotors and the guns only after someone with white camouflage paint smeared in irregular lines across his face dug through the wall with his bayonet and stood, silently staring for a minute, before sweeping me over his shoulder and out.

I yell, "Fuck you!" and the ringing continues once, then stops. I close my eyes and feel the gentle swirl of Indian summer breezes on my legs. Then I hear doorbells ringing all over the apartment, remote but very clear; still, it lasts but a few seconds. Then I hear the low buzz and the click of the safety latch.

People are basically so stupid.

I hear the slow, labored footsteps in the stairwell, in the hallway, stopping outside my door. Shit! It's like too many things, scary stories like "The Monkey's Paw," Sharp and me looking at each other from our hammocks before getting that set of sealed orders that did us in.

Then I hear Stern saying, "Jones, you asshole. I know you're in there. It won't do you any good to hide out. I'll camp on your doorstep till you come out." I want to ask why but I have nothing to say to Stern. He's comfortable to have around sometimes, like a broken-down old couch or, I suppress the laugh at what the hell I'm thinking, a well-worn John the Conqueror. Well. So.

So instead I say quietly, weakly almost, "Jones is gone for the day—all of it. This is his personal masseuse and light housekeeper."

"Well, listen to me, you faggot. Let your 'master' know I'm here and open the goddamn door!"

"Not likely." I think and rethink and try to leave the dream behind.

"Open up, man. I can't stand out here all day."

I don't want to talk to him through the door forever so I get up and swing it open. Stern is still red in the face from climbing the stairs. He doesn't look too happy. He's wearing his best near north outfit. It doesn't fit on this side of town.

"Stern."

"How you been, Jones? Haven't seen you in a couple weeks. I keep calling and getting weird recorded messages. Really have to answer the phone more, TJ, or at least return your calls."

262

He's walking in a circle around the room, stopping to peer at the spine on a book or the inscription on a plaque.

"Why?"

I sit back down and prop my feet up.

Stern stops and looks at me, then continues, mopping sweat from his neck with a monogrammed handkerchief.

He steps into the kitchen. "Getting a beer, man. Want something?"

I ask for ice water and he returns with an oversized can of malt liquor and a huge green glass filled with ice.

"Where's the water?"

"I thought you'd kind of just let the cubes melt," he said. Shrewd. Smartass.

"So what's the story, man? You been busy, out of town, crazy, or what?"

Stern frees a button on his tight off-white shirt, then leans my way, really expecting a specific answer.

"Just busy, I guess."

"Not at your office. I tried you there."

"I didn't say. My work takes me across the city. Anyway, I wouldn't lose any sleep over it."

He looks at me, then works on the beer for a minute.

"Sure looks like you have."

"Have what?"

"Lost some sleep over it. Over something."

"Just old illnesses sticking up. They don't know when they're defeated."

"Yeah. I guess so." He pauses, takes another pull. "Saw your friend downstairs."

"Who's that?"

"What's-her-face. The one with the great tits. You know, the professional tanner."

For a minute I think he's talking about Kathleen, and I

don't like it. And that surprises me. But it's Susan he means.

"Oh. Her. She's bizarre. Starts on that in April and is still out there in November. I think she goes to a tanning salon in the winter. It's too bad."

"Oh?"

"Early cancer."

"Oh, yeah, right."

Stern drinks and looks around, drinks and looks at the floor. He's uncomfortable, and that isn't like him. At all.

"Listen, Stern, I probably should get some sleep, try to fight this malaria off. It just comes up once a year or so." It's a lie but he doesn't know the difference. He just sits and looks at the floor when he answers.

"Actually I came over here for a reason. I ran into Tom Patrick at the Yacht Club yesterday and he asked me to come talk to you."

I look at him and then through him.

"I don't know what all he was talking about, but he said you'd want to know even if you said you didn't. Shit, I don't even know right now what that means, but he said you'd want to know."

My voice is very low, very calm, very smoothly modulated, the model of decorum, of control, of cool.

"Tell me what he said, Stern."

Stern gets up and walks around, stopping to look out the windows.

"He didn't say this, but you know I saw some of your football games the last couple years."

"Sure. I know."

"And I don't know all the guys on the team, or in your league. I just like to watch the game."

He paces and I nod.

"I do remember Patrick from the games . . . not just

264

from the social circle I run in. I know we've never talked about it. Anyway, it's hard to ignore the quarterback. Or the best little receiver in the league."

"You know who that is, I assume."

"Well, I really didn't till yesterday, but when I heard the name I suddenly knew why he was so good. All-pro that soon. Great hands, always. Anyway."

He stops and looks at a pile of letters stacked neatly on an end table. I'm afraid he will pick them up and leaf through them in his nervousness.

"Get on with it, Stern." The sweat has come on again and there is a ringing in my head. The pills are all in the bedroom and bathroom. Most of the sweat rolls off my back where he can't see it.

I remember a day when I thought I would drown in my own sweat. It wasn't too long after the starving patrols straggled back into base. I let Sharp report. He knew about the malaria, had known for some time and hadn't reported it to base hospital. I told him not to. But he didn't know about some of the complications. Just me and a medic who didn't know enough to countermand my orders.

Four or five had made it in. One of the privates had bruises from the heavy jungle growth all over his face and arms. Something had cut into his leg. It was badly infected with what I knew was pseudomonas. The pus oozing from the wound was a bright blue and a dull green in color. But he didn't know any better than to stand under the trees with me.

None of us had eaten enough for almost a week. Water had been limited. I was too weak to do anything but stand under that tree and sweat off what little water I had. I poured the last of my water onto a long black strip of cloth and handed it to the private. He squeezed water into his mouth and over the leg gash, then wiped my face before he put the headband across his forehead and eyes.

I saw the rainbow flashing in the insufferable heat, from the diseased leg of the man standing next to me. The sweat poured off me like a shower when I hobbled out into the sun to find Sharp, to get a medic for the man standing alone under the trees, smiling, balanced on one leg.

They cut his leg off at the thigh that night. We all heard it.

That was real. Listening to Stern was not.

"Okay. Patrick wanted me to tell you that he's 'come to terms,' as he put it, with your friend Billy Priest. And he expects you to be ready to play by Sunday."

There's a haze in the air outside. It looks like the end of Indian summer. The end of another season. Over there, there was no end to anything, not even on the commercial jet back.

I need the pills in the other rooms. I have to get well for a while. I have things to do.

"Well?" Stern is looking up at me from the floor, where he sits cross-legged, leaning back against a stereo speaker.

"Well what?" I hold his gaze, level.

"Are you going to play?"

I get up. "I need some pills." I get what I need from the bathroom and take them with my ice water. The bathroom mirror shows a face with red in the eyes, black around them, the lips a thin line of determination. My hair is dampened on the ends and curls up on my forehead, my neck, my shoulders.

Stern is where I left him when I return and sit back in the rocker. I rock for a moment, watching beads of water sweat off my glass and drip soundlessly onto my legs.

"Let me tell you a story I've never mentioned to you, Stern. In fact, I don't think that I've told this story to anyone." I think, but my memory is cloudy; it is clear like glass about so much, and dim about other things I wish I knew.

"One night many years ago a friend and I went out to dinner. We had seen each other only once or twice since we'd come stateside, and this was before the war ended. But for us the war had been over for a long time. And all I mean by that is that we had been home for years. The war *still* isn't 'over.'

"His name is Jim McCoy. Back then—maybe 1974, 1975—he'd just moved to Chicago. Still lives here. I see him every few months, mostly when it occurs to *him*. I knew him *real* well—I can't tell you, and that's not even the point—but times change.

"McCoy picked me up at my apartment, this was when I lived on Roscoe. I wanted to buy him a dinner so big even he couldn't eat it all, and Jim has always been able to pack it away. So I told him on the phone we were going to Pheasant Run. Nice place, I told him. Grounds. Big dining room. A theater if we wanted to see a show, which we didn't.

"He picked me up and we drove out there. I had a nice pair of pants and shoes on, a tie, a sport coat. McCoy wore a suit. You gotta know how to dress when you mingle with the rich and famous, don't you, Stern?"

He doesn't look away. My eyes are burning with the light blaring in through the windows, from the white walls that I've thought about painting a darker color, any other color. I don't need landlord hassles, so when it gets to me I retreat to the bedroom, painted a cool blue, and sit in the rocker there by the window.

"And it wasn't just the meal, the food. Lots of places

serve huge helpings of food. I wanted to welcome him to Chicago. I knew old times would come up, but back then I believed we could forget. We could try. We *had* to try. That's what I believed then."

Droplets of water and sweat combine and fall from my legs into a little pool on the floor. Stern stares like he's viewing an autopsy from the laboratory's theater window.

"Well, we'd just pulled into the parking lot and man, was he impressed. Wasn't like the only fancy restaurant he'd ever seen, but it's a nice place, you know.

"We got out of the car and had just gone through the doors to that classy, long, glass-enclosed tunnel that runs from the front door all the way to the building itself. I don't even know if it's there anymore, but back then it was the ultimate convenience for the restaurant patron. You could get out of your car, walk a few steps to this little hallway, and walk the rest of the way to the restaurant without getting rained on or snowed on or anything. And when you left you'd go the same way, and have your husband or chauffeur or whatever pick you up under the awning outside of that clear glass tunnel. Great convenience. Even had flowers planted in rows on the inner walls, and windows that would ventilate without getting anyone wet. Class, real high class."

Stern starts to look a little uncomfortable, but so what.

"So we'd just stepped into this little fishbowl when a whole bunch of people came pouring through the doors at the other end. They were maybe fifty feet away—it was a long tunnel—and obviously had been doing more than eating.

"But we didn't pay much attention to them. They were loud, but we were talking, I think about where McCoy was going to live. He was staying with relatives. Well, we'd gotten almost halfway through this terrarium, when these folks walking our way just stopped. Most of 'em stopped talking. They stood where they were. That's when I first paid any serious attention to them.

"Actually, it was four couples, four men, four women. They weren't real young, either, maybe thirty-five average. The men wore suits. The women were all high-fashion, not that I remember what, exactly, but I remember the makeup and the pearls and the classy dresses.

"They were pretty drunk but that was nothing to us. We started to pass the first guy and his wife or girlfriend, and he kind of lurched over, his arm wrapped around the woman, till they were leaning against the glass wall on our side of the enclosure. There was no way we could get by.

"I remember stepping back a pace or two to see if that guy was really drunk and staggering around or to see if he had other ideas. He had, he and most of those he was with. There was one woman way in the back who never smiled or said a word. I always wondered what she thought, why she was with these people.

"I saw a look in McCoy's eyes that I hadn't seen since the jungle, and that scared me bad, man. Not for me, and not for McCoy. I was afraid for those people.

"I guess I should have expected the rest. I suppose we should have gone into the city, to the Blackhawk or someplace like that. But it's supposed to be a free country.

"So we played along, even McCoy for a minute. Sometimes you peg a situation wrong, or hope you do. But not me, not this time.

"We moved over left, tried to go by on that side. Two of the other three men slid over and blocked our way. Their women went with them. And then I told McCoy I'd go through first, slip past them if that's what they wanted, just to make us feel like dumb shits.

"The guy with the woman way in the back moved in

and blocked the only crease through the wall-to-wall people.

"So I backed off and told McCoy, 'I think we're about to get a good line,' and he said, 'Sure as hell are, brother.'

"And the man in front said to his little group, something like, 'Well, friends, appears the standards of this establishment have dropped severely. Looks like they let hippies and nigras in now. I just don't understand why these people would want to come here. Don't got their kind of food. Or sour mash liquor, or LSD.'

"McCoy was standing there as calm as I've ever seen him. I just sighed and leaned against the wall, looking at the expensive flowers lining the tunnel from one end to the other.

"He kept on, slurring a word here or there, the other people laughing, especially the women. I tried to think about something else, considered turning around and walking out, wondered what would happen if anyone else came into the walkway. But no one did.

"I was still standing there, head down, when I heard the big man in front say, 'Save all their welfare checks for a month just to come here, this freak and this slack-jawed black nigger,' and McCoy didn't turn an inch, just said, 'You go left and middle, I'll go right,' just as it had been ten years before in a place that bore no resemblance to this sheltered lily-white country club, and I didn't even look up, just said 'Go,' and when he moved I moved.

"It's a cliché but this time I think it is true: they didn't know what hit them. One minute we were standing there, looking relaxed, while they bottled up the entranceway. The next McCoy had taken the big man with the mouth and dropped him to his knees with a foot sweep while I threw two elbows simultaneously and one of the others doubled over. The other one went through the glass, shattering a wall-sized pane outward as he held his kidneys. I pushed the two women out the hole in the wall onto the glass before they could even scream.

"McCoy stood there as the smile on the woman's face faded. Then he put a hand out and placed it an inch or two above her breasts, onto her pearls. He smiled and fingered them, playing them over her cleavage. She was scared, all right, her man on the ground heaving for air, half the group down or out the window, but not too scared to start to call McCoy something he distinctly did not like.

"He dropped her next to her man with a straight fist to the stomach. The man in the middle, the one who had filled the crease, was waking up. He was supposed to be mine, but as he started forward with his fists up, the guy I'd kidney-chopped grabbed my pants and pulled. I couldn't believe it when I heard the rip, from the knee to the ankle. So I put that foot into his throat and he was down to stay. But the other one was past me and heading for McCoy.

"McCoy never looked up, just laid out a forearm shiver across the neck that twisted the guy's head back. I'd seen him going for McCoy and had laid a side kick across his sternum.

"You were talking about football, Stern. Well, there it was, the classic old defensive hit, high and low at the same time. They don't get up from that combination, and this guy was no exception.

"That left the girl standing wide-eyed beyond it all. To her credit, she never backed away. She just stood there staring at us and the seven people littered across the entranceway, lying in pools of glass, scattered several feet outside in the grass.

"McCoy looked at her but didn't take a step. The expression on his face had never changed.

271

"I leaned over and fingered the material of my pants. I remember saying, 'Shit. I just bought these pants to take you out to dinner,' and McCoy laughed his big laugh and said, 'Appears a bit too crowded here, Jones. Probably have to wait to be seated, anyway. Bring your pants and I'll take you to a nice quiet little place on the west side of the city.'

"He turned and walked back the way we'd come in, not looking for any trouble, no special treatment. That young woman stood still, looking at me, ignoring the noises of her hurt friends.

"So we walked out the way we'd come in. We went to dinner and had a pretty good time."

I pause and wait.

"That's my Pheasant Run story. I've been thinking of it more and more lately."

Stern is quiet, sitting against the speaker.

"I guess you didn't get the point of my little story."

"I guess not."

"The point is that I try real *hard* to stay away from trouble, but when it comes chasing after me, eventually I turn around to meet it."

"You're not going to play ball."

"Not me, and not Billy Priest. I just wish Patrick had let it be. I told him. I told him too many times."

"You want me to talk to him? I know him pretty well, maybe I can—"

"No, man. That time is over. He's been fucking around with my friends. That I don't forget."

It is the grip of the war on me, something Stern has never seen. He sits. I can feel veins throbbing in my shoulders as the sweat dries and my body takes on its load.

Stern says, "I'm sorry for you, Jones."

I say, "Save it. Someone else is gonna need it."

Halloween. It's early afternoon and the sky is a pale pink.
The trees are perfectly still. I sit on a hill in Grant Park,
arms wrapped around my knees.

Leaves line the sidewalks and snap and crash with
every footstep taken through them.

There is no need for a Halloween in Southeast Asia.
You think we took it all so seriously? Visit any bar any
night and you'd find a ghastly Halloween celebration, a
good old American party, with the grotesque faces and
costumes, and the drinking and screwing in back rooms.

Over there all of it was customary and every day. No
one called time out or labeled it for convenience.

The last October I was there I lived with the woman I
simply called the French girl. I'd been sent back to base
for treatment of wounds, malaria, and superinfection of the
kidneys and pancreas.

I hardly looked at the nurses and checked out on a
pass as soon as they finished with the blood workups. They
didn't care as long as I stayed in the city and checked in
regularly.

That's how command was with us. There were only a
few of us left who'd done the sorties north, and the C.O.'s
all acted like we didn't exist. So we found other things to
do. We didn't talk among ourselves very much, didn't
search other guys out. Buddies stuck together, but I didn't
go looking for Corporal Wolf. We'd worked together on
escape and evasion. And he was in the city. I left him alone.
I went looking for the French girl.

On the outskirts of the city was a row of fine colonial
homes. Not mansions, not really. Homes. Big, tall old
houses, some four stories high, all surrounded by neatly
trimmed grass, set back from the city proper by a block or
two.

Every soldier who went drinking, whoring, or trying to

score a little THC or heroin had to walk past those homes. You'd be in the ugliest, most squalid place you'd seen outside of a Chicago housing project and staring you right in the face were those nice clean homes.

Ask anyone and he'll tell you that the enemy never touched them, never so much as cut across a corner of that property when they came in on sapper attacks. Finally, in 1975, we saw footage of tanks and half-tracks rumbling over the lawns. That sight bothered some guys I know more than seeing the city in flames, watching that last gunboat leave. And some of us, those of us from the north in the early to mid-'60's, just knew that wasn't the last gunboat or, as the newsmen put it, "the last Americans to leave the city."

Everyone associated with it called it the French Quarter. It wasn't even in the city, and it wasn't like what it sounds. It wasn't some area where there were stores and restaurants and bakeries with croissants and café au lait and petits fours.

It was a row of unconnected homes that had remained standing, untouched, for decades.

One night, before I crossed the lawn to the French girl's house, I saw and heard the incoming artillery flatten the bars and buildings just a few dozen meters behind me. It was directed fire, hitting key parts of the city, which meant anywhere they might find our soldiers. Not military targets like ammo dumps or airstrips, but bars and opium dens and little apartments where a soldier would pay a dollar and a couple cigarettes to a fourteen-year-old girl for a blowjob.

That night some men died in those places, and our artillery lobbed up over those colonial houses into the dark. Recon planes spit out coordinates, but we just lobbed those shells over the houses, like tossing a fresh egg from one hand to the other, afraid it might break.

That night, like the first day I had a chance, I went to the home of the French girl and knew I was safe.

I met the French girl after McCoy took me past the houses that time. It didn't seem anything special then. I had liberty and had put a tracer out through a friend of mine at radio HQ, a line on Sharp and where he was staying. And I finally caught up with Sharp. He was never far away.

But that month, that year, I had some time. I went to a few bars and waited. I went back to the place McCoy had taken Ringo and me, but it had taken a direct hit. There was nothing left. I looked at the houses, serene in their constancy, in their peaceful image broken only by the flashes of yellow and orange and white at night when the big guns popped off. I used to like to stand in an alley, braced against a building, and smoke a cigarette down to the fiery end, watching those houses lit up like the cigarette illuminated my blackened face in the shadows. Here one second, gone the next.

I met the French girl in the market across the alley from the rough bars. The market was poor, but it sold fresh fruit and an occasional chicken or pig. We went to the outskirts for fruit not torn up inside, and for meat that hadn't been dead two weeks.

McCoy had told me what he knew about the houses that the war didn't touch, that they were there even before the French takeover, but that forever after they'd been associated with the French.

No one really knew who lived there, how, or why. All the servants were gone. Still, the grounds stayed clean, kept up. The peddlers throughout town knew the people from the houses but would never admit to it. The owners were like ghosts, but alive, somehow surviving unscathed in the midst of death, disease, destruction.

The girl I saw that fall day was no ghost.

In the early '60's some of the old traditional ways persisted. This was before the days when women would fight openly in the streets over a cup of rice. The war had brought money: tremendous wealth to some, stability to others. But the outskirts were poor. In spite of the poverty, the women dressed well to shop. Shopowners and market vendors closed during the heat of midday and remained open long into the cooler evening.

I was the only American there that day. I'd sacked out in my fatigues and timed it so I'd get there just when the market reopened. It worked. I stood in line with a dozen women—me, smelly and unshaven, a big tall American in boots and fatigues and a sidearm, and them, short, older women mostly, dressed in floppy hats and colored print blouses and big, wide, long black skirts.

I paid for my fruit and slipped down against a wall to eat and watch. The day was clear and still; there wasn't much going on. I heard helicopters infrequently, and there was no firing at all.

Across the way the leaves on the trees on mansion property didn't move. Neither did doors or windows, shades or blinds. They were ghost houses, reminders of Dien Bien Phu.

And then, suddenly, from nowhere, there she was, standing in line with the other women. The French girl.

Before the six weeks were over—six weeks of tests and probes and stool samples and doctors who didn't know one end from the other—I lived in her house. I slept there, ate there, almost learned to relax there. She treated me like a man. Not a soldier, or an invader, or an American, or a killer, or anything specific. Just like a man.

That day we talked. I tried broken French and she answered with perfect English. She had been born there but had gone to school briefly in Lyons. She'd come home in spite of war, in spite of the French withdrawal. All the servants were gone now. A handful of French citizens occupied the houses on the city's edge. She lived alone in hers.

I remember her best sitting on one of the verandas at dusk on a humid night. It was quiet, and patches of fog rolled in across the river. Far to the north we saw the smoke rising in the air to obscure the moon. A light rain pattered down through the trees, soaking the clipped green grass.

She had hazel eyes and hair that waved on top and curled when it reached her broad shoulders. Her hair was brown. I can't remember its exact color.

She'd sit in jeans and a white shirt, barefoot, against a pillar and look out across the city, at the sky. I'd sit on the railing or on one of the porch swings.

Occasionally we'd hear bursts of gunfire from along the perimeter, or from the bars a few blocks away.

At first I talked, asked questions, tried to find out more about her. But if she answered at all, she'd just turn the questions around, aim them at me. There was so much I couldn't say: so much I was forbidden, so much I wanted to forget.

When night came on and the colors of the sky faded to black, broken by flashes of light from our battery positions, she'd take my hand and lead me through the floor-length screened-in door to the living room. There she'd unbutton her blouse and unsnap and unzip her pants. She let me do the rest, to take my time. I let her do whatever she wanted.

277

I'd wake early, reacting to the drugs, and usually she was pulled in tight against me, an arm thrown limply across my body, her hair falling over her face.

On the worst nights she rubbed me down with alcohol. Her house was well stocked with medicines, food, the ordinary things we take for granted in a civilized country. She rubbed me down till I broke into sweats, the chills around my joints feeling as if someone were slowly cracking a bone in each joint.

Then she washed away the sweat, keeping cool cloths on my forehead, even draped over my chin and mouth when the humidity was too high to stand.

They stabilized my condition at base—no cure, of course—and repeatedly offered to send me home. I refused.

Four days into that sixth week I got papers sending me back north. I was to work with an elite group. The names listed for liaison and contact were McMichael, Miller, Davis, and Sharp. All veteran corporals but Davis. He was the sergeant in charge.

We didn't talk much that night. She knew from my olive drabs and the machine gun I carried that I was leaving.

We went to the market and later ate chicken—coq au vin—with wine from her cellar. We even ventured outside the city, as far as we dared into the forest. I wore clothes left in a closet—a ruffled French shirt designed for parties and old corduroy pants. I slung the moray and a revolver on under my shirt. She carried two matching pearl-handled .25's in her high riding boots.

We wanted to make love under the trees but were afraid. My hand never left my shirt. Her pockets bulged with extra bullets.

That night I woke in a light sweat and knew she wasn't

on the floor with me. I saw her standing, naked, against the louver doors, watching spotlights in the sky. I walked silently up behind her and pulled her back sharply against me. I put an arm across her shoulder and my other hand around her, gently cupping her breast.

She turned her head only once, to look at my eyes. Hers were shaded in the unnatural light, but they were more than tired. They looked like they were dying, and I pulled away then, but she drew me back against her, and we stayed like that, fucking furiously, until first light.

When I left to take the shots I would need before flying out in two days, she sat in a chair, drinking wine and juice mixed, clad in an unbuttoned shirt.

She said, "They are so happy in France that the Americans are here." I stopped and just looked at her.

When I returned that night she was gone. She didn't return the next day, and I couldn't find her anywhere.

I saw her eyes, so quietly sad, and heard her voice when the gunboat lifted off.

Though I returned twice to the city, and searched the French Quarter and the houses, I never saw the French girl again.

There are hours till dark and the children in costume are starting to make their rounds. I have a bowl of wrapped candy near the door—M&M's, Snickers, Mr. Goodbars. We never get many kids in the apartments. Partly it's the neighborhood, partly the anonymity. We all get the children of good friends who live in the area, but most kids won't go into an apartment they don't know, and if they take the dare, they almost never go beyond the first floor.

I'm dressed in black for this night—boots, pants, T-shirt. My leather jacket is on a chair by the door.

Ray Sharp's letters are spread out on the coffee table

279

in front of me. They go back ten years, but there can't be more than thirty. In fact, I know exactly how many there are: twenty-eight, including the new one that arrived in today's mail.

I've refolded each letter carefully and replaced it in its envelope. That way I can match the undated letters with their postmarks. I've folded and unfolded most of the letters so many times, I've had to tape the folded edges back together. I haven't opened the new letter.

I can hear children on the first floor, their shouts and screams. Someone buzzes my apartment, and I start to get up to answer, when I hear the buzzers in all the other apartments go off all in a row, like sirens. I rest my tired hands on my knees and think of the simplicity of games.

Just seeing the new letter, alone in the mailbox, touched off some gland inside, some physical impulse, a neuron pattern, a jump off the synapse. My gut is strangely cold. Usually it burns and then cramps, but today it is cold as that first splash of water in winter. The codeine I've taken is fighting it, and I tense and relax muscles like they taught me in the hospitals.

For each of the letters spread out before me I've written four or five. At first it seemed like a waste of time, but I stopped feeling that way a long time ago. Sharp isn't wasting time reading letters from me, and never would. *Never* would that be a waste, of his *time*.

The new envelope is small—one of the cheap little ones with his block letters spelling out my name and address, a stamp with Roberto Clemente's face in the upper right corner. Blocked in as return address is "Lock Box A, Knoxville, Tennessee." Such ironies. I wonder what he thinks about when they make him write that.

The smell of dead grass and leaves drifts in through the window. I know that if I look up I can see the trees and the sky beyond the trees, maybe even the sun going down.

Ray Sharp. Five of us came back. Only five. And somehow Sharp and I both made it. But like the song says so well, "For What It's Worth."

I tear the envelope open slowly so it doesn't fall apart. Inside is a single sheet of ruled notebook paper. I unfold it and spread it flat against my knees and begin to read:

T.J. How are you, man? I got a couple letters and haven't gotten around to answering. Sorry, man. Maybe I'll do better. I don't have much to report. I took you up on the exercise plan you mailed me. And my library grows every day. Some of the money I save goes for books, and we get 'em cheap in here.

The shrink sees me every day now. Wants to know what makes me tick; you know. So I talk and talk, sometimes tell him really how it is. Sometimes I lie. I know how to mix it up from the white room you had. Taught me a lot. How to make it. I don't need their pills.

If you come down in December watch the roads. Freezing rain here, the exercise yards are shit for months.

I wish they'd let me keep plants in my cell. Can you bring one down? Maybe they'd let it in if it's from you.

Last week a guy tried to take me down with a shiv he made from a file. Right in the yard, front of everyone. I *had* to turn it on him, man. I had to. It's what I do, what I did best. You and me. And Ringo.

They gave me an extra ten when he died. Don't know what they expect, what they want from *me*, man.

Hey, don't worry. I'll be out on the yard by the time you come. Take you on in the 100.

See you buddy. Stay out of the rain.

—RAY SHARP

All the letters but the first two are from the Tennessee State Penitentiary. Sharp did okay for a few years, then got

281

into a little trouble. He kept moving around, couldn't keep a job. Then he moved to Tennessee and one crazy night broke a table over a deputy sheriff's head down in some little bar. He was in the middle of one of those "country boy" disputes.

The sheriff almost died, they charged Sharp with attempted murder and armed violence, and before I even knew about it they'd given him twenty to thirty years, no good time, no parole. Psychiatric observation. And now you can add ten to that.

I remember Nixon's face on TV before I got the first letter and the "last helicopter" out of Vietnam after.

Five of us "elite corporals" came out.

I see Sharp once a year. He looks the same; exercises as much as he can, still has the reflexes of a coiled wire. They usually leave him alone in there, and that's how he likes it.

We don't talk much. When we do it's usually petty stuff, work, the weather, sports, books.

Sharp's a cook in the Pen. Someone over here has put his skills to use.

Ten more years.

I leave the letters out, swallow capsules without water, grab my jacket and leave. It's dusk.

I pat the jacket pockets like a man checking for money and walk past a bundle of children begging for treats next door. One of them is dressed like a soldier. He could be eight or nine, has greasepaint on his face, and carries a plastic M-14 with a banana clip.

They never get any of it right. I pull the collar of my jacket up and walk toward the el.

*Lake Point Tower is a fortress, designed to be one. Sur-*rounded by thirty-foot-tall walls of sheer concrete, three of its four sides are totally enclosed. The fourth side contains the multiple entrances and drop-off zone for vehicles. There is enough security here—doormen, electric eyes, bulletproof glass—to stop a terrorist attack.

Inside there are apartments, of course, and also stores, beauty parlors, maid service, restaurants, fully-equipped gymnasiums—even a small park on the second or third level, full of grass, trees, and bushes, but accessible only to the lucky few who can afford to live there.

Tom Patrick lives there. It figures.

I'm waiting on one of the dirty and torn side streets so incongruous next to the Magnificent Structure. Maybe Orleans or even Grand. The street is ripped up, one sidewalk just jagged cement blocks, constantly in a state of disrepair. It's dusty and littered with garbage.

The sun's been down for an hour, maybe two. I've lost track. I've scouted him and know he has to walk down this street to get into the building. It's the only way.

It's cooler and the haze hangs a bit more heavily near the lake. It's perfect Halloween weather.

An occasional car braves the potholed streets. Mostly cabs bounce up and down the avenue, picking up and dropping off the rich and famous. Some are dressed for the occasion: fancy, expensive costumes from the best specialty stores.

I look up at the wall and wonder how long it would take me today to scale the thing, with the proper equipment. It's been a long time.

I lean in to the cold concrete and keep an eye out down the block. I know he'll come from down the street, so I ignore most of the stragglers cutting across or turning onto my block from the crosswalk.

Through the soft haze I track the moon and the stars.

There were nights like these overseas, but I push them back and focus on tonight.

A high-priced hooker cuts the corner near me and walks slowly by. She has all the natural equipment of a real model and the accessories of a young executive on the rise—the right shade stockings, the hairstyle, the handbag. But she wears a black leather jacket half unzipped with nothing on underneath. Her auburn hair's color is a little off. And the heels on her shoes are just a bit too high. She's worth good money to some fat ass in that building.

She gives me a look and I return it, then glance at my watch. It's near nine. I don't know how long I've been standing almost motionless on this darkened, decrepit street, waiting for a man.

The night is cool and hazy, but it's Halloween, and that makes it clear, protective, understandable. I don't have to think about the war twelve thousand miles away and almost twenty years ago, about sealed orders, about an elite unit of "killer corporals," about what we did over there, no matter who gave the orders or why.

I'm home, it's Halloween, and I've got business.

I wait and eventually, as I knew he would because I've watched him, Tom Patrick comes walking down the street, my way. He's on the other side and appears to be trying to sober up after a heady costume party. He doesn't see me cross and follow him toward his building, even when I loop around behind. Then he crosses the street back and I go with him and I know he's seen the shadows trailing.

He turns to face his assailant and I finally understand his costume. It looked like he was dressed in ordinary baggy clothes—all green and with lots of zippers, but nothing too weird. But he also appeared to be carrying an oxygen tank on his back and pieces of some sort of hose. A deranged vacuum cleaner salesman? Dustin Hoffman in

The Graduate? Nah. He's a Ghostbuster. And the fright I saw etched into the lines on his face is replaced by relief.

"Shit, Jones, don't sneak up on someone like that." He wraps the hose from his uniform back around his shoulder. I suppose he would have tried to fight with that stupid thing. "You had me going. I saw you cross over and then follow me. I'm not *that* out of it, you know."

I can smell liquor but the walk has done him good. Knowing Patrick, he'd never get so sloshed he couldn't make it home. At playoff games he always had the coolest head around.

He looks at me curiously. "So what brings you to where the better half lives, Jones? I don't suppose you want to play a little ball and couldn't wait to tell me?"

"That's not exactly it, Tom."

"I don't believe in coincidences."

"Me either."

There's silence as we look uneasily into the other's eyes.

"What then?"

"I got to clear something up with you, that's all."

"Now?"

"Now."

"Here on the street? You waited for me out here tonight?" He's looking around to see who's in the neighborhood. Cars. Only cars. Cars with darkened windows and chauffeurs.

"That's right."

"You could have gone in to wait."

"No. It has to be here, right here on the street. A street deal requires a street deal in return."

Patrick belches and brushes away an inadvertent tear.

"No idea what you're talking about, man. You must be loose tonight. Hope your party was as good as mine."

285

He turns to go and I twirl him back with a gentle hand.

"No party, man. Nothing loose. I've just been waitin' here for you."

He steps back and fixes his gaze solidly on me. His eyes aren't bugged out, and I can see a glint in them. He isn't drunk at all. It's all show, to get him by. I don't know about any party, but he's as sharp as I am right now.

"All right, Jones. Speak your piece."

"Word is you've been tampering with a very good friend of mine, and I think you know who I mean."

"So?" He leans against the cement wall and watches me with veiled eyes.

"So. I told you specifically that I wasn't gonna play, that you better leave Billy alone, that you keep your hands off."

"So?"

"So you put your fuckin' hands on, asshole. It wasn't very smart." The adrenaline runs, my face flushes with heat, my temples throb. I've felt it all before, but it's been a while.

"Look, Jones. We didn't fuck with *you*. I talked to you a few times, yeah. And that's all. What we do with Billy Priest is none of your fuckin' business. Don't tell *me* to stay out of it. *You* stay out of what *we* got goin'. I'm talkin' championship season here, Travis boy. Don't get in the way."

Patrick turns to go and I spin him around again. This time, before he can even think to react, I've got him up against the wall with my knee tight against his groin and my forearm pushing hard against his neck. He doesn't move, lets his hands fall limply to his sides.

I haven't been so angry for longer than I can remember. When I found out that Ray Sharp was in prison, I drove down to Tennessee to go his bail and argue his case. I was stopped twice for speeding and tore up the county courthouse when they wouldn't let me see him. It took me a year to pay off the damages. And I spent the weekend in a cell across the hall. We had a good time for those two days.

It's the same kind of anger.

"Now, listen to me, scumbag. You're tryin' to get to that man, maybe already have, using the only way you know how. I pulled him out of the gutter with a needle in his arm and I ain't lettin' you send him back. I don't care what it costs you or what it costs me. I just don't care anymore, Jack, you got that? You got it?"

The knee and the forearm both push until Patrick wheezes and starts turning colors. I continue.

"You know what I can do when I get pissed. You remember the game with the guards back in '79, don't you? Well, dude, I got a message for your limited brain: I'm *pissed*."

With my free hand I slip a switchblade from my jacket pocket and touch the button. Patrick's eyes bulge with fear.

"Stories you don't know about me, Patrick. Things I did and things I saw. Things no man can forget. Billy Priest doesn't know the half of it, what it was like. There was a bunch of us. We didn't even *know* it, you asshole, you stupid little creep. Killer corporals. That's what they called us. And they sent us in on purpose, sent us in again and again till there were only a few of us left. Used us up and threw us away. Another grand military experiment.

"But the things we learned, Tommy boy. You don't want to know the things we learned."

I can feel the sweat rolling down my temples, can feel

the heat in my head, the aching and throbbing. Patrick's eyes are glued to mine. His face is purple and white. I haven't seen that look in a long time. His shallow breath comes in wheezes, gasps.

"Two of us walked out of those jungles together, Tommy. But the jungle never left us. We carry it around inside. Over there they used to call us something because we were so good at it.

"Do you know what they called us, Tommy? Do you know what the grunts would say when they saw one of us comin' or when we were assigned to one of their units?"

He doesn't even try to answer.

"They'd say, 'We got us a cut man,' or, 'There's one of 'em. Cut man.' Everyone knew what it meant.

"Maybe you'd want to find out tonight just what they were talkin' about, hmmm, Tom, old boy? You great gross quarterback asshole."

I lean over and whisper in his ear, the six-inch blade dancing in the streetlight not three inches from his nose.

"I can cut a man's spleen out in ten seconds and you'd think a surgeon had gone in. I am quite ready to offer you a demonstration. Feel ready to donate a kidney to the cause of human rights, and all 'cause you want old Billy to play a stupid little *game* for you. High price, Tommy boy. High. But it's your choice."

He twists his head back and forth.

"That s'posed to mean no, I bet."

He tries to move his head up and down. I drop my forearm and Patrick twists his head every which way, slowly brings his hand up to rub his neck. He has a crazed look in his eye. It's pure fear. It's what I want.

The knife twirls between my palms in front of his face, I flip it onto my finger and balance it, blade down, then

288

juggle it along my fingers to my other hand. My eyes never leave his face. The blade never draws blood.

"You tell me now, tonight, that neither you nor any of your boys will *ever* mess with Billy Priest *ever* again."

"I promise."

"What?"

"I promise!"

"You sure you make that statement without a hint of duress, Tommy boy?"

"Yes! We leave Priest alone. You too. It's the last time I'll ever bring it up. Now just let me go. Please."

The fear has moved. He sweats and shakes. The sweat is rancid. My business here is almost done.

"Okay, Tom. I'm just sorry you never quite got the *point* before tonight."

Patrick is wrapping his arms around his sides. I ease back, let his groin breathe. I slowly close the blade and zip the knife into a pocket.

Patrick looks so absurd. He's white as a starched sheet and shaking in his silly Ghostbusters Halloween outfit. Somehow, though, it fits.

"Can I go now?" He stumbles to get it out.

"Why, sure, Tom. You could have gone on home anytime you wanted. Just remember. I know where you live, and if you ever move, I'll find you."

He gives me one last look and starts slowly for the entrance to Lake Point Tower.

I say, "One more thing, Tom." He doesn't turn but stops, and I wait patiently. Finally he starts to turn to face me and I aim a kick right below his left kidney. It connects and he's on the pavement retching, doubled over, holding the side he'll remember me by for some time to come. I see the look. He doesn't know why. He really doesn't.

"Come on, Tom. Think about it. You just kept pressin' your luck till there was nothin' left to do. Think of it as a Trans-Pacific gift. Twelve thousand miles, to be exact."

I leave him there and walk for the el, tossing capsules down, that refrain infecting my head: "Who you gonna call? Ghost-*busters!*"

The cut man dream begins, as I knew it must. It had been chasing me for too long—this time, I had put it off for, literally, years. But I knew I could not hold out forever.

In a way, the dream reminds me of the clinic, the white room. None of us ever really escaped that place. And so does the dream stalk me.

Sgt. Davis took us on an extended march through jungle too thick for helicopters to penetrate. It was Sharp, Miller, McMichael, me. Davis had the orders. All he told us was to keep slogging. We had a mission beyond the jungle and only two days to get there.

McMichael followed Davis and carried the MZ-84. He had a pair of M-14's strapped to his shoulders. When we reached the swampy part of the "trail" that Davis followed, McMichael passed the bug juice back to the rest of us. Davis never stopped, just stepped through the mud and pools of stagnant water heavy with mosquitoes and flies as big as small birds.

Miller brought up the rear, hurriedly covering our trail when he could, slopping mud or moss over the new breaks in green branches. Sharp and I, in the middle, carried his equipment for him so his hands would be free.

The jungle was dense, but somehow the sun found us and added to our misery. We didn't stop except to urinate. We had taken diphenoxylate tablets for a day before we started and took more with the chocolate and crackers we ate whenever Davis gave the sign. Our shit would just have to wait till we got to wherever we were going. Davis kept walking. No stops.

We plodded on through darkness until Davis couldn't even see over the brush and trees. Without the sky as a tool, we had to rely solely on the trail. And the trail had run down to a snake's path sometime that afternoon. After an hour Davis stopped and let us come in.

We stood silently in water up to our calves while Miller looked for higher ground, somewhere to dry out. Our faces were pasty white in the darkness. Sharp noticed, so we all smeared mud on our foreheads and pulled the bandannas up over our noses.

Miller gave the sign—the broken branch code we'd worked out long ago—and we sloshed through water and muck to a little island of grass and dirt, but no mud. It felt spongy beneath my boots, and I was glad rain wasn't in the forecast, and that we were leaving at first light. We dumped equipment onto the driest land and Sharp and I took the perimeter search, a 180-degree sweep by each of us fifty meters out.

Just as I turned back in toward the tree we'd marked with one slash of Sharp's knife, the ground gave way beneath me and I was floundering in slime and water past my waist. I knew Sharp was completing his half circle, that he'd be looking for me, so I waited, holding my M-16 over my head, trying to catch onto something, anything, with my feet, looking for a piece of wood heavy enough to heave myself onto.

I felt like I was walking on air, in slow motion. I wasn't sinking, really, just slowly subsiding into water heavier than the water I knew, into land lighter and soggier than any land I'd ever known.

Then without a word or sign Sharp was before me, testing the earth with the toe of his boot. I wondered how much he could feel, just how close the toe was to the end of that boot. Funny how we think sometimes.

And as if in answer to my thoughts, Sharp stretched back and lay flat on his chest, inching ever closer, now probing the swampland with one of his knives held at arm's length ahead of him.

All I could see was the body crawling closer like a big tropical snake—slowly, as if stalking wary prey. Even the knife blade had been blued so it wouldn't glint. All of our blades had been.

Then he found it: the last firm piece of ground before the invisible dropoff. He stood up and I could see the whites around his eyes like two marbles with spots in the middle, rolling in unison in the darkness at an impossible height.

He was only a meter away.

Sharp was working something loose from his hip pack. He hissed a signal to me and I tossed him the gun, which he stacked next to his against a tree stump. He was fastening something to an irregular plank of wood when we heard the code from Davis, not twenty meters away. It was taking us too long. Sharp kept tying something to the wood, and I could picture McMichael and Miller methodically setting up the MZ-84 and the collapsible mortar for crossfire, ready for the fiercest black attack in decidedly unfriendly country.

Just as response time wound low, Sharp dropped the piece of wood and answered in code on the tree stump: "Okay, coming in, ten minutes." Davis answered. We knew if we weren't in in those ten minutes, Davis had to believe they had either our code, or us, or both. He'd have no choice but to sink farther into the swamp and light up the night with flares before they could be overrun. Sharp had to work fast.

He clicked his fingers and was ready for the toss. The bar of heavy wood landed to my left, but I pulled it in and got it out of the mire in a second. I scooped slime off of its ends and discovered Sharp had tied onto the wood on both ends with some kind of wire, heavy stuff. I looked over for a nod, for some idea of what he had in mind, but he was gone. The rifles were gone. I felt a moment of panic deep in my gut but I couldn't let it take over. I pulled gently on the bar of wood and the wires tensed, then relaxed, tensed, then relaxed.

Sharp was still there, somewhere, in the fetid black illness of the jungle, ready to help me out.

Sweat was pouring down the heavy lines below my cheekbones, beneath the dark cloth. I couldn't feel anything below my chest. It was as if I were weightless. Then I felt Sharp's final tug and I grasped the piece of wood until my knuckles begged to pop through my skin. And I felt a tremendous tug at my shoulders and my waist at the same time. Somehow, I'd moved a little closer to drier land.

The next yank almost popped one of my shoulders, but I knew how to jam my arm down to stop the shoulder separation even while it was happening. I was a meter closer to Sharp, and a few more millimeters out. My boots still couldn't find anything solid. They walked in place through the deep water as if it were air.

Now I could see Sharp. He was facing away from me, on his knees, both guns wrapped against the back of his neck and held in place by his shoulders and his arms hanging along the barrels and stocks. His head was down and he wasn't moving. Just barely I saw the wires stretching from the guns to my plank of wood.

He looked like the figure of Jesus in the Church of St. James the Apostle, the Anglican "high church" in Chicago that my mother had insisted we attend once each year

293

. . . till one year, when I was sixteen, I refused to go and never set foot in an Episcopal church again.

Sharp got up, slowly, and hunched his shoulders for another pull. He lurched ahead and I tried to help but time was running out on us, and it was all Sharp, straining, doubled over, jerking each shoulder back and forth to try to pry the mud away from my right or left side long enough for me to reach land.

I dove headfirst for the oily, grassy slick. It was a dangerous move: either I'd make it or find myself face-down in the swamp with all my weight pulling me downward and backward.

But with that dig I'd launched myself far enough so Sharp could drop the guns quickly and wedge them between two trees. Just as I started to slip under, his arms were beneath my shoulders, pulling, before I lost all balance, and I knocked the bar of wood away and dug into the soil with both hands. I looked up into Sharp's eyes and pulled even harder until I felt my legs again, squirming up onto the grass.

We were drenched in sweat, sprawled out across a patch of firm ground in the middle of water that looked like land.

Finally Sharp stood up and helped me to stand. We stood there like thieves, only our eyes visible to the night, and I thanked him without a word.

He pitched me my gun and we double-timed in. Davis had given us twelve minutes, not ten, but it was a tense camp. McMichael had lodged his machine gun in the fork of a tree. He dropped down from a branch as Davis waited for the report.

Sharp whispered, "Nothin' within sixty meters, maybe more." I nodded. Davis looked at me. Sharp said, "Sinkhole. The trail's the only safe way." I scraped mud and putrid strings of moss and decayed vegetable matter off my fatigues. Davis looked me over.

"You be okay till we can dry you out in the sun?" He didn't whisper. He was satisfied that we had a decent perimeter to talk and work within.

"No problem," I muttered as Miller cut vines and trailers from my legs with a knife.

"Take some penicillin anyway. Your kit's strung up in the tree. Can't afford to lose a man, no matter how." His voice was weary, more burdened than I'd ever heard it, so I nodded without an argument and Sharp threw me the pills and a canteen of fresh water.

Davis looked at his watch and said, "I'll do the cigarettes but fast. Sixty meters isn't far. Line up and roll up your sleeves and your pantlegs. Then empty your boots."

McMichael rolled up his sleeves. We could see leeches six inches long feeding around his massive biceps. Davis burned them off with a cigarette tip and stepped on them when they fell.

It took three cigarettes to clear us. Strangely, I had the fewest—only three. We had picked them up and had been carrying them half that day from the fresh water areas of the trail.

Sharp was last. He said his legs were clean as Davis burned them off his neck. I took the cigarette and did Davis, then dropped it into a dirty pool of water. The ground was covered with the bloody, pus-filled half bodies of dead and dying leeches.

Davis hustled Sharp and me into the highest branches of the tree that would hold our weight, then climbed onto lower branches across from Miller. McMichael pulled ground duty. Leeches, bugs, snakes, bothered him less than the rest of us. He just reached out and killed anything that bothered him.

There'd be no guard tonight. We all needed the sleep.

The last thing I saw before I nodded off was Ray Sharp cutting a long black leech off his leg with his moray knife.

Light had hardly suffused the horizon when we set off along the trail that had narrowed even farther. It couldn't have been a foot wide. The marshland slowly disappeared as we entered a forest of broken bamboo. It slowed us tremendously. Just a prickle from a bamboo shoot would break even McMichael's tough skin, so we had to go slowly to avoid the sharp branches on both sides.

The sun was high when Davis raised a hand for a rest. We sat gingerly among the bamboo. We looked like some great sign of death, sitting there quietly within the garden of brown and white bone. A large bird flew silently over, alone, but did not block out the sun.

Miller said, out of the blue, "I've got a bad feeling about this one, boys," and then was silent. He spoke to no one in particular.

Sometimes it happened. Everything would be going smoothly and all of a sudden, out of nowhere, a guy would start talking like that. Some guys would give away their most private possessions. All of them grew pensive and quiet. They were, in some ways, the scariest times I have known from the war.

Hearing it from Miller—reliable, wisecracking Miller— put us all on edge. Davis told us to saddle up and move out. We had an hour or two at most to get where we were going. Only Davis knew where that was.

We moved a little faster now, in the same order, and soon we were past the bamboo forest and walking a widened, firm jungle trail. The only dangers we could see now were occasional snakes, small but venomous, that whipped like little pieces of rope across our boots.

Miller lagged behind, straightening elephant grass,

splinting broken green branches with bits of vine. When the path widened, Sharp and I trudged along together, peering back at Miller, who knelt in the brush at the side of the trail.

I never heard the shot, but one second Miller was kneeling there and the next he was gone and the unit was in the brush at the side of the trail, and Sharp was dragging me down after him.

It was quiet then. There were no more shots. After a few seconds the birds and reptiles and insects began their clamor again. Davis signaled Miller with the new code, twice, but we heard no answer. We looked up into the great leafy trees, strewn with vines and foliage growing up trunks and along branches, making it twice as thick as ordinary trees. Nothing.

Sharp was flat on his back with field glasses, scanning the trees over and over. McMichael cradled the big machine gun, ready to swivel it wherever Sharp pointed. Davis was studying the trail maps to see how far out we were, to see what it would take to come on in. That left me with nothing really important to do, so I took an M-14, got up on my knees to see where Miller had gone down, and stood up and ran high and fast to that spot.

I heard Sharp's shout behind me, just once, and McMichael pulling his gun's bolt. I was running hard across the packed earth, not even bothering to weave, just looking for a soft place to land.

It couldn't have been more than forty meters, and the land was level, so it might have taken me five, six seconds from the moment I stood up to the moment I burst upon the two figures stalking each other, only meters apart. All I had time to do was see which one was American. I emptied all twenty rounds into the other one, who convulsed and jumped and started to crawl away and then stopped.

I stood over him, forgetting there could have been—probably were—more out there. He had been a short man, about five feet tall, and he wore friendly army fatigues with the sleeves and pantlegs cut off. A Russian sniper rifle, scoped and heavily padded in camouflage cloth, lay at an angle across one foot. The flies were already doing a dance on his face and chest and I turned to Miller as Davis came up slowly, Sharp on the flank, McMichael back with the monster machine gun. Davis was looking up and Sharp was looking down and I was looking at Miller.

He'd been creeping forward in the tall buck grass, pulling himself along with his knife. His gun lay some five meters back on the trail. He was flat on his back now, eyes closed, smiling, gulping breaths.

He didn't even open his eyes when he said, "Shit, Jones, you do tend to arrive quickly, don't you? Mind, I'm not complainin', but you almost killed me with a heart attack. Just when I was ready to finish that dude off too."

I monotoned, "Miller. You didn't even have a gun. Why'd you leave your *gun* back there, asshole?"

He jumped up and sheathed the knife. "Maybe I wanted to join you 'elite cut men,' man." He picked up his rifle. "And maybe I didn't have much choice in the matter." A steel-jacketed round had cut into the stock of his rifle just above where his right hand should have been.

Davis came up and asked, "You okay, Miller?" Miller nodded. Sharp was checking the body for papers or ID. Davis tossed me a full clip and I switched them.

I told Miller I'd take last man duty. Davis signaled us out, following McMichael's huge form taking up most of the trail.

"You know, Jones," Miller drawled from up ahead, "I feel a whole lot better about this mission now." He was counting detonators as he walked, oblivious to heat, the jungle, everything.

"Nice to hear you say so," I muttered, and tossed twigs and grass where Miller was leaving a track. Looking back on it now, I sometimes think I should have known something about the mission, but I didn't. Not any more than anyone else.

The outrider from the base spotted us at exactly the same moment Sharp, out on point now, saw him. Everyone quickly found cover till Davis and the sentry exchanged codes at least three times. We had to be certain the codes hadn't been "compromised," as they said at HQ. We'd been losing patrols and even bigger units through bungled communications and stolen codes. Rumors had come down to us and we sat on 'em. There was enough pressure already on the privates and Pfc's.

The sentry was a corporal from a unit that had been stationed far to the west for several years. That's all he told us before bringing us into base in dead silence.

Base was small and thrown together. They'd shored up a stand of wood against a thick patch of high thatch, grass, and other foliage, so we had one side protected. Two tents had been pitched against the backdrop. The rest of the area consisted of dirt, mud, a latrine in the wood, and a number of sleeping holes.

We dumped our stuff while Davis went to find the C.O.

"Shit, man, this is worse than that piece of crapola we had last year," Sharp complained. He was sitting on his helmet, which rested on a tree stump on the edge of camp. He took vicious strokes out of a piece of soft wood with one of his knives.

Miller added, "Well, gentlemen, I have seen worse. At least we're not living in a swamp." McMichael had lain down next to Sharp and trained his big gun on the rest of the camp. He tilted his helmet down over his eyes.

"I don't like this, Jones," he drawled. "Let me know if Davis gets jerked around or if you see somethin' funny. I got it covered." Then he appeared to doze off.

The camp was too quiet. Davis and the sentry had gone into one of the tents to report, and there was no one else in camp. We knew there were supposed to be three groups similar to ours already in, and one or two more were expected. So where were they?

I took the field glasses and scanned the brush on all three open sides, as well as the trees. I traded the M-14 for an M-16—more rounds—and was leaning down to whisper into Sharp's ear when Davis and the sentry emerged from the larger of the two tents.

Miller kept stringing detonators together with malleable fuse and packets of plastique every meter or so. I tapped Sharp on the shoulder and he sidled over to the left, near the edge of camp, as Davis plopped down on another tree trunk, took his helmet off, and scratched the lice and insects out of his hair.

"C.O.'s sick. Dysentery or somethin'. As if he's the only one." Davis didn't notice the sentry ease off into the brush again, but the rest of us did.

"Well, coach, what's the plan?" McMichael mumbled it out so you could hardly tell he was awake.

"I guess we wait for one more unit to come in. Then we break the seal on these orders." Davis pulled a long brown envelope, sealed, and wrapped in watertight plastic from his shirt. "Funny. That Frog wanted me to turn them over to him till the other unit comes in. I said no way. Strict orders about that."

Miller kept stringing the explosives from his pack. "Always by the book, eh, Sarge?"

300

Davis just looked at him.

But Miller was onto something, so he took it, aired it out. "Frog, you say, sir?"

"Don't call me sir!"

"Right. Frog, though, eh? Don't suppose it's the same guy Franklin told Jones here and me about late one miserable night back south. Tall dude, black beret, no insignia, shoulder-holstered Parabellum?"

Davis poured water across his face. "Hate to disappoint you, Miller. This Frenchie's short and squat, speaks with an accent, carries no sidearms. Just what the *hell* are you doing, Miller? Those aren't exactly toys you're foolin' with there."

"Excuse me, sir, but I'm afraid you've been a sergeant too long. I told you I had a funny feeling about this mission. Doesn't it strike you as odd that there are *no men* in this camp?"

McMichael mumbled, "Already *struck* me."

"There's supposed to be fifteen or twenty, like us, here."

Sharp called over from the side, "They can't all be on sentry, or patrol, or out collecting firewood."

Davis put his helmet back on and twisted around, surveying the camp. He looked tired, surprised, worried.

"What about you, Jones?"

"The salami ain't kosher, coach. We better be on our way till we know what's what."

Davis stood up, saying, "But Lavey told me the camp—"

I cut him off. "*Who?* That dude in there is a Frog named *Lavey?*" I held Davis by the arm.

"Yeah. He said—"

It was cut off by a series of pistol shots from one of the tents and Davis's chest burst open in front of me. He fell

301

straight down at my feet, already dead. For one second there was silence. Then we all dove in different directions, all except McMichael, who pushed his helmet back and raked the tent twice. There was no response.

I saw the sentry run in. I saw the confusion on his face, and we held off shooting. When he reached the center of camp, just when I thought he'd have to make a decision, a tripod-mounted M-60 placed somewhere near the doorway of the other tent cut him down, dropped Miller where he knelt trying to reel in his detonation chain, followed my backward flip into the underbrush. I knew Sharp was moving that way but I had to get to Miller, and McMichael put fire down so I could.

I cut behind him as the two guns choked and spat at each other at almost point-blank range. When I reached Miller he was lying on his side, shielding the explosives from the M-60 with his body, and as I lifted his head up, the M-60 sputtered and stopped. McMichael's MZ-84 kept raking both tents for a solid minute and then was silent.

I smelled shell casings and blood and bent down to hear Miller cough and whisper, "Deliver this present for me, will you, Jones?" I opened his shirt but there was too much blood. He put a bloody hand onto mine and said, "I told you I had—"

Sharp's grenades took out both tents as Miller's body convulsed once. His muscles all relaxed suddenly. I drew the chain of explosives around my arm like I was hauling in lengths of rope. Sharp was walking cautiously toward the tents, bayonet ready. McMichael sat behind his gun, lighting a cigarette. He called out, "Sharp. Better check that sentry on your way back in," and then returned to the cigarette, just sitting.

I was trying to piece it together but too much had

happened too fast. Sharp came out of the tents at a run and stopped to look the sentry over. I piled Miller's stuff into a rucksack and hitched it onto my pack. I heard Sharp come up, heard him say, "Just dumb hill people. Sentry's dead, looks righteous," and he started to tell McMichael he was one lucky bastard when he stopped.

I picked up Davis's sealed orders and stuck them in my shirt, picked up an M-16, and shoved extra clips into my thigh pockets.

"So it's just us. Let's get the fuck out of here." I was looking around like a kid afraid he's lost a toy, when I saw Sharp standing, just leaning on his gun, looking from McMichael to me.

McMichael was saying, "You three dudes get out of here. Not that it hasn't been my pleasure, but I'm hunkered down here and feeling real restful. Take them orders and do her right."

I walked around in front of him and saw how the machine-gun holes had crisscrossed his chest. The bullets would have cut a smaller man in half. There was no way McMichael could still be alive.

"I know Miller's probably screwin' off in the woods with that damn plastic of his. Collect him and get out."

Sharp looked at me. McMichael couldn't turn his head at all.

The ash of the cigarette dropped into a puddle of blood on his chest, hissed, and disappeared. Sharp lit him another cigarette, put it in his mouth. McMichael's fingers were locked around the MZ-84's trigger guard.

"Need some cover, maybe." He looked up at me, with difficulty. The blood formed a muddy little pool on both sides of him. "You are three tough bastards. I knew enough about you, Jones, when I saw you doggin' my jeep into camp." He'd puff on that cigarette and look from Sharp to me. He couldn't move anything but the muscles in his face. "I'll be cool."

Then his face froze, his lips clamped onto the cigarette, his eyes halfway between Sharp and me. I reached down and took the cigarette out of his mouth and threw it into the dirt.

"*What* the *fuck*, Sharp! *What* the goddamn *fuck*!"

Sharp grabbed a pack and an M-16. "Roll, Jones. We got somethin' to do."

His voice was quiet, distant. Sharp was his most dangerous when he sounded like that.

We headed out 180 degrees from the way we came in. Sharp was saying in that same monotone, "No tags. We got the orders. You got the C-4. McMichael holds the base for us." I nodded. He looked alive as anything, propped up behind his big gun.

"Sharp." I'd almost forgotten.

"Yeah."

I had to ask. "Lavey?"

"Gone. No sign."

Somehow I knew. We walked on into the jungle.

About ten klicks out we slowed, took bearings, looked at the trail map. We were clear, we figured, but we wanted at least a day's forced march between us and whoever had broken the code and set us up.

A kilometer farther northwest the marsh began to suck at our boots again. We kept on, shoving the vines away from our faces with gun butts. When it got so tight we could barely squeeze through, we still kept on, Sharp hacking away at the trailers strung with moss with one of his knives, his longest and thickest. He was like a surgeon snipping and gouging, as if the patient otherwise would surely die.

There were only the sounds of the jungle—the jungle and our boots being pulled downward and the faint sound of the blade carving us a path to the middle of the swampland.

We stopped instantly, as if we could read each other's thoughts, when we found the perfect place to bed down. We were standing in water a foot deep. No fading sunlight penetrated this enclosure. We couldn't see the trees even four or five meters away for the lushness of vegetation.

Three trees formed an odd little triangle before us: two side by side, maybe a half a meter apart, and another two meters away. There was no solid ground, but the branches in the trees could be clipped safely without our losing any cover.

We silently strung up hammocks from our packs, fishnet-style army issue hammocks that weighed an ounce and could hold two hundred pounds. We tied them from the pair of trees to the other tree, head to foot. The trees were too skinny to hold us, and we needed the sleep.

We stashed everything together in one pack and hung it by nylon cord from the third tree—everything except our guns. We talked in low tones about trying to dry our boots off during the night that was advancing like a dark cloud over the swamp, and rejected the idea. If we were surprised, we'd be dead.

So we sat in uniform, boots on, even helmets on, bandannas up against the mosquitoes. I pulled Davis's sealed orders from my shirt, slit the waterproof plastic with the moray blade, and carefully opened the envelope.

Inside was a single piece of paper headed by an unimpeachable code, all numerical, that we'd all memorized back in Monterey. It was used only for the most important and secret communications. I read the orders once, again, and again, then handed them to Sharp.

The sun was down. He read them in the dark while I closed my eyes and tried not to think. And then he whispered them out loud, in disbelief:

DATE RECOUNT REPORT: BRITISH OFFICER JONES
FRENCH OFFICER LAVEY COMPROMISED.
TERMINATE IMMEDIATELY WITH EXTREME PREJUDICE
REPEAT DATE RECOUNT CODE COMPLETED.

We lay in the hammocks awake for a long time. There really wasn't a whole lot to say.

An hour before first light we slipped into the marsh water and aimed ourselves back east, and north. Most of the equipment we left in the tree. We carried guns, the pack of Miller's explosives, food and water, and Davis's trail maps.

This was one sealed order that we were going to carry out ourselves.

The way back wasn't too different from the way out. Same terrain, same heat, same snakes in the water and hanging from the trees. As we veered north we found more arable, tillable land. The pockets of marsh water disappeared. We found ourselves trying to stay concealed up on a rolling plain that reached over low hills toward China.

I let Sharp take point, by a few meters, just a precaution so we wouldn't both be cut down by the same gunner, or grenade. But I was right on behind him, dogging his footsteps.

That might be how I remember Sharp best, though I carry a lot of images of him around with me. No matter what anyone tells me, no matter what the nightmares say, Sharp will always be the point man to me.

Sometimes in dreams I see us as if from the air: two stick figures moving slowly along a series of green, rolling hills. On one side there is the impenetrable swamp. On the other the green stretches away forever.

The sun was bright and harsh at first, but as we traveled, a crosswind picked up, and though it can't be called cool, it was then to us. A few hundred meters to our left a ridge appeared and paralleled our trail, what we had worked out by the maps that morning.

Sharp veered in toward that ridge, which was sparsely populated with dwarf trees. I followed him in, and we were relieved to dump our packs, guns, helmets, to drop the bandannas and eat a lunch of dried fruit, chocolate, and water. We ate without speaking, then pulled out the maps to chart what we planned to do.

"We're a few hours from the Huo Kang River. I figure we might find Lavey there." Sharp hadn't even reconned the area, so he spoke quietly.

"Why the Huo Kang? Maybe he slipped farther east: shit, he might even have gone south."

Sharp's mouth was set in a line. He rubbed dirt out of the sweat covering his neck. "If he went south, we'll find him. But he didn't. It doesn't make sense. The Huo Kang is the only navigable river in the area. If he went straight east he'd be in swamps too dense to land a gunboat into. He needs someplace to hide, man. He's got to know his friends didn't get us all. He's got to know about the orders."

I dug through the medical kit looking for the antibiotics as he spoke. I found some sulfasalazine and swallowed a handful of tablets.

Sharp said, "How you doing, Jones?"

I closed the kit and swung a pack up on my back, put my helmet on, strapped my rifle across my back. "Roaches doin' a tap dance on my intestines. Let's get outta here, Sharp. If you're right, we'll be there by dark."

Sharp got up off his helmet and saddled. We stepped away from the trees into the glare of sunlight and we kept the bandannas down.

Not an hour later the green grass and brush turned even richer. We could see the dirt change shades just about every kilometer.

Two hours later we were climbing a low rise and could hear the quick click of the language. We crawled to the top and looked over, grass and weeds netted into our helmets.

There was a narrow plain below, covered with flowers, all in long rows. The plain looked like it had been carved out of the grass with a machine. It was too perfect. The rows were also precise, long, heavily dotted, with flower growing right on top of flower.

At the end of the strip farthest from us, four women stood amid the flowers, chattering, arguing, laughing as they pulled flowers away from their leaves, looking quickly beneath each leaf, inspecting each one.

I tapped Sharp on the helmet and we bellied back down the rise and double-timed a parallel path a few hundred meters to the west.

We skirted the women and their patch of pretty flowers.

Sharp asked, as soon as we were safely by, "The women?"

"Hill people. Don't know which tribe, which dialect. Picked up some snatches. Nothin'." I was getting a bad feeling about this. I wondered if it had been the same for Miller.

"Sharp."

We were slowing, walking back toward our river path, and we stopped dead when I put my hand on Sharp's shoulder.

"What? We gotta *go*, man."

"Those women back there."

"Yeah." He was cleaning mud from the action of his M-16.

"That was *opium* they were harvesting back there."

"*What?*" He just looked at me, the gun barrel cold and dark against his hands.

"Opium. Opium flowers. They were weedin' out dead leaves. Givin' the good plants a chance to grow."

"Shit."

"I figure it's one big opium field from here to the river and beyond. That's why the land's so good. That's why it hasn't been farmed. This is somebody's private opium paradise."

"Oh, shit." It was rare that Sharp let you know what he was thinking by the tone of his voice, but he did it this time.

Then he almost spat out, "So from here to the river we're gonna see these women—men, kids, troops, shit, who knows who—workin' on those fields. Guns?"

"Probably troops too. Definitely guns. Looks like a rich crop, good year. These will not be friendly hill people."

Sharp looked around like he was trying to find something he'd just lost.

"What do ya say?"

I pulled out the map we'd figured would lead us to the Huo Kang. I flipped it open but didn't really look at it very closely.

"I say we sneak around 'em, go through 'em, cut 'em down if we have to. I say we go. All the way to the Huo Kang."

Sharp looked at me closely. "Orders?"

I folded the map and pulled the bandanna up. "Sure, orders. Let's go."

Sharp wasn't ready. "You knew that British dude. I don't believe you, man."

I looked him hard in the eye. "I knew 'em both. Now, let's go."

Sharp pulled his bandanna over his mouth. This time I took point.

By dusk, we'd passed a half-dozen opium farms, each one larger and deeper and better protected than the last. We passed them close enough to smell the guards' cheap cigarettes. We tried to go in farther east and found the vegetation even more lush, even more dense. We crawled slowly down the rows at the periphery of one field when we found both ridges guarded by hill people and brown uniforms with AK-47's.

We were almost strolling past the guards of a plot that strung out acre by acre, when Sharp and I smelled it at the same time: fish. Raw fish being eaten by some of the guards at their posts. No one in Southeast Asia ate fresh or raw fish in the interior. We had to be within a kilometer of the Huo Kang.

The brush and trees were more dense the farther we went past that one last farm. We pulled over and checked the gear. We opened the medical kit and split it: morphine, syringes, drugs, rubber hose to tie off with, all went into one of my thigh pockets. Gauze, cotton, bandages, antiseptic, and tape went into Sharp's left thigh fatigue pocket.

I took the maps and chocolate and zipped them into a sleeve pocket. Sharp took the dried meat squares and dried fruit. Before pitching our packs and the canteen, we both took long hits of fresh water. It was the last we expected to taste for a couple days. Or ever. Luck was the unspoken factor. That and skill. I took another small handful of sulfa tablets, and we both liberally fertilized the area. The diphenoxylate can't keep your shit in you forever.

310

And Sharp rigged a fast *punji* stick with an extra knife blade he always carried, coating the blade with shit and suspending it with a piece of elastic at groin level under the biggest tree around, the kind of place troops might be likely to frequent.

"Mean little bastard, ain't ya?" I whispered.

"Just wanna let 'em know I was here."

We checked the guns and clips. We took as many as we could carry with our arms free and buried the rest. We split a dozen grenades. And we checked our knives. We'd probably have to use 'em.

I carried a boot knife and a moray down my back in a neck sheath. Both blackened, both double-edged, razor-sharp. And I had a razor sewn into my fatigues, secured in cork.

Sharp carried two morays, one in his neck sheath and one in a shoulder sheath. He carried a boot knife with a nine-inch blade. And on his belt he had a folding commando knife. It wasn't much more than a straight razor. That's how he liked it.

All of his knives had been blued and sharpened until there was nothing more you could do with them.

We put our helmets on and fixed the chinstraps. Double bandannas covered our necks and faces both. Then we worked on the small areas of flesh that showed with a heavy mud paste of that rich, dark earth.

And we left. Sharp went first because he'd memorized the landmarks to the river and because I carried the only pack left: Miller's long string of plastic explosives, fuse, and detonators, all wired together to blow any one of a number of ways.

Kilometers are short distances, even when you're pussy-footing along, as we were. We looked for rocks and broken tree branches. We slipped through patches of moonlight

311

toward the leafiest trees, those that provided maximum cover. But in ten minutes, maybe fewer, we started to smell the river. Partly dank. Partly fresh. A breeze hit us in the face. The breeze meant the river was probably wide, and fast, and deep.

We heard voices beyond the next tight band of trees. When we huddled, Sharp told me they had to be on our side of the river. I told him they sounded Thai or Chinese to me but I couldn't be sure.

We bellied through the light grass. It was like being home, that grass—not elephant or bush grass. It felt like it had been *cut*, it was so smooth, so soft, so green. I could see the color vividly even in the blackness.

And then I saw Sharp check his boot knife. And I remembered the order. And the sentry being cut down. And Miller dying in the forest. And Davis, the only sergeant I ever really liked. And last, but most, McMichael. McMichael was who sent me in. Later I thought of the nuns carrying Lavey's satchel charge, the dope being sold on the streets of the cities over there, orders, duty. But that was later. I went in because of the last thing I saw on McMichael's face.

Everything checked out right and we went for the voices. Crawling side by side, we had only gone a couple hundred meters when we saw the camp. Several tents had been pitched against the outline of the moving water. A short guard tower, maybe fifteen meters tall, stood up on the camp's left perimeter. On the right, where an old Huey sat on the bare ground, boxes of ammunition had been piled high.

Low gasoline lanterns lit up the camp. It was big enough for twenty, twenty-five men. The guards wore brown uniforms and fatigues. All of them had automatic weapons on their shoulders. One man sat on the railing of the guard tower. His still form silhouetted the sky.

I looked over at Sharp. He was a black form lying perfectly still in that low grass. Only his eyes moved, almost imperceptibly in the dark.

The guards spoke a Thai dialect. Four of them stood around one of the gasoline lamps, smoking. One or two of them appeared to be drunk, or high.

Similar lamps lit up three of the five tents. Vague forms moved in shadowy patterns inside.

Boxes were piled around the tents. Some were standard U.S. army issue food and drugs. Others were lettered in Chinese, and several were blank.

We could hear the rushing of the river's current now. It must have been partially dammed upstream; usually the current would have been lazy, but it virtually roared along only a few meters from the camp. The camp had to be temporary, new, or the tents would have been replaced by hootches on stilts.

Luckily the breeze blew in our faces. I doubted that they could have picked up our swamp stink anyway, but Thai opium farmers can smell almost anything anywhere. I guessed that they were Thai, no matter what the uniforms said.

So we studied the scene for quite a long time. A guard tower had been likely, and the river was expected. We didn't care about the number of men. But we hadn't counted on a helicopter. We had to blow it for sure.

I leaned over to Sharp and in the faintest of whispers suggested a plan.

"We need to get the sentry and the chopper," I hissed over the short, clipped phrases of the guards and the gentle roar of the river water.

Sharp studied the distance between the two. His voice was a hoarse rasp.

"You blow the chopper. Set a charge for two to three minutes after we hit the tents. I'll take the sentry down and meet you behind the tents."

We both knew this was how it had to be—Sharp was the best cut man and we needed the sentry dead silently. We didn't discuss what we'd have to do once we met behind the tents. We never talked about it, before that moment or since. Simply, it was clear.

I interrupted Sharp's memorization of the camp. "I figure the river is our best bet. Right direction, good speed right here anyway. She curves around down south and narrows. We take her in the dark, we might make it." I could see Sharp's nostrils flare beneath his bandanna.

He said evenly, quietly, "Don't use all the C-4 on the chopper. Bring what's left around back with you."

That was all. All we could do was hope we hadn't missed periphery guards, hope those by the tents would keep talking, hope there were no wrinkles. And hope that the men we'd come to get were in one of those tents. Maybe that was hoping a lot, but there was never a doubt in my mind. It all added up to Lavey and Jones sitting on camp stools smoking their pipes, figuring how much crop their farms would produce in the markets of Southeast Asia . . . and probably elsewhere.

In spite of the breeze, sweat ballooned under my armpits, around my thighs, down my back. I felt the brown envelope of orders covered in plastic in my shirt.

Sharp hissed at me and pointed to the "9" on the face of his watch. That was our sign to go, when the minute hands swept around to nine.

With just a whisper of movement, just a rustle, Sharp

was off for the guard tower and I was digging through the grass, crab-scuttling, knowing what I had to do and what would happen if one of us were seen, or if Sharp got his man too fast before my job on the chopper was complete. I hadn't seen any floodlights, but one flare would do it to us just as easily.

The grass was cool and soothing to my face. Before I could think, my hands were on the base of the old chopper. I twisted around, saw the guard in the tower, pulled a length of C-4, fused, from the pack and cut it free. As I clicked the detonator to five minutes I saw something black, quick as a cat, scramble up the ladder to the guard post.

Briefly, only for an instant, two men stood there. Then there was one, and then none, and I was skirting the chopper and the boxes of ammunition, dropping detonators in among them, a bit of freelance since I was in the neighborhood. I didn't waste time bellying. I ran, low to the ground but fast, my gun in both my hands, the noise of the river on rocks and wood a music to my ears. It wasn't nice music.

The guards' voices were louder and I could pick out phrases, whole sentences. Stuff about going down with the sweetest and youngest farm girls. I'd heard it all before, all but one who talked about the best whore he'd ever had, in Malaysia. Malaysia?

I threaded a natural path along the river's shoreline and saw Sharp coming toward me in the darkness. We dropped down together behind the brightly lit tents and struggled to catch our breath.

Some of the details of dreams are clear and interminable. They play themselves out over and over until you think you will die. It might be preferable to the dream's incessant repetition. And other parts have dissolved into the remains of memory, dormant or gone. So it was with the cut man dream.

I still remember very vividly the dark rushing current of the river. But for the babble of dialects around the tents we lay behind, and the hiss of the lanterns, the night was quiet. Peaceful.

Sharp was pointing with a bloodied knife blade to the tents. I knew he wanted to blow the camp, and I strung what was left of the plastic explosive gently around all of the tents, lit and unlit.

We were losing time but still we waited. If we chose the wrong tents, we'd be caught in the dark or blown up by our own munitions. I motioned left and slipped my boot knife out. Sharp nodded to our right and we went, slitting the back panels of the two darkened tents with the same smooth, deft motion.

I dove in, knife in the blade-up position, looking wildly for men, for cover, for the business I came for. Nothing. It was a half-empty supply tent. I slipped back out where Sharp crouched waiting for me. I looked at him.

"Opium," he whispered.

I whispered back, "Just supplies."

"We gotta *go*, man," he hissed, pointed to his watch and looked at me closely. His face was dark—not just from the mud and camouflage and bandanna—dark in the pupil, dark in the iris of the eye.

I saw several silent shadows move in one of the remaining tents, pointed my blade, and we went.

I slit the back panel from ground to shoulder height and Sharp was in. He had the Frenchman Lavey by the mouth when I climbed through. That's when the British officer we knew only as Jones kicked my knife from my hands.

316

We stood facing one another, Sharp collaring Lavey, Jones facing me barehanded. And for some reason I've since tried to figure out, the Britisher never cried out to the sentries. I still don't know if he recognized me, but I knew him.

It was them, all right, just as we had hoped, as the seconds ticked down and we were stalemated. Our eyes locked in patterns of the darkest fear, hate, anger, resentment. It was the most depraved moment of my war.

Then the first helicopter charge exploded. Sharp hissed, "*Sealed orders*," just once, and that was enough.

I saw him cut Lavey across the veins in his throat and into the windpipe before the first charge was through. The Britisher looked away for a second and I had the moray knife from my neck sheath and I lunged forward, slashing the arterial veins across his neck as he tried to turn his head back toward me. Blood splashed over my hands. I stood for a moment looking at him, his body facing me, his face turned the other direction, as he slowly crumpled into pools of his and Lavey's blood.

Sharp grabbed my arm and pulled me from the tent just as guards burst through the canvas flap doors. He sprayed all three tents with his M-16 as I clicked on the detonator for the last batch of plastique.

We ran for the river, hearing scattered shouts in Thai behind us. I dove into the water and Sharp was right behind me, but he'd picked up a huge tree branch, its leaves still intact. We hung on and tried to hide behind the leaves as light machine-gun fire stirred up the already fast current, and as the camp reverberated with explosion after explosion.

Only when the sky was lit by burning canvas, supplies, and exploding ammunition did I notice my knife was still in my hand. Sharp saw it too. His knives were already sheathed, very businesslike. He gently pried it from my fingers, dipped it deep into the water that swirled around us, dragging us downstream, and handed it back to me.

His eyes had changed color, from black to a pale, almost translucent gray. I sheathed the knife while he continued to look at me. Then he said, so simply, "cut men," and turned away.

He said it again and again that night as we spun downstream. By dawn we were both saying it, even after we came across friendly villagers who fed us and provided an escort to an American base camp a half day away.

I could still smell the burning opium that afternoon.

I wake up. In the hospital I used to babble, or shiver, or wake and suddenly be completely aware of my surroundings. That's how the dream was for a long time. Now I wake quietly, outwardly calm, feeling the dampness of the night.

Sharp and I spent most of the rest of our tours training recruits. They debriefed us at city HQ, with civilian CIA types present, then kept an eye on us. They did full psychiatric workups, physicals, everything. And then they let us be until our detachment orders came through.

We never talked about it. Someone did, though. We heard about the American soldiers who slit their allies' throats, protected orders, the group of ruthless killers who called themselves cut men. We were the evil that they felt but could not see.

We did our time and came back to the States. The rest is just memory.

Someone has put up a wind chime outside a window nearby. It rattles and sings incessantly.

When Ringo, McCoy, and I took extended liberty, wind chimes hung out of all the windows. In the night heat they'd lull you to sleep.

A year later, after the city was hit that night, a squad of Marines went from street to street, cutting them down. We were told they were distractions. On a windy night no one would hear the sappers coming in.

The French girl loved wind chimes. We'd lie together in bed or on the floor and listen to them till morning, caught in a world of serenity and music for those hours.

When the wind shifts to the north they are silent. It is a silence I can grasp and understand. I am a long way from other silences, but they are here with me in my apartment, with me when I walk down the street.

I wear a new knife manufactured in Germany in a shoulder sheath when I go outside. It hangs blade-up beneath my armpit.

Silence is oppressive like noise is. Spring steel is a comforting horror.

It is December and cold. I've worked late and have had to slip through the crowds of Christmas shoppers to get to the subway. I've been home for an hour trying to get warm.

Something is happening within my body. I have sweated through several T-shirts and now wipe the sweat away with a towel. It is the clarity of heat, interior and exterior, with which I must reason.

But each step is old news to me. When the sweating stops, I slip into a bathrobe and wrap myself within a snap-up comforter.

Monday Night Football pits the Los Angeles Raiders against the Pittsburgh Steelers. Franco Harris is gone. Freddy Biletnikoff is gone. Gone are the Steel Curtain and stickum. Lester "the Judge" Hayes still plays on the false greens of the football field, still won't tuck in his jersey.

I smile, shiver, and shake. Rock and roll. The only light in my apartment comes from the television tubes. Their garish neon jumps and jerks in weird reflections about the room. My clothes and shoulder sheath lie in a heap against the wall.

Here, on the mattress, I wrestle with disease and memories. My jaw aches from the pressure of the bite. Pain racks my sides, my lower back, my abdomen.

Then, suddenly, it is gone, a reminder that it will be back, but somehow gone. I drink down a glass of water while staring at the telephone next to my bed. Sometimes it is hard. Sometimes it is almost impossible, knowing it will get harder.

I remember what I had told myself one day, not so many days ago: the real fear is the dream of a day I cannot control. I sit up in the half-dark and think of Linda Duncan, her voice, the smile, and the words she would say if I would only call her. The words she will say when I call her.

But not tonight. Not tonight. I am neither warm nor cool now, and I sit up against the wall without the bathrobe or comforter. I swallow a capsule without water and reach over to change channels.

It's *The Outlaw Josey Wales.* There's the sound of burning and shooting and the screams of people being killed.

Some things are too familiar.

Outside the wind howls and clatters but the wind chimes have ceased their singing.

About the Author

John Jacob was born in Chicago in 1950. He worked as a social worker with hardcore delinquent children in the 1970's, worked as an intelligence analyst in state government, and was a hospital fundraiser. He has published five books of poetry, one of which won the 1980 Carl Sandburg Award. He has taught at six colleges and universities since 1972, most recently at the University of Illinois-Chicago and Northwestern University, where he teaches writing. For four years he has been a member of the Etonic Shoe Company's national track and road racing team.